STRANGERS
AND
COUSINS

STRANGERS

AND

COUSINS

LEAH HAGER COHEN

RIVERHEAD BOOKS

New York

2019

RIVERHEAD BOOKS
An imprint of Penguin Random House LLC
penguinrandomhouse.com

Copyright © 2019 by Leah Hager Cohen

Library of Congress Cataloging-in-Publication Data
Names: Cohen, Leah Hager, author.
Title: Strangers and cousins: a novel / Leah Hager Cohen.
Description: New York: Riverhead Books, 2019.
Identifiers: LCCN 2018015113| ISBN 9781594634833 (hardcover) |
ISBN 9780698409644 (ebook)
Subjects: LCSH: Domestic fiction.
Classification: LCC PS3553.O42445 S77 2019 | DDC 813/.54—dc23
LC record available at https://lccn.loc.gov/2018015113

Printed in the United States of America
1   3   5   7   9   10   8   6   4   2

Book design by Gretchen Achilles

To Osva

והרגל שלנו

STRANGERS
AND
COUSINS

❦ · 1 · ❦

Episode One. Monday.

Four Days Before the Wedding.

"The redcoats are coming! The redcoats are coming!"

Pim sounds the alarm. He's decked out in Minuteman regalia: his sister's old blue windbreaker, too big for him (mercifully, since it's all he has on and Aunt Glad could arrive any minute now). Even so, the pale cabbage of his bottom flashes beneath the hem as he gallops along the upstairs hallway. The dark wainscoting and wooden floors are giving off a swollen, spiced scent and the window at the end of the hall shows a square of glaucous sky. It's been raining for days.

Bennie, his mother, catches sight of the self-appointed sentry as his mission takes him past the open bathroom door. She's kneeling on the bath mat, helping Mantha wash her hair. Mantha, previous owner of the windbreaker, is eight and would normally be able to handle this task on her own, but in her current state, sporting a blue fiberglass elbow-to-wrist cast on her left arm, she must submit to her mother's assistance. She sits in the tub with her head thrown back, eyes pinched shut, mouth a perfect prune.

Pim, recently ejected from the tub himself, doubles back long enough to thrust his head in the doorway and repeat his echoic warning, and Bennie glances up at him, at five her youngest, hovering there still pink-skinned, damp hair sticking out every which way, imploring her to—what, exactly? express alarm? muster arms?—and a current of amusement ripples through her (his urgency, his nudity), but she issues only a short imperative: "Pajamas," before turning back to her daughter and tipping a potful of water over the cream-rinse-clotted hair.

"When are they coming?" asks Mantha after she is done spluttering. She splutters ostentatiously after every potful, no matter how carefully her mother ensures the water does not run over her face.

"When are who coming?" Bennie, picturing redcoats, frowns.

"Everyone."

Oh. Right. The invasion. Everyone—or something very close—will be descending on them in the coming days, summoned together by the impending revels: Clem and Diggs are getting married.

Clem, the oldest of Bennie's four children, is planning, at the ridiculously tender age of twenty-two (never mind that Bennie was a bride at that very age), to wed her college girlfriend in four days' time. Bennie still can't quite believe it. With a not-uncheery sigh, she runs through the list of expected arrivals, a helpful reminder for herself as well as Mantha: there's Aunt Glad, speeding here at this very moment (Walter left over an hour ago to pick her up at the assisted living center in Fishkill), then Clem and her two bridesmaids, due later this evening. Spread out over tomorrow and Wednesday, Bennie's siblings arrive: Lloyd with his daughter and Aunt Carrie with her brood—

"What's a brood?" Mantha wants to know.

"A whole bunch of chicks. Or in this case, Aunt Carrie's kids."

"She only has two."

"I was being ironic."

"What's ironic?"

"Actually, maybe I was being sarcastic."

Mantha tallies the kids in her own family: Pim, her, Tom, and Clem. "Are we a brood?"

"And how."

Mantha laughs.

Anyway—Bennie resumes her itinerary—Thursday is when Diggs & Co. arrive, driving up from Falls Church, Virginia.

"Who's Co.?"

"Short for company." In this case, Diggs's father and step-mother. The "& Co." contingent, along with various other less intimately connected family members and friends, are putting up, thank goodness, not here but at the Garrison Inn in town. The future in-laws had been invited to stay here, but their demurral came, quite frankly, as a relief (a reflection not on them but on the haphazard hazards of daily life behind the scenes with the Blumenthals; Bennie doubted the Digginses would be well-served by witnessing at this early juncture just how chaotic a family their daughter was marrying into). Even so, their own house has been tasked with accommodating nine extra people in addition to the six who officially live here. Live(d) here. Because Clem, after next weekend, won't.

What almost no one knows is that Clem is the tip of the exodus. It isn't simply that Clem will presumably, in the natural order of things, be followed by the next oldest, Tom, and eventually by Mantha here and one day even by that little half-naked militiaman tearing up and down the hallway now hollering—what is he hollering?—*Grab your muskets, men!* It's that very soon none of the family will live here anymore, here in the house where Bennie has lived her whole life, and where her mother grew up as well, and before her, Aunt Glad, who is in fact Bennie's great-aunt. Walter and Bennie have agreed not to say anything until next week, after the wedding, after the meeting with the real estate agent.

For years they've had a running joke about putting the house on the market—mostly taking the form of idle quips about abandoning ship in the wake of some new thing going wrong, some not inconsiderable plumbing bill or carpentry bill or masonry bill (not to mention the great bat-exclusion fiasco, which led to the great chimney-rebuilding fiasco)—but over the past six months the conversation turned serious. And it wasn't any longer just the house they spoke of leaving, but Rundle Junction itself.

Still, it hadn't become real until the evening—less than a week ago—when Walter came home close to midnight from the village meeting, bearing a conciliatory pint of burnt caramel from Piccolo's. Bennie had kept herself awake doing combat with the Thursday crossword; he found her glowering at it on her old wooden clipboard. "Sorry I'm so late." He sat heavily on the edge of the bed, handed her one of two spoons and dug his own into the ice cream. "Public comments went on forever."

She listened as he recapped the evening's revelations, at the end of which she gestured with her spoon. "You're saying it's really going to happen."

"I'm saying it already is. Ben—right down the road, you know Garvey's old place? As of last week there's a new family living there."

"Black hat?"

He managed to combine a confirmatory nod with a reproachful wince at her use of the slang. Never mind that she'd picked it up from him; Walter had grown up around Orthodox Jews in New York.

"You're saying it's time, then. For us to move?"

He let a few more seconds elapse, out of respect or as a kind of condolence—after all, she is the one with roots here—before granting, "I am."

She'd called the Realtor the next morning. Not being one to wallow.

So that's two secrets she's carrying around now—the second quite literally: she is ten weeks pregnant. Walter knows. And her ob-gyn. No one else, not until after the wedding. What a thing! Another fact she can hardly believe. As soon as she'd seen the plus sign on the stick she'd felt herself blush with the preposterousness of it, the unlikely foolishness of finding herself pregnant at age forty-four. And yet she'd felt this, too, in that first instant: utterly flush with good fortune.

In a gesture that is semi-involuntary and wholly uncharacteristic, Bennie now lays her hand flat against the wall at the end of the tub and runs it down, as if stroking the flank of some loved, ailing creature. In so doing she dislodges (oh yay) a few more flakes of paint where the wall is distended and discolored: signs of one more leak they've never quite managed, despite periodic attempts by assorted handymen, to vanquish.

"What are you doing?" Mantha queries.

"Oh you know"—airily—"just feeling the wall!"

"Whatever. Anyway, who comes then? After Diggs & Co?"

"Nobody much," says Bennie. "Just all the wedding guests."

For the wedding is happening here at the house, or at any rate on the lawn, on Friday at five o'clock in the afternoon; Clem had gotten it into her head that it would be auspicious to wed on the eve of the summer solstice.

Down the hall comes a tread too heavy to be Pim. Bennie looks up to see her older son toting the pretty leaded-glass reading lamp she asked him to bring down from the attic hours ago.

"Did you remember to bring down the night table like I asked?"

"Yes, Mother!" he flings back in a falsetto as mellifluous as it is unconvincing. Tom is sixteen.

They've decided to install Aunt Glad on the first floor of the house, in the room that has always been called the office but which has devolved over the years into more of a cold storage room, a place for stowing excess produce and off-season clothes. In preparation for Aunt Glad they've made it over: earlier Tom lugged down the folding cot and Bennie, in a rare instance of going beyond the minimum requirements for cleanliness and comfort, made it up with freshly ironed linens spritzed with lavender water. Mantha had plucked a nosegay of violas and put them in a jelly jar on the desk (these are already wilting; she having forgotten to add water) and even Pim had made a contribution: a windowsill tableau of battling plastic dinosaurs.

Back in 1920, the year of Glad's birth, the residential part of the house had been entirely confined to the second floor, with the downstairs functioning as the village post office and general store. Photographs in the powder room off the foyer show what it looked like then—with the old service window that's been reimagined as a pass-through between the kitchen and dining area, and the shelves where dried beans and coffee and rolled oats were once displayed now transformed into a pantry. One photo shows Bennie's grandmother Joy and Aunt Glad as little girls out in front of the house. Glad sits in a Radio Flyer wearing a pair of fairy wings. Joy, holding the wagon's handle, is costumed in a white dress with a diagonal sash that reads: *Two o'Clock*. The photo, as every generation of inhabitants has been able to recite, was taken on the occasion of the Spirit of Progress Grand Community Pageant of 1927, in which nearly the entire village was said to have participated.

More pageant pictures decorate the powder room, one whole wall of which is practically a shrine to that unabashedly multifarious event: here are men costumed as Wappingers paddling canoes across Ida Pond; there women in Grecian robes, posed Isadora Duncanesquely on a hillside; here Morris dancers with bells on their knees; there children skipping round a maypole; here a float carrying nymphs and satyrs; there—jumbled together in a single frame—a skeleton riding a donkey, a pilgrim churning butter, and a man dressed up as Father Time, cradling an hourglass in his arms.

All of the photos, it goes without saying, had been taken during the first four days of the pageant, before, that is, the fifth and final day, when an explosion in the grandstands killed eighteen children and injured some three dozen spectators of all ages. Collectively then, the photos, while portraying only the most shining achievements of the historic civic event, prefigure in some way the tragedy that was to cap it—at least for anyone who knows the story of that fateful day, as all Rundle Junctioners do—and this unarticulated presence, the weight of the event not depicted but nevertheless lurking within the proud images, lends the powder room gallery a faintly funereal dignity.

Among the children in this household, it's the photo of Glad and Joy that compels the most interest, less for the sisters themselves than for the way it shows the exterior of their very own home looking at once the same as it is today and not. It gives them the chills. It's like a magic mirror in which they can glimpse—not their fate, but what might have been their lot, if only the timing had been different. Over the front porch, for example, they can make out a sign that isn't there anymore: ERLEND'S STORE * DRY GOODS * SUNDRIES * VILLAGE POST. Also they can see an elfin version of the shagbark hickory that stretches high above the roof today (or "in real life," as Mantha insists on putting it, no matter how often people remind her life was real then, too).

In the foreground Joy stands with her shoulders back and her toes turned out, regarding the camera levelly, whereas Glad, in the wagon, has an arm flung across her eyes, either to shield them from the sun's glare or to flout the photographer's attempt to capture her. The seated girl appears, to her great-grandnieces and -nephews, defiant, mischievous. More interesting than her sister. She looks like a girl who might hit you if provoked, and they have each in their turn admired her for it.

MORE THAN EIGHT DECADES have passed and still, as the car conveying Glad Erlend back toward her family home rolls slowly past the sloping Green, marked at one end by the ruddy sandstone village hall and at the other by the moon-pale public library, the old alarm clangs in her marrow, scampers through her blood.

But why?

Beyond the sopping grass, down the hill, the surface of Ida Pond is sequined with rain. Glad finds herself straining to see through the drop-studded pane, intent on making something out, searching the visible curve of shore for the fatal spot.

Fatal spot?

She cannot pinpoint the source of her dread. It's a smudge at her periphery. When she tries to get a better look it darts away. It breathes unease, flickers and fans up the side of her face, blazes across her shoulders, crackles against her breast. With a whoosh her ribs flare beneath her blouse.

Glad lifts a hand, presses it to her sternum. Her fingertips are cool.

Now she is passing the center of the Green, where a hulking granite monument displays a plaque.

A plaque?

No plaque is visible through the rain. Memory supplies the element she cannot see, affixes it to the rock. A copper plaque gone lichen-blue. Engraved with eighteen names.

GLAD IS SEVEN, Joy nine. Everyone in the village is here. Many more people from out of town are here, too, come by train and car to see the spectacle, which has been advertised as far south as New York City, as far north as Poughkeepsie:

THE SPIRIT OF PROGRESS GRAND COMMUNITY PAGEANT

OUTDOOR DRAMA OF RUNDLE JUNCTION'S PAST,

PRESENT, AND FUTURE PERFORMED DAILY BY ITS

RESIDENTS ON THE SHORE OF IDA POND

JUNE 20-24

It's Friday, the last official day of the weeklong extravaganza, but post-pageant celebrations are set to continue into the weekend (at their own house they have a party planned; Mother is baking an angel food cake with penuche frosting), and already, this early in the morning, the path to the grandstands that have been specially built for the occasion along the eastern shore of the pond is thicker with foot traffic than on any of the previous days. The Garrison Inn is full to capacity. New Ashkelon and other neighboring towns' inns have no vacancies either; some residents have rented out spare rooms to strangers.

The mist is still rising off the pond, the sun just beginning to make butter on top of her head (this is what Joy calls it when you reach up your hand and feel the oveny hotness there), and it's rousing, she loves it all, the feeling of importance, the hordes of strangers that, having heard about the great thing her village has done, have flocked here from afar, masses of people milling on the sidewalks and streets and making their way across the Green, a great pinwheeling confusion of trousers and skirts. Above her head their voices interlace and ricochet, a potpourri of human tongues, some speaking in unfamiliar accents, some in unfamiliar languages. Voices thick and sweet as condensed milk, voices soft as ashes swept from the grate, voices like salt and pepper, voices like a box of tacks spilt across the floor.

Stay close, Gladdy, Mother keeps reminding. *It's your responsibility not to get lost.* It's her responsibility to keep her eye on Joy's lilac sash, the trail blaze she has picked to follow as they thread through the crowd. Daddy left before sunrise to assemble on Moose Island in the middle of the pond along with the other men playing Wappingers. Their part is to paddle canoes across the water during the second episode. What a revelation it has been to see their ordinarily practical and retiring father transformed by the fringed trousers and beaded tunic Mother sewed for him. Mother is the only one in the family not acting in the pageant (*As if I don't already have enough to do*), but she has taken on the task of chairing the Costume Committee and serving on the Public Communication Committee; in addition she has been in the kitchen all week, turning out batch after batch of hermits and her famous no-bake chocolate oatmeal cookies for the Performers' Refreshment Tent.

Glad and Joy hold hands while Mother carries her bundle and together they make their way, along with the multitudes, across the Green to the path that wraps around the pond, heading as they have on each of the four preceding mornings toward the grandstands. The dancers in the first episode, "The Birth of the Hours," assemble on the far side of the stands under the copper beech tree. Joy in her lilac sash is one of the Hours: Two o'Clock. Glad, initially pouty over being informed she was too little to play an Hour, has come to relish her part, which, anyway, has a longer, fancier, and more romantic name: Little Fairy Attendant Upon the Hours.

She may not have a sash like Joy's, but she has something better: wings. Mother made them out of wire and netting and decorated them with cloth flowers and real feathers, the latter gathered and contributed by Glad herself (*Wherever did you find these?* Mother had looked askance: *They're sure to be riddled with contagion,* but Glad begged, *Please, please, I promise they're clean, won't you sew them on?*). The wings are attached to an elastic harness that fits around her chest and crisscrosses over her shoulders. The elastic bites into the side of her neck every time she turns around, which she cannot help doing often, in an effort to admire them. She stops in order to adjust the elastic, trying to route it along her dress instead of her bare skin, but it keeps working its way back up against her neck. Finally she succeeds in securing the collar of her dress underneath the elastic. That's better.

When she looks up her limbs go hollow.

She is lost. Not lost—she knows where she is—but although her feet have not budged it's as if she's traveled to a distant land, for the crowds have continued to flow around her and no one looks familiar. She's become dislocated while standing in place. *Mind you keep up,* Mother'd said. *It's your responsibility.* She tries to think matter-of-factly. When you're lost you're supposed to stay put. Or no: you're supposed to find a policeman. Failing that, a woman with children. Failing that, a kind-looking woman. Failing that, a man with children. She looks around. Such a terrible abundance of faces and fabric, hats and gaits and voices and smells, such a dizzying thrum. Her stomach spins, her gorge rises.

And then: Joy. Through the crowd, Glad spies her sleek brown bob, her organdy dress. She darts forward, frantically pushing past waists and bottoms until she catches up and with a flood of relief seizes her sister's arm. But the girl who spins around is an impostor. She has Joy's dress, Joy's height and hair, but—the vision assaults Glad with a kind of hallucinatory violence, a nightmare logic—she is Joy wearing the head of a stranger. Not-Joy glares. Glad releases her arm, and someone brushes roughly against her and a few feathers tear loose from her wings and drift to the ground.

Then, sweetest of sounds, she hears her own name—*Glad! Gladdy!*—and running, overcome with gratitude, dizzy with it, she dodges legs, pushes without pausing to say *excuse me* and arrives, panting, tears threatening, beside the real sister, her own Joy, who, taking her by the hand (not without a reproachful squeeze), tugs her forward.

But whose voice called *Glad! Gladdy!* for it wasn't Joy and it wasn't Mother—it was a boy, surely, a little boy with a voice like a silver trumpet. Who could've called her? She searches her memory (but this is old Glad now, the nonagenarian craning her neck to see out the window and straining to remember as she glides through the center of the village in the rain in the car all these decades later, searching, scouring the recesses of her mind for something that belongs there, something that should be there but is missing, has been irrevocably lost. Or not irrevocably. For it's something to do with the voice, isn't it? *Little boy blue, come blow your horn.*

But we mustn't speak of that.)

Only once they reach the old copper beech on the far side of the grandstands does the forest of bodies thin out enough for a small person at last to breathe freely and perceive the wider view: the three maypoles that have been erected along the shore of Ida Pond, their Easter-egg-colored streamers rippling in the morning breeze; the brass band on its wooden platform under the crooked willow whose branches weep into the shallows of the pond; the tents set up behind the red sandstone Village Hall, which serve as dressing rooms for the performers; the vendors assembling along the snow fence—installed to control the crowds—just beginning to set out their concessions: sandwiches, popcorn, lemonade, and bags of peanuts in their shells; pageant ears to enhance one's hearing; celluloid eyeshades and paper fans to mitigate the effects of the midday sun; and souvenirs for children—handkerchief-size Old Glories on sticks, clackers, toy horns, and pinwheels of red-white-and-blue.

What on earth did you do to your costume? Mother tuts. She sets down her heavy bundle (Whatever *is* she carrying? Old Glad, peering uneasily down the narrow corridors of memory, cannot make it out) and stoops to reshape the wire frames on Glad's back. Then she rotates the child, inspects her front, and straightens the dress collar. Licks a finger to tame the cowlick that will within minutes reassert itself in the center of Glad's bangs. While Glad submits to the grooming, not altogether begrudgingly (For how often does she receive Mother's undivided attention, not to mention her touch?), she squints into the grandstands, interested not in the bodies seated upon it but in the dim recesses beneath. Already half a dozen children are playing within that cavernous hidey-hole, which has served all week as the private domain of the children of Rundle Junction.

Joy and Glad, like most of the children in Rundle Junction, have bit parts early in the pageant but are not required for the rest of the performance, which stretches out over the course of each day, broken up by intervals during which spectators promenade about the pond or partake of picnics on the Green. On Monday, opening day, the sisters had watched the entire performance, but as early as the second day they, like many of their peers, had already grown bored by the long, slow repetition of the numerous episodes and tableaux, and preferred to spend the hot afternoon in the cool dim area beneath the grandstands.

To their surprise, Joy and Glad have not been forbidden to play there. It's the sort of activity Mother would ordinarily declare off-limits on the grounds of its being dangerous, dirty, and unsupervised. But she has been unusually lenient this week, swept up like everyone else in the spirit of novelty and adventure and community effort. She has seemed younger, looser, has smiled more, laughed more; the sisters even saw her weep, openly, without shame or embarrassment—she was not alone; many of the townspeople touched handkerchiefs to their eyes—during the final episode on the first evening, as the sun lowered and reflected off the pond and the clouds bled apricot and cherry and the chorus sang an original composition by Mr. Frank M. Brown, the high school music teacher and organist at the First Methodist Church. How luminous, how soft and strangely pretty their mother has appeared to them this week.

In any case, she has allowed Joy and Glad uncommon liberty— *Be responsible! Make sure to stay together!*—and they have taken advantage of this to clock many ungoverned hours playing with their compatriots in that place of mystery whose terraced ceiling, the inverse of the raked seating above, is so low at its lowest points that even the littlest children have to crawl and at its uppermost extreme rises to a vaulted, churchly height. Some direct sunlight comes through at the back, yet even there it remains relatively dim and atmospheric, for bales of hay have been stacked high all around.

Who stacked them there?

Who knows.

Bales of hay on either side of the grandstand serve the purpose of providing extra seating; those who don't arrive early enough to secure a spot on the bleachers can clamber up on the hay to get a view of the pageant proceedings from there. But the bales stacked in back? Perhaps their placement was intended to prevent people from doing precisely what the children of Rundle Junction have done: gaining access to the space under the stands. Or perhaps they were simply extra, an excess of hay having been hauled over from neighboring farms that answered the call for donations. Perhaps they wound up forming a wall along the back of the grandstands merely for convenience's sake, to avoid taking up space needed by the performers, the vendors, and the police who are responsible for maintaining clear paths of ingress and egress for all the spectators (over two thousand each day so far, according to official reports, with this final day of performance—word of mouth having spread—expected to draw close to double that number).

Who could have foreseen what would happen?

Only in hindsight would it seem inevitable that children would find a way to burrow in. Only in hindsight would it seem foolish that no one thought to question the prudence of encircling the spectator seating with all that flammable material.

It was a sixth grader named Percy Oglethorpe who, a little past noon on that Tuesday, discovered that if he shouldered through a narrow gap between two stacks of hay that had been set down at a slightly cant angle, the opening quickly widened into a passageway, which led in turn to a fantastically capacious arena, shaded and hushed, directly beneath the main mass of people attending the pageant.

Once in, he gave a whistle and within a minute was joined by three of his more rowdy friends who, muscling after him, widened the gap between the bales. Upon registering the magnitude of Percy's discovery they'd issued whoops, inadvertently or not summoning other children to come see what merited such fuss. Soon the space was full of kids of varying age and size. Some discovered there was decent treasure hunting to be had here directly beneath the audience: coins, buttons, an embroidered handkerchief, the odd hair ribbon or pocket comb. Others yanked out handfuls of the already blanched, sun-starved grass to clear the way for games of marbles, readily produced from trouser pockets. The older girls established their own separate territory within the dimmest recesses of the place. In the days to come, this would be encroached upon, timorously at first, then with greater boldness, by their male counterparts; in time an empty pop bottle was introduced, along with some resultant kissing. But because the entire realm was a contiguous open space, it offered no real seclusion; the intermingling of little and big kids seemed to ensure a kind of wholesomeness, which was likely why, although a handful of grown-ups did poke their heads in briefly from time to time to gauge the nature of the goings-on within, no one ever thought to issue an out-and-out ban.

It was as if the whole town had caught pageant fever.

PERCY OGLETHORPE. One of the eighteen names on the granite monument that marks the center of the Green. He'd been twelve that summer, practically ancient as far as a seven-year-old was concerned, and certainly not anyone Glad knew well, yet the population of Rundle Junction was small, and after all they'd attended the same elementary school, played on the same playground, walked the same sidewalks, swum at the same sandy beach down at the western edge of Ida Pond in the summers, and as she is being conveyed past the Green now, these eighty-seven years later, the car maneuvering carefully down the rain-slick street, tires swishing round the curve beyond the Village Hall, a surprisingly clear image presents itself. Tousled carroty hair. Copious freckles. Jutting ears. A narrow face that tapered to an almost elfin chin. A perpetual squint. Perhaps—the thought occurs to her with freshness and vigor, as if it were important, as if it mattered one jot— perhaps if he'd lived longer he'd have wound up with glasses.

A granite monument with eighteen names, eighteen lives, all belonging to children.

Or rather: each belonging to a specific child. Each child possessing a singular assemblage of features, idiosyncrasies, memories, hopes, a distinct lineage, a unique destiny. But that's oxymoronic, no? What is the word for a destiny that never comes to pass?

And what of her own scars prickling as the car rolls past—do they really prickle, does her rib cage really kindle? Do the shiny pink-and-white gathers of skin on her face and neck and side really tighten? Or is it only her imagination, a trick of the mind? These many years later.

Glad has studied herself all too closely throughout the years of her life; she no longer needs a mirror to picture just how the burned areas look, the white parts ropy as curdled milk, the pink parts livid as baby mice. The scars are the sole part of her skin that has never noticeably aged, the sole part of her that remains preserved almost exactly as it has been since she was seven.

Yes, she remembers being there. Under the grandstand. The magnificence of that cool, inverted space with its soaring ceiling, its great private mote-streaked dimness. She remembers the mounting trepidation and excitement she felt as she and Joy burrowed in past the packed bales that first time and found themselves in that child-only underworld smelling of dirt and hay. She remembers the way each subsequent day they felt more at home there, more at ease, more entitled. All of them, collectively, developing pride of ownership in the space they'd conquered and settled. And she remembers how the pale golden spears of light had slanted down to reach them there, slanted down, far down through the firmament formed by the tiered seats, the mystery of those shafts of light cast from so far away, beyond any space they'd ever traveled or known.

Of the explosion she remembers nothing. Has only the vaguest memory of the fire, vague jumble of flame and smoke and heat, of children's cries and screams within what had become a deadly enclosure, of panicked adult exhortations from without. Who knows what of these memories is real and what conjured, suggested, subscribed to after the fact? Only Joy she knows she remembers for sure. Joy holding on, squeezing her hand so hard it hurt. Joy not letting go. (*It's your responsibility*, Mother had reminded them, and Joy was good and minded her responsibility, she got Glad out of the fire and would later be praised. *Thank God, thank God*, people would say, *Thank God Joy at least was responsible*. No one would ever call Glad responsible on that day.) Joy pulling her with two hands away from the darkness of the blaze, away from the choking foul grit of the smoke, out into the open, out into the brilliant smash of cymbal-throb sun and lung-shock blue. (But whose hand had Glad been meant to grasp, who had she been meant to hold on to and not let go?) *Open your eyes, Gladdy.* That had been Joy. *Open your eyes, you're safe, I've got you.* And somewhere the sound of a siren, and somewhere the sound of bleating.

But where is the little boy tending the sheep?
He's under the hay-cock fast asleep.
Will you wake him? No, not I,
For if I do, he's sure to cry.

Scientists, she has read, say memory does not exist independent of thought. Any notion of it as a separate entity, a substance that can be secreted away in the body like bits of grain, is fallacy, fantasy. Romance. Memory's sole physical province, they insist, is the brain. Yet Glad does not believe this. Glad has never shaken the conviction that her body harbors memories long hidden or lost from her conscious mind. Could it be a coincidence that the body repairs its wounds by forming something called granulation tissue? Granulation, grain. The fine grain, the fineness of grain. To be engrained. Of all the words she never wanted to learn— *debridement, necrosis, proud flesh, grafting, adhesion*—of all the words she was subjected to, words that issued from the mouths of doctors and nurses for many months afterward, words that became part of her parents' vocabulary, and Joy's, and her own— *granulation* was the one that seemed to hold some promise, some consolation.

Glad touches the fingers of one hand to the scars on the side of her face, glides them lightly down her neck, over her heart, across her breast and ribs and around beneath her arm—a gesture so commonplace, so many times repeated over the course of so many decades, it holds the unconscious grace of ritual, of rite.

"We're almost there."

She startles. But of course: a car cannot drive itself. She swivels toward the driver's seat. A large, jovial-looking man with a sonorous voice and a head of thick silvery-white hair, rather too much of it. His face more youthful than his hair would suggest. She cannot place him, quite. For some reason he makes her think of a walnut.

"Pardon?" Glad, who has excellent hearing, finds it sometimes useful to feign otherwise. A stalling technique. She dislikes these moments of disorientation, but has learned that with time and patience she is often able to gather clues from her environment. Surely she ought to be able to piece together enough information to recall who she is with, why she is here with him, and where they are driving. She has a sudden inspiration—might he be taking her to the train?

Lately she has been visited by a not-unpleasant dream in which she is in some kind of station. A vast metal-and-glass structure alive with porters and pigeons, plumes of steam and plaintive whistles. Sunlight streaming through a skylit atrium in steep silver-white shafts. In the dream she is standing under a wooden departure board, whose split-flaps make a great rattling noise every time the schedule is updated, and she is trying without success to decipher the numbers of the platforms and the destinations of the trains, all of which seem to be written in a language—an alphabet—she does not recognize. And yet she is devoid of anxiety. She is filled with the peaceful knowledge that she will recognize her own train when it comes.

"We're almost at the house," the driver says.

"I know that." A little tartly, it comes out. She didn't mean to be rude. But the sound of her own voice pitched in such a manner turns out to be comforting. It reminds her of something about herself, makes her feel capable, unassailable.

Sure enough, now a piece of the puzzle presents itself:

By "house" he means home. As in her childhood home. The white clapboard building whose first floor houses the village post office and general store, and whose upstairs houses the private rooms where she lives with Mother and Daddy and Joy. Or lived. She doesn't live there anymore. She is returning as a guest, returning for a celebration, some sort of reunion or gathering . . . a holiday . . . a festival? A wedding! The wedding of her great-grandniece, the eldest of all the great-grands. Clem, Clementine, a skinny little thing with hay-colored hair. Who must be in some way connected to this man—she glances over again—this rather nice man driving her; she knows he is someone she feels warmly toward. Even if he could use a haircut. But what is his name, this nice, large silvery fellow who reminds her for some reason of a walnut?

And who is the interloper?

For a wedding always involves an interloper. By definition. A wedding means a stranger getting inside the gates.

Surely someone has told her the name of Clem's intended. She could ask. Could inquire of this man; probably he would know. But—with a little jolt it hits her; she almost gasps—why, he is himself an interloper! The only reason she's in his car now is that he married Bennie, her grandniece. That's who he is, her nephew-in-law. What is his name? She peers at him. Surreptitiously, she thinks—but no. Instantly he responds, turning to her and daring to grin broadly.

"Watch the road!"

He laughs. Obeys.

Well that was more than tart. She was overly severe. Really quite rude. Ought she apologize? She steals another glance. He appears to be biting back a smile. No, then, she decides. And scowls out the window. *After all there are rules to follow, proprieties to observe.* And now for no apparent reason (sometimes it works this way, the mischievous, on-the-lam facts just surrender themselves, turn all of a sudden meek and compliant) his name comes to her: Walter. He is Clem's father and Bennie's husband and his name is Walter. Walter the Walnut. In spite of herself she lets loose a great chortle. And then—how undignified, how merry—they're in it together, the two of them, Walter and Glad, not exactly kin, not exactly strangers, joined in helpless, primitive laughter.

BENNIE EMPTIES A LAST POTFUL of water over Mantha's head and rubs an expert thumb across her daughter's crown. "Squeaky," she approves.

"Can I stay in?"

"Better not. Water's getting chilly."

"It's summer!"

True, or nearly true. The first official day of summer is Saturday. But how dark the sky looks outside the bathroom window, and how unseasonably cool it is. Both sides of the indoor-outdoor thermometer have given readings in the sixties all day. If the rain doesn't let up, Clem and her bridesmaids may have to abandon their plan of staying in a tent out back. Bennie can see it now: everyone crammed inside the house, sleeping bags unfurled in every bedroom, wet towels draped over the furniture, clumps of mud and sodden grass tracked in faster than they can be wiped up. All of which would be headache enough even without a wedding, a wedding over which she has little say, for—despite bountiful inquiries and offers of help—the happy couple has insisted on handling all the planning and preparation themselves. Bennie is certain this includes zero provision in case of rain.

Another sigh, not not-uncheery this time.

"Hop out now," she insists, for no real reason except that exercising control over something at this juncture, even a proxy something, seems a good idea. She plucks the rubber stopper from the drain and rises, slowly, a hand on her lower back, making careful allowance for the recent shift in her center of gravity.

Mantha's bottom jaw slides forward in her trademark sulk but she obeys, leaning her good arm on her mother to leverage herself upright. Water sheets oilily off her skin, which glistens from the bath bead they dissolved in the tub. At eight, Mantha is still wholly without a sense of physical modesty and everything is on careless display: the frank curve of her stomach, the nearly color-less flat nipples, the florid welt on her left buttock where an insect bit her. Her hair, normally a wiry mop, cleaves to her scalp. She smells of strawberry (the bath bead) and coconut (the cream rinse) and her indifference to her own loveliness produces in her mother a wistful flare of feeling that wicks out again without ever taking form as thought.

Now, as a hundred times, a thousand times before, on so many other evenings, with this child or that, Bennie shepherds her daughter through the familiar routine, which has the pleasing rhythm of a shuttlecock: out of the bath and into a bath sheet. Out of the bathroom and into the bedroom. Out of the bath sheet and into pajamas. And, "Hey," Bennie calls to the other one, still streaking up and down the hall, "out of that jacket now, young man"—("Mine!" Mantha protests)—"and put on your pajamas before I have to say it one more time."

"One more time, one more time," parrots Pim, coming to a brief halt in the doorway of Mantha's room. He flirts with obedience—letting the windbreaker puddle to the floor—only to eel away again naked.

"Your rotten brother," Bennie observes.

"I know!" They listen to his wayward footsteps clomp down the stairs. Then Mantha covers her mouth and joggles her shoulders up and down, a pantomime of laughter: *yuk yuk yuk.*

Everything is vaudeville in this house.

Bennie drapes Mantha's head with the bath sheet and towels vigorously. Flaps it away. Damp thatch sprongs in every direction. "Comb," prompts Bennie, holding out her palm.

WALTER'S MONDAY-NIGHT RITUAL is making baguettes. Ordinarily three; tonight five times that number, in anticipation of the delegations of glad-tiders set to arrive this week. Originally he'd envisioned doing all the baking for the wedding celebration itself: bread and rolls, a ricotta orange cake, rosewater and spice cookies, a blackberry galette. This was a couple of months ago, when the RSVPs started rolling in. He'd begun sticking little torn-newspaper bookmarks in cookbooks, making and revising lists, asking whoever happened to be passing through the room, "What do you think about hazelnut torte with espresso frosting?" and "Does this sound good: lemon and almond semolina cake?"

"Are you demented?" Bennie'd inquired. "You're going to bake desserts—excuse me, not only desserts but also breads—for fifty-odd people? Have you been laid off work and forgotten to tell me?"

It had taken considerable effort to talk him down, but in the end he'd consented to stick to baguettes and let the cake, singular—"One wedding, one wedding cake," Bennie decreed—come from a bakery.

He fills the kettle and sets it over a medium flame, preheats the oven, ties on his blue-and-white-striped apron. Removing the tea towel from the bowl of dough he'd left rising before heading off to Fishkill, he lifts the yeasty mass onto the counter and begins working it with the heel of his hand. Soon the air is particulate with flour. Walter sings as he shapes three more loaves, lays them on the oiled tri-part pan, scores them, slides them into the oven. His bass-baritone does not so much rise over the chorus of rain bearing down on the porch roof as join it in song. The Warsaw Ghetto resistance song. He substitutes freely for the Yiddish he can't remember: "*Zog nit keyn mol az du geyst dem letstn veg / Something himlen blayene something bloye teg / Something something undzer oysgebenkte sho / Ah la lum tee dum tee dum: mir zaynen do!*"

The kettle shrills; he fetches a mug and pours Glad's tea, sweeping aside the baguettes he baked earlier that afternoon and taking the cover off a new bowl of dough, each action flowing so smoothly one into the next they feel of a piece, feel like one large continuous action; already he's forming the next trio of loaves. A fat bottle fly buzzes around his head. His is a large head, thick with prematurely snowy hair and well-balanced by a barrel chest, a hefty girth, thighs like fire hydrants. He carries thirty more pounds than his doctor would like, but he carries them well. Even the fly becomes part of his seamless choreography; he swats at it with a tea towel, keeping time with his song. He might be conducting rather than shooing. Now in English. "*Oh never say that you have reached the very end,"* he sings. Singing is not the right word, though. Insufficiently oomphy. He bellows, he booms. He rends the air, swirling the flour motes into hoary whorls. *"Though leaden skies a bitter future may portend!"*

Another balletic swoosh of the rag; once more the fly is diverted. In English, too, he is untroubled by forgotten lyrics. *"Ba dum the hour we bee da dum will arrive / And our marching steps will thunder: We survive!"*

Tom saunters in from the porch chewing a long stem of wild onion grass, his T-shirt darkened with spatters of rain.

"Prop that door open, will you?" Walter doesn't glance around. *"Zog nit keyn mol . . ."*

"Mom says keep it closed so flies don't get in."

Without breaking tempo, by brandishing his tea towel Walter indicates the extant fly.

Tom shrugs, props the door, then comes around the counter. "Hey Dad. We getting one of those signs?"

Walter finishes the verse before inquiring, "What signs?"

Tom, having faithfully if delinquently set up both the reading lamp and the night table in the office, had rewarded himself by going out to sneak a smoke in his usual spot, around the side of the barn, from where he'd spotted in McElroy's yard an unfamiliar object: a large corrugated plastic lawn sign. McElroy, their nearest neighbor, an unsmiling widower with a putty-colored crew cut and an unwavering allegiance to Chevrolet, is nothing if not reliable. Every two years he replaces his pickup with the latest-model Silverado, always in black. Every four years he plants in his front yard a sign promoting whichever presidential candidate the Blumenthals are not voting for. Today's sign, unrelated to any election cycle, had not been there on the occasion of Tom's last cigarette, meaning McElroy must've staked it sometime this afternoon. Meaning in the pouring rain. Meaning with some degree of dedication, or passion, or something. "They're kind of every-where," says Tom. "Have you noticed? Like overnight everyone got one. It's weird."

It's true. Along with all the American flags that have prolifer-ated in recent weeks, flapping from porches and garage roofs and on lawns (but this is a regular seasonal occurrence in the weeks leading up to the Fourth of July), another emblem has spread pro-digiously throughout the village, a spate of corrugated green signs with gold lettering: CITIZENS FOR THE PRESERVATION OF RUNDLE JUNCTION. Below that, in smaller font: SAVE THE SILVER MAPLES. "So are we?" repeats Tom. "Getting one?"

"No."

"How come?"

"It's not—"

"We're anti-preservation?"

"It's not really . . ." But here Walter trails off under the guise of multitasking. Nestles newly formed loaves in the spare pan. Grabs the mister, opens the oven, spritzes the batch currently baking.

"Not really what?"

"It's less about actual concern for the environment than about political opposition—or really, ideological opposition—to the new devel—"

"Oh I know, I know about this," Tom interjects. "The new housing complex. They want to build where the wetlands are." Truth be told, a month ago Tom hadn't even known there were wetlands in Rundle Junction. But in May his bio class took a field trip to the swampy tract out behind the dead bowling alley, and lo and behold: it turned out to extend fifteen acres, all the way to the shore of Ida Pond. These wetlands, Ms. Srivas had explained, functioned as a natural sponge that helped keep the residential and business districts of Rundle Junction from flooding. And the silver-maple forest provided a wildlife corridor for all sorts of other animals—otter, mink, coyote, fox.

"I'm impressed with your knowledge," says Walter, with a small and un-ironic bow.

"And now some developer wants to convert it all into luxury apartments."

"Well," says Walter, "it's a little more complicated than that. For one thing there's also a class component here. An issue of economic diversity."

"What do you mean?"

"There's a shortage of affordable housing in the area. The plan is for a new development to include subsidized units for low-income families."

"Which is a good thing."

"In my view."

"Dad." Tom sounds offended. "Mine too. But don't you think . . . I mean not at the expense of the environment, right? Because mainly"—he repositions the onion grass in his mouth—"mainly this is about saving the silver-maple forest." Close listening reveals this to be a question. Lately Tom has taken to inflecting his questions in the manner of statements.

"Mainly"—Walter pauses to run his tongue contemplatively along his teeth—"mainly it's about the Jews."

The developers are said to be Haredi—or at any rate to have close ties to the ultra-Orthodox community. From Brooklyn to New Jersey to Rockland County and beyond, the various Hasidic sects—Satmar and Belz, Vizhnitz and Skver—are bursting the seams of their environs, and the fast-growing community nearby in New Ashkelon is rumored to be seeking a foothold in other towns with affordable housing and space for shuls and yeshivas. This, Walter says, this specter of invading Otherness, more than concern for wetlands or wildlife, is what Citizens for the Preservation of Rundle Junction is really about.

"Come on, Dad." Tom pulls a face. "No one's like that."

But Walter can vouch for it. Playing to anti-Semitism is precisely how Jeff Greenberg stirred up opposition to the developers' plans at last week's village meeting. One might think with a name like Greenberg he'd be less quick to play on people's vilest, most deep-seated aversions, no matter how assimilated he himself may be, but he hadn't hesitated to fan unrest with talk not of silver maples but of Jews. Greenberg had hung his hand patiently in the air until he was recognized by the chair, then stood and dropped his bombshell in a move you could call a reverse-Tom: putting a statement in the form of a question. "Is it true," he asked, "that the new development's going to have two kitchens in every unit?"

Two kitchens? The whispers licked like flames around the room as people turned to their neighbors for clarification.

One for dairy, Jeff explained—he sounded almost embarrassed—and one for meat. Jeff Greenberg, built like a crane, unimpeachably unimposing in his faded dungarees, his faded plaid shirt. His wife's father's friend knew the building inspector or the village engineer or some such; at any rate someone had reportedly seen the floor plans and every unit had been drawn with two kitchens. "When we think of other communities," he'd continued in his reedy voice, "where large groups of ultra-Orthodox have settled, when we look at the impact such influxes have had on schools, property values, local businesses, even local governance . . ." And here he'd paused and spread his palms in a great, fatalistic shrug.

There was no need to finish the sentence; everyone in the room was surely envisioning New Ashkelon, whose school board and town council had, over the past decade, become majority ultra-Orthodox. As the demographic had shifted—and with the birthrates being what they were among the Haredim, the shift was swift; the joke was that the community's median age, fourteen, was also the average number of children per family—the character of the town also swerved dramatically. More and more of its local businesses had begun closing early on Fridays and remaining shuttered all Saturday in deference to the burgeoning Haredi clientele, who boycotted stores that stayed open during the Sabbath. Public school enrollments had declined and property values had first soared, then plummeted as non-Orthodox families moved out, leaving one of the elementary schools to be converted into a yeshiva and freeing up houses for the growing Haredi population, who received tax breaks for designating them places of worship. Driving through New Ashkelon on any given afternoon had become an exotic experience, an inadvertent form of tourism. There was a newly built *mikveh*, and *eruv* wires had been strung around a nine-square-block section of town. Even Walter felt unwittingly voyeuristic, seeing groups of men in fur *shtreimels* and *peyos* walking along the side of the road, with separate groups of women in dark, loose-fitting clothes and flocks of children in long sleeves, long skirts or long trousers, no matter the time of year, no matter how high the mercury in the thermometers.

Without making explicit reference to any of these factors, Jeff had simply paused, then added, again with near-apologetic gentleness, "I think we'd be making a grave mistake if we didn't ask ourselves whether that's what we want for Rundle Junction."

You had to hand it to him, he was good.

"But there's public money going into this," someone said, already with—not a snarl, not yet, but certainly a tone of indignation. Righteous indignation. "I mean, fair housing laws and all. Right? They can't just rent exclusively to their own kind; wouldn't they have to allow anyone who qualified based on income?"

Jeff—really he was a canny sonofabitch—hadn't even needed

to respond to that—not verbally, anyway. Nodding, he'd mashed his mouth up against his teeth in a kind of rueful grimace—*In theory*, he seemed to be saying. *And we all know that and a buck fifty will get you a cup of coffee*—then slunk back down in his chair as other voices around the room took up the debate, the hashing and rehashing of intention and actions, the statutes on the books versus the reality of human behavior, the law of the land versus the law of numbers, until the chairman of the meeting had to call for order.

That night the citizens of Rundle Junction sat in their kitchens and discussed kitchens with a fascination they could not recall the subject ever previously warranting. They sat in their kitchens and also in the booths at Shady's Coffee Café and on the benches outside Piccolo's FroYo, and they stood outside their cars in the lot behind Village Hall, the weight of their keys forgotten in their hands as conversations between spouses and neighbors and friends lengthened and divided, some shaping themselves around terms like *tax base* and *high density* and *public assistance*, others around *hats, wigs,* and *shawls*, and still others around *melting pot, freedom,* and *democracy*.

Walter insisted on telling Bennie all about it when he arrived home, disregarding for once her well-established indifference to civic affairs. Whether despite or because of the fact that Rundle Junction was Bennie's lifelong home while he was only a transplant, it was Walter who had always felt impelled to invest in the community, subscribe to the local paper, and keep abreast of zoning changes, budget override votes, yard waste collection dates, police blotter items, food pantry needs. Over the years, anytime he suggested she accompany him to a village meeting (*This'll be an eventful one—they're going to discuss whether moneys donated to the schools can be earmarked for specific sports teams*), she'd scoff. More precisely: she'd close her eyes and fake-snore. Stalwart, she liked to call him, at once a blandishment and a jibe. As in, *You go, Stalwart. You go and keep our village safe.* And she'd slip into a kind of botched frontierswoman accent. *Ah'll stay home and tend to the young 'uns.*

If she's always treated his sense of civic engagement as a source of amusement, lately she has expressed blatant incomprehension. Ever since their late-night, hushed conversations about selling the house (whose deep family history has become dwarfed by its deep structural problems, which they now understand have flagrantly outrun the capacity of their bank account ever to remedy) have come to include not simply leaving the house but also the village, and to use the parlance not of *whether* but of *when* (these discussions shaded in turn by the growing certainty that sooner—before the character of the town is patently altered—rather than later will likely result in their getting a better price), Bennie has treated his continuing attendance at village meetings—his continuing allegiance—as a cause for something like baffled pity. Walter himself can't explain why Rundle Junction's future remains important to him. He's not even sure what motivates him more: the well-being of the village itself, or his need to regard himself as a good steward.

"Dad." In the kitchen, Tom recovers his wandering attention by clapping a hand on Walter's shoulder: universal sign of masculine solidarity. With this as with so many of his gestures these days, it's hard to tell whether he's trying on the vestments of manhood in earnest or spoofing them in wiseassness. But when next he speaks, he sounds sincere. "I think it really is an environmental thing. Ms. Srivas says there's something like fifty species of birds alone that live there."

Walter registers the clumsy puppyish weight of his son's hand and looks him in the eye. Tom's face has morphed rapidly this past year, the twin promontories of jaw and brow asserting themselves more squarely. His neck has thickened; his nose, too. Who needs time-lapse photography? Just get yourself a teenager and pull up a chair. "Maybe." Walter doesn't believe it for a minute but wants to be fair. Or at least model fair-mindedness. "Maybe," he allows, "for some people that is the concern."

Tom responds with kindly reassurance. "I've never experienced any anti-Semitism in Rundle Junction."

It's frankly rattling, an upset to the natural order, to be comforted—condescended to—by one's own son. The implication being that Walter's getting doddery, susceptible to paranoia. With a deliberate exhale he changes the subject. Working to keep his tone neutral, unedged by accusation (but really, could anyone fail to notice the tobacco on Tom's breath, even under that masking whiff of onion grass, even under the mingled scents of June rain and yeasty dough?), he says, "What were you doing out in the rain just now?"

"Me? Nothing—uh, Mom wanted me to count how many folding chairs we have in the barn."

The delivery's a little too quick to be believable, but Walter lets it slide.

"WHAT'S THAT?" Pim, bare-bottomed, sits on one hand. With the other he points to the shiny pink splotch on Aunt Glad's face. It spreads down her neck and disappears beneath her blouse, as if someone threw an egg and it broke against her cheek and ran down and never got washed off.

They're side by side on the ancient gold settee. Aunt Glad holds open on her lap a picture book, *Ant and Bee Go Shopping*—Pim delivered it so she could read to him, but it turns out he is not very interested in the story.

"What's what, dear?" Aunt Glad gazes at his finger, then turns to follow its aim. He seems to be pointing at nothing more specific than the south-facing living room wall, which is covered with little brass doors, a hundred fifty-six of them. This is another number she knows by heart, or by marrow, by her very grain. Each door bears its own tiny pane of glass and a combination lock in the shape of a ten-pointed star, its points labeled *A* through *J*. "Why, those are the letterboxes," she says. "People come to collect their mail from them." Even as she speaks she feels the dials between her fingers, the specific resistance of the cool brass knobs as she turns them. She and Joy do this when their parents are busy or elsewhere; they've taught themselves how to pick the locks, how to feel the wheels catch as the notches line up on the other side of the door. They do this not to remove the letters (if they wanted to steal mail all they'd have to do is sneak behind the counter and pluck it from the open back side of the boxes; however this, they know, would be not simply mischief but an actual federal offense), but for the spark of elation that comes with success, that little in-sip of victory whenever a lock releases and the door yields.

"No," says Pim, "what's *that*?"

She turns back, trying to see what else the child could mean, and his fingertip grazes her face. She has a quick urge to bite it. Instead she places her own hand, heaped with veins and animated by a benign tremor, over his and guides it to his lap. "Don't point, dear." It has been thirty-four years since she taught kindergarten. She retired in 1980, at age sixty. They gave her a pension and a party with sherbet punch and hummingbird cake. Mr. Striker, the music teacher, choked on a piece and turned red as the punch.

It must be the pecans, someone says. But could that be true? This is before the days of nut allergies. *It must have gone down the wrong way*, someone says. He has to be guided to a chair, have his tie loosened, a cup of water held to his lips. Someone is kneeling before him—is it she? *Mr. Striker, are you all right? Feeling better now?* He is the only male teacher at Rundle Elementary—the only man in the whole building except for the custodian, Mr. Mangoli, whose teeth are stained brown and who keeps a spittoon in the boiler room.

Pim decides it must indeed be naughty to point out Aunt Glad's eggy splotch. He'd had a notion it was, had a notion his parents would reprimand him for it. Also he decides that she herself must be unaware of the splotch, which fills him with such pity that he reaches out and pats her arm.

"Well!" Aunt Glad gives a pleased little cry.

Her skin is a fascination to him. Not only the pink-and-white part that runs down the side of her face and vanishes beneath her blouse, but all her skin, the way it drapes from the bones, cross-hatched by tiny grooves, as if someone took a fork to candle wax, the way it smells like the inside of the linen closet upstairs when you slip in and latch the door behind you in a game of hide-and-seek.

For her part Aunt Glad peers at him, her chest suddenly tight. There is something familiar about the child, the sweet rudeness of his stare, the dampness of his hair, the way his whole body, all that translucent bare skin, the whole package of his body, seems to flicker. She has a quick conviction she is responsible for him. His name is on the tip of her tongue.

Then the small book in her hands recalls her to the moment, to the matter at hand. "Now, where were we?" And turning the page, she resumes reading aloud. "'Then Ant and Bee and Kind Dog went to choose some fruit. And Ant and Bee and Kind Dog all chose . . . plums!'"

But Pim has lost every ounce of interest. He reaches over and presses the book shut.

"Oh," says Aunt Glad, extracting her thumb. "Gently."

"My sister is being a bride," he informs her, hopping off the settee.

"Yes."

"Mantha is being a flower girl."

"Mm-hm."

"Tom isn't being anything."

"He will be a proud brother of the bride."

"I am being a soldier."

"Not a ring bearer?"

"I have a rapier and a musket and a lightsaber and a crossbow."

"My."

"It shoots real marshmallows. I will shoot everyone that comes that I hate."

"Oh! Well . . ." Aunt Glad feels suddenly tired. "I suppose no one will come whom you hate."

The little boy is hopping about the room, slashing the air with an invisible sword. His body, though no longer damp from the bath, is slippery-looking, nimble and bare, flitting through the watery greenish light of the downstairs. *Little boy blue, come blow your horn.* Rain drums on the flat porch roof, loud as the leaden feet of toy soldiers. The soldiers they make out of lead, she and Joy, pouring the molten stuff into casting molds, molds that make members of the Coldstream Guards in five different poses. Molds that had originally been a birthday gift, or were going to have been a birthday gift, molds that had already been wrapped in colored paper and tied with ribbon, intended for a little boy—*but we don't talk about that.* Daddy works his jaw quickly as they unpack everything from the kit: molds, clamps, ingots, a special little pot and ladle. It's after supper, wintertime, the corners of the room webbed with shadows, the Glendale stove giving off its heat.

Mother, sitting on the new gold settee, reaches into the basket of mending at her feet. Carefully Daddy and the girls lay the pieces on the long wooden table.

You go ahead and put one in, Daddy tells Glad. Mother sucks in a breath like a needle of air. *You're not going to let her do it.* Meaning Glad, home at last after so many months in the hospital, after so many operations. *She can do her part,* says Daddy softly. He clenches and unclenches his jaw so fast it looks like he has a heartbeat in his temple. *You go ahead and put one in,* he tells Glad, holding out the pristine little pot, and she picks up an ingot—round and fat as a shortbread cookie—and plunks it in. He sets the pot on the Glendale and begins to speak in an almost mechanical rumble. As if for no other reason but to banish the silence. *We call this a melting pot,* he says. *For reasons that are clear. But it also happens to be what we call our country. A nation where people from all different lands come together as one.*

A queer, muffled sound from Mother on the settee.

Glad's skin prickles. The graft scars tighten around her neck and ribs, squeeze like an angry grip, punishment for something no one will name; the shadows at the edges of the room dance.

Daddy goes on. *The metal we use*—interrupting himself to clear his throat, *baharruum!* like a bullfrog—*is part tin, part lead antimony.* When the ingot has become silvery-black liquid he says, *Come, Joy. You can pour the first batch.* With an abrupt, ragged sound, Mother leaves her sewing and the room. Daddy holds his big hand over Joy's small one and together they pour what will become soldiers.

In front of her, the naked little soldier boy hop-pirouettes, kicking out violently behind him. "Hi-*yaa,*" he says, baring his teeth. He repeats the move several times, completing a tour of the room before turning to Aunt Glad and confiding in her severely, "The Han army is on the move." Hands cupped in her lap, she watches him continue his maneuvers, faintly aware of being the recipient of his chivalry, for which it is her duty to pay grateful attention. In truth, she is a little bored. Pim's penis flops around independent of the rest of his body's torsions, a scrap of whimsy at the center of an otherwise bellicose display.

"William Myron Erlend Blumenthal!" The roar makes them both jump. Bennie stands at the bottom of the stairs holding the bath sheet still damp from Mantha. "Oh, Aunt Glad, hello! Hello! How was the drive? Have you been here long? I didn't hear you come. And you're sitting here all alone!"

"Oh!" Glad gives a little laugh as if to say she's undeserving of such fuss. "Tom was here just a while ago. He stopped for a chat."

Bennie stoops to kiss her great-aunt and breathes in her smell, a scent that is neither good nor bad but cherished by virtue of familiarity, some mixture of school paste, lemon drops, and Vapo-Rub. "Sorry, Aunt Glad."

"Whatever for?"

Bennie narrows her eyes at the naked boy. "That scoundrel."

Pim shrieks delightedly at this. He does another twirl, shows off his deadliest kick.

"One," counts Bennie, spreading the bath sheet wide.

From the kitchen comes Walter's voice, resounding with enjoyment of its own virility. *"Spanish heavens spread their brilliant starlight / High above the trenches in the plain!"*

"Spare us," mutters Bennie, "the Spanish Civil War songs."

"He was just telling me the Huns are coming," explains Aunt Glad, making a valiant if vague effort to connect the dots.

"The *Han* army!" Pim corrects.

"Two," counts Bennie. How she despises herself for resorting to counting out loud. In front of this gentle soul who famously taught kindergartners for thirty-three years without once (the story goes) having to raise her voice.

Walter, sonorous, from the other room: *"From the distance morning comes to greet us / Calling us to battle once again!"*

Bennie draws a deep breath, clear harbinger of "three," and Pim at the last moment dashes into her arms. She wraps the towel around him, pinning his limbs so that he can safely pretend to struggle while she growls with her lips just touching the rim of his ear, "I've got you now, my pretty. You'll never get away."

MANTHA IN HER BEDROOM gazes down upon them all. She is the one. The grand surveyor. Good elbow on dresser top, chin on fist, she squints into the dollhouse that has perched there since before she was born, mentally locating the members of her family in the rooms they inhabit at this very moment in Real Life.

Real Life is a distinction she insists upon because there are so many other kinds. For instance: Past Life, Future Life, Dream Life, Make-Believe Life, Private Life. Pim lives in Make-Believe Life most of the time, except when he is sleeping. Aunt Glad drifts between Real Life and Past Life; sometimes you can actually see her crisscrossing. Tom lives with one foot in Real Life and the other pitched forward into Future Life; this, too, you can see with your own eyes, the way he tests the ground ahead of him, trying out new walks and voices, new ways of presenting and absenting himself. Her parents most often and quite categorically claim the territory of Real Life. This is why, whenever she chances upon them believing themselves alone, it produces an elevator-drop sensation in her stomach: to glimpse them inhabiting Private Life. To glimpse her mother, reading a paperback on the couch, break into a smile of such rare tenderness over—what could it be? a line, a phrase?—and then gaze into the middle distance, working her lips almost imperceptibly. To glimpse her father doze off with the newspaper in hand, to see the paper fall aside and his mouth go slack, to see nothing but slits of white between his eyelids for a moment before he jerks awake, clears his throat, returns to the article at hand.

People in the same house, at the same moment—even immersed in the same conversation with each other—can be inhabiting different realms. Mantha alone, by studying the special dollhouse until her eyes go out of focus, has the ability to locate the members of her family in their various realms.

The dollhouse is special for the following reasons:

1. Her grandmother built it. Her grandmother who died when Bennie was just nineteen. Many years ago, when her grandmother was no older than Mantha is now, she built it with the help of Aunt Glad, the same Aunt Glad who is at this moment sitting downstairs on the gold settee with her sparse cottony hair and her goldy-brown eyes and her small feet that do not quite touch the floor. They built it together, just the two of them.

2. They did not use a kit.

3. It's this house. Not only is every room replicated in miniature, with aspects of the old post office faithfully included; so, too, are many of the actual furnishings they still have today. The cane chair on the porch. The clawfoot tub in the bathroom. The Morris chair in the living room. The floor lamp, with its stained-glass shade decorated to look like a bowl of fruit, that stands beside it. (The miniature version is molded sugar. Mantha has touched it with her tongue.)

The house is split and hinged like a bivalve. Its permanent position is wide open, everything on view. At night from her bed she can see into the tiny replicas of rooms set aglow by the moon-shaped nightlight plugged into the wall. Every night from her bed she performs this ritual preamble to sleep: she travels through the rooms, through the house that passes generation to generation, she flies down the staircase and up again, in and out the windows, over the roof, over the moon.

The house is doll-less. At least it came to her unpopulated. Two years ago, when she was six, Mantha claimed a pair of wooden clothespins from the laundry basket and made them her children. One has a bit of yellow yarn tied around its neck, the other a bit of red yarn. Their names are Fear and Sadness. *Hello, my Fear*, she'll murmur, she'll coo, even today, picking up the one and placing it softly in the white bathtub carved from a bar of soap. *Good morning, little Sadness*, she'll greet the other, giving it a kiss before propping it up against the tiny perfect maple-stained balsawood kitchen table in the breakfast nook. *I made your favorite, toast and eggs.*

"Isn't it strange?" Bennie'd said at the time to Walter. "Isn't it worrisome?"

"What are your dolls' names?" she would ask Mantha (who was still called Sammy then) from time to time, hoping the answer might have changed.

It never did.

"Would you like another clothespin?" Bennie would offer. "Do you think they might want a sister named Happiness?"

No was ever the answer.

She didn't seem like a depressed child.

"Do you think she ought to see someone?" Bennie said to Walter.

The pediatrician referred them to a psychologist who specialized in play therapy. She was a grandmotherly sort with an Israeli accent who watched Mantha-then-Sammy take apart and reassemble separately a set of *matryoshka* dolls. *Do they have names?* the psychologist asked.

Yes.

Can you tell me what they are?

They were Jenny, Judy, Jean, Bobby, and Foofoo.

Do you have any dolls at home?

Yes.

How many?

Two.

Will you tell me about them?

They're sisters.

What are their names?

But Mantha-then-Sammy appeared not to hear this question. Having finished with the *matryoshka* family, she moved on to a box of little wooden cars, which she began to unpack onto the richly colored kilim rug.

What do you do when you play with them?

She arranged all the little cars in a ring before answering. *Take care of 'em.*

How do you take care of them?

Oh—now she was driving the cars one by one out of the ring, parking each on a separate part of the kilim—*cuddle, sing songs. Take 'em to the zoo. Cook 'em pudding.*

What kind of pudding?

Lima bean. Popcorn. Beep.

I see no reason for concern, the psychologist told Bennie and Walter after two more sessions. *I find her to be securely attached. Able to self-soothe with imagination and creativity. Also—but I don't need to tell you this—she's a pip!*

Before Mantha was born the dollhouse had belonged to Clem, just as this room had once been Clem's, and the apple-and-pear-patterned wallpaper, and the bed and the dresser and the radiator and the window seat and the closet and the mirror that is so old the silver backing has come off in places so whoever is being reflected is afflicted with vacancies like a leper or a ghost. Before Clem, the room belonged to their mother and Aunt Carrie. Before that, to their grandmother, who died before they were born. Even longer ago it was shared by another pair of sisters, Glad and Joy, their great-grandaunt and great-grandmother. And one day Mantha herself will be the mother who comes into this room to kiss her own little girl good night.

Now, beyond the drumbeat of rain, which has been falling for days, hammering the roof, swelling the doors fat against their jambs, making chocolate soup of the bald parts of their lawn, Mantha listens for clues as to what is happening throughout the house. She hears:

Pim and her mother in the living room (there is his piglet squeal; there Bennie's low, matter-of-fact retort).

Aunt Glad on the settee (her throaty chortle; Pim must have done something funny).

Her father in the kitchen (caterwauling one of his protest songs).

Tom on the stairs (here he comes galumphing).

And now an engine (growing louder: coming up the drive)—and Mantha gives the shout: *Here's Clem!*

THE CAR, a long-nosed Buick wagon, lurches to a stop. The rear passenger door opens. A foot, Doc Martened, plants itself in chocolate soup. "Shit." This is Hannah. "Thank you for parking in the Hudson."

From the front passenger door another foot emerges, this one bare, balletic, describing an arc over the puddle. The rest of the body follows as if poured. "I have to pee, I have to pee!" This is Chana, owner of the car but (as she readily professes to any and all) an abominable driver ever grateful to default to the passenger position. "I'm serious, you guys, I really have to pee."

"So pee," Hannah tells her.

"I have to!" She gallops laughing toward the house.

Now the engine cuts off. Headlights, too. The driver's door opens. Out steps our ingénue.

Let's give her a real entrance. She's twenty-two, yellow-haired, brown-eyed, with the tiniest gap between her top front teeth. Seven weeks ago yesterday she strode across the stage at her small liberal arts college, wearing a shiny black gown and a mortarboard upon which she'd glue-gunned a dozen real mauve tea roses, and received a diploma conferring upon her the degree of Bachelor of Arts (concentrations in anthropology and theater, senior thesis: "From Flash Mobs to Pop-Ups: Paratheater Since Grotowski"). Since then she's been crashing on Hannah's couch in Brooklyn, helping her make jewelry out of playing pieces from vintage board games (Risk earrings, Trouble necklaces, Life charm bracelets), then helping her sell said jewelry at farmers markets all about town. Hither and yon. In neighborhoods she'd never heard of, one day in a magical pocket of green space, the next on a baking expanse of asphalt. Evenings they'd either meet up with Hannah's friends or stay home and cook great unbalanced meals. They developed an obsession for experimenting with outlandish pestos (mint, parsley, ramsons, beet, even—surprisingly fabulous—blueberry), concocted from whatever had looked good at that day's market, then twirl up their pasta and suck down cold forties out on Hannah's fire escape, barely big enough for two plastic milk crates, a potted grapefruit tree strung with colored lights, and a life-size cardboard Betty Boop who watched over them like a patron saint. She has, in other words, these past seven weeks, been marking time.

Now she can hardly wait to get on to the next thing: four more days until her Chosen Life begins! Not that she doesn't love Hannah, not that the Bushwick interregnum wasn't a lark, but truth be told it had started to wear thin, an undifferentiated, aimless string of peripatetic days and beery nights, as if life were no more than a single extended improv, all spontaneity, zero goal. Whereas Clem has a very definite goal, an immediate goal. That is, to wed. In a manner of speaking. In an irreverent manner. In a manner in keeping with all the convention-flouting, pot-stirring, expectation-upending character of the love she and Diggs have for each other in the first place.

Clementine Esther Erlend Blumenthal, firstborn child of Walter and Benita Blumenthal, soon to become Mrs. KC Diggins (not that she's actually changing her name)—at any rate soon to become her college girlfriend's wife, her helpmeet, hausfrau, old lady (how thrilling, all the words she will soon be able to apply to herself, even the distasteful ones, especially the distasteful ones!—it has become a private joke between her and Diggs to refer to each other as chattel, even calling each other by the pet name Chat—a sign of their temerity in looking the history of bride-as-property dead in the eye, a sign of how freely, cheekily, and brazenly they choose to assume the mantle of this ancient, oppressive tradition: not haplessly but subversively, not as defectors but as infiltrators!), this maiden, this bride, bedecked in clogs, cutoffs, a Mr. Bubble tank top, a belled ankle bracelet that tinkles when she walks, and a tiny peridot stud glinting in her nose: our ingénue steps from the car, spreads her arms and throws back her head to receive the rain on her face.

"Yo, Gene Kelly," Hannah says. "Want to pop the trunk?"

So she does, and the girls (they still default to thinking of themselves as girls, try as they might to get into the habit of referring to themselves as women) each retrieve an armload of gear and scurry up toward the porch.

THE ROOM IS FULL, as Aunt Glad remembers it frequently being, and that in itself feels right and calming, even though there is nothing especially serene about the medley of voices and confusion of faces tonight. A basket of hot bread has been passed around and now sits on the coffee table, giving off visible threads of steam. Aunt Glad has demurred; Walter's baguettes are too crusty for her, hurt the roof of her mouth, but she feasts on the sight of the children devouring it, the youngest girl with the cast on her arm slathering far too much butter on her slice, and crumbs exploding willy-nilly whenever someone takes a bite. Walter, still in his apron, sits in her father's old Morris chair, a bottle of beer on his knee.

The little boy has finally been persuaded into pajamas, which are decorated all over with some kind of machine she doesn't know the name of. He is no longer fighting armies but leaning against his mother at the other end of the settee, sucking his thumb. "Perfume'll cure that," confides Aunt Glad. She keeps a bottle of Nuit de Longchamp in her desk for just that purpose. Whenever one of her students turns out to be a thumb sucker, she calls the boy or girl over, speaking to them always in private, never to shame, and explains, before applying a drop to the troublesome digit, *The taste will help you remember to keep it out of your mouth.*

The young ladies sprawl inelegantly around the coffee table. The little lithe one who bounded in ahead of the others, trumpeting without embarrassment about her dire need of the powder room, sits cross-legged on the floor. The one wearing men's boots, her legs splayed wide, is taking up half the couch. She looks like she belongs to a game of checkers, with her hair and boots so black and her lipstick red as crayon. Clem sits beside her, looking almost lovely. The length of her bare limbs, the length of her yellow hair—nearly to her waist. What a shame about the thing in her nose. Glad keeps wanting to offer her a handkerchief, only to remind herself it's a piece of jewelry.

And where is her friend Tom? She looks around for the older boy. There he is, he's brought a stool in from the kitchen and perches up high, laughing at something someone's said. The way his jaw opens reminds her of something—one of Lester Vilno's marionettes. Several dozen of them he must have made, each adorned in an elaborate costume he stitched himself. *Wickedly clever contraptions*, Mother calls them. Every year at Christmas he gives a show in the children's room at the library. All the characters speak with the same accent (Lithuanian, some say, or is it Latvian? something foreign anyway, full of lilting vowels and crimped consonants), but they each have their own personality. Some perform tricks: the mouse marionette pedals a wooden tricycle; the ballerina walks on her toes; the boy with measles drops his jaw and unrolls a pink felt tongue for the doctor.

There are those who cast aspersions on Lester Vilno; Glad has heard them cluck their tongues (*Queer old bachelor to invent all those fanciful figures*). Others speak with sympathy (*Poor fellow lost his entire family back in the old country, struck down by disease or something worse; What's worse?* Glad asked, only to have Mother shoot Daddy a look—*Little pitchers!*—before answering, *Never you mind*). In any case the sight of Lester Vilno riding his bicycle, long black coat fluttering out behind him, long grizzled beard reaching midway down his chest, is familiar to everyone in the village, and even those who disparage him do so with a kind of pride, as if to say, *He may be strange but he's our stranger.*

Glad cannot recall when he stopped coming around the post

office or how much time passed before it occurred to her he was gone for good. Did he vanish gradually, or all at once? Even this she does not know. Eventually she had become aware that it had been ages since he'd come to buy twine or tea or sandpaper, ages since she'd spotted him pedaling along the streets of Rundle Junction, ages since he'd stopped giving his annual Christmas puppet show. By the time she got around to asking *Whatever happened to Lester Vilno?* she wasn't really surprised that Mother, darning socks by the fire, answered simply, *Gone.*

Gone where? No one knows. Mother sews. Daddy feeds the fire another log. The pine sap pops and the rain drums and Glad's head bends forward until her chin reaches midway down her chest.

Clem's leg stretches forward. Her bare toes prod her sister's back. "Hey Sammy. How much longer you gotta wear that thing?" Meaning the cast.

"Mantha," corrects Mantha. She is kneeling rather territorially in front of the bread basket, swabbing butter on a torn hunk.

"Mantha!" Clem smacks herself on the forehead.

"That's my name, don't wear it out."

"I keep forgetting that's what we call you now."

"What are your pronouns?" asks Hannah.

With hauteur: "That's for me to know and you to find out."

"How much longer with the cast, honey?" repeats Clem.

Mantha, shoving bread in her mouth, hums the three-note melody of *I-don't-know.*

"We go back to the doctor in two weeks," answers Bennie. "Hopefully he'll take it off then."

"Two weeks! How you s'posed to be my flower girl with that thing on your arm, huh? How'm I s'posed to get married if you can't perform the duties of flower girl?"

"Clem," chides Bennie. "Don't."

"She knows I'm kidding. Don't you, Man?"

Mantha, with exaggerated dignity, rises, brushes crumbs off her pajamas, hooks the handle of the bread basket on her cast-arm, and mimes strewing flower petals with her good one. "What do you say to that?"

"Phew." Clem wipes her brow. "I can breathe easy."

Mantha gives her a neat kick.

"A better question," says Bennie, "is how are you going to have an outdoor wedding if this rain doesn't stop?"

"Oh it will," promises Chana, very earnest. "It's supposed to!" Working her smartphone, she rattles off: "Twenty percent chance of thunderstorms Tuesday, fair on Wednesday and Thursday, Friday just partly cloudy."

"Anyway," declares Clem with blithe optimism, "there's always the barn."

Bennie indicates the utter preposterousness of this suggestion by altering her expression not one whit.

The barn's list of woes has grown dramatically since Clem first left for college. Dry rot, leaks, fungus, broken windows, partial foundation collapse, carpenter ants. But it's the list to the west that's most dramatic: it looks like a lover going down on one knee. Or at dawn, with the mist rising off McElroy's field, like a ship being tossed at sea. A few years back they had an engineer out to inspect the structure and give an estimate for repair. When he explained the only viable solution was to tear it down and start fresh—and named the cost of such a project—Walter and Bennie decided on the path of benign neglect. Ever since, whenever the subject of the barn comes up, they've made a sport of indulging in a kind of gallows humor. It's as if, having resigned themselves to eventual catastrophe, they're impatient for it to occur. After a big storm one of them might say, "How's the barn?" which is the cue for the other to respond, "Critical but stable. We'll know more if she makes it through the next twenty-four hours," or, "There's no medical explanation for it, but she's still hanging on." Once Walter obtained a real DNR form from his primary care doctor, stuck it to the barn door, and managed to keep mum for two whole weeks until Bennie noticed. He was rewarded by a hoot of laughter so loud he heard it from the kitchen.

"Whatever," Tom says now. "Umbrellas, people. Chillax."

"We brought a chuppah," mentions Hannah.

"Really?" says Walter.

"Yeah, we made it."

"Out of clay," Clem cannot resist chiming in.

"Out of cheesecloth," says Hannah. "In actual point of fact." It had given her a kind of masochistic pleasure to construct it for Clem, whom she loved, during their time together in Bushwick. She had trimmed it with classic board game pieces, metal Monopoly tokens and the tiny weapons from Clue.

"And cheesecloth will keep the rain out how?" Bennie wonders.

But, "Really?" Walter repeats, his voice dense with emotion. "You made a chuppah?"

"Yeah," says Hannah.

"You guys are Jewish, aren't you?" asks Chana.

"*Más o menos*," says Tom.

"It depends," says Clem.

"On what?"

"Who you ask." In truth—and perhaps irrationally, since she'd been raised outside any religious tradition—she was still kind of stung from the time the Chabad guys, on campus with their mitzvah tank, refused even to speak with her after she answered truthfully that her mother wasn't Jewish.

"If you ask Hitler," Mantha interjects knowledgeably, "we are."

"Basically," Tom qualifies, "we're Jew-*ish*," indicating the amount between finger and thumb.

49

Bennie's ancestors, the Erlends, originally hailed from Norway; they'd arrived in this country in the late eighteenth century as— at least nominally—Lutherans, but any adherence to that particular denomination had faded into WASPy generality soon thereafter. What vestiges of their old-world rites had endured (the felted gnome ornaments they hung on the Christmas tree, the cardamom-scented gløgg they heated each New Year's, the wildflowers the little girls picked and tucked under their pillows on midsummer's eve) harked back more, in any case, to paganism than church. Nor had Bennie herself ever technically been an Erlend, that name belonging to her maternal side. Before becoming a Blumenthal she'd been a Jansen, thanks to a father of Dutch descent; *his* religion, as he'd never tired of informing all who inquired, was football.

Walter's family, the Blumenthals, had arrived in the New World from Czernowitz much later, in 1915, and had remained observant—if to a steadily diminishing degree—almost up until the current crop of kids. Walter's great-great-grandfather was said to have been a rabbi in the Old Country. His great-grandfather Chaim had kept kosher. (Walter has a single dim memory of a wordless figure sitting hunched in the kitchen of some relative's row house in Flushing, disdaining the *treyf* everybody else was eating and accepting only a baked potato, which he'd eaten with a plastic fork off a paper plate.) His grandfather David, who lived until Walter was well into his teens, had gone to shul on foot every Sabbath, no matter the weather. Even his father, Myron, who as far as Walter knew harbored not the merest shred of belief in a divine being, never once entered or exited their apartment without reaching up to touch the mezuzah nailed to the door frame, then kissing his fingers.

Walter has vague recollections of his own years at Hebrew school: the classroom smell of sweaty boys, sweaty Converse, and disintegrating books. He remembers the wet-palmed struggle to learn his haftarah portion, the halfhearted slog of composing his *d'var* Torah, the feel of the necktie against his newly protrusive Adam's apple, but somehow nothing of the bar mitzvah itself. All that remains of his Judaism now is a handful of Yiddish songs, some commemorative fasting on Yom Kippur, a weakness for pickled herring, and a pronounced socialist bent.

Nevertheless—or perhaps all the more—now, sitting with his daughter days before her wedding, he is touched by the idea of Clem's wanting to incorporate something of his religious tradition into the ceremony.

"That's very nice." He takes a long, rather misty swallow of beer. "And you made it yourselves."

Hannah, bowing, gives a courtier's flourish with her hand.

"Dad's gonna cry." Tom the Comedian.

Walter spreads his arms: *So sue me.* "I'm moved."

"Do you know," Aunt Glad remarks with sudden interest, "I think Lester Vilno might have been Jewish." Heads swivel in amusement. Hadn't she, just a moment ago, been fast asleep?

"Who's Lester Vilno?" Mantha wants to know.

"Oh . . ." She trails off uncertainly, seems to search the room for an ally, someone who might help her explain. Finding none, she says, a touch reprovingly, "*You* know. He always sits right there"—gesturing toward Tom.

A current of giggles—quickly transformed into coughs—flows through the room. Tom, marvelously straight-faced, thumps his fist twice against his chest and flashes Aunt Glad the peace sign.

Devilish Tom! She has at least one like him every year: cutups, in need of careful monitoring and frequent reprimands, but how lively they are, how—she tries not to let on how much claim they have on her affection—delightful to be around, with their cockiness, their pluck.

Now Tom turns to Walter and asks with a concertedly ingenuous air, "Gee, Dad, think it's safe to use a chuppah where the neighbors can see?"

Of course this sets off among the bride and her maids a flurry of questions, and a briefing on the local political scene ensues: the Citizens for the Preservation of Rundle Junction signs are described, McElroy's allegiance noted, the wetlands and silver-maple forest explicated, the proceedings of the most recent village meeting recounted, the two-kitchen apartment plans detailed, Jeff Greenberg's reedy voice mimicked.

"I don't get it," says Clem. "Are you saying this is anti-Semitism? Or there's real environmental concern?"

"There's real environmental concern." Tom shoots a look at his father. "With a little anti-Semitism on the side."

"It may be that there's both," Walter concedes. "But I find it hard to believe there'd be this much energy around the silver maples if it weren't underpinned—maybe unconsciously—by anti-Semitism."

But: "I don't think it's either," says Bennie. They all turn toward her, those who know her long-standing indifference to local politics with added curiosity.

"No? What do you think it is?"

She meets her husband's gaze from across the room. "Justified wariness."

Tom lets out a low whistle. He might be being funny, but by the time it peters out, nothing feels funny about the tension in the room.

Bennie goes on: "Of an influx—"

"Of anyone different," proposes Clem.

"No . . ." Bennie speaks as if finding her way word by word. "I don't think Rundle Junction is categorically unwelcoming of difference. Look at the Freedom to Marry Ice Cream Social. Look at

Cuentalo en Español." Referring, respectively, to the annual gay marriage celebration held on the lawn of the Unitarian Universalist Church and the bilingual story hour held Thursday afternoons at the public library; she still takes Pim to the latter. "What I was going to say is an influx—"

"Of high-rises," tries Tom.

"Of just more people?" guesses Mantha, buttering more bread.

"An influx an influx an influx," Pim chants softly around his thumb. He leans against Bennie, nestled into the soft, warm meat of her arm.

"Shh—she's getting mad," Clem admonishes, only half joking.

Bennie sets her jaw. She looks not unlike Mantha when Mantha is doing her sulky face.

"What were you going to say, Mom?" Tom, angelic on a dime. "We really really want to know."

A dignity-reclaiming pause. "I was going to say an influx of fundamentalists."

"Fundamentalists," Walter echoes. Now he is the one to set his jaw.

"Yes. I think it's wise to be wary of fundamentalism. Of any stripe."

Walter gives a short, wounded laugh. "What about the fundamentalism of not wanting the demographic makeup of your town to change?"

Bennie opens her mouth. Closes it. Seems to have a new thought, tries to catch his eye. But Walter has become preoccupied with the label on his empty beer bottle.

They all feel it, the rift. Even Aunt Glad, who isn't following the content. Even Hannah, who didn't grow up with the Blumenthals and might not be expected to pick up on nuances. Even Chana, who's never met Clem's family until this evening. Walter and Bennie are the custodians of this house and home, the paired sentinels who guard the gates. Their children are accustomed to thinking of them as a unit, a single continuous entity. Even when discord unsettles an entity it remains an entity, one thing. This is different. Never before has it struck the children so clearly, the vast distance separating the realms from which each parent hails: Bennie of the Erlends, established for generations in Rundle Junction; Walter of the Blumenthals, one family among myriad wandering Jews.

Inharmonious silence coats the room. The rain, dauntless, continues to play its four-piece timpani: roof, panes, branches, earth.

Of all people it's Chana then, funny little Chana with her cloud of marmalade hair and her wistful cluelessness and squeaky voice, the most outsidery person in the room, who suddenly has the clearest vision of what is happening in it. It sweeps her up, the funny-sad timeless truth of it. Us-and-them-ness. "It's the old Mel Brooks routine!" she blurts. They all look at her, nonplussed. Turning bright pink, she nevertheless presses on: "The 2000 Year Old Man? When they ask, 'What was the first national anthem?'" Still nothing but dull stares from all over the room, but she cannot extricate herself from finishing now. Her own nervous laughter punctuates the punchline: "'Let 'em all go to hell. Except cave seventy-six!'"

Clem looks flummoxed; Hannah, scornful; Bennie, inconvenienced; Walter, distant. Tom laughs but only because he's embarrassed for her. Mantha laughs but only to be like Tom. Glad emits a ladylike snore, which makes Mantha laugh harder. Then she proclaims, "Well I'm striped."

"Huh?"

"Mom said 'of every stripe.' Like me." She stands to display her pajamas, which are indeed candy striped. "And Dad. He's striped, too."

They all look at Walter, who glances down at the blue-and-white-pinstriped apron he still has on. "So I am," he says. "So I am."

Bennie extricates herself from sleepy Pim, gets up, and crosses to the Morris chair. She removes the empty beer bottle from her husband's grasp and replaces it with her hand. Is this détente? In its inelegant deliberateness, it is perhaps the most intimate gesture the children can recall ever having witnessed between their parents. And while none of them is privy to the wealth of history behind it, while none has knowledge of all the secrets Walter and Bennie have shared, or indeed knows that in this moment they happen to be holding between them two rather important secrets that will in time affect all their lives, still it is not lost on them—anyone can see—how firmly they are clasping hands, how deeply meeting each other's gaze.

"Aw shucks," says Tom. "Looks like weddings just bring out the romance in everyone."

The young people laugh. Bennie brings Walter's empty, along with a few spent glasses, into the kitchen. The sound of the sink, the sound of dishes.

"Guess I better take that one to bed," says Walter, nodding toward Pim, who looks to have fallen fast asleep. He hoists the little boy from the couch, limbs loose as sacks of flour, and starts toward the stairs. The movement causes Pim's thumb to fall out of his mouth, waking him just enough to mumble a warning to the room at large. Or is he talking in his sleep, speaking from within the pocket of some dream?

"The black hats are coming, the black hats are coming!"

Clem goes googly-eyed and claps a hand over her mouth.

"Did he say black hats?" whispers Chana.

"Where'd he pick that up?" Tom tries not to laugh.

"Where *did* you hear it, Pim?" Walter asks.

But the little boy's eyelids have drooped inexorably shut, like the weighted lids of a doll.

FIRST NOCTURNE

THE MOON

The stationary front responsible for four straight days of rain over Rundle Junction finally ends. Around two o'clock in the morning the waning gibbous moon, color of butter, appears over the old post office.

Bennie wakes lucid and all at once. This is how she always wakes, never any groggy in-between for her. But what has summoned her from one state to the other at this moment, what has changed?

Beside her: the long, sloping mountain range of her husband's body rises and falls, emitting low rumbles so familiar to Bennie they're no more than white noise. On her other side: the plump hillock of Pim, who nightly vacates his own bed to come burrowing in beside her. Little does he know how imminently he's about to be evicted from this spot. For now, his untroubled breath ruffles delicately in and out between his parted lips: a tranquil taffeta snore. Bennie listens for another sound, a top note of distress coming from one of the children's rooms or from Aunt Glad—what if she's awake and confused about where she is?

But no.

Nothing.

There is light on her face, light streaming across the bed.

Always they sleep with the curtains drawn across the lower sashes but the top portion of the windows left uncovered. Rising up on her elbow now in the narrow channel left for her by the blithe sprawl of these two bodies, she spies the moon. Freshly scrubbed, throwing off a light so piercing and pure for a moment she thinks she hears it: a struck bell.

It's the silence, she realizes. The absence of the drumbeat of rain. This is what has changed. She inhales: the air is fresher, finer than it's been in days. Thin as skim milk. She falls back on her pillow, instantly asleep once more.

MEMORY

In fact Aunt Glad is awake, as she often is at this and many other hours of the night. Wakeful moments pock her sleep like holes punched in the lid of a box. (Like the holes she and Joy make for the salamanders they collect. *So they can breathe*, says Joy. *And so they're not in darkness*, adds Glad.) The inverse is also true: dream moments pock her waking hours and light shines through those holes, too. Light from life and light from dreams filters back and forth, and in their needle shafts of illumination, specks of memory and mismemory mingle and mill.

She lies on her back under the departure board, listening to its wooden slats rattle, trying to read the names of trains and their platform numbers as moonlight streams through the glass atrium, blinding her.

She lies on her back under the grandstand, listening to the pageantgoers' muffled cries, trying to see through the smoke whoever is calling her name as a tiny toy trumpet drops out of the sky.

She lies on her back on linen sheets as soft as cream, listening to footsteps travel through the house, trying to track them, to suss their aim as they move back and forth, nearer and farther, round and round. Always she is unsuccessful. Always she falls asleep again before they find their destination.

They've put her in the office, though it isn't an office anymore. Mother used to sort the mail in here, and frank the envelopes and file the receipts. No mail's come through here for years and years now. But she can still see the bins they'd use to store incoming and outgoing first-class. She shuts her eyes and sees them, and the canvas mail sacks with their tare weight stenciled on, and the stacks of catalogues that pile up: Montgomery Ward; Sears, Roebuck; and—Glad and Joy's favorite—the seed catalogues, Burpee; Farmer's Wife; Childs; Dominion. Shelves of parcels too big to fit in any letterbox. For a week or two in early spring the room is filled with peeping: cartons of live chicks. Sometimes an order of bees.

But what is that noise she hears now? Neither chick nor bee. From behind her head, from within the wall behind the cot they have set up for her here: miniature clicking, ticking sounds. At first she thinks she must be causing them herself, setting the bedsprings, the old rusted coils, against one another. But even holding perfectly still she hears them. Quick little movements, efficient, industrious. A mouse's jaws, its tiny mandibles, its exquisite, minuscule paws. A vision of a sunflower seed and then she cannot imagine the sound linked to anything else. Certainly it must be a mouse, a fat gray fellow settled on the tripod of haunches and tail, whiskers quivering, cracking one by one its stash of seeds and nibbling, nibbling.

THE MOUSE

In fact it is a mouse, a young female who gave birth to her first litter last week on the night when the rains began and who lost all five pink hairless pups to flooding before they'd opened their eyes, before their ears came unstuck. She'd built her nest underneath the porch, where the water swirled up fast on the second day of rain and washed it away. She's begun constructing a new nest in this drier place between the wallboards, and has paused her work not to crack a sunflower seed but to eat a beetle that happened by.

THE LOVERS

And in fact Glad had heard footsteps, real footsteps in real time. In the living room now Clem is talking softly, privately, in the dark. The oblong moon hangs like the palest of apricots in the sky. Clem speaks barely above a whisper into the cell phone pressed to her ear. Every sense is heightened in the smallness of the hour. Her own voice arouses her, its vibrations traveling through her chest and throat, across her tongue and lips. Everything is erotic, the shadows and the breeze. She's lying across the settee with her head thrown back, long hair dangling over one end, long legs dangling over the other. She is saying *I can't talk any louder, Chat, it's a house full of people . . . No, I'm in the living room . . . because my aunt's sleeping in the next room . . . a T-shirt and underwear . . . I don't know, I don't memorize these things . . . my my how insistent we are . . . all right, hold your horses . . .* She shines the light of the cell phone on her crotch, brings it back to her ear. *They're blue . . . I don't freaking know, rayon maybe, okay? What about you? . . . Oh Chat, I miss you so much . . . I missed you like crazy the whole time in Bushwick . . . mm-hmm . . . that's right, baby, I missed your bush, your cinnamon spice—yo girl! . . . que te es méchante! . . . not if I lick your wick first . . .* Hushed laughter. Clem switches the phone to her other ear.

Now her voice softens and slows, and she utters these next words in measured, attentive cadences, as if the person on the other end is saying them, too, reciting in concert with her; it is impossible to tell who has initiated the move, so smooth is the shift from spontaneous conversation into this poem, this canticle, these words of prayer: "*I am come into my garden, my sister, my bride: I have gathered my myrrh with my spice; I have eaten my honeycomb with my honey; I have drunk my wine with my milk.*"

A pause. During which Clem does not speak. Neither do any words come through from the other end of the line. A shared silence, pregnant with peace and longing. Then Clem sighs. A whispery voluptuous sound. And resumes talking, barely above a murmur she says, *Ah, Chat, when are you getting here? . . . it's okay, she's like a hundred years old, I think we're good . . . no, no, I couldn't stand staying there a minute longer. I love Hannah but it got seriously old, her place, her life . . . all those damn farmers markets, for real. Oh wait I have to tell you something important, okay? May I tell you something deep? With profound implications for our future conjugal bliss? We are never going to make pesto together . . .* More soft laughter. *I do love Hannah . . . I am not a mean friend . . . no I'm not, I was just so homesick for you . . . I know . . . I know! I know, but baby? It's hard to feel at home when you know it's only temporary.*

BUT THAT ISN'T TRUE, thinks Aunt Glad with clarion conviction from her cot in the next room. Ninety-four years old she may be; nevertheless she retains excellent hearing. She half rises, as if to go into the living room and tell Clem she is wrong. For a moment she feels driven, feels it's imperative she explain, her responsibility to make the child see. *It's your responsibility,* Mother is telling her, and Gladdy is saying dutifully, *I know, Mother,* yet something always manages to distract her, or her memory manages to fail her, and oh won't Mother be disappointed in her now, oh won't she be furious. Won't she be racked with grief.

Somehow, despite her intentions, Glad has let the mattress receive once more the full, if negligible, weight of her body, has let the creamy sheets soothe and cool her burning skin. It isn't time, in any case—she's gotten her timetables confused. Clem's too young to hear the truth (How could one so young be expected to understand?), that the world itself is no more than temporary.

❧ 2 · ❧

Episode Two. Tuesday.

Three Days Before the Wedding.

Midmorning finds Bennie in the breakfast nook, a scum of cream on what remains of her now-cold third cup of coffee (a blunder, is her stomach's verdict, but then these days her stomach is supremely finicky), an assortment of to-do lists on blue notepaper fanned out before her. There's something she needs to add to the shopping list, only she can't come up with the word. *Pregnancy brain.* Her hair is still slightly damp from the shower; she likes letting it dry slowly in the luxury of sun now shining in again after so many days of rain. All the windows are flung wide— she did the flinging herself first thing this morning, going from room to room to let the leaping breezes whisk away the fungal mustiness that had built up over the past few days—and the new air is so buttery and blue she could weep for joy. If it weren't for feeling she could weep from despair, that is.

Rein in those hormones, she scolds herself. No need to be melodramatic. Groan from exasperation, more like.

It's all very well for Clem to declare that she and her friends are *in charge of everything, Mom, you won't have to worry about a thing!* They're too inexperienced to understand all the backstage work involved in hosting a wedding. They wouldn't know to think about things like do they have enough seating for all the older people, and who's going to clean the bathrooms and make sure there are fresh hand towels. And although they've promised they have all the food under control, what could that mean, really? Have they any idea about things like quantities? And food poisoning? How to keep cold things cold and hot things hot? Have they given thought to coolers and chafing dishes, ice and—what *is* that chemical jelly stuff called?

Sterno. She adds it to the list.

From where she's sitting she can see chocolate smudges on the freezer door, a rubble of bread crumbs under the toaster oven, a pileup of Matchbox cars wedged behind the radiator. A glance heavenward only reminds her of the disaster of the ceiling, where some hidden source of moisture has caused an interesting work in progress: what started a year ago as a spreading pointillism of discoloration began to be punctuated this winter by dark, fringed craters where the plaster is bulging loose; in recent weeks a few chunks have actually broken off. In fact—*What is that?*—she leans over and peers at the butter dish and, yes, extricates from it another ceiling flake. The most overwhelming part is that all these flaws are merely the ones visible *from where she's sitting*: multiply them by a hundred, at least.

Ah well. Soon these problems won't be theirs. Assuming they can get a buyer. *We know we can get a buyer,* Stalwart said. Meaningfully. Meaning the Haredim. *But shouldn't we at least try to sell to someone . . . you know, just regular?* she said. It's not that she doesn't acknowledge the strangeness of her position. She, who's never lifted a finger for the village, who's never expressed any particular allegiance to it, siding with those who hope to keep its character intact. She's not sure why she feels this pull. Some latent sentimentality she never knew she possessed, some crumb of pre-nostalgia shaken loose by the decision to move? Or is it a biological imperative, heightened by the fact that she is, once again, with child—a primal desire to root for the continuation of Our Kind?

Could such primal desire, come to think of it, be the cause of her husband's equally surprising position: his blanket defensiveness in the face of concerns about the newcomers? For even though he was the one to initiate the talk of moving, he won't brook a negative word about the Haredim. She is puzzled, troubled, by the lump of resentment he seems to have been nursing since last night. Stalwart, ordinarily so open to engaging the many sides of a complex problem, seems in this instance reluctant to grant that a person could oppose the new housing development for any reason other than knee-jerk bigotry. She thinks of all the evidence—information *he* has shared with her—about what the Haredim really might do if they reach critical mass in Rundle Junction: vote as a bloc to change zoning laws; slash public school budgets while sending their own children to yeshivas that prepare them not to become productive members of the workforce but to devote themselves full-time to religious studies; decimate public coffers with all those large families living below the poverty line. Generalizations, yes. Stereotypes, admittedly. But generalizations and stereotypes based on what is actually happening in other villages and towns where they have established strongholds. Based, as Mantha would say, on Real Life.

Funny—no, not funny: awful—to think of him thinking of her as his adversary. She recalls the story Walter told her years ago about an old couple. Were they people he'd known or was it a fable or a midrash or something? Anyway, the wife has something wrong with her foot, and together they go see the doctor. The doctor says, *What brings you today?* And the husband says, *Our foot hurts us.*

Our foot.

Bennie would very much like to ask Walter if she's hurt him. Ask him, *How's our foot?*

Oh well, she can't, not now. Stalwart, that cad, has deserted her. Absconded as usual on the 6:54 to Grand Central. He is—big breath here for the official title—Chief Information Officer at the Ujima Collaborative, a Nonprofit Social Research Organization Specializing in Developmental Programs for Underserved Youth. Or as Bennie likes to say: *Other people do important work and Walter talks about it.*

Joking, of course.

So Walter's gone—he's taken off the rest of the week for the wedding but had to go in for a board meeting today—leaving her to hold the fort. (*You mean rule the roost,* he said when she grumbled about it earlier this morning, an amendment she'd accepted with an if-the-shoe-fits grin.) Bennie taps the eraser end of the pencil against her teeth and frowns at the top of the door frame, which seems to have grown a furry gray coat of dust. Maybe she can put Lloyd to work when he gets here. Can one do that? Greet the brother you haven't laid eyes on in nearly two years, not since his wife abandoned him in a foreign country, taking their then-nine-year-old child, by saying: *Hey Lloyd, long time no see, sorry about your marriage,* then sticking a feather duster in his hand? Better yet: *Hey Lloyd, you don't mind helping clean house, do you? By the way, this might be the last time you ever set foot in it.* Of course she won't say anything like that last part. She feels a twinge of guilt at withholding the fact that they're putting the house on the market. But why should she? Her brother's never shown any affection for the place. Couldn't wait to leave it behind, and hardly ever comes back to visit.

Poor old Lloyd, always just a little morose, just a little inert even on the best of days. Somehow her imagination has him wearing Walter's pinstriped apron, the strings long and droopy in back. Eeyore's tail. Oh dear. If Carrie were here they'd be cackling. Or working to suppress cackles. Meticulously avoiding each other's eyes. They are well practiced, the sisters, in the alternate arts of making sport of their younger brother and leaping righteously to his defense. Poor Lloydie.

But why poor? More to the point, why should it be Carrie's and her job to cosset him? Hadn't he grown up with the same advantages as his two sisters, there for the having, if only he'd accepted them? It had been his choice to reject them—*them* the advantages and *them* the family. He's the one who turned his back, went off of his own volition and squandered—not their love, perhaps, but their bequest. Refusing all that would have been provided for him if only he'd expressed the desire, if only he'd deigned to hunger for the things they'd all been raised to expect: an education, a good job, a reasonable place to live, a network of helpful contacts. The support of a community that cared about him—indeed, had a vested interest in him, having poured resources into him in order to create him as one of their own.

Even after their parents died, especially after their parents died (dramatically, you might say: two cancers in three years— first Dad, at age forty-seven, after months of feeling run-down and ascribing it to not getting enough exercise, had gone in for the routine physical he'd long put off and came home with a death sentence: stage four colon cancer—only to be outdone by Mom three months later, diagnosis: pancreatic cancer; she was dead within seven months; he wound up trailing her by two years), they did not lack for support, emotional, social, or financial—all were offered in quantities frankly too great to manage from family, friends, even from the village itself. The local chapters of the Elks and Rotary clubs established scholarship funds for the kids, all of whom were still in high school when their mother died. Lloyd, the youngest, was the only kid still living at home, a senior in high school, when their father followed suit. The sisters kept in touch as best they could manage from college, and of course they saw him on holidays, but it had been Aunt Glad, moving back into her childhood home, who provided Lloyd with daily companionship through the last bit of his childhood.

During the worst of it the siblings used sports terminology. With the reckless bravado of adolescence they relied on morbid jokes about the "rivalry" between their parents, their "race toward the finish," the way Mom "came up the backstretch to beat the odds," the way Dad "almost scored a hat trick" when, after his initial debulking surgery, he coded twice in one day. Other people—neighbors, aunts, and uncles—looked askance, but it gave the kids a carapace they could retreat inside and it drew them together in a way that kept others out, which felt necessary, sustaining. And it had worked, after a fashion. At least Bennie and Carrie had done all right, but somewhere along the line Lloyd had fallen off course. Or not fallen—if that were the case they might've turned back and propped him on his feet and kept him on the team. What he'd done was something more like turn and traipse off the field midplay. A thing he used to do, come to think of it, as a little boy, during informal games of baseball or soccer. At some point he'd just plunk down in the grass to pick dandelions, or wander away without telling anyone. When people would yell at him, *But you're on second base!* or *You can't just leave the goal untended!* he would only grimace—the famous, squinting, equivocal smile part of his MO even back in his towheaded boyhood—with a look of something like commiseration. As if to say, *Sorry, I know it's bad manners, but it's how I am.*

And after their parents died, it had been more of the same

genteel abnegation: *No thank you* he'd said to college. *No thank you* to culinary school and forestry school and even to a funded gap year abroad. *No thank you* to first and last month's rent plus security deposit on a studio apartment near the commuter rail. *No thank you* to meeting with any of their parents' friends who would have been more than happy, truly delighted, to put him in touch with other offers and help him find his way.

Never: *Leave me alone, quit bothering me.* Always: *No thank you.* Delivered with unfailing sweetness and regret. That was the thing about Lloyd, the thing that made him at once irremediably lovable and irremediably infuriating: the graciousness of his demurrals, which made you always yearn to offer him more, or offer him something different, always in hopes that you'd come up at last with the elusive thing he might actually accept, so you'd keep striving for this, failing to acknowledge its certain futility.

Well—but he had accepted the invitation to Clem's wedding. Managed to RSVP and everything. They'll be here today, he and Ellerby—another thing to prepare for. Even if she does wind up roping them into lending a hand with the scullery work later this week, she does at the very least need to have beds made up for them when they get here. Not to mention have dinner to serve. And, asterisk to that: her brother's ever-changing dietary preferences to cater to.

Fake butter, she adds to one of her lists. Soy/almond milk.

Speaking of brothers: "Where's your brother?" she demands of Mantha, who's wandered into the kitchen and is poking around the fruit bowl. "What are you looking for?"

"A plum that isn't squishy."

"Well stop that. Just take one. You're making them all squishy. Where's your brother?"

Mantha takes a plum and gives it a distrustful, millimeter-long lick.

"Wash it first."

Mantha takes it to the sink.

Bennie sighs. "Samantha Rachel Erlend Blumenthal. I'm not going to ask you a third—"

"There." Pointing.

Bennie looks over her shoulder through the screen door. Pim, in purple bathing trunks and the jacket of Tom's old *judogi*, is busily arranging his toy soldiers along the porch railing. From the steady movements of his lips he's either narrating or doing their voices. Aunt Glad's out there, too, dozing in the cane chair.

"Not that one," says Bennie.

Mantha bites into the plum and it gushes all down the front of her. "Tom? I don't know. Still in bed."

"Libel!" As of recently, Tom's first-thing-in-the-morning voice is pretty much basso profundo. Its unfamiliar depth stirs in Bennie an inappreciable flutter. He appears in the doorway sporting boxer shorts and a jaw-cracking yawn.

"I think you mean slander," says Bennie.

"Blasphemy!" he barks in Mantha's ear. *"Sacré bleu!"*

She elbows him with her fiberglass cast.

"Dude!" he yelps, suddenly a tenor.

Simultaneously Bennie cries, *"Not* with the broken arm!"

"That thing's a weapon." Tom, rubbing the injured rib, strolls fridgeward.

"That thing," says Bennie, "cost two hundred dollars out of pocket."

Tom glugs milk directly from the container. "It's almost empty," he breaks off gulping to gasp, thereby forestalling Bennie's rebuke.

And then he goes on standing there, draining the carton, one hand resting carelessly on the still-open door of the fridge, his bare torso ridiculously lean, his sternum tufted with toffee-colored floss that continues in a line vanishing down inside his

waistband. The muscles on his raised arm stand out in crisp definition, biceps smooth as river rocks. And the spread of his shoulders, the swell of his neck: When did he become this splendid,
hulking other? His very body a kind of eloquent repudiation. Of
what? Of the little boy he no longer is. But also it's a repudiation
of her, no? The body that bore him, the younger softer greener
woman she once was.

CLEM WAKES TODAY, three days before her wedding, much as she
does every morning: impatient for her life. Impatient to make her
entrance in it. Standing on the threshold of what Mantha would
call Future Life. The Main Act. She feels the impatience as a
physical sensation. In her fingers, mostly, a kind of distant throb-
bing, as if she had a buildup of sap in her veins and it needed to
flow. Once when she was younger, maybe twelve—and still believed, just automatically, never having taken the time to consider
otherwise, that her mother, simply by virtue of being her mother,
was like her: a native of the same landscape, familiar with all the
same sensations and perspectives—she'd said, *You know that thing
where your fingers hurt and you try to stretch them?*

Arthritis?

*No, I mean the thing you get where it's like an ache deep inside
and it's kind of psychological because it's connected to like a homesick feeling but it's not that because it can happen even when you're
home?*

No. I don't know that thing.

A slap that stung the more for having no malice in it; Clem
didn't doubt that Bennie was telling the truth, that she really had
no idea what Clem meant.

Now she starfishes her hands open and shut, wrings them softly
to ease the ache. She looks around. Hannah and Chana are both

still burrowed, only their heads—razored raven chop and tangerine frizz, respectively—sticking out of the tops of their sleeping bags. It had been raining much too hard last night to even consider setting up their tent; they'd camped instead in one of the attic rooms, their sleeping bags sardined horizontally across a mouse-chewed futon, one wobbly standing fan and one ancient box fan stuck into the window no match for the marshy atmosphere.

Who knows, maybe she does have arthritis, or some rare bone marrow condition confined only to her hands. When she wakes beside Diggs she often kneads her awake, pressing her fingers against the muscles of her beloved's warm, smooth, pudding arms and the wing-nubs of her scapulae, until Diggs mumbles, "Still sleeping here," although on some mornings, given the right sort of provocation, she'll deign to roll over and pounce. To sit astride, looking down with regal curiosity, and lace her own strong fingers through Clem's.

Their differences are legion. Beginning, most obviously, with the black-and-whiteness. "*Pudding?*" Diggs repeated the first time Clem used the word, and arched one eyebrow suspiciously. "As in chocolate pudding? As in some Kozy Shack? You my little race-fixated cracker-girl?"

But "No, no!" Clem protested. "Don't call me that, Chat. As in pudding-smooth, creamy, and custardy. As in delicious and yummy and good and . . ."

A few seconds later, more honestly: "All right, maybe I was thinking of chocolate pudding. But not in a fetishy, exoticizing way."

And after a few seconds more: ". . . and anyway certainly not Kozy Shack. If anything, Swiss Miss."

A mighty roar from her beloved then, hot breath in her ear, claws on her thighs, wild laughter erupting from both as they tumbled and scratched and got each other off.

This is what's so great about them, what makes it work and keeps it strong: when race comes up they talk about it, address it head-on. Anyway, that's not even what Clem thinks of as their biggest difference. The main thing is how practical Diggs is, how logical and well-equipped to navigate worldly matters, to believe in worldly matters *as* navigable (even now, she's at her summer job with the ACLU's Program on Freedom of Religion and Belief, a paid internship between her first and second years of law school), while Clem is more disposed to see life as ambiguous and absurd, a sort of indistinct *mush*, one gigantic, swirling, unpredictable concoction the point of which is to surrender to it all your heart and all your might, not knowing—not even presuming to ask—where it's headed. *To surrender,* as Clem put it in the introduction to her senior thesis, *the ego's designs to the eternal truth of uncertainty.* Diggs says this difference is actually related to race, says Clem's loosey-goosey approach to career is at least in part a function of her privilege and not everyone has the option to major in an artsy-fartsy field.

Which Clem gets. Totally. Which is part of what she'd like to help change. *Through* art. Art is not frivolous, she tells Diggs, quoting her thesis adviser. Ignazio Leopardi: about a million years old and still crazily rakish, with a tiny yin-and-yang stud in his ear, purple eyeglass frames, a frankly libidinous laugh. Art is not an accoutrement, she tells Diggs, not an indulgence, but a societal expedient, a tool of social change! It's like the leopards in the temple.

The whose in the what?

The leopards. In the temple. Kafka. She says it as if she has known it forever, but in truth she never read a speck of Kafka beyond Gregor Samsa until this past spring.

Theater is like the leopards, Clem told Diggs. *It disrupts the status quo,* she tried. *Until its ideas bring about lasting change by getting incorporated in society.*

Maybe. Diggs lubricated her skepticism with diplomacy. She's good at that. *But if we're talking expedience, law has it all over art, bambina.*

Okay, Grandmaw. Diggs, who'd been a year ahead of Clem in the same small liberal arts school where they met, is older by all of thirteen months. *If that's what they're training you to believe.*

Clem's not altogether impervious to the reality of daily life outside the bubble of college. Her dream is eventually to be involved in some kind of Theater of the Oppressed–type work, maybe work with incarcerated youth—but she's not all moony about it; she knows that when she first moves to DC, into Diggs's apartment—or rather (she's got to practice thinking this way!) into the place Diggs found but which will soon be their shared abode—she'll likely wind up waiting tables or temping first.

They've had some of their best (read: thorniest) conversations about this very issue: How do you balance dreams and reality, ambition and uncertainty, the exercise of free will with the willingness to be swept along by the current?

"Here's the new rule," Clem proposed one day last winter when they were trying to figure out in practical terms what their lives would look like post-wedding. *"Break the wineglass and fall toward the glassblower's breath."*

Diggs did her single-eyebrow thing.

"That's Rumi," said Clem. "Pretty good, no?"

"So are we falling toward marriage"—Diggs embroidered her skepticism with air quotes—"or choosing it?"

"We might *feel* like we're choosing . . . "

"Nuh-uh. Feel, nothing. Fall, nothing. I have agency. I do things by choice."

"You do, huh. Everything?"

"Yup. Free will, baby."

"It's all about intention."

"You got it."

"Very romantic. So are you saying you *chose* to fall in love with me?"

"Never said I fell in love with you."

Tears sprang to Clem's eyes.

Diggs watched in astonishment as they welled and overflowed before she moved in to stroke them away with her thumbs. "Lord, girl, you are sensitive. I *rose* in love with you."

More tears, hot and copious. These Diggs drank. Murmured, "That's Toni."

Little beat. ". . . Orlando and Dawn?"

"Morrison, white girl. Pretty good, no?"

Now in the little attic room longing shoots bodily through Clem, painful and lovely. Oh hurry up, she thinks, a bossy little prayer: please let these last few days hurry by. It isn't even precisely Diggs she's impatient for. Or at least, not only. It's herself—the fully formed self she's waiting to discover, waiting to become. At the end of the aisle, under the chuppah, after the vows. In the act of becoming—choosing—her adult role.

"When"—she actually put this question to Diggs the last time they were together, right after graduation; she had thought she might feel it that day, the sense of becoming finally evident to herself, fully assembled, not hypothetical, but no—"when do you get to the part of your life that's really real, the part when you know you've arrived?"

"What do you mean, *bambina*? Arrived professionally?" Cocked head, a single, prolifically expressive eyebrow arched.

They'd been sitting under a tree, Clem still in her commencement gown but unzipped, revealing a Jiffy Lube T-shirt and cutoffs underneath. Diggs had put Clem's mortarboard on her own head, where it looked ridiculously stylish in an outré sort of way, wilted tea roses and all. "No. Oh—is that what it is for you, though? You think? Like once you've gotten your law degree? Or passed the bar?"

"Depends what you mean by arrived. I mean"—and here Diggs had done that lovely shimmy thing she does with her shoulders and neck—"I *arrived* the day I came out my momma."

Clem believes it. Diggs would have arrived in the world whole and intact, united already with the root of who she was and would forever be. Even as an infant she would have been in full possession of herself. It's a cinch to imagine newborn Diggs serene, even dignified, in her swaddling clothes.

Her fingers, she furls and unfurls. The sap, the sap.

"Quit pokin'," grumbles Hannah beside her.

"Morning, Glory."

"'S not morning."

But it is. Something has changed in the night; the rain moved on and the air being pushed through the fan's blades now is dry and fresh, the light diamantine, and the great expanse of the backyard, with its sagging barn and unmown grass and jungly, vine-choked copse beyond, all gleam golden-green.

Clem unplugs the fan, wrests it from its spot, and thrusts her own head and shoulders into the space between sash and sill. "It's clean!" she trills. "Everything's clean and new." And spinning around she claps her hands, stamps a barefoot flamenco around the sleeping bags. "Get up, get up, you sleepyheads! The rain has stopped—we can set up the tent!"

NOW WHOEVER CAN THIS BE, Glad wonders, this fellow coming up the front walkway (which nobody ever uses)—and what is that object under his arm?

Lester Vilno, by the lopsided gait—but Lester has a beard and all that wiry hair, while this man is clean-shaven and bald. He ought to be wearing a hat, whoever he is, that much is certain. He's shining pink on top. Daddy'd never be out without his Panama on a day like this. Mother'd never let him.

Her view is partially obstructed by the petunias and begonias trailing from hanging baskets and the sweet peas twining up around their strings (the one like stalactites and the other like stalagmites; she's taught legions of pupils to remember which is which by using the mnemonic *c* is for ceiling and *g* is for ground), and she has to bob her head around to keep track of his progress. As he gets nearer the front of the house he slips right out of sight. Aunt Glad rises from the cane chair, using the porch railing to steady herself, and—land sakes! The little boy's soldiers. Half of Charlie Company goes skittering into the spirea. Ah well. They're only poor things, plastic, not like her and Joy's Coldstream Guards, so dashing in their glossy bearskin caps and scarlet tunics, each one painted painstakingly by hand. Confounding how ugly today's toys are.

She peers over the railing into the bushes. Doesn't spot a one. Good camouflage; she'll grant them that.

From out of sight comes a knocking, then a "Hello?"

She makes her way toward the end of the porch, replies through the azaleas: "Hello!"

"Oh. Hello there!" Rather a nice-looking man, lean, crinkle-eyed, in a peach shirt and tan slacks. Now she sees he does have some hair, but what little there is has been shaved to a whisper of velvet, the kind of elective baldness men sometimes choose to diminish evidence of the real thing. Shading his eyes with one hand, he waves with the other. "I rang a couple of times . . ."

"Well the bell doesn't work at all!" With an edge of exasperation, as though she's reminded him before. "No one uses that door!"

He laughs.

It occurs to her who this must be—one of Joy's suitors. No wonder he's so bumbling and confused. He's probably nervous about meeting Mother and Daddy. "She's just getting ready!" Glad assures him. "You'd better come round to the side!"

She makes her way back along the porch, hidden by the screen of foliage, which hides him, too, as he cuts a parallel route across the lawn. She reaches the side entrance just as he comes bounding up the porch steps. Not a young man, but something springy in his step. And that shirt. Peach-and-aqua plaid. Rather festive.

"Jeff Greenberg." Extending his hand.

She hopes he won't have one of those painful grips. Hearty men so often miscalculate how much of their enthusiasm to channel into physical expression. "Glad Erlend."

"Delighted to make your acquaintance." Oh he just drips manners, doesn't he? If he were wearing a hat, he'd have tipped it. "And you must be visiting from . . . ?"

"But I live here," she corrects him, and a great breeze blows then through the trees, the tall pines that line the drive, rustling their branches, and the departure board makes its rattling sound as all the wooden slats turn over and a whole new set of trains is listed, a whole new set of platform numbers. "Hardly what you'd call a visitor. I do stay over in Fishkill now . . ." She trails off, momentarily absorbed by the image of a room with a cot and a white trapunto coverlet, dinosaurs on the windowsill—where in her life, when in her life is such a room located? ". . . and again. Very hospitable place. But Rundle Junction is my home. In fact, *this*"—fluttering her hand at the structure behind her—"is my home. Of course all homes are no more than temporary. Of course"—she leans forward confidingly, suddenly and inexplicably full of warmth toward this stranger—"life itself is temporal!"

He looks surprised, then laughs again.

She isn't normally this chatty but there's something so solicitous, so inviting about his manner. Or is it his shirt?

"Are you from around here?" she inquires. Perhaps she knows

his people. Greenberg doesn't ring a bell, but. Perhaps she should ask how long his people have lived here. Perhaps—should she ask him to sit? Offer him a glass of punch?

"I am." He doesn't elaborate. His eyes linger on the side of her face. She has grown less self-conscious over the years but on occasion, often when meeting a stranger, she is reminded of how her appearance makes others uneasy. There's a shift in his manner now, as if he's eager to get on with the business of why he's come. Of course: Joy—perhaps she ought to run inside and fetch her sister.

"I was hoping to catch Walter—is he around?"

"Oh! No, no . . . I believe he's gone to work."

"In that case I guess I'll . . . or maybe"—the way he pauses, frowning, then brightens as if with a sudden inspiration, ruffles her feathers a bit, although she'd be hard-pressed to say why; perhaps it all seems a bit contrived?—"maybe you'll let me leave this with you?" He takes the object he's been toting from under his arm: a plastic lawn sign on wire stakes, dark green with gold lettering. "Or better yet, right here?" Propping it against the railing. "And would you be so kind as to let Walter know I'll give him a call?"

She casts a doubtful eye at the sign, which is triggering, or rather falling just short of triggering, something, a memory of the conversation last night when everyone had been sitting around the living room and there'd been a kind of breach, a vague imprint of displeasure. What had it been about? Stripes. Who was wearing stripes and who was not. And . . . Lester Vilno. He had been part of it, too. Blamed for something, wasn't he? Hated and vanished, Lester Vilno, whom she has not seen in years.

"You can try," she tells him doubtfully. "Of course it's awfully busy here this week, what with my grand-nephew coming in this afternoon, and his little girl, and then my grandniece and the twins . . ."

"A real family reunion!"

"Isn't that the way with weddings."

"Ho! Someone getting married?"

Could he be a little dense? Or has she made a gaffe? Misread the train schedule? What made her assume he'd have known about the wedding? It's his air of familiarity, of convivial ease. Feeling duped, she allows tersely, "Their eldest."

Now a whole pack of young people come banging out the screen door and Glad, relieved to extricate herself from what has become an increasingly laborious encounter, heads back toward the cane chair, into whose sweetly mildewed cushions she sinks. The man in the festive shirt is trying to make small talk with the young people, pumping hands like a politician, explaining about his sign and giving them messages to pass on to Walter. Good, the young people know how to handle the situation. There's Clementine, and her heavyset friend the checkers girl, and the little curly-topped one who'd made such an impression last night—running into the kitchen proclaiming her urgent need for the powder room—oh and there's her friend Tom, too, although he seems to be going the other way, coming from the direction of the barn and passing that Greenberg fellow on his way up the steps. Peals of laughter, *Mazel tov!* footsteps crunching on gravel, the distant rumble of a tractor, voices high and low interweaving like the colored ribbons on the maypoles as the children dance round and round at the shore of Ida Pond . . .

"Aunt Glad?"

"I wasn't sleeping." She opens her eyes. She'd let them close for just a second. It's Clementine, kneeling before her. How lovely this great-grandniece is. That thing in her nose is really very tiny. It could be mistaken for a piece of glitter. Goodness knows, she's had her own fair share of errant glitter stuck to her. Around the holidays she's always coming home from a project with her kindergartners to find the shiny specks attached to her person.

"Aunt Glad?" Clem says again, soft as the first time. What a great, gleaming girl she is. And so young. Not much more than twenty, surely. To think—just think!; it's barely imaginable—to get one's mind around all the things a young person doesn't yet know. All the suffering. All the hopes and dreams that never come to pass. The sudden losses, the sudden swerves. The forks in the road. Looking back over your shoulder at the roads you never explored. The choices you make and the chance events you never get to choose. Clementine. Darling Clementine, like the song. *Oh my darling, oh my darling*. Glad looks upon her as through a sudden mist, a viscous light full of dust motes, silver notes, *you are lost and gone forever*.

"Your parents," Glad tells her, "will miss you . . . a great deal."

Clem gives a tinselly laugh, charmed and uncertain. "Lucky for them they've got three more. Aunt Glad, are you all right out here? Would you be more comfortable lying down inside?"

"Oh no. Thank you. I'm comfortable right here."

"Can I get you anything? Something cool?"

She spies her tumbler on the wicker table and replies triumphantly, "I see I've still got some tea!" Iced tea, this time, or sun tea, as the girl who delivered it earlier—the curly-topped one—had called it. "You go ahead, dear."

Of course it's only the way of things. Of course they're not meant to know everything so young, everything all at once.

"It's all right," Glad assures her. "You go be with your people."

MANTHA IS SUPPOSED to be cleaning her room. Ellerby is being plunked on her in an hour's time without anyone's having thought to ask her opinion, never mind her permission.

"Oh Mantha, for heaven's sake. I don't have time to discuss this with you," is what her mother said just moments ago while wrestling a fitted sheet over the mattress. "You have the trundle bed, you're a girl, you're practically the same age, end of story."

"But my arm!"

She's been milking the broken arm for five weeks now to great effect; it seemed worth a try.

But no. Bennie'd swept out of the room without another word and now Mantha lies on her own unmade bed, dangling one leg over the side and letting it swing in such a way that her big toe, with each extension, messes up by increments the blanket on the freshly made trundle.

Through the window she hears Clem and the Ch/Hannahs doing something with an aluminum ladder on the front lawn. Earlier they'd set up their tent out back, an orangey dome with windows that zipper open to reveal screens and a jaunty tarp sort of thing lipping up over the doorway in case it decides to rain some more. She'd asked if she could help and they'd said, "We got it." She'd asked if she could be part of whatever they were doing next and Clem said it wasn't really a kid thing and besides it involved use of a ladder and she didn't want to get in trouble for Mantha breaking any more bones.

Ellerby is eleven, three years older than Mantha. Her mother claims they've met but Mantha has no memory of it. Her mother says the reason they haven't seen Ellerby in so long is because she lives with her mother, Tía Violeta, an immigration lawyer. Now they live in Yuma, Arizona, but Tía Violeta was born in Nicaragua. Which means she is an immigrant herself. According to the world map on the wall beside the stove, Nicaragua is a violet-colored piece of pie between North and South America.

"Is her mom coming, too?" Mantha'd asked in the kitchen this morning.

"No. You know Lloyd and Violeta are divorced. Ellerby is just spending a few weeks with her dad."

"Where does Lloyd live again?" Mantha asked, braceleting one of Bennie's sturdy wrists with both of her own hands, measuring the circumference, marveling at the difference in size between her wrists and her mother's.

"Don't *hang* on me, Mantha." Bennie shook herself free. She wasn't the biggest cuddler in the world to begin with, but lately she seemed even more averse to being touched.

"But where?"

Bennie sighed. "We've been through this before. New Mexico. At the moment. Uncle Lloyd gets around a lot."

"Why does he get around a lot?" Mantha wanted to know.

"That," said Bennie, "is what we call the sixty-four-thousand-dollar question."

PIM'S GOT HIS BUGLE on a ribbon around his neck. The *judogi* came off hours ago, when the afternoon heated up; now he wears just plastic jelly sandals, his purple bathing trunks, and on his head a cap of blue felt stuck through with a feather. He's slinking around out back in the unmown grass, tall enough to hide him when he crouches on all fours. The tops, gone to seed, tickle his bare chest.

His quarry: that alien orange creature in the clearing by the barn. It hadn't been there when the sergeant called him in to lunch (and kept him under strict surveillance while he ate every bit of it: a hunk of cheese, an apple, and a piece of hardtack spread with raspberry jam). It simply materialized during his absence, assaulting his eyes when he headed back out on an important solo mission for which he will need not only his bugle but also his dagger. He feels his waistband to make sure it's still there where he tucked it. Check.

He advances cautiously, trying to decide what nature of beast the orange thing is. Whatever it is, a brightly colored thing like a cockscomb or crest rises evilly from its head. The danger is increasing. He pauses to transfer the dagger from trunks to teeth, then slinks along several yards more before freezing—what was that noise? Sniper? Rock python? Fokker Triplane with mounted machine guns buzzing overhead? He scans the land, scans the sky. Sweat trickles with gratifying authenticity past his ears. *All clear, men. Follow me,* he commands. *Steady on, men. Watch the rear, men.* An excellent word: *men.* Sometimes his internal patter consists just of the single word *Men! Men!* He crawls along to the euphonious silent chant, biting down on the gray plastic blade, until he reaches the verge of the tall grass, the boundary line between neutral and enemy territory. Here he halts. *Hold up, men!* Through the curtain of bearded spikelets he scowls at the orange hump. A breeze skitters through the poplars, flips all the leaves around to silvery paleness. A damselfly stitches its way toward him, carrying silent warning.

The thing is breathing.

He crawls into the open. *Stay back, men.*

Rising, transferring dagger from mouth to hand, wiping the drool from it, he advances toward the thing, which abruptly inhales, fills its lungs, balloons ominously, and lunges at him. *Hi-yaa!* He leaps, stabs it in the throat.

Quelled, the creature collapses back into its earlier shape. He steps closer, peers inside its belly. Sleeping bags, knapsacks, a welter of boots, flashlights, towels, books, provisions . . . What a clever disguise! He shakes his head in grudging admiration: not beast but bastion. The crest on its head a kind of banner, a pennant. The enemy's ensign, no doubt. Over his shoulder he hollers: *We've found it, men! Their secret headquarters. Cover me, I'm going in.*

He undoes the zipper and slips through the flap as if into a giant pair of pants. Inside it turns out to have creaturely aspects after all, its walls made fleshy with the sun shining through, its atmosphere muggy as breath. *All right, men, the coast is clear. Hurry, before they get back: let's porridge.* This is what Vikings do upon reaching a foreign enclave, go porridging for food or weapons or treasure. He pokes his dagger into pillows and packs, then fishes around in the guts of them with his bare hands. *Nothing of value . . . hold, what's this?* Object of interest: a sneaky little weapon, flat, no longer than his palm, sandpapery on both sides with a mean little point on one end. He sticks it in the waistband of his trunks. In the next he finds—*Zounds! Poison!* Poison tablets in neat pink rows, crackling evilly in their individual plastic compartments. *And lo—three are missing! We must alert the king!* These, too, he shoves into his trunks.

But it's porridging the last sack that yields the most important find: a black thing like a velvet lump of coal. He pries it apart on its hidden hinges and there—*Men! Men!*—sits the crown jewel, stolen from the palace last night. It's real all right, a golden band supporting a milky stone shot through with circus colors. The whole kingdom has been out looking for it all day and now Pim and his loyal band have found it. *Good work, men.* They grunt modestly, trying not to show how much they love it when he praises them. *Now—let us hie from here.* Stashing the jewel, too, inside his waistband, he slices at the door flap with his dagger and hurtles back into the fresh air. *Quick, like the wind,* he orders, and his men, heeding his wisdom as always, stay close at his heels; together they pound across the meadow with its tall grasses once more like lashes tearing at their flesh, the enemy in hot pursuit. Only when the last of his own has crossed the drawbridge does he bring the portcullis down and raise the bugle to his lips.

GLADDY! GLAD!

Glad's head jerks up. All around her a muzzy scrim of green.

Clatter of hoofbeats. The iron horse. Urgent and distant, still a long way off.

But what is this green? An emerald opacity she knows she knows . . . the nameless lake. Garvey's Puddle, Daddy calls it for a joke. You cut through McElroy's and then across Garvey's farm, find your way along the swampy bit where the skunk cabbage wilts to slime in summer, scramble over the old stone wall—being careful not to drop your bundle (an old towel Mother doesn't care about wrapped around a book and a bottle of Nehi)—and there it is: patch of pebbly beach where she and Joy stretch out and read until it gets too hot to stand.

Then Joy wades in, wincing, always mincing over the sharp pebbles, but Glad takes the swashbuckler's route, walks the gangplank of toppled spruce that points its majestic finger toward the center of the lake. At its tip she bounces until the dead tree groans and then she jumps, her body slicing the glossy surface. And plunges down until her toes stir the cold silt soft as a pelt; then rises slowly through the green murk and sees, with eyes wide open, an underwater orchard, rows of bubbles like apple blossoms scattering on currents of wind. When the water parts open the other way, divulging her once more to the air's slippery whisk, she rolls on her back and floats, lung-dazzled and deaf, a blanket of water lapping up over her ears. Her closed lids make fireworks of the sun.

Here in Garvey's Puddle she is not the burns, not the scars, not the shiny, puckered, pink-and-white congealings of ruined skin. No more does she swim at Ida Pond. No more will she bare herself before so many people, no more be that poor child over whom people cluck their tongues. The girl who reminds them of their own grief. Here in Garvey's Puddle she is barely even a girl, barely even a human. Here she is little more than breath, spangled lungs and fiery eyelids. She is her soul, just.

Gladdy! Glad!

There it is again, but who could be calling her out here in the woods, out here in Garvey's Puddle with her ears underwater? She blinks her eyes open. Bit by bit she is returned to herself, here in the present (to what Mantha would surely call Waking Life). To now. The solidity of the cane chair, the arid weave of the June air. Oh. The waving tendrils of green all around her are not pond water after all, but the cascading curtain of hanging plants and climbing vines that enclose the porch.

Toot toot! The whistle blows.

But it's not a train whistle, it's the little boy blowing his horn. A searing grip squeezes her chest, her neck. The side of her face curls, at once melty and taut. *Come here*, she struggles to say. He is her responsibility. She wants to clutch him by the hand, pull him toward her, but she cannot make her fingers work, cannot lift her arm. *Make sure to stay together.* The boy is wearing a cap stuck through with a feather. Around his neck a ribbon, attached to a toy horn. Whatever is his name?

"Pim," her bearings supply.

(He is a different child, then. Not little boy blue.

But we mustn't speak of that.)

At the sound of his name he looks at her sharply, sideways, head cocked. Not quite with a smile but with something canny, something half-expectant at the corner of his mouth. As if alert to possible advantage.

"No," she tells him. He has the snapping brown eyes of the child who will line up first for recess, the same child who will not hear the bell when she rings it for them to come back in again. "I have nothing for you, young man."

But he has such a lively face. And does not run away.

"Come over here."

She does not presume he will obey. Yet he does, comes to stand coolly before her, the horn dangling from its ribbon around his neck, a plastic dagger thrust in the waistband of his trunks.

"Can you recite?"

He stares at her, lips parted. She can smell his lunch.

"Young man, do you know any poems?"

He blinks.

What on earth are they teaching in kindergarten these days? "Do you know how to make a rhyme?"

"Eeny meeny miny moe."

"That is not—"

But he cuts her off to crescendo cocksure, "Catch a tiger by the TOE!"

Well then. She closes her eyes and pronounces in a fine, formal voice, "The Cow." Then, clearing her throat, fixing upon him her deep-set eyes:

> "The friendly cow all red and white,
> I love with all my heart:
> She gives me cream with all her might,
> To eat with apple-tart."

Pim, drawing the dagger from the waistband of his trunks, responds, "Onepotato twopotato threepotato four, fivepotato sixpotato sevenpotatomore!"

Aunt Glad:

> "She wanders lowing here and there,
> And yet she cannot stray,
> All in the pleasant open air,
> The pleasant light of day."

Here she gives a little nod as if to say it's his turn.

Lofting his dagger heavenward, Pim cries, "Fuzzy wuzzy wuz a BEAR! Fuzzy wuzzy had no HAIR! Fuzzy wuzzy wuzn't fuzzy WUZ HE!"

Undergirded by a blossoming grin, surpassing him in dash if not in decibel, Aunt Glad rounds the bend into her final verse:

"And blown by all the winds that pass
And wet with all the showers,
She walks among the meadow grass
And eats the meadow flowers."

"DUDE, YOUR AUNT AND BROTHER are having a total poetry slam." Hannah, returning from the Buick, which is parked up near the barn, is weighed down with a quantity of eco-friendly shopping bags.

Clem and Chana loll on their backs at the foot of the ladder, which leans against the black walnut tree that holds dominion over the front lawn. If it can be called a lawn: really more of an alopecic quarter acre of dirt and crabgrass.

"Up on the porch. They're like, taking turns reciting at each other."

"What, Glad and Tom?"

"No, the little guy." Hannah unbracelets herself, allowing all the bag handles to slide off her wrists, then settles her own body beside them with a grunt. "I'm telling you, the atmosphere's infuckingtense. Pim's got his dagger out."

Clem laughs.

"I love Aunt Glad," effuses Chana. In her adorable squeaky way.

Hannah looks to catch Clem's eye, but it's not happening.

Clem either isn't attuned or is actively declining to acknowledge that the two of them have spent hours privately dissecting Chana's too-readily tendered declarations of love. She's like one of those crazy lawn sprinklers, broadcasting identical drops of affection in every direction: she "loves" this eighties movie, that psych professor, the guy who makes the omelets in the cafeteria, your purple Danskos, her horoscope, your tweet, your status update, your Snapchat, your hashtag, Ashtanga, quinoa, chia, acai, chai, Gaga, raga, crab Rangoon, the harvest moon, how you rearranged your room. What is she seeking with her affections, her affectations; what is she hoping to gain?

"It's not real," Hannah has judged.

"It is real," Clem has countered. "Just naive."

"It's facile. Glib."

"It's a little glib."

"It's manipulative."

"What makes you say that?"

But here Hannah has sidestepped. What she doesn't say: that it's a kind of performance, a way of demanding *Love ME, love ME.* Funny, batty, sprite-like Chana twirls about spreading her fairy dust of loving everybody and everything, and doesn't it work, doesn't it goddamn *work*, isn't she appealing? (Right down to her conspicuous magnanimity with the Buick, handing over the keys to any and all with that giddy, self-deprecating laugh: *Please, I suck behind the wheel!*) Coating herself with blithe iridescence. Making herself lovable at every turn. In a way the more stolid Hannah (stolid in spirit, stolid in body) could never be. Even for tell-it-like-it-is Hannah, putting all this into words would cut too close to the bone. To the big-boned bone.

Which is why, when Chana squeaks, "I love Aunt Glad," Hannah replies, "Really? What do you 'love' about her?"

If Chana detects the quotes she doesn't let on. Instead, sitting up, wrapping her arms around her knees, she answers wonderingly, "I don't know. She seems like such a free spirit. I mean—obviously she's old but she seems youngish, or ageless, or something. Unhobbled. Unfettered by age."

A gust pushes through the canopy of the black walnut, showering them with a windfall of drops. Hannah lifts her face and lets them land there, plump and cool. She opens her eyes. The tree is an astounding specimen—according to Clem's mom over a hundred years old, probably closer to two—with profuse, spreading, muscular limbs. They've spent the past hour binding its limbs with strings of tiny amber lights, then hanging great paper lanterns from its lower branches. Clem and Chana scampered about up high, fleet-footed and sinuous, even simian, while Hannah, built for ballast, anchored the ladder and handed up supplies. The tree's natural ornamentations, the golden catkins it puts out in early summer, were dashed by the rain; they festoon the ground around them now like furry caterpillars. Hannah picks one up and shreds it.

"Do you know," says Clem, still lying on her back, "I've sometimes wondered if she's gay."

"Chana?" asks Hannah, lying down beside her. She adds a footnote just in case, "Yuk-yuk," to clarify it's a joke. A mean-ish joke. Chana has been ardently, unequivocally out as a lesbian since the middle of her sophomore year, when she joined the staff of the Womyn's Center, got a half shave, and began wearing her magenta equals-sign sweatshirt every single (at least that's how Hannah tells the story) mofo day. Never mind that any actual sexual encounter has yet to occur in the life of Chana Naomi Metzger. Hannah knows this because she's grilled her little Ch-inflected counterpart. And why has she grilled her? And taken such pleasure in it, persisting until Chana, flustered and abashed, confessed to being inviolate, still pure—as Hannah insisted on putting it, as

if astonished, as if needing to make sure she was indeed understanding correctly—as the driven snow? *Uh, technically.* Did it
make Hannah feel better to establish this fact? Did it comfort her
in some way? Is she just a rotten person? Perhaps. Perhaps just
torched with loneliness. And the secret that she has pined for
Clem since their freshman year.

But, "No, Aunt Glad," answers Clem. "You know she's really
my great-great-aunt, right? She's never been married, which obviously doesn't mean anything in itself. But back then, I mean I
think basically everybody got married. Unless they were a nun.
And it's not just no husband—I've never heard mention of any
man in her life. Ever."

"Imagine being a gay woman in her time," says Chana. "I literally can't." She, too, lies back down again. She follows everything
Clem does. Well, to be fair, she follows everything anyone else
does. They are spokes on a wheel, the three of them: heads close,
feet distant, all gazing up into the immense fretwork of branches.
"Can I ask, what are all her scars from?"

Clem sighs. "So, she was in a fire when she was little. A famous
fire, here in Rundle Junction. Eighteen people died, all kids."

"Jeez—it happened at school?"

"No, it was some kind of outdoor performance at the lake. Actually a pageant. Like the whole town was in it, and those who
weren't in it were at it, and supposedly on the final day there was
an explosion and all these little kids in the audience got trapped
under the bleachers."

"And she was one of them?"

"Yes. Her sister, too. Her big sister, Joy, is the one who pulled
her out."

"Glad and Joy? That's awesome."

"But what did you mean 'supposedly'?"

"I don't know, I think they never proved for sure what caused the fire. Some people said there was a bomb."

"Like—terrorists?"

"Maybe. Maybe anarchists? Whatever they had back in the twenties."

"That was Prohibition."

"Bootleggers, then."

"Whatever, I don't know. They never even proved it was a bomb."

"What does Aunt Glad say?"

"Oh, we don't talk about it. I mean! We never—I actually don't remember anyone anytime in my life ever mentioning it in front of her. Or even when she's not around, it's not something that ever gets discussed. Like, by my mom or anything. It's weird, I suppose."

"What?"

"Well. I guess the fact I never thought of it as weird before. We just grew up knowing this big tragic thing had occurred. And that it was something we don't talk about."

"Can you imagine, though?" says Chana. "Living through a tragedy like that? I literally can't."

The repetition of this phrase causes a new twinge of irritation in Hannah. "Life is tragedy," she says.

"Life is a cabaret," corrects Clem.

"I thought it was a bowl of cherries?" ventures Chana.

"You guys, you guys." Hannah slaps her forehead. "How many times I gotta tell you? It's a cereal."

"This is terrible," says Clem, "but when I was a kid I always figured the reason she never had a husband was because of her face. How shallow am I?"

"But maybe there was a woman," says Hannah. "She could have

had a Boston marriage—any domestic companions? Any Sapphic suspects in her life?"

"Not that I know of."

"What a lonely life," says Chana.

"She could be a ghost bride," says Clem.

"What's that?"

"Like in China. Didn't you—they cover this in Intro to Gender, Sexuality, and Women's Studies, no?"

Chana shakes her head.

"Well I've been reading up on marriage customs recently, maybe that's where I learned it. It's this practice of marrying a living person to a dead person, originally to appease the dead person's spirit, but it also became a way for a woman who didn't want a husband to avoid getting married and still be like, honorable."

"Dude—think she's a virgin?" Hannah's question prompts a contemplative silence, which she ends with a low, trailing whistle. "Now *that's* a lonely life."

Clem says, "Maybe it's linked to her longevity."

"Like Darwinistically?" Hannah wrinkles her nose.

"I was thinking more spiritually. Like forever youngly."

"As in Carl?"

"Say what?"

"Because you said Jung. Never mind."

"No, no, no!" Chana cuts in. "I totally get what you mean. She's like literally ageless. She's like an older lesbian Peter Pan."

Hannah makes a great farting sound with her mouth. "Okay, first of all get your facts straight. Peter Pan *is* a lesbian."

This gets a big laugh. Damn right. If there's one thing Hannah's (relatively) secure about, it's her drollery. Too, her command of authority. Which she exercises now, sitting up, brushing bits of catkin from her hair. "A'ight, bitches. Let's get this show on the road." To Clem: "When are you going to fill us in on the plan here, anyway—I mean beyond just the lanterns and chuppah, all the Martha Stewart stuff? What's the actual ceremony going to look like?"

But Clem clamps her lips together and bats her lashes. "All in due time, my pretties."

BENNIE, HAVING JUST COME IN from the backyard where she'd been taking laundry from the line, dumps her load onto the bed. Her marital bed, as they say. A quite nice bed, actually, she's always liked it, cherrywood, a splurge back then. It had been their first major purchase together. Well—if you didn't count the juicer. Which had felt major at the time, the juicer they'd bought jointly even before they were sharing an apartment. The joke—tentacled with meaning, for a formal proposal of marriage never passed between them, never issued from either of their mouths, so if anything it was the slapping down of both their credit cards at once at the Sears checkout counter on that fateful rain-soaked morning in the kitchen appliance department that signaled the seriousness of their intentions to join their lives not just for the moment but for the future as well, in fiscal, nutritional, and all respects—the joke had been that they would split custody of the appliance, one month at her place, one at his, until they eventually merged households. In reality, once they'd lugged it up five flights, unpacked it from its cardboard-and-Styrofoam housing, and assembled it on her butcher block island (she had the crummier apartment but the bigger kitchen), inertia set in and the juicer stayed put.

How insufferable they must have been! She extracts a pair of bedraggled pajama bottoms from the pile—Pim's, the elastic fairly shot and a hole in the crotch—and briefly considers relegating them to her rag bag before deciding they have not quite outlived their utility as apparel. How insufferable she and Walter both, first with the overscrupulosity of their research on the health benefits of fresh juice, then with their proselytizing to friends, family, anyone who would listen. She recalls all too well the strident tone with which she'd rhapsodized about its merits, spreading the good word, aiming for converts. Thank goodness that phase had been cut short. A few months into it, morning sickness arrived with a flourish.

What d'you want to do today? Walter had asked one bright spring morning as they lounged in her bed. He had the paper open to movie listings.

Anything worth seeing? She'd been up twice already to vomit.

He mentioned the Spike Lee and the Woody Allen before casually adding, *We could just get married.*

She considered a moment, then responded with equal economy of affect: *'kay.* It wasn't utterly spur of the moment. A couple of weeks earlier they'd gotten the license. Good for sixty days. They weren't planning anything fancy. They weren't *planning* anything at all. Their only plan: to forgo planning. *We'll just do it when the time's right,* they'd told each other, stashing the document in the silverware drawer (to this day the spot where they toss important scraps of paper: behind forks, spoons, and knives).

When the mood strikes, added Walter.

When the fat lady sings.

When the iron's hot.

When Niagara falls.

When the stars align.

When pigs fly.

Hey!

Kidding, she said, and kissed his ear.

It was as if they were trusting something to fate. Something so large it could be apprehended only out of the corner of their eye. As if their method of selecting a date needed to acknowledge that the act itself was a gamble, marriage so preposterous a proposition there could be no logical, no direct way to enter into it. You had to stagger in obliquely, roll in randomly, like the ball on a roulette wheel. Their method of picking had the charm of a children's game. That one where you spin the globe and blindly stick out your finger to stop it, then open your eyes to see where you'll end up living out your days. Usually somewhere in the ocean, oh well.

So they'd headed downtown and gotten married. Clem was born six months later. One day, when Clem was old enough to contemplate the implications of the gap between the date of her parents' anniversary and her birthday, she inquired whether she'd been a mistake. "Of course not," Bennie told her. "Unplanned is not the same as a mistake." She'd been twenty-two when she had Clem, twenty-eight when she had Tom, thirty-six when she had Mantha, and thirty-nine when she had Pim. She'll be forty-five by the time this next one is born.

"For a practical lady, you don't bring a whole lot of rhyme or reason to the way you space your kids, huh?" Carrie had said over the phone upon learning Bennie was once again with child.

If there was a critical edge in Carrie's comment, Bennie elected to overlook it. A touch of jealousy, maybe. Such a leaky emotion, jealousy, it always showed through, like grease on a paper bag. It wasn't hard for Bennie to summon compassion in this case. Where she enjoyed such an embarrassment of riches, Carrie had long suffered deprivation. She and Graham had endured a lot of travails— not to mention laid out a lot of cash—to have the twins. Anyway, she wasn't wrong: Bennie *is* a "practical lady," generally prone to exercise control over as many aspects of life as she can get her hands on. Except one.

Her own wedding day had begun with Stalwart holding her

hair back while she threw up. Then on the way downtown they'd ducked into the Korean grocery by the subway to buy a bunch of gerbera daisies. She'd stuck one in his buttonhole and one in her ponytail. Then they'd gotten lost looking for the City Clerk's Office, and then they'd gotten the giggles and the clerk had rolled his eyes at them, and then they'd gone to the movies after all, where they gave the daisies she was tired of carrying to the ticket seller and sat through both the Spike Lee and the Woody Allen, and then back in their own neighborhood had gone for Reubens at the Last Bite Diner, where she'd nodded off over her egg cream. Back at the apartment Stalwart had run a bath for her and while she was in the tub he rescued the limp flower from her ponytail holder and put it in a shot glass on the bedside table. And what strikes her now, as she folds the laundry, what hits her about this string of snapshot memories (the closest thing she has to a wedding album) is their childlike quality.

Perhaps it isn't unusual for a young couple to *feel* young, to feel like children on their wedding day. But Bennie and Walter hadn't simply been young; they'd been orphans. In choosing to make each other kin in the manner they had, absent any family members or even proxies from their community of friends, in joining themselves together in a manner that underscored, that proclaimed their aloneness, they'd brought into the ceremony the experience of having been abandoned, set prematurely adrift.

Perhaps this is why, if it gives Bennie satisfaction to manage matter-of-factly the quotidian aspects of life, it gives her another kind of pleasure to reserve this one area for relinquishing the illusion of control: for once not to feel competent! For once to let herself be scooped up, overruled, held by something larger. In the realm of creating life, of letting herself be bound repeatedly, even cyclically, but unpredictably, to a baby, she takes her deepest pleasure in surrender.

Now, folding a pair of Tom's gym shorts, she finds his plastic mouth guard fused to the pocket. Oh joy. No way that union's being sundered without scissors. She sets the shorts aside, then goes to the window, drawn by a burst of laughter. On the lawn Clem and her friends are playing with a big aluminum ladder they must have gotten from the barn, a mass of paper lanterns, and a daunting tangle of extension cords. She can't help thinking of it as play. Some kind of elaborate make-believe. She still hasn't drawn a bead on what this wedding means to Clem, let alone to Diggs, whom she's met only twice but who strikes her as much more serious and adult, frankly more rooted in reality, than Clem. Truth be told it's Diggs's involvement in the whole escapade that lends it any gravitas at all. Clem and the Ch/Hannahs seem to be treating it as a lark. Even as they set up decorations for the event, their antics seem to indicate the event's underlying unseriousness.

Look at them now, shambling around the lawn, letting the ladder tear up clumps of grass for heaven's sake (oh lawn, ever-unthriving: they've tried sod and seed, bluegrass and ryegrass, chemical fertilizer and white clover—nothing works and she's almost given up on caring except that she just put down seed in what—she *swears*—was her final attempt to fill in the bald spots *expressly for the wedding*—forget about ever achieving what real estate agents call curb appeal; maybe they'd be better off waiting to put it on the market until winter when there's a picturesque—not to say obfuscating—blanket of snow), she's reminded of the made-up chores of childhood, the über-important trundling from room to room of chairs and blankets from which to fashion forts, and into which would disappear—oh, all manner of thing: books and dolls and bedside lamps, a mug of pencils, the tape dispenser. What else? A telephone (clunky, rotary-dial, missing its cord). Parcheesi. Band-Aids. Bag of marshmallows, can of navy beans. An entire loaf of sandwich bread and—what is that? The cooking sherry? (*But I need those things!* Clem, age five, had howled when Bennie confiscated these last several items. *Excuse me, you do not. You can't just raid the pantry, Clementine.*)

Clem had liked playing wedding, too. Or not so much wedding as bride. In Bennie's old smocked nightgown, hemmed with a couple of safety pins, and a pair of Bennie's high heels—a bridal essential, to judge from the protestations when Bennie balked, putting to Clem the prospect that she might trip and break her neck. (*Mamaaaa! I'll be careful!!*) And careful she would be, treading slowly, even grimly, the length of the living room. Her face tilted slightly upward, as if the object or force summoning her hovered around where the wall of mailboxes met the ceiling.

That was the extent of the game. She'd reach the end of the room, drop a curtsy, and be done. You'd see it, the visible shedding of the role, the dissolution of the imaginary world. Never did she incorporate into the ritual any kind of make-believe ceremony. No recitation of vows. No pretend officiant, no ring, no kiss, no bouquet toss, no dancing—no joyousness, even. It was all about the walk, the long, solemn, solitary walk down the ersatz aisle. Yet for all its minimalism, its lack of evident drama, the game held inscrutable allure. Clem played it again and again, with a kind of ferocious dedication, almost a frightening intensity.

Once while Bennie stood watching, not so much indulgent as bemused, from the kitchen doorway, Stalwart had come up behind her and slipped his arms around her waist. In the cadences of an old filmstrip narrator, he'd intoned, *In primitive cultures young girls were offered as human sacrifices to the gods in hopes of ensuring a plentiful harves—oof!*

That would be her elbow in his ribs.

Though she had to admit he'd nailed it. That was exactly what it made you think of: submission, surrender.

Walter. Good old Stalwart. A nickname more aspirational, she sees in retrospect, than descriptive. Although back in the day—on the day they first met!—how beautifully firm he had seemed to her then, how resolute, ethical, and brave. She'd been twenty-one. He twenty-five. She in her last year of undergrad, majoring (for lack of real interest in anything else) in English. He a grad student in Mass Communication, one of the leaders of the campus anti-apartheid movement. She all lip gloss, mousse, and bobby-socks-with-Birkenstocks. He all scruff and stubble, exuding the rank appeal of the honorably unwashed. Literally honorably unwashed, for she met him outside the tent he'd been headquartered in, from which he'd conducted all his work—scholarly and political—ever since fall break, when the shantytown was erected on the plaza in front of the administration building. On the November morning when they met he had not showered (she later learned) in four days. The shantytown comprised a single plywood-and-cardboard shack that looked like a child's playhouse, along with five or six tents pitched hither and thither around it.

Walter had been sitting cross-legged in front of the foremost tent—the black, green, and gold flag of the African National Congress flying from its peak—brewing coffee on the most perfectly diminutive camp stove Bennie had ever seen. She smelled the coffee before she spotted the one brewing it. She'd been heading to her early-morning Tuesday-Thursday seminar, The Woman Question: Gender, Class, and Rights in Victorian England. By this point in the semester it was still more night than day when she set out for class—streetlights on, a few faint stars loitering overhead—and she enjoyed taking the opportunity to pretend *she* was in Victorian England. In her head she substituted cobblestones for concrete sidewalks; suffrage petitions for the books she clutched to her chest; gaslights for incandescent bulbs; the clatter of wagon wheels for the wheezing brakes of the campus shuttle bus.

Then she smelled the coffee, looked round, looked down, and

there he was—looking up at her. With a kind of ease, a familiarity, as if well-accustomed to the sight of her, as if he'd been regarding her for ages. Upon seeing her notice him, he broke into a grin that was sheepish yet not.

"'lo." Even with that first utterance, frogged with sleep and kept to a single syllable, his voice did something to her, resonated, rang. He had a large head of scraggly curls and wore a colorful Andean serape.

"You're up early," she retorted, and blushed. How inane! As if she were claiming to know his personal habits, when he ordinarily rose. Of course all she'd meant was that at this hour she'd assumed the shantytown would be dormant. Indeed, vacant: she hadn't realized anyone actually stayed there overnight. In the afternoons and evenings she had seen it swarming with activity, scores of students sitting around with their backpacks and hand-painted signs, smoking and talking, strumming guitars and playing djembes, striding around the plaza handing out flyers full of unwieldy combinations of letters: ANC, UDF, COSATU, or else massed on their feet, facing the flak-jacketed student leaders on the steps of the admin building, raising their voices in call-and-response: *Stop Blood Money, Divest Now!*, and *Amandla! Awethu!*

Yet here was this man by himself, the plaza deserted except for a few isolated figures trudging stiffly to class at this unpopular hour. Such a big man he was to sit with his legs crossed like a child's, tending with casual propriety to the littlest camp stove imaginable. It was darling. It belonged in a dollhouse. During the day, with its acronym-strewn signage and staticky bursts of megaphone, the shantytown had an ugly utilitarian air. But in the half-light of the streetlamps and the predawn celestial glimmer, it appeared whimsical and ambiguous, a setting from a dream. The cold stung her nostrils and heightened the fragrance of the coffee in its aluminum pot. A cowboyish odor, beany and thick. She didn't even drink coffee in those days—stuck to cocoa or tea—but in that shivery violet hour it smelled good to her.

She fell for the coffee, she fell for the stove: this was what she liked to say later, when retelling the story of how they met. She fell for the tent. It was true in a way, although there wasn't a thing special about it, the tent. Only that she wanted in.

"Do you live here?"

He laughed. Creases like parentheses appeared on either side of his mouth.

"I mean—but you stay out here all night?"

He shrugged assent. "Admin's been threatening to bulldoze it. Kind of need someone here around the clock."

"They won't bulldoze with you in it?"

"Here's hoping."

"But isn't it freezing?"

"The sleeping bag's good for twenty below. The tent holds in a lot of body heat."

She felt a temperature surge in her own body then, despite the fact that her teeth had begun to chatter in the morning's raw damp.

"But yeah," he went on, and there was the grin again, sudden and crease-framed, "it is getting pretty fucking cold. Witness all my hearty comrades." An arm came out from under the serape; he gestured at his invisible cohort.

"So it's just you out here?"

A little bow. It had a bit of the showman in it and a bit of the monk.

"You're the stalwart, then."

Thus she pronounced him. Gave him what would become his lifelong nickname even before she'd learned his name.

A cacophony of shrieks yanks her out of the memory and directs her attention back out the bedroom window onto the lawn, where the aluminum ladder wobbles, then topples, tossing a passenger to the ground—this mishap the result of Hannah and Clem attempting to "walk" it across the lawn with Chana hitching a ride on top. Is anyone hurt? Chana's prostrated; Bennie can see her full gypsy skirt arrayed all around her like a mushroom's multicolored gills, but no: she's a dancerly little thing and tumbles up fluidly, like a film run backward, unscathed, arms wide, triumphant. Laughter peals across the yard.

What's the *matter* with them? They're *clowns*, she thinks, with irritation. But what's the matter with *her*? The better question, perhaps. What is this about, her own sourness? Why can't she love their effervescence, let herself enjoy it? She and Stalwart, after all, had made of their own wedding a private idyll, following in the footsteps of no venerable tradition. But its playfulness had been hard-won, even deliberate—a kind of refutation of sorrow—and it had been birthed in the shadow of overmuch suffering, overmuch loss.

Whereas Clem and the Ch/Hannahs (frankly at this moment even the decision to have homophonic bridesmaids rubs her the wrong way, as if it's just a bit of cleverness, another jokey gimmick) are going about this as if none of it counts, as if it's all a lark, gauzy, make-believe. As if it isn't a matter of lives at stake. As if no long and serious story is about to take root. As if they lack all sensible fear of the future.

THE MUSTANG COMING UP the drive is asymmetrically two-tone—rusty maroon and gold—though it surely did not start life this way. In dire need of a muffler job, it knocks along at a pace that would be too fast for the gravel even if not for the groaning struts, before lurching to a halt up near the barn. Its open windows a referendum on the state of its AC. The late-day sun streams across

McElroy's fields, backlighting tall swaying wands of grass. The engine cuts out and in the sudden quiet a black-capped chickadee proclaims the arrival of these pilgrims with its short, piercing song: *fee bee!*

From the driver's side: bare feet. Frayed jeans. Lloyd unfolds. He is tall and too lean, always has been, with a concave chest and sugary stubble and pale eyebrows that somehow incline toward the center of his brow in a perpetual wince. Or perpetual thought. Or as if the difficult, intricate, ceaseless involutions of his mind cause him a kind of delicate, desirable pain. There is a kind of woman who finds this irresistible. Lloyd does a yoga-type thing, stretching out his back, then an un-yoga-type thing, reaching across his narrow chest and scratching his armpit.

From the passenger's side: green imitation-snakeskin cowboy boots. Brown legs, stained pink shorts. Ellerby slides out. Frumpy and grumpy. Messy obsidian hair. Looks like she's been scissoring bubble gum out of it. She plucks her sweaty underwear out of her crack.

Lloyd opens the trunk. They each heave out a bag, start toward the house. Halfway there Ellerby stops, runs back to the car, opens the door, grabs a turtle-shaped knapsack, slams the door, opens it again, grabs a cowboy hat, slams the door, runs back to where her father is waiting. They resume walking.

Porch: vacant.

Kitchen door: open.

Lloyd peers through the screen. "Hello?" Looks around at Ellerby, who raises her eyebrows as if to say, *I'm just the kid, re-member?* He pushes it open, enters. "Hellooo?"

Thieves could not creep more stealthily through the kitchen. They peer around the door frame into the empty living room. The famous preserved wall of brass mailboxes, each rectangle of glass glowing rose-gold with the sun's slow-sinking light. Lloyd circles the room as if casing the joint, Ellerby close behind him. Together they come to a stop before the geometry of boxes. Lloyd puts a hand to his chin and Ellerby follows suit. He tilts his head to the side; she does the same. A pair of after-hours prowlers in a secret gallery.

"Freeze!"

They swivel. They have been addressed by some kind of warrior. Fugitive from a portrait by Hokusai. He stands on the bottom tread of the stairs, pointing at them a wooden sword. Bare-chested, ski-masked, clad in purple bathing trunks.

"Lay down your weapons," he commands.

Lloyd and Ellerby lower their suitcases.

The warrior: "State your business."

Lloyd bows. "We come in peace."

Ellerby raises her empty hands, positions them as if holding a camera to her face, and with a motion of her index finger and a click of her tongue, snaps a picture.

The warrior glares at her. A tense interval. Then he sheathes his sword. Austerely he announces: "You are welcome here."

"Much obliged." Lloyd hazards a guess. "Ninja?"

He is remonstrated. "Samurai."

Lloyd bows again, and the samurai bows back.

Bennie comes down the stairs behind a full basket of dirty laundry. Fugitive from a Pissarro. "Lloyd!" She sounds at once welcoming and miffed. "I didn't hear you! For heaven's sake! How long have you been here?" Skirting the samurai, she comes all the way into the room, sets down her basket, hugs her brother, hugs her niece, then steps back, uncommonly flustered, brushing non-existent crumbs from her skirt.

"Hope it's okay," says Lloyd in that vexing, hangdog way of his, sliding his hands into his pockets, "we let ourselves in."

Bennie's face pinks. She emits a short, pained laugh. Oh, Lloyd.

Why must he—after all, he grew up here! She says it aloud, "Don't be silly, it's your house!" The family manse. It's not as if she's the gatekeeper. She's his sister. His big sister. She laughs—makes herself laugh—again and puts a hand on his shoulder (*But he's all wire! All wooden dowel and wire underneath his shirt*), declaring in a way meant to sound funny and hospitable, "The prodigal returns!"

He shrugs. A small movement of his shoulder, and she can't tell whether he's conceding his own ridiculousness or flinching at her touch.

"How are you, Lloyd? What's"—she tries to think of the way he might phrase it—"your passion these days?" And knows instantly she's bungled it.

Now he laughs, barely. Sound of a dry leaf falling. He understands the question as an effort to probe tactfully into his livelihood, to ascertain without seeming to grill him how he's paying the rent. Importing Nicaraguan coffee, he says. Fair trade, Rainforest Alliance certified. From Matagalpa and Jinotega, mainly. Might begin working with a women's farming collective in Estelí.

"That's great," says Bennie, with a jot too much enthusiasm. "Good for you." What does that even mean, "importing coffee"? Is he actually hauling beans into the country himself? Distributing them to warehouses, retailers? Is he employed by someone else (*please yes*), sitting behind a desk all day in some leased commercial space, taking orders, managing accounts? Or is he winging it, is this some solo Lloyd venture, some far-fetched half-baked dream being presented as a fait accompli but in fact just-hatched and bound to fail within a few months?

She doesn't ask follow-up questions. It's too pointless, too frustrating, he's only just arrived, why spoil things immediately? He'll get defensive, think she's putting him down, being defeatist. Accuse her of lacking imagination, lacking faith. Or else she'll get defensive, see his enigmatic smile as a mask of superiority, a form of condescension. Of mocking her, ridiculing her stable (read: stodgy) life. Little does he know.

Anyway Lloyd manages. Somehow. Always has. She glances down: there are his long, narrow, for some reason unshod feet, coated with yellowish driveway dust. Next to them: Ellerby's fake-snakeskin cowboy boots, cheap green plastic-looking things with pointed toes, surely bad for her feet.

"You must be exhausted. What do you need, guys, cool drink? Food? Shower? How long have you been on the road?"

"Left Albuquerque Saturday."

"And today?"

Lloyd consults Ellerby, who perhaps transmits a telepathic response, for he nods and says, "Yeah, about ten hours. Started out from the motel in Columbus around eight. Stopped once for lunch, once for gas."

Ellerby jabs her index finger in his direction.

"What?"

She makes a face: *You know!*

"Oh yeah. We stopped for ice cream, too."

The samurai, abruptly reanimated, yanks off his ski mask. Sweaty hair spikes out around a hectic red face. He pulls a handful of his mother's skirt. "Can I have some ice cream?"

Bennie looks down, takes unhurried stock of his avid expression, all the while exploring a back molar with her tongue. "After dinner."

He gives a whoop and bolts upstairs.

"Excuse me!" At her cry he halts as if javelined in the back. "Get back here and pick that hat up, please." He clatters down, swipes the ski mask off the stairs, clatters up again, vanishes. They can all but see the cartoon speed lines in his wake.

Bennie, with comic dignity: "Pim, meet Lloyd and Ellerby. Lloyd and Ellerby, Pim."

IS SUPPER THIS EVENING a festive affair?

Mantha ponders. Undeniably it's beginning to feel momentous, with each subsequent night more people gathered around the table (this afternoon she'd put the leaves in herself; she'd been supposed to do it with Tom—the leaves are solid oak and heavy—but he was nowhere to be found and Pim was too little and Aunt Glad too old and Clem too selfish; in the end Chana had helped), and lots of chatter—endless, it seems—about the wedding, from symbolism to brass tacks, all the supposedly millions of chores still to be done. There's certainly something in the air—but is it festivity? That's the question.

Tom got to the table late and disorganized-looking, his T-shirt ripped at the shoulder, his cheeks ruddy the way they get whenever he's exerted himself physically or emotionally. He's said nothing since an initial mumbled "Hi," and is just sitting there now shoving absurdly big hunks of baguette into his mouth. "Pretty," commented Clem a moment ago. He'd rewarded her by opening his mouth and displaying the masticated mess inside.

Beside him Aunt Glad also eats bread, but at the opposite end of the manners scale. She tears off flakes and crumbs, which she places at slow intervals on her tongue. Each time she inserts a new piece her whisky-colored eyes gleam like embers flaring up before a draft.

In addition to the freshly warmed baguettes they are having sausages and peppers Bennie did on the grill, along with tomato and feta salad, roasted cauliflower and peas, and tofu and pineapple kebabs for the people who don't eat meat, namely Lloyd, Clem, and Chana. Mantha, having decided tonight that she doesn't eat sausages, tofu, tomatoes, feta, cauliflower, or peas, is making a supper of grilled pineapple chunks, which she dips into the large puddle of ketchup squirted in the center of her plate.

Down at the end of the table, the three young ladies (already Aunt Glad's term for them has been absorbed and put to use, albeit with a glaze of irony, by everyone else) show evidence of their unladylike afternoon, all that dragging around of the ladder and scrambling through the trees and falling down and laughing so honkingly that every time they erupted anew Mantha imagined a V of geese. They look messy and sunburned, Clem's hair stuck with catkins, Hannah's eyeliner gone racoonish, Chana's fat braid wisped apart like smoke. All their antics have left them far from tired, though, to judge by the way they are dominating the conversation, with great animation and an unsortable pidgin of academic-ese mixed with hipster jargon. Syllables fall on Mantha like glittering geodes, enticing and sharply excluding. Sentences rush by studded with odd phrases: *dialectic of function, court-involved youth, reverse appropriation*. Mantha tries out a few for herself, mumbling under her breath: *Optically white. Body shaming. Microaggression.* The syllables unyielding in her mouth, like Grape-Nuts.

Pim, beside her in his junior chair, is wholly absorbed in his cauliflower and peas, which he's segregated into squadrons and now—humming "When Johnny Comes Marching Home"— arranges into battle lines.

"Take a bite, now," directs Bennie every so often, each time leading to a reduction in the ranks of one or the other fighting force.

Directly across from her sits Lloyd. Each bite he inserts in his mouth gets chewed an exorbitant number of times, during which time his fork rests on the plate, and his hands rest in his lap.

Oddest of all, he chews with his eyes closed. When, swallowing, he opens his eyes to find Mantha staring, he gives her a small smile, as if granting her permission to be amused. She looks away. Beside him Ellerby is his opposite: she rivals Tom, pounding away at great wads of sausage and bread, shifting them from one bulging cheek to the other while pineapple juice oozes down her chin, which she swipes every now and then with her paper napkin.

Walter's chair remains empty. He called a little while ago to say he missed his train and will catch the next. Poor Dad. Always working so hard. Never mind that *Poor Dad, always working so hard* is a phrase she learned from Bennie herself; she compares the two now unfavorably in her head. Her mother's baseline is grumpy. Her father's is jolly. Even when he's not being all stalwart like his nickname, all noisily singing in the kitchen and everything, he rarely gets mad. When he is mad, he just gets quiet and serious. The way he got last night, come to think of it. What had been the deal with *that*—the silent weirdness between her parents, all because of—what? Fundamentalists in stripes?

She leans across the table toward Ellerby. "Are you Jewish?"

Ellerby looks inquiringly up at her father, who shakes his head no.

Mantha hoots. "You don't even know?!"

"Samantha," says Bennie.

"How could she not know that?"

"Why'd you even ask her, stupid?" says Tom. "Dad's the one who's Jewish."

"So?"

"Lloyd's Mom's brother."

"So? Her mother could be Jewish."

"Her mother's from Nicaragua."

"So?"

"In my day," interjects Aunt Glad, with her old kindergarten teacher's knack for being amiably censorious, "it was considered impolite to talk about religion at social gatherings."

"Where is your mother?" Mantha leans again toward Ellerby, as if the answer might be whispered in confidence.

For a moment Ellerby appears frozen. Then she sets down her fork, picks up her invisible camera, and snaps a "photo" of Mantha, who blinks just as if a real flash had gone off.

"In my day," continues Aunt Glad, "it was considered impolite to ask any questions of a personal nature at the dinner table."

"What?" Mantha appeals to the table at large. "I just wanted to know where her mother is."

"Mantha." Bennie's voice is a shot fired across the bow.

"What?! What's personal about that?"

"Your shirt," Bennie says, her voice dangerously stripped of inflection, "is in your ketchup."

Snorts of laughter from Tom.

Mantha whacks him with her cast.

"*Hey!*" Tom massages his shoulder extravagantly. "Did you see what she did?"

"Mantha, leave the table."

"Me?! Why *me*?!"

Tom sticks a finger in each ear. "Duuude. You trying to torture the entire canine population of Rundle Junction?"

Mantha scrapes her chair back violently. "Why don't you ask *him* what *he's* been doing all afternoon!"

The pause that follows is interesting. Mantha's outcry had been a wild shot, but from the ruddy splotches reestablishing themselves on Tom's cheeks, it seems she might have struck upon something. All three young ladies stop their gabbing. Lloyd, for the first time all evening, attends with curiosity to the conversation. Ellerby angles her invisible camera at Tom. Pim looks up from his battle of vegetables. Aunt Glad, like the last person to realize the others have stopped passing cards in a game of spoons, looks around the table and emits a little sound, something between a cough and an *oh!* And Bennie—for it all comes down to the mater-familias here; what will she do, in which direction will she steer the action?—takes temporary cover behind one of her trademark unfathomable stares.

What ultimately breaks the silence, however, is the bang of the screen door followed by the appearance of Walter: sports jacket slung over an arm, tie loosened, brow pleated, hot, tired, and—despite Mantha's recent ode to his never getting mad—visibly angry.

With one hand he's still clutching his briefcase. With the other he holds up a green-and-yellow lawn sign. "Anyone know anything about this?"

"That guy dropped it off earlier today," offers Clem.

"What guy?"

Bennie has set down her fork and knife and placed her fore-arms and palms flat on the table. The tiniest vertical showing be-tween her eyebrows. She glances toward Lloyd and Ellerby, then back at Walter with an in-sip of breath, poised to interrupt if only she can catch his attention, but he stands glaring—really, there is no other word for it—at Clem.

Who, shrugging, says, "You know. That guy you don't like. Tall, thin. You once called him a sycophant? Kind of bald? Works for the town?"

"Jeff Greenberg? He doesn't work for the town." Walter has set down neither the sign nor his briefcase. He's not trembling, ex-actly, but something along those lines. Imperceptibly vibrating.

"Oh yeah, Jeff Greenberg. Well you know what I mean. He's like, civically *involved* or something."

"So let me get this straight. Jeff Greenberg just came and stuck this"—Walter gives the sign a shake and a few bits of earth fall from the wire stakes—"in our lawn?"

"Walter." Bennie stands.

"What?"

"Hello."

The look on his face is the same one Pim turns on her whenever she rouses him from a bad dream: as though she is the source of what afflicts him. Then, slowly, he is recalled to his surroundings. Something coiled releases. "Hello," Walter responds, and he takes in the room, the various people arranged around the table, adjusting his mien as he registers the newest newcomers—"Lloyd! Ellerby! You made it"—and sets down his briefcase, and laughs. "Sorry, folks."

"He didn't stick it in the lawn, Dad," says Clem.

"What?"

"Jeff Greenberg didn't put it in the lawn, he left it on the porch. I saw him. He asked if he could leave it and if you'd give him a call."

"He was wearing a festive shirt," contributes Aunt Glad.

"He said mazel tov about the wedding."

"He said mazel tov."

"Yeah."

"Uh-huh." Walter sucks his teeth. "If he didn't put it in the lawn, how'd it get there?"

"Maybe it blew?" says Mantha, whose mother's injunction to leave the table seems to have slipped her mind.

"Maybe it flew." Pim, fresh off the poetry slam.

"Maybe it grew!" Mantha and Pim laugh uproariously.

"It was stuck," says Walter, "into the ground. Out by the road. Someone put it there."

"I did," says Tom.

In the silence that follows, everyone's breath seems amplified.

"We will not. Have it. In our lawn." Walter's delivery, though quiet, is unwontedly authoritarian.

To the rest of the family's surprise, Tom persists. "Why not?"

For one moment, gloriously and precariously, they can all picture him as a man.

"You know they're racist?" says Tom. "In New Ashkelon the ultra-Orthodox hung an effigy out the window of a man in dreads and a rasta hat."

Walter squares his shoulders, opens his mouth.

But: "This needs to wait," says Bennie in a voice that could cut brick. She alone is privy to the complexity of all Walter is grappling with: not only the village politics of newcomers and locals, race and religion, who belongs and who gets to say so, but also the particular politics of their selling the house, the implications of having the sign on display, and the signal it might send to potential buyers, whoever they may be. But he must not give vent to all that here and now. Not before the kids, not before the company, not before Aunt Glad, and not before the imminent celebration. She lasers her gaze, charged with telepathic warning, at her husband.

Who receives it. Whatever he had been going to say comes out instead as, "I'll go wash up." He heads to the powder room.

Bennie, with something like concerted breeziness, says, "Tom, please fill Dad's water glass. Aunt Glad, can I serve you a little more salad?"

Mantha gives it a moment to see if she remains exiled. Only when Bennie has sat back down and resumed eating, without evidence of remembering her decree, does Mantha slide her chair back up to the table and stab another pineapple chunk.

"OW," MUTTERS HANNAH. "That used to be my foot."

"Sorry," whispers Chana. Crickets are chirping and out along the county road the occasional sound of an engine dopplers in and out, but other than that the night is quiet, as she herself has been striving to be.

"What are you doing?"

Rummaging through her duffel in the tent in the dark. "I forgot to take my pill."

Hannah grunts.

Chana keeps delving as noiselessly as she can, searching with her fingers for the stiff plastic rectangle, smooth on one side, the other side having twenty-eight raised bumps. "Sorry, Hannah, can I check your bag?" she whispers.

Another grunt, crankier.

"Sorry, sorry—I just can't find it and I'm thinking maybe it accidentally went into yours." Is it her fault Hannah's bag is equipped with literally the loudest zipper ever?

"Oh my God," moans Hannah. "What do you need it for? Are you dying?"

This time it's Chana who doesn't answer.

"It absolutely has to be right this second?"

"It's just that I'm supposed to take it the same time every day."

"What's the matter?" Now Clem's awake, too.

"Sorry, sorry, you guys," Chana whispers.

"Bo Peep here lost her pills."

"What are they for, Chanaleh? Can we help you look in the morning?"

"I guess . . . I swear I put—"

"Baa-aa."

"Do you think you left them in the room we slept in last night?"

". . . maybe." Oh God, did she? Dismay flares in her mind like a sparkler: oh let it not be harbinger of a migraine! Clem's uncle is in that room now, so it isn't even like she can dash back and check. Of course it's nicer here than in that stuffy attic, with the tent windows unzipped and the damp odor of the earth, even if it is spooky staying next to that big carcass of a barn, even if there's a mosquito trapped in the tent with them (its whining in her ear is what made her wake up and remember she hadn't taken her pill in the first place), if only—*Breathe, Chana, stress'll only make it worse.* Going on the pill has made all the difference with her menstrual migraines; she's afraid if she gets off schedule she'll be in for a doozy. Oh please let these spurs of light not be migraine aura! She wouldn't mind explaining about her meds to Clem but not in a million years could she do it in front of Hannah, who for some reason doesn't like her and never has: if Hannah knew she was a lesbian on birth control she'd never hear the end of it.

It's hard being here in the midst of someone else's family, especially when it's her first time meeting any of them, especially when none of them know her. What more acute loneliness than to be a stranger in the midst of a group of people who are knitted together in the most intimate way? It's even hard here in the tent with Clem and Hannah, especially when she understands she's the second-best friend, the second-choice bridesmaid, chosen perhaps as much (she's not an idiot) because she has a car as because Clem wanted her here. She's been working hard to fend off the shameful secret that dogs her: at nineteen she still battles severe and occasionally debilitating homesickness. Besides her therapist the only people who know are her mother and father, who have been countless times the recipients of her middle-of-the-night weepy phone calls. Not weepy: sob-clogged, gut-stinging, anguish-riven. She tries channeling them now. *Shuush-shh, Chanaleh, don't do this to yourself,* she can hear her mother say. Then her father's voice: *Try to breathe, honey, that's it. Take another. Deep breath now.*

"We'll help you find them when it's light," promises Clem, burrowing back down in her sleeping bag.

"Thanks," whispers Chana. But already she's getting the feeling. It's coming, it's already here. A mournful metallic tang in her mouth. Flashbulb geometry in her skull. The assault from within: it creeps with undeterrable fortitude through her limbs, fizzles like Pop Rocks in her blood. She wraps her arms around her knees, lets escape a tiny whimper.

"Leave them alone," Hannah murmurs into her pillow—is she being nice? "And they'll come home, wagging their tails behind them."

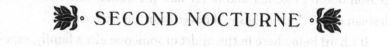

SECOND NOCTURNE

THE MOON

On this June night at three a.m. the moon, that lithe trespasser, gains access to the Local Archives Room on the third floor of Rundle Junction Public Library. It sends one narrow column through the fan-shaped window to cast a rhombus of light across a study carrel, on which several items have been left: a cardboard file box labeled *True List of Persons, 1917–present*; a lipstick-stained Styrofoam cup (this despite food and beverage not being permitted in the Local Archives Room); several index cards covered with pencil scribbles; two tattered clothbound volumes, titled *Handbook of American Pageantry* and *Spirit of Progress Grand Community Pageant, Rundle Junction, N.Y., 1927*, and a smattering of diminutive black grains . . .

THE MOUSE

. . . which are in fact rodent droppings, excreted by an elderly doe mouse who makes her home together with a couple of younger females near the hot water pipe that runs behind the baseboard of the Local Archives Room. She belongs to the same species, *Mus musculus*, as the young mother mouse we met earlier, the one who lost all her first litter to flooding and is now building a nest in the wall behind Aunt Glad's cot. Although they are genetically alike and physically almost indistinguishable, although they live less than two miles apart, and although in a broad sense they might be considered members of the same tribe, in a conventional human sense they could not be called relatives. That is, if it were possible to draw the extended family tree of each, even going back as far as a dozen generations (much further, as a point of reference, than either the Blumenthals or the Erlends could possibly trace their own ancestries), one might find no overlap.

This particular mouse (now, after only three years on earth, in her dotage) first became a mother at twelve weeks of age. She has fulfilled her evolutionary purpose by giving birth to more than three hundred children. She and her domestic companions (both descendants of hers) nurse their babies communally in a nest composed chiefly of chewed-up paper.

At the time that the moon is sending its lozenge of light into the Local Archives Room, the mouse is making her usual rounds, flitting across the stacks, scavenging for crumbs (happily for the mice, the no-food-and-beverage rule is routinely disregarded) and nest-augmenting materials.

This is the final night of her life. She will expire of natural causes by morning.

Now on the study carrel she climbs the small edifice of tattered volumes, displacing a few index cards as she does, and stands on her hind legs to sniff at the lipstick on the rim of the Styrofoam cup.

One last time her whiskers touch moonlight.
They quiver.

MEMORY

The Styrofoam cup and the index cards had been inadvertently left behind the previous day by a historian researching the early-twentieth-century American cultural phenomenon of civic pageantry for an intended monograph of which she has not yet written a single word save the title; she is planning to call it *Pageant Fever.*

Although the historian's stock in trade is stories, and although she herself has, like anyone else, a life rich in stories, as a character she does not figure in this one. But her notes do. A sample of her misplaced jottings:

"A map of the United States dotted at every point where a pageant has blossomed during the last decade might be as thickly-speckled as a fertile meadow in the season of dandelions."

—Ralph Davol, *A Handbook of American Pageantry*, 1914

ABSTRACT:

Nearly all pageants shared same general plot → Grand Course of Progress from Forest Primeval to City Beautiful. Regardless of variations, end goal of pageantry movement was uniform: "to stoke in citizens a deepened sense of fellowship and to minimize differences among them, whether of class, politics, race, religion, or ethnicity."

PAGEANTS AS NURSERY OF PATRIOTISM

- threat: "our foreign citizens after years in this country are still our foreign citizens"
- solution: use pageants as tool for encouraging assimilation, allegiance, national solidarity
  - educate/inculcate the "foreign-born element," glorify traditional hierarchies, squash discontent
  - depict anyone rising up against government as villains
    → ultimately vanquished by forces of good

o o o

Ex.: 1920, Miami, Ohio—"good people" fight off band of red-capped gnomes "who wander about in the dark, stirring up trouble and unrest"

o o o

Ex.: 1921, Nassau, Long Island—member of the "Black Hand" carries concealed explosives, is apprehended/interrogated by police

o o o

Ex.: 1925, Lexington, Massachusetts—scarlet Fan of Unrest attempts to rally workers against bosses until Freedom comes along and persuades them to act as individuals, rather than organize as revolutionary masses

o o o

Ex.: 1926, Stoughton, Massachusetts—Spirit of Anarchy tries to get recent immigrants to accept Red Flag, before being defeated by Spirit of Liberty and removed by uniformed soldier and sailor

○ ○ ○

Ex.: 1927, Rundle Junction, New York—(unscripted*) conflagration breaks out beneath grandstands during fifth and
final performance, eighteen spectators dead (all children),
thirty+ injured; usual suspects: immigrants, socialists, labor unionists, atheists, bachelors, artists, Jews

*though not part of official pageant, tragedy co-opted to
fit/reinforce traditional pageant narrative →

- officials declare cause of fire "indeterminate" despite accounts of blast (explosion/loud noise). possible explana-
tions: fertilizer bomb, Molotov cocktail, "pyrotechnic
paraphernalia gone awry," anarchists, communist agita-
tors, Freemasons, anti-Prohibitionists
- another theory—though unpopular—was natural causes;
spontaneous combustion possible if hay baled too wet
or green
- eventually becomes settled opinion that tragedy caused
by an isolated "malefactor"
- this individual (never found) deemed "unnatural, mon-
strous, beyond the pale"

BEYOND THE PALE, said the men gathered around the old Glendale.
The men: regulars who came to Erlend's to pick up their mail and
stock up on razors and thread, saltines and seeds, then pulled up
chairs and whiled away a morning exchanging gossip and news.
The old Glendale: cold and unlit because it was summer. Still, the
very position of that fat black iron stove in that building that had
official status—for it was, despite its homeliness, a federal space,

recognized and sanctioned by the great republic for which they all stood, for which they all sprung gladly to their feet whenever the band struck up "The Star-Spangled Banner"—made it a natural place to gather.

Beyond the pale, they repeated, taking up the refrain, passing it around like a flask. As if no other words could approach the degree of loathsomeness, the extent of reprehensibility: to cripple with grief fourteen mothers and fourteen fathers (for two pairs of victims had been siblings and one couple had lost all three children in the fire); to think—as the men sitting around the Glendale tended to—of the mothers, as the loci of the village's collective anguish, brought to their knees at grave sites, taking to their beds in the invalidism of suffering, eventually rising again but forever changed, crimped by sorrow—all this was nothing if not *beyond the pale*.

Pale from *palus*, a wooden stake. Driven into the ground to mark a boundary. Or a series of stakes to make a fence. To be within the pale is to be within the jurisdiction, within the region governed by law and protected by society. To be beyond the pale is to be by definition lawless, uncivilized, lost.

In the absence of any concrete suspect, and unwilling or unable to envision him as anyone they knew, the people of Rundle Junction fell into the habit of referring to the malefactor as "the person from away."

It was axiomatic: the evilness of the deed made the villain by definition unfathomable. And in the days and weeks and months following the tragedy, the men who smoked and chewed tobacco around the cold iron hearth of the Glendale (the men whose circle, if you happened to notice, no longer included old Lester Vilno, the bachelor or widower, depending on what story you'd heard and believed; the odd fellow who lived alone and made marionettes and did puppet shows for the area children; the small, stooped figure who was never exactly one of the regulars gathered around the Glendale, but who frequented Erlend's just the same and was often to be seen lingering on the porch, whittling some hunk of wood, or perusing with prolonged and concentrated interest the jars of penny candy before making his small purchase; the foreigner with the long beard and hooked nose and accented English and heavy, dark, liquid eyes—and hadn't the part of Europe he was supposed to have fled, come to think of it, been called the Pale of Settlement?) with their very words, their refrain, its choral repetition—*Beyond the pale, Beyond the pale*—edged the villain farther away, distancing and transfiguring him into something at once more and less than human.

Until he was neither a living being to be contemplated nor a problem to be puzzled out, but a chimera, a thing that doesn't exist, or exists only as a symbol, terrible, fantastical, yet eminently practical, for its one vital use: to remind us why palings, why fences and boundary lines, must be established, must be well-kept.

THE PRODIGAL

Lloyd lies on his back, sleepless, in the hottest room of the house. The wedge of attic where Clem and her bridesmaids slept the night before. His childhood room at the back of the house, now shared by Tom and Pim, had always been the coolest of the bedrooms. It was gloomy in winter but sweet in summer, with the towering pines shading the tiny screened balcony.

It's three in the morning but the room is lit almost brazenly by a lemon-drop moon floating smack in the middle of the curtainless window. Lloyd is naked but for his watch, an old analog on a cracked leather strap. Because it's beat-up people assume it's an heirloom. Many have asked its story. Women, men, strangers he's met in bars and roadside diners, at free outdoor concerts and at the put-and-take section of the dump, at the plasma bank and on protest marches, and at the giant flea markets he likes to frequent, with their endless aisles of junk repurposed as wares. All those flea markets where he has been known to score a good deal, turn a decent profit. Or just as often lose his shirt.

But because Lloyd is Lloyd he is always well-received. Even when he owes money, lenders find themselves bending over backward to give him a break. Even when he's broken his word, shown up two days late, dented your car, lost your keys, forgotten what he promised, changed his mind. Even when he's ripped you off— not by conning, he never cons, unless you count his indolent charm a form of con, but he never lies outright, never schemes, just has a particular talent, a native grace, a knack for parting fools and their money—even then people can't help but feel fond toward him. Want to buy him a drink, cook him a hot meal, follow him home— or, more likely, take him into their own homes, their own trailers or apartments or motel rooms for the night.

The thing about Lloyd is that he's eminently adaptable. He knows it, too, knows how to work it, knows it works for him wherever he goes, his chameleon nature, his tractability. His appeal the appeal of an orphan, a cipher. Unthreatening, impermanent, consistent only in his willingness to vanish. His commitment to vanishing. If he had a family—not Ellerby, she doesn't count, being a child and a bit of a wraith herself, a dark-eyed hoverer who spends most of the year out of sight and who, the few months she is with him, floats silently alongside, taking invisible pictures with her imaginary camera—but if he had a real family, a tribe he truly belonged to, he wouldn't be able to slip in and out of other people's stories the way he does. It's only by virtue of all he's declined that he remains free.

He brings his watch around to his face and in the light of the moon reads the time: 3:07. He stands, pulls on his jeans, takes the book he has been reading—an old liver-spotted copy of *The Tibetan Book of the Dead*, rediscovered on a living room shelf—and treads lightly downstairs. On the second floor he stops in the bathroom and without bothering to turn on the light, pees. The bathroom smells of the cool, cracked porcelain tiles he can see perfectly in his mind as he feels them underfoot; of the rusty water in the tank; of mice. Always mice, this house has always smelled of mice. Throughout his boyhood: their caraway-seed droppings in the pantry, spring traps set with peanut butter, sounds of scurrying in the walls.

He makes his way down to the kitchen where he drifts toward the fridge, leans into its cold yellow light. A jar of olives, a block of Parmesan. Bunch of mint. Ceramic bowl of raspberries red as mouths. The myth of Persephone comes to mind, the garnet juice bursting between her teeth, the mistake that condemned her to eternal return. Not that Rundle Junction's Hades. Not that he had an unhappy childhood. He just never cast anchor here. Some kind of abstemiousness in his nature, some asceticism necessary to keep his mind clear, his path unimpeded, for hadn't he always been aware—from the very earliest moments of his awareness— that there was somewhere else he had to go, some distant destination he had yet to find?

He fills a mug from the drying rack with water from the tap. Manages the screen door to the porch with such experienced delicacy it does not squeak. Goes to sit in the old cane chair and nearly has a heart attack.

"Hey," says Tom, already occupying said chair.

"Jesus H." Sits in the rocker instead.

The moon filters through the curtain of hanging plants in streamers and scraps, like bits of paper torn and tossed across their laps and scattered on the floor. Insects chirr. Treetops stir. Lloyd can feel Tom waiting, braced: *A grown-up* . . . Can feel his mute expectation: *Questions shall ensue.*

More than a minute goes by. Lloyd takes a swallow of water. Who is he to question Tom? No one, hardly. No one at all.

Tom extends his palm: pair of hand-rolled cigs. "Smoke?"

"What is it?"

"Tobacco."

"No thanks."

Tom rests one on the arm of his chair, lights the other for himself. "I can get weed." Part etiquette, part boast.

Lloyd's smile's lost in the darkness. "I'm good."

Another thirty seconds pass. "So you're not going to interrogate me about what I'm doing up at three?"

"You want me to?"

"No. That's cool." After a bit: "So you've been involved in like, activism, right?"

"I've marched here and there. Held a banner or two."

"Ever been arrested?"

Lloyd blows a little air through his nose. "Not for that."

"For what, drugs?"

At that he laughs outright. "What does your mom say about me? Or—never mind. Guess that's obvious."

"No! No, she hasn't said . . . I mean—I don't know . . . it just seemed like a reasonable guess."

Lloyd nods, sucks his teeth. After a moment volunteers: "I've never been arrested. I was taken into custody once for trying to help some people who came here illegally, but there were never formal charges."

"What happened?"

"Too long a story for three a.m." And now he does ask, "What about you? Law on your tail? Or is this just garden variety insomnia?"

Tom takes a drag, exhales, and examines his cigarette, rotating it between forefinger and thumb. "Actually," he confides, "I was just over at the site of the new development. The thing from dinner—what all those signs are about?"

"The thing that's got your dad so up in arms."

"Yeah. I wanted to check it out for myself. See if the units really do have two kitchens and whatnot."

"How'd you get there?"

"Biked."

"How much could you see in the middle of the night?"

"Not much. I, uh—climbed around a little, but I couldn't get into any of the units. I tried to figure it out by the gas lines."

"And?"

Sheepishly, "I couldn't tell which pipes were which."

Lloyd can feel Tom's desire. It's like a damp pressure, a bottled breath. Some new-hatched thing with untested wings. He's not sure what the desire is for. He's not sure Tom knows. But how well he recognizes it. How it brings him back. "You care."

"What?"

"You care about this thing, you're invested."

"I don't know if I'm invested. I'm curious. Do I care about Rundle Junction? Do I care about hate crimes? Do I care about killing the planet?"

"Do you?"

"Of course. But caring's easy. Knowing what to think is harder."

"And?" inquires Lloyd. "What are your thoughts?"

"I don't know. At first I thought my dad was dead wrong." Tom reaches into the recycling bin, feels around and extracts an empty tuna fish can. He ashes into it, holding it cupped there in his hand. "About it being anti-Semitism. I thought the main issue really was the environment, the wetlands, the silver maples and that." He takes a drag, exhales. "But then I was talking with Chana earlier tonight, you know? She's from New Jersey. She's like super-Jewish, right? Goes to temple with her parents, goes on marches with Jewish Voice for Peace, the whole nine yards. And she says the ultra-Orthodox have basically taken over this town near where she lives and it's literally a travesty. Her words. She says they basically impose their religious beliefs on the whole town. They boycott shops that won't close on the Sabbath, put them out of business. They send their own kids to yeshivas but meanwhile they get themselves elected to the public school board and basically turn the public schools to crap, cut the budget for sports, music, APs, stuff like that.

"So now I'm thinking, maybe it *is* anti-Semitism. Maybe Dad's right. Maybe the whole environmental thing is bull—a smokescreen, a way to fight them legally. But here's the thing: sue me, but I don't really want them to cut AP classes and sports and stuff. Even if I graduate before any of that happens, what about Mantha and Pim, you know? Dad says if you believe in democracy you have to accept it on its terms. Majority rule, everyone's allowed to run for the school board, everyone's allowed to vote how they want. Shop how they want. Live how they want. Which—I mean, yeah. Obviously. That's what we believe in, right? Except, being totally honest, I don't really want the Haredi taking over my town. You know? And if talking about the silver maples is the best way to stop that, maybe I'm for it. Even if it's sneaky."

Tom puts out his cigarette in the tuna fish can. "You think I'm being disloyal." It's that thing he does of asking a question but inflecting it like a statement.

Lloyd makes a small sound, neither cough nor laugh.

"What?"

He holds up his palms: *I didn't say anything.*

"I am, technically," decides Tom. "Being disloyal."

"Maybe," says Lloyd, "you're being aloyal."

"What's that?"

He shrugs. "I just made it up. But there's immoral and amoral, right? So maybe there's disloyal and aloyal."

"What's the difference?"

"Are you opposing your dad for the sake of opposing him? Or do you actually have your own thoughts that differ from his?"

"I have my own thoughts. That differ from his. How is that not the definition of being disloyal?"

Lloyd gives a rare belly laugh. "What if it is?"

Tom frowns at the tin of ashes.

"Look, maybe loyalty's overrated," Lloyd goes on. "What does loyalty ever do but cloud our perception? Muck up our thinking— *replace* thinking—it marries us to an ideal and blinds us to what's actually there. And for what? What's the great payoff?"

"But—"

"In and of itself, what does loyalty serve? It doesn't serve truth. It doesn't serve justice. It doesn't teach, or heal. Or create growth. It's not a real virtue. It isn't even a form of love." Lloyd is speaking so softly now Tom has to strain to hear. "Though it sometimes gets dressed up that way. Though it often gets dressed up that way."

Tom is hungry, thinks Lloyd. That's all. Everyone is. Every healthy person hungers. To know things for himself. Form his own questions, test his own ideas. Funny how a person's own family is often the first to punish him for that.

"The only thing loyalty serves," Lloyd says, "is loyalty."

Five and a half years from now, as a senior in college, Tom will take this question as the basis for his honors philosophy thesis. A dozen years from now, as an intern at a Brussels-based venture on conflict mediation and alternative dispute resolution, he'll explore how the question is affected by cultural and situational variables in real-life case studies. Forty-three years from now, as an internationally renowned expert in the field of transitional justice and reconciliation, he'll fly from Jerusalem to Arizona, where he'll re-tell the story of this conversation as part of the eulogy at his uncle's memorial service.

On this June morning he digests it in silence.

Astronomical twilight has begun. Astronomical twilight: the twice-daily period during which the geometric center of the sun is between twelve and eighteen degrees below the horizon. In the morning this period is succeeded by civil dawn, the moment when the sun reaches six degrees below the horizon. At this moment, in clear weather conditions, solar light becomes sufficient for conducting most outdoor activities. In several countries civil dawn is the basis for laws related to aviation, hunting, and the use of headlights.

In Rundle Junction, night loosens its grip. The sky, like blotting paper soaking up ink, begins drinking in the light now draining from moon and stars.

❦ · 3 · ❦

Episode Three. Wednesday.

Two Days Before the Wedding.

"**O**h! The Bible with a bullet in it!" Aunt Carrie lays a hand upon her breast. "Otis, Hugh! Come, you've got to see this!"

They're in the Rundle Junction Natural Historical Museum, no more than a couple of rooms in the basement of the public library. Aunt Carrie positions her boys in front of her where they can see inside the glass case containing artifacts of local history, including this pocket-size Civil War–era Bible butterflied open, the better to display the bullet embedded in its pages.

"I always loved this. Has Pim seen it? He must have."

"I don't know," says Bennie doubtfully. "I'm not sure *I* ever have."

"What are you talking about? Of course you have. Didn't we all have to take a field trip here in fourth grade? And how could you not have brought Pim, with his love of all things military? Pim-Pim, come!"

Carrie and the twins flew in from Cleveland this morning,

Walter driving through rush hour to ferry them up from LaGuardia. Carrie had been typically thoughtless about picking a flight that got in at the worst possible time, but it allowed Walter to come across as a hero, not to say martyr, and at the same time to escape the franticness at home, which is to say Bennie's franticness, since everyone else has been drifting around pretty tranquilly—this fact itself no small contributor to Bennie's franticness. Carrie's husband, Graham, is missing the wedding, purportedly because he can't get away from work. He's a probate attorney. Bennie, who can never remember what that means (frankly it just makes her think of prostate), considers Graham's absence no great tragedy, and yet the thought niggles: If Clem were marrying a man, would he have rearranged his schedule? Carrie herself speaks of the wedding in a tone that suggests she doesn't consider it quite legit. *Remember on Friday Clem is getting "married" to her "friend,"* Bennie overheard her brightly telling the boys, the aural quotation marks unmistakable.

Of course Carrie's always ever so slightly overacting, always playing to the peanut gallery with her blandly pretty features. She's not so much a ham as a perennial overcompensator. Compensating for what, exactly? Graham's permanent veneer of disdain, no doubt: making it up to the boys, going the extra mile to ensure they're exposed to the recommended minimum daily allowance of enthusiasm. But it predates Graham, this inflated merriment; it was a role she played, a task she shouldered, in childhood, too. Tall, strapping Carrie with her taffy ponytail, her blue-gumdrop eyes, her bubble-gum lips that always form each word as if for a hard-of-hearing person. She's been here a whopping three hours and already Bennie could use a break.

Lunch had been a flurry of cheese sandwiches, after which Bennie and Carrie had piled all the younger children—Pim, Otis, Hugh, Mantha, and Ellerby—into the car in order to go "tire them out" (Bennie's phrase) at the playground on the shore of Ida Pond, where the sisters lounged on a bench for what felt like the merest of moments before they were beset by the children, who came back one by one to heap up beside them, offering their scrapes to be evaluated and clucked over, their thirst to be assuaged (Bennie'd brought a string bag full of juice boxes), their shoes to be dumped free of wood chips. Someone said something about the ice cream truck and they all began whining for treats, even though the mothers maintained they lacked the ability to make the ice cream truck magically appear. "All other rumors of our greatness are accurate," Bennie hastened to assure them. It was Carrie who suggested, when the kids refused to be cajoled to go back out and play some more on the hot climbing structures, that they see if the museum was open.

The way from the playground to the library took them past the granite monument, and Ellerby paused to read the oxidized copper plaque:

IN MEMORY OF THE 18 CHILDREN

WHO PERISHED BY FIRE

ON THE SHORE OF IDA POND

JUNE 24, 1927

"Oh, that's a famous story," began Mantha proprietarily, but Ellerby, who hitherto had uttered so little that various of her cousins had wondered if she had some kind of speech impairment, did not let her cousin elaborate, but read aloud, in the unhurried manner of her father, the names and ages listed below. The boys, trailing grass-stained and sweaty behind them, caught up now with the girls and, without quite knowing why, organized themselves into a formation of solemn attention.

Otis, ridiculously cherubic with his sunlit curls and cheeks like pink hams, stood with his feet apart and clasped his hands behind his back. Hugh, younger than his brother by seven minutes, sallow and slender everywhere Otis was fair and stout, used his middle finger to push his glasses up the sweaty bridge of his nose before following suit. Pim, the littlest, stood erect, chest thrust forward, chin held high. As a kind of afterthought, his right hand floated up and covered his heart.

"Maxwell Abbott, seven years old," Ellerby intoned. "Cecily Cartwright, eleven years old. Clara Cartwright, nine years old . . ."

"Okay, okay, we get the picture."

". . . Winifred Dempsey, eight years old. Benjamin Erlend, two years old."

"So young." The mothers had strolled up behind them; it was Carrie, of course, who made the sentimental observation.

But, "Erlend!" exclaimed Mantha. "Nobody ever told me we were related to one of the kids who died in the fire!"

The mothers looked at each other.

"It's a coincidence . . ."

"How's it spelled?"

They inched forward, leaning over Ellerby's head to decipher for themselves the letters, partly obscured by lichen and rust.

Ellerby stopped reading and turned to inspect her aunts' faces. All the kids turned to look at them.

"Huh," said Carrie. "Huh, huh, huh."

"Weird neither of us ever noticed it," murmured Bennie.

"I don't remember ever reading the names. I mean, we all just knew what the memorial was; I don't remember *anybody* actually reading it."

The sisters mirrored each other's frowning visages.

"We would know . . . " Carrie reasoned, sounding patently unconvinced.

That was enough to propel Bennie into certainty. She told the children, "There must have been another Erlend family."

It was Ellerby who commented: "It's the same name."

"Hel-lo-o!" Mantha made three syllables of it. "I said that already five minutes ago."

But, "The same as you," said Ellerby, extending the tip of her pointer finger toward Bennie.

Bennie regarded her niece. Their faces, while betraying nothing of their shared blood—the child's face being smooth and brown, the woman's harried and blotched with heat—were identical in their expressionlessness. If they shared a genetic trait it was the cool way each masked her thoughts.

Carrie, whom that gene had skipped, exclaimed, "She's right! That's crazy . . . Benjamin, Benita—it *can't* be a coincidence. Oh my gosh, you guys—we have to ask Aunt Glad!"

Her sons were less swept off their feet by the prospect of sharing a familial tie with one of the ancient dead. "I'm thirsty," said Otis. But the juice boxes were gone. "I'm thweaty," said Hugh, and pulled on his mother's arm: "What are we doing now?"

Bennie sympathized with the itch to change the subject, not because she found it dull, but because it was so freighted with strange implication, and with questions she'd prefer to sift through in private. *Was* there a family tragedy, long since hidden away? *Was* she the namesake of an unfortunate ancestor? And why had no one thought to fill her in, if so?

Ellerby lifted her imaginary camera, which evidently went everywhere with her on an invisible strap around her neck, and snapped a photo of Bennie looking pensive next to the plaque.

"Come on then," said Bennie brusquely. "Let's go see if the museum's open."

So they all trooped over and found that it was.

"How lucky!" chirped Carrie.

Now, inside, they are at least out of the sun. In fact it is bliss-fully cool in here. The rooms have that soporific smell produced by old wood and varnish, and the fragrance draws both Bennie and Carrie back through the decades—isn't it the very quintes-sence of their childhood? An olfactory bridge to selves that no lon-ger exist—and has a complicated effect on the children as well, at once muting their vigor (a contagion of yawning passes among them) and producing a sluggish form of restlessness. A scuffle breaks out between Otis and Hugh as they jockey for position in front of the display case, and Hugh gets pushed into Mantha, who whacks him with her cast. "Ow!" he cries, and Bennie in a voice like distant thunder says, "Mantha, so help me, if you keep this up . . ." and lets the rest of that thought dangle ominously.

"Pim," declares Carrie, scooping him into her arms (her go-to parenting technique: deflection, redirection), "see that little book with the pellet in it?" By some magic she is able to both lower her voice conspiratorially and project it for the benefit of the other kids, who, scenting something of interest about to begin, abandon their squabbles and draw near. "Well that little book saved a sol-dier's life."

How? she can feel them wondering, *how could a little book save anyone's life?*

Fed by their raptness, she imbues her voice with color as she fills in the details, makes her voice climb and dip, tack and clip in a way she has known to intoxicate small children and dogs. She is better at this than Bennie. Bennie may have twice the number of children, Bennie may be more unflappable, run a tighter ship, but Carrie is the enchantress: pliant, enticing, transmitting her own pleasure for the children's sake. She boosts Pim a little higher on her hip. "It's a Bible, a tiny, little Bible"—on *tiny* and *little* her voice shimmers—"that he always kept right in the pocket of his shirt. And when he got shot on the battlefield"—she bends to read—"'wounded at the Battle of Franklin in Tennessee on November 30, 1864,' the book actually *stopped* the bullet, just before it would have entered his heart! See?"—her voice throaty now with sudden emotion—"There it is, you can see it . . . stuck in the pages . . . nothing but that little bundle of paper to shield his heart . . ."

On the other side of the room, perusing fossils, Bennie stifles a yawn. *Mucrospirifer brachiopod.* The index card gone ochre with age. *Early Paleozoic Era.* How dull, the items under glass. Elevated by having been placed under glass, but how dull they are, little lumps of pocked gray shale and sandstone. *Streptelasmatidae,* reads another card, *Middle Ordovician–Middle Devonian. Conularia formosa.* All the Latin makes her eyelids droop. The cards, typewritten, look fossil-like themselves, browned and brittle, stuck with T pins to black felt. In the neighboring case, artifacts of the Wappinger people, thousands of years old—stone scrapers, bone needles, flint points. Quill and antler tools. Pendants and pipes. *Pre-contact,* they are labeled, and Bennie thinks, *Contact with what?* then realizes *Oh! With us! Before we came along with our smallpox and guns and changed everything. How different is it,* she muses, *from what is happening now on this same piece of land, a new group of people moving in, the existing residents up in arms?*

And if she and Walter have decided not to fight the change but to accommodate it—even hasten it—is that really weakness? Or is it realism? Knowing one's place in the world. Knowing the impermanence of one's place.

Mantha, materializing at her side, rubs her face against Bennie's shirt.

"Are you wiping your nose on me?"

"No!" She backs off, affronted. But she is in a clingy mood and almost instantly leans in again.

Bennie pulls away. "It's too hot."

Ellerby glides over and, with a movement of her index finger and an accompanying click of her tongue, documents the Wappinger tools.

Mantha glares. "Anyone can do that," she whispers.

Otis's voice, petulant, from across the room: "Where are the dinosaurs?"

Don't whine, Bennie would say, but he is not her child.

Carrie soothes, "Fossils, darling—not dinosaurs. Fossils of sea creatures."

After the fossils come cases of local fauna: taxidermied mammals and birds, a whole series of Odonata specimens impaled on acid-free paper. "Ith the pinth what killed them?" wonders Hugh, and Pim envisions a dragonfly taken down midflight by a pin shot from a tiny bow.

They drift limply through the exhibits, the children's disappointment palpable. Once again the grown-ups have promised delights that turned out to be paltry in real life. And whatever happened to the ice cream? Didn't someone say there was going to be an ice cream truck?

"Oh my gosh, kids—it's Aunt Glad!" sings Carrie from the back room. They flock in her direction. Aunt Glad's not as good as the ice cream truck, but still it's a novelty to think of finding her at the museum when they all remember having left her back at the house. How did she get here? And why?

But except for Carrie the tiny back room is unpopulated. Also dank and poorly lit. The entire room is devoted to the events of 1927—the pageant and the tragedy that ended it. The children thread past cases of artifacts that make real, that complicate and lend dimension to, the names of the children Ellerby so recently read off the copper plaque on the granite stone in the center of the Village Green. Among them: an ornately inked booklet (labeled

Pageant Program), a cardboard cone (*Pageant Ear*), a trio of trinkets—paper fan, toy horn, handkerchief-size American flag—(*Pageant Souvenirs*), a piece of charred wood (*Remnant of Grandstand*).

The walls are covered with old-fashioned photographs; it's before one of these that Carrie stands. "Look, kids—recognize anyone?"

"We have that picture!" Mantha is quick to claim. "In the powder room. Only ours is smaller."

This one has been blown up to nearly life-size.

Carrie points to the winged child sitting in a wagon. "Who's this girl?" she asks in an intoxicating hush.

"Who *ith* it?!" Hugh whispers back. He has some of his mother's theatricality. His eyes are enormous behind his eyeglasses.

Everyone else already knows. They feel bad for him, almost—why, she's their very flesh and blood! *Aunt Glad*, they tell him, shaking their heads and giggling behind their hands.

The children pay hardly any attention to the adjacent photograph, a wide-angle shot of the grandstands taken on the morning of the final day of the pageant: little more than a grainy sea of blown-up humanity, faces and bodies all but indistinct, a common blur of black and white. That Lester Vilno—who paid for a ticket like anyone else; who brought from home a frugal lunch of fresh radishes, celery, and two boiled eggs, all wrapped in a checkered cloth; who furthermore brought with him several sheets of paper and a pencil, at the ready in his pocket, that he might sketch any ideas that might come to him as he watched the proceedings, inspirations for new marionettes; and who would later be, if never officially blamed for what happened on the final day, scapegoated as a walking emblem of foreignness, as a vessel of suspicion—that he is among the people captured in this photo was lost on everyone at the time. It would not be verifiable even now, regardless of today's advanced technology, since no other record of his visage exists. As it happens, the only remaining record of Lester Vilno's existence is contained within the memory of one Glad Erlend. And that is fading fast.

SOMEONE HAS PAINTED SWASTIKAS on the new development.

"What do you mean 'on' the new development?" asks Bennie.

"On it, Ben—on the walls."

"I thought it was still just being built."

"That doesn't alter the fact," Walter, rarely snappish, snaps.

"No, I just . . . so it has walls already?" She tries to visualize it. Were the marks spray painted on girders? On Tyvek wrap?

"They painted two swastikas on the foundation walls, one on the contractor's trailer." His T-shirt shows dark moons at the armpits and collar, dark beehives on the chest and back; he has been mowing the front lawn with the old push mower, whose blades have not been sharpened in years. If they had a power mower he likely wouldn't have felt the vibration in his pocket until he'd finished the job. As it was he'd paused to read the text, from, of all people, Jeff Greenberg, and was so distressed he left the job unfinished, the lawn mohawked: a single band of high grass splits it now down the middle. Bennie, coming into the kitchen to start dinner, had found him pacing, a bottle of seltzer in hand, trying to decide whether to call Marty.

"Who's Marty?"

Martin Stein; old college friend; you remember him, Ben, we were at his wedding; works for the Anti-Defamation League. Walter speaks in bullet points while swiping through contacts on his phone. "Maybe I should get more details first."

"What do you think it means?" asks Bennie.

He looks at her, incredulous.

"No, I mean—in this context. Who do you think is responsible?"

"Gee, Ben, let me think. How about anti-Semites? Whether it's coming from the Citizens to Preserve Blahblahblah People or not, it's obviously a hate crime—what?"

For it's obvious she's thinking something, the way she's standing there with narrowed eyes, one arm propped against the door frame, chewing her bottom lip.

"Nothing."

"*What?*"

"Just, it's a little convenient, no?"

"What are you talking about?"

"To happen at just this moment. When the village finally seems to be mounting some solid opposition, with the whole wetlands thing. Seems like a campaign that might really have an—"

But here a great eddy of children gushes in under her arm, as if the kitchen were a tidal pool and she and Walter, on dry land a second ago, were now inundated with a swirling wave of voices and bodies and paraphernalia: paper, pencils, a shoe box full of glue sticks. They take over the breakfast nook; it's all the little ones minus Pim (who can be spied at this moment through the many-paned bay window of the breakfast nook, striding about the lawn with a sailor hat and a bandanna knotted loosely around his neck).

"Wait, you guys—what's going on?" Bennie demands. "This isn't the art and crafts room."

"They're playing post office!" declares Carrie, bringing up the rear with an armload of supplementary materials: stapler, tape dispenser, can of markers, pack of construction paper.

"What are you, their minion?"

"It's just like we used to play!" she rhapsodizes. "Remember, Lloydie?"

For Lloyd has just appeared, too: he hovers on the threshold, looking almost comically mortified to find himself in the presence of so many people. Poor hapless Lloyd. His hair going every which way, his stubble glinting coarse and whitish (*When did he get so old?* both sisters think), a red welt on his cheek that would be mystifying if they didn't know him to be an insomniac who always disappears for long stretches in the middle of the day only to show up bearings the marks of napping.

"What are you looking for, Lloyd?" Bennie asks. "Coffee?"

"Remember?" Carrie continues. "Lloydie would always insist on being postmaster!"

"Lloydie, Lloydie," chorus the twins.

He gives a shy, pained grin—a grimace, really.

"Lloydie!" All the children take it up.

"Stop that," she tells them. To him again: "What do you want? Coffee, juice?"

"Uh, just water, thanks." He accepts the glass she hands him with a sleepy, grateful look. Takes a swig. Apologetically, "Didn't sleep much last night."

"You always don't sleep much," says Ellerby.

He aims his index finger at her: *Right you are.*

"So here's how it works," proclaims Mantha. "Everyone gets a mailbox—"

"I know this!" says Otis. "We did it in school. For Valentine's."

"This is different," she informs him. "We have real mailboxes." And points with her scissors (eliciting a swift maternal *Don't point with scissors*) toward the wall.

One entire wall of the kitchen, formerly the inner sanctum of the post office, is studded with cubbyholes that correspond to the wall of little brass doors in the living room. Whereas in the latter they constitute a kind of idiosyncratic decorative element, in the former they are strictly utilitarian, housing such items as spices, birthday candles, tea, pot holders, dish towels, matches, a vegetable peeler, a lemon zester, a strawberry huller, a garlic press; also there are bandages, Mercurochrome, aspirin, rubber bands, paper clips, hair grips, playing cards, cootie catchers, and business cards for all varieties of home repair.

"That's where you put the letters for the customers to take out on the other side," Mantha explains. "The doors are locked but I know how to pick 'em."

The cousins beg her to show them how, and Mantha, pretending reluctance, heaves herself up from the breakfast nook and leads the way into the other room.

The grown-ups acclimate themselves to the relative stillness of their wake.

Then Walter picks up the thread of the interrupted conversation. "You were saying?" he prompts Bennie, sliding into the vacated breakfast nook. "About the swastikas, and the convenience?"

"Right." She sits opposite him. "What I was thinking is, who stands to gain? From the vandalism. Not the Citizens to Preserve Blahblahblah People. Even the perception of anti-Semitism would hurt, not strengthen, their cause. Right? And on the other hand, doesn't a hate crime automatically generate, if not outright support, then at least sympathy?"

Walter, who sees where this is headed, pretends not to. "Go on."

"What do you mean?"

"Finish the thought."

"I did."

"Uh-huh."

"I did, Walt. That's the extent of my thought, at the moment." She purses her lips. Of course that's not the extent of her thought. But she won't be bullied into saying the thing he'll find most objectionable. "Is there something you would like to add?"

They stare each other down, the air fairly crackling with the obviousness of what neither is willing to voice: *Could the Haredim themselves be behind the offensive graffiti? As a way to upstage and derail environmental objections?*

"What?" Carrie's gaze is ping-ponging between them. "What are you guys talking about?"

But neither Walter nor Bennie gives any sign of having heard her. Both are thinking of what only they know, the thing that even in this moment of friction unites them: the fact that after the wedding they're putting the house on the market. The fact that the timing of their decision (over which they have labored long and hard: after all, why not wait until Tom, who has only two years of high school left, graduates? why not wait until Glad, who cannot be much longer for this earth, passes on?) has everything to do with their own strategic interest and not the good of the community. The reason they are electing to abandon Rundle Junction now, rather than sticking around either to rally behind the wetlands *or* pave the way for friendly relations with the new-comers, is strictly financial: they're hoping to get out while the housing market's good, before demographics shift and property values drop.

What they alone understand: any opinion either of them has about the unfolding drama involving swastikas and lawn signs is inevitably tainted by self-interest, the desire to get a good price. And they sit there now, regarding each other across the old scratched table in the breakfast nook, united by guilt. And even though Walter is defensively, tribalistically angry at Bennie's un-spoken insinuation and Bennie is angry at Walter's resistance to even considering the common sense of what she has so far tact-fully refrained from explicitly suggesting, they are bound by their shared sense of guilt; it lends the air between them a frisson of intimacy, which Carrie senses, so that when she asks again, "What?

What's going on?" there's a note of jealousy in her voice, a hint of the old kid sister don't-leave-me-out petulance.

Bennie sighs. "Someone put swastikas on the new housing development."

Says Lloyd, "When?"

His sisters' heads swivel toward him in tandem: Can this really be Lloyd? Expressing interest in a local matter?

"Last night," Walter replies.

"What time?"

"I don't know, what do you care?"

"I don't."

Not for an instant do his sisters believe him.

But he is saved from further scrutiny by the entrance of Aunt Glad, who pushes the screen door open and comes in with her glass, nothing but melted ice and a wilted sprig of mint left in it. The sight of her reminds Carrie to ask about the name on the plaque.

"Hey, we have a question for—" she begins, only to stop herself when she sees her sister shooting her a look.

Not now, Bennie mouths.

It's true: Aunt Glad is looking rather frail, a bit pallid, actually, at the moment—never mind that she still moves as nimbly as ever, dainty as a damselfly even as she nears the century mark.

Walter has already risen and gently removed the glass from her hand. Cupping her elbow he conducts her past the litter of construction-paper scraps on the floor. Carrie and Bennie murmur solicitous inquiries: *Can we fix you something to eat, Aunt Glad? Would you like to lie down?* Lloyd just crinkles his eyes in his sweetest smile as he bows out of her path.

"Thank you, dears, no—I just thought if the young people are playing post office"—they exchange marveling glances: *What outstanding hearing she still has!*—"they ought to know how it's done. I want to show them how Mother and Daddy did the mail, how they weighed it and franked it, I mean." She pats Walter's arm, releasing him from assisting her, and continues independently on her way, adding, "We had some of that in our day, too."

"Some of what, Aunt Glad?" They exchange mystified glances.

"Feeling against the Jewish people," she calls back; already she's crossed into the next room. "It's nothing new."

"Hey," says Lloyd, "should the little guy be up there?"

They follow his gaze out the bay window. Pim is mounting the big aluminum ladder left out on the lawn by Clem and the Ch/Hannahs. They watch as he climbs. Up he goes in his white seaman's cap. Hand over hand he ascends, somehow managing to carry, tucked under his armpit, a spyglass (the cardboard core of a paper towel roll) as well as a wooden sword. Higher and higher— surely he must be nearing the point labeled *Do Not Stand Above This Step.* Surely he must have passed it. A collective gasp in the kitchen as his mother, father, aunt, and uncle see the ladder wobble.

PIM, SAILING THE HIGH SEAS, knows how to ride the swells. Reaching the crow's nest, he finds his balance and proceeds to look out for the foreign elephant. The man said to. This morning on the radio while his father was shaving and Pim was sitting on the hamper. Almost every morning they do this: Pim and his father get up early while the rest of the house is still asleep, and Walter shaves and Pim sits on the hamper and together they listen to the news. Walter concentrating on his reflection in the mirror while Pim concentrates on his face in the flesh as it reemerges, stripe by pink stripe, from beneath the white foam. Pim loves the news. The gravity of the voices, the sense that elsewhere in the world people are in charge, grown-up men and women tending to things, managing things, discussing things in a language he can't fully follow, a gray wash of gobbledygook. Every now and then, a phrase emerges, glistening clear and pink, for him to seize. That happened this morning when the man had said, *How concerned are you about the foreign elephant?* And the other man had said, *Well obviously without taking our eyes off the threat of domestic terrorism, I think we need to pay close attention to the foreign elephant.* Ever since, Pim has been on the lookout. Paying close attention. He expects it to look something like the elephant on the Parcheesi box, garbed in tasseled robes of pink and blue.

Reaching the crow's nest, he raises his spyglass and scans the roiling ocean. Nothing but waves as far as the eye can see. But wait—what's this? Glinting off to starboard, can it be? Something large and gray? Something tasseled and tusked? "Ahoy!" he cries. He feels the tossing of the waves. From behind him come startling shouts: "Pim!" he hears, and swivels. The sea swells. The ship lists. "Pim!" the beast trumpets.

And he falls . . .

immensity of earth

immensity of sky

. . . lands on his back, cupped between the two.

I'm okay, he means to say but cannot, he's caged, his lungs are caged, trapped behind iron bars, he cannot move, he's squashed flat. Then all at once air swooshes in, the cage melts, and a sob flutters free.

He scrambles to his feet. His sailor hat's come off; his neckerchief's askew. There on the ground: the spyglass, crushed.

A shadow stretches over him. It's his father, wearing the complicated look of a large man who's been running hard and now, having brought himself up short, labors to appear calm. "You okay, bud?"

Pim nods scornfully, only to burst into tears.

The gathering up. He does nothing. Needs not ask or reach or even see; he is simply lofted and held in his father's arms, his father's massive and massively strong arms, stronger than any ship, stronger than any ocean, and he is burying his face in his father's neck, being tickled by the coarse hairs that sprout everywhere on his father's body, which Pim both loves and reviles. Every night when he wakes and pads down the hall to burrow in with his parents, he takes his place in a landscape at once familiar and peculiar. Perfumed with skin and hair and breath and secretions not his own, a landscape formed of elbows and bottoms, stomachs and shins, warmly shifting bulks punctuated by the audible breaths his father emits, the damp plosive sound of each exhale as it blows open the valve of his lips, and the softer purrs his mother makes at intervals deep in her throat. The parental bed, his homeland, the cradle of his civilization, grows day by day more strange to him as he becomes more adept at noting its particularities and his own.

But now as he is carried across the just-mown lawn Pim relinquishes all such noting and sorting. His separate selfhood is of no interest to him at this moment; he savors instead his passivity even as he savors the taste of his father's neck, salty and slippery with his own tears. It is not a smooth ride—he is not cushioned from jolts as he would be if his mother were carrying him (she has a way of fitting him into the curve of her hip, and a more graceful gait besides, although of late he has not been able to get comfortable in her arms)—but his father's tread is full of power, of solidity. Sturdiness. His mother calls him Stalwart. She says it means steady and firm, lasting. His father sings in a sturdy voice while he bakes bread. He sings, by his own assessment, *fortissimo!*—and the way he says it, pinching his fingers together with his thumbs and shaking them in the air, always makes Pim laugh. He sings *We shall not, we shall not be moved* and also *Rocka my soul in the bosom of Abraham* and his voice fills the house and Pim doesn't know who Abraham is but he understands *bosom* must be an old-fashioned word for arms, and he knows his father's arms, his father's bosom, is wider and stronger than anyone else's in the world.

"NOW WHAT?" says Bennie in dismay. She's looking through the breakfast nook window, tracking Walter and Pim's progress as they make their way toward the house—Walter giving a thumbs-up so they know Pim is fine—but her attention's diverted by the car chugging up the drive behind them.

Rattletrap station wagon plastered with stickers, a mound of bundles bungeed to the roof. Stopping near the house, it discharges its load of three—no, four people, none of them recognizable except in the generic sense. In the generic sense they are members of the Clem and Ch/Hannah coterie. A bare-chested boy with hair as pale and curlicued as ramen noodles. A person of indeterminate gender with a buzz cut and overalls. Another with cornrows to her waist. And a bearded fellow wearing—what is that?—a baby carrier on his chest. Complete with baby. Not four people, then: five.

"It's like a clown car," says Carrie as a sixth body emerges, this one shaggy and four-legged.

"Oh Clementine," sighs Bennie.

They converge in the yard, Bennie and her siblings, Walter and Pim, the newcomers, and, a bit tardily but making up for it by the frolicking way they dash across the lawn from the direction of their orange tent (wherein, to judge by a whiff, marijuana has recently been partaken of), the trio of bride and bridesmaids. Squeals of joy from the young people; a flurry of introductions— the names bandied about seem to be Dave-Dave, Val, Maya, Banjo, Richard, and Harriett, but by the time all the hugs and handshakes have been exchanged, it's anyone's guess which name is attached to which body. The obvious is confirmed: these are college friends, here for the wedding.

"They do know that's two days away, right?" Bennie mutters at Clem.

"Mom! They're here to help set up."

"And who is this?" asks Bennie, bending toward the little one whose anemone hand now closes around her proffered finger.

"Harriett," somebody says.

Harriett regards her with that brazen baby clarity, so tranquil as to border on impudence. Her eyes like wet stones.

It's all perfectly ordinary—the palmar grasp reflex, the unwavering infant stare—yet Bennie, like most highly defended people, is total mush beneath the carapace. Babies are her underbelly. Perhaps now, with the voltaic secret of new life forming inside her, she is especially susceptible. For a prolonged moment she feels a quickening, a glimmer of some profundity she'd once known, now beyond her recall.

The baby, still holding fast to Bennie's index finger, opens her mouth, or rather lets her mouth fall open slightly. A bubble of saliva blossoms between her lips.

Pim lunges from his perch in Walter's arms toward his mother—*his* mother!—and makes a whimpering sound. "Don't whine," murmurs Bennie, even as she pries her finger free from Harriett's grasp and, without looking, receives her boy, fits him neat as a jigsaw piece upon her hip.

Now the ramen noodle fellow extracts a French horn from the backseat and blows into it, producing the first four notes of the "Wedding March." *Here comes the bride.* The person in overalls gives him a poke and the last note ends in a squawk. "What?" protests the musician. "It's festive!"

Chana hoists herself onto him piggyback. "It *is* festive!" she concurs. "Give me a ride, Dave-Dave!" and he obliges, setting the instrument on the ground and galloping her across the lawn where they collapse at the foot of the black walnut tree. The dog, with a loose-hipped, shambling gait, goes over to sniff them for damage.

Over everyone's heads, Walter is beaming a look at Bennie. *What gives?* it's asking. *Are they planning to stay here?* She telegraphs back, *I know.* She telegraphs, *You're telling me.* And for a moment they are in it together, mutually put-upon, and she envisions them joining forces to announce, with benevolent regret, that their house is stuffed to the gills and can't possibly accommodate more guests.

But in the next moment—oh, she could throttle him, or throttle herself for being so dumb because after all he is Stalwart, ever the emcee, she should have seen it coming—he is inviting everyone inside, inquiring about the length of their drive and whether they're thirsty, whether they need anything to eat.

So it falls to Bennie to say to Clem, "Could you hold back a minute?"

She sets Pim down and waits until he's caught up with the others before turning to her eldest in order to enumerate her rapidly growing list of concerns. Where to begin? Perhaps she won't have to, perhaps Clem is about to tender an apology, a sheepish or even tearful admission that they are in over their heads, a plea for help with the wedding, or a confession—is this what Bennie hopes?—that it's not *really* a wedding, but only a game, a frolic, a farce. An elaborate piece of performance art.

What Clem tenders instead is the Last Straw. With a bland smile she inquires, "What's up?"

"'What's *up?*'" Bennie echoes. The world tilts. The very horizon comes loose at its seams.

Here they are: late afternoon, late June, two days before the wedding. Here they stand on the lawn fragrant with fresh mowings, enveloped by a breeze as lilting as a song. Bennie imagines the scene as it should be. As one of the pageant photos, a tableau titled "Mother and Daughter on the Eve of the Daughter's Nuptials, an Idyll of Great Poignancy Attended by Love, Fear, and Hope" (these represented by three children in gauzy frocks posed accordingly about the two main characters). She sees it unfold in mawkish pantomime: Mother and Daughter both, with stylized, synchronized gestures, brushing tears from their eyes, swanning into fond embrace.

"What do you *think* is up?"

Clem blinks. The blink is an act, a faux innocence, an aggressive innocence. Just beneath is a steely shell; Bennie feels it and is enraged and wounded by it and cannot fathom its provenance. Resentment is steaming off her daughter like vapor off dry ice, but what on earth does Clem have to feel resentful about?

"First of all," Bennie says, hating how high and breathy her voice sounds but being powerless to amend it, "who are these people just showing up at our house? And when were you going to inform us about them? Or excuse me—stupid question: clearly you weren't. Clearly you didn't feel the need to tell us. Let alone ask. How could it not occur to you to ask if it would be okay to have more people over before they just show up? Before they just waltz into the kitchen where, incidentally, I guess I'm now about to start preparing supper for"—she does a quick calculation—"nineteen." On and on she hears herself go, cringing at the merry-go-round inevitability of her tirade even as she is helpless to rein it in. ". . . and don't think it's not obvious you've been getting high in the tent, after I told you I don't want anyone doing drugs on our property, especially so close to McElroy's, but even more now with all these kids around—"

"I haven't been, Mom, honestly. Hannah smoked a bowl but

that's it, it's gone now, that's all she brought with her. I wouldn't even know who to buy it from up here."

"That isn't the point, it's your selfishness, Clem, your obtuseness, your utter disregard—I mean it's mind-boggling! Yet again a decision you make, apparently without a qualm, to go expressly against what Dad and I said. And where are they even planning to stay, your friends? In Rundle Junction? Has anyone bothered to check whether the Garrison still has vacancies? Because I very much doubt—"

But this Clem interrupts with an airy wave, gesturing toward the station wagon with its pyramid of bundles strapped to the roof. "Relax," she says. "There's plenty of room to pitch their tents next to ours. They'll be self-sufficient."

"Clem!" It hits her like a two-by-four, less the news than Clem's blasé delivery. "Do you have any concept of what self-sufficient means? You told them they could camp here? Tents, *plural?*"

"What do you care if it's one tent or two?"

"That's not the—they're going to be using our bathrooms, our towels, our kitchen, wanting showers, wanting, wanting—I don't know—*coffee*." Pronouncing *coffee* as if *a kidney*. "Just for starters. For heaven's sake, there's a baby! What about"—she is spluttering now—"what about diapers? What about spit-up? Do you have, I mean remotely, any idea how much laundry a baby makes?"

"Mom." Clem winces. "No offense. You should hear how bourgeois you sound."

Bourgeois! she wants to say. *I fell in love with your father when he was living in a tent fighting apartheid. He hadn't showered in days. Our first apartment didn't even have a table, we ate our meals on a door taken off its hinges and laid on milk crates.* Bennie's queasy with the injustice. The basic misapprehension of who she really is.

But, "Really," her daughter is saying, sounding not just unruf-
fled but—and this is the real Last Straw, the real insult to injury—
compassionate. Yes: *gently* now, Clem breaks the news: "If you
could hear yourself you'd be embarrassed."

Bennie breaks. Just breaks. Tears crowd in tight behind her
eyes until she submits to them, gives up trying to master herself.
She brings her hands to her face and weeps. Bent, racked, before
her placid eldest, her pretty, lissome, straight-backed, butter-
wouldn't-melt-in-her-mouth eldest, she lets her mouth crumple
and her eyes and nose flow.

There, there, she used to say when Clem was little and the disaster was a skinned knee, a popped balloon, a dropped ice cream
cone. *There, there*, meaningless syllables but with a softness to
them, and Bennie would cradle her girl in her lap and pat her
curved little back and murmur *there, there*, more a cadence than
anything, low in her throat like a mourning dove cooing, and of
course *there, there*, had really meant *here, here*, as in *Here I am* and
Here you are and what could be amiss in such an equation? It had
been enough. Had been plenty. The crying, the cooing, and the
little curved back: always her cup had runneth, then, for what joy
it is to have the ability to comfort your own.

Perhaps it's for the loss of this ability that Bennie weeps now.
She feels a hand placed, rather too lightly, on her shoulder. One
cupped palm of lukewarm consolation. Two little pats. And now
gulping, now using her shirt to wipe her face, she thinks, *So this is
how it happens. The rift. This is how your children separate themselves from you at last: with the cruelty of indifference.*

"ANY FOURS?"

"G'fish."

"Any jacks?"

"G'fish."

"How 'bout sevens?"

It's a kind of music, the slip-slap of cards being laid on the rug, gathered up, fitted into fans in children's hands.

Glad sits on the gold settee, her small bony feet up on the footstool Tom so thoughtfully brought her. Tom that gallant boy. They are gathered in the living room, the whole ever-expanding lot of them; she has all but given up keeping track of which ones are her blood and which ones strangers. Bennie (she of course is blood, not only blood but the very heart that pumps it, the very keeper of the hearth) sits at the other end of the settee, her face clouded, though when Glad inquires if anything's the matter she replies she's just a touch tired. Walter in the Morris chair, bottle of beer on his knee, also looks tired. Carrie and Lloyd and Tom have claimed the sofa, and Clem and her clan are either on folding chairs brought in from the barn or sprawled on the rug, all except the bearded fellow, rocking the baby in the rocking chair. The tall boy is strumming a miniature guitar. It has its own name, she used to know it. A lute, maybe? No. A yule? Not that either. There's a dog, too, queer-looking creature—like one of those flip-book chimeras, part bear, part sheep, part camel, or like a piece of licorice allsorts (they sell these from a big glass jar next to the cash register, five cents for a little paper bagful).

"We used to gather in just this way." Glad addresses the room in her clear, oratorical kindergarten teacher's voice. "Back when it was the post office. And Erlend's Store."

From the way they turn to her, nodding and smiling, she has the impression she must have said this before, perhaps just minutes ago, and she blushes, less from embarrassment than chagrin. To be caught out, discovered in a memory lapse, is no great shame in itself. It's the loss of currency she minds, the understanding that each time such a lapse registers on the others, she is placed in their minds a little farther apart, sent floating down the current of irrelevance, set adrift . . .

The little ones don't notice her gaffe, so deeply immersed in their game of cards on the carpet. Really it's a pretty sight, the circle of them sitting crisscross-applesauce there under the stained-glass lamp. (In her day you said "Indian-style," but that's frowned upon now.) *Though I don't know why,* she says aloud. *Daddy played an Indian in the pageant,* she reasons, and the big boy sitting nearest her offers a smile without (she can see) understanding what she's talking about. (At least it might be a boy; to be honest she isn't sure. The hair's worn short as a new recruit's but under the bib of the overalls—is that a bosom?) *A Wappinger Indian,* she goes on. *Mother sewed his costume herself—she put a row of fringe on each leg of his trousers. And made him a tunic out of a burlap sack embroidered with beads from the store—we used to sell them here, you know, beads and buttons and you should've seen her working at the table late into the night, bent over with her poor eyesight and the floor lamp drawn up close.* She hears herself . . . surely she's speaking aloud . . . but no one is paying any attention. Then she realizes—it's a peculiar feeling, not nice at all: she hasn't been moving her lips.

Still, it's true. Mother stitched his costume, working by the very same lamp that is right now shining on the hair of the boys and the girls (the boys' hair longer than it used to be when she was their teacher; the girls' messier, untamed by ribbons and pigtails). Earlier this afternoon she'd given them a lesson on the postal system and how it used to work. She'd directed the wiry little girl—whose is that child, by the way? is she kin? the others call her cousin but she looks nothing like an Erlend, not with her hair black as serge and her skin brown as toast; she is what Mother would have described as "a foreigner," or in a gentler mood, "from away"—to climb up on a chair in the office and feel around on the uppermost shelf of the storage closet, where, sure enough, the Pitney Bowes was parked, just as it has always been. The children had all seemed surprised when it turned out really to be there where Glad directed, especially the girl with the blue cast on her arm. She lives here year-round in the very room Glad and Joy used to share, with the walls papered in apples and pears, and her eyes had gone wide and she'd puffed out her cheeks, saying, *Why didn't I ever know this was here?* as if she were in charge of everything in this house, and then she'd tried, as the dark little girl (*she* looks like an Indian, come to think of it) lowered it carefully, still standing on the chair, to take it from her, but Glad had said in her schoolteacher voice, *Let one of the boys do it, dear,* and then quickly, lest she be accused of favoring boys, *It needs two good arms.*

One of the boys, the one with the cheeks, set it on the desk and they'd all gathered around while Glad explained what franking was and how it worked, and everyone got a chance to run an envelope through the meter, which had no ink but still made its satisfying *chunkety chunk,* and when Carrie came in to see where the children had disappeared to she, too, had been amazed (*I remember that old thing! Who knew it still existed . . .*) and demanded a turn putting an envelope through herself and the children all talked over one another, practically fighting to be the one to repeat what their great-grandaunt had told them, that the machine had been approved by the U.S. Post Office Department in 1920, the very year of Glad's birth.

Without any detectable form of communication—perhaps they signaled to one another in the pheromonic manner of bees, thought Glad, drawing upon some hidden store of rudimentary entomological knowledge—they had transferred their mail-making materials into her room then, arranging themselves at the desk and on the floor, and one of Carrie's little boys (the one with the glasses and the lisp) climbed right up on the foot of the neatly made cot and made that his work space, while Glad herself reclined at the head, her legs stretched out (*Oh how good that felt*) beside the child, her bare toes curling and flexing in the June breeze—flattered by the children's having gravitated to her, flattered but not entirely surprised, for was she not a much-beloved teacher?—and nominally oversaw their operations. Said operations consisting mostly of cutting and folding and taping and pasting, a little bit of scribbling, too, although the lexical content of these missives was plainly ancillary to the crafting of letters as objects—*objets*, Glad's memory supplied. *Objets de vertu.* She scanned the children bent over their paper constructions. The smallest great-grandnephew, the little warrior, squatted on the floor with his scissors and paper, breathing as if he were climbing a mountain, flushed with effort. The Indian-looking girl stood at the desk, creasing her paper into an envelope, on one foot only: the other was hooked around the back of her knee, like a crane. Again Glad tried to remember who she was, how she fit in with the others. Lloyd's adopted daughter? The imperious child, the one who lives here, the one with the blue cast on her arm, was filling a sheet of lined paper with writing and singing softly under her breath. (*Debout! Les damnés de la terre! Debout! Les forçats de la faim!*) One of her father's songs, no doubt; Walter was always belting something out.

Allowing her head to rest back against the pillow, Glad had closed her eyes for a moment. Sounds of snipping and scrawling, breathing and sighing, sniffing and swallowing—one of the twins had a cold or perhaps hay fever; she ought to tell him to use a tissue but was too peaceful to fuss, too peaceful even to open her eyes—sounds, too, of the breeze rustling the venetian blinds, the sound of the slats fluttering, tumbling, a new list of trains on the departure board, and now the sound of a fly buzzing, bumping fruitlessly against a pane; she imagined it trapped between the screen and the glass, she ought to open the screen and close the glass so as to help guide the poor thing out into freedom, but again found herself too peaceful to translate intention into action.

Excuse me, a little hand patting her, little finger pecking like a chick at its shell, about to be born: *Excuse me, please, Aunt Glad, do you have an eraser?*

Shh, she's sleeping; can't you see her eyes are closed?

But I'm awake, she wanted to tell them, *I hear everything you say*; only she was too far away to open her mouth, too far away to open her eyes; aware of yet detached from her body on the cot in the warmth of the June afternoon. She was far away but not alone. She felt herself accompanied. It was Joy beside her, Joy composing a letter in her new fancy style (*It's called cursive*) that Glad couldn't read. *Who are you writing?* she asked. *I can't tell you*, said Joy. *It's private.* So Glad took her own sheet of paper, her own pencil, began her own letter. *Who are you writing?* Joy asked; when Glad said hers was private, too, Joy peered over her shoulder. *That's not even writing.*

Is so—it's in code.

No it's not. You're just making scribblescrabbles.

Am not.

Are so.

Am not.

Are so.

The very fact of Joy's continuing to bicker instead of withdrawing from the argument was a victory and should have contented Glad, but she was not disposed toward contentment. She couldn't help it—Joy had a special talent for riling her—really, she was practically forced to jab her older sister with the pencil, whose point, breaking off in Joy's wrist, would leave a blue-black remnant there, a crumb of graphite lodged deep in the derma. The blemish, which for the rest of Joy's life people would take for a birthmark, was a source of queer satisfaction to Glad, herself so egregiously blemished compared with her pretty older sister. Joy never told on her, so only the sisters knew it for what it was, a battle scar, and although Glad supposed it ought to have made her feel guilty, it did not. She couldn't help that either.

Glad opens her eyes (*How long have they been shut?*) to find herself not in the office on her cot but in the living room on the settee, and the children are playing not post office but go fish. The floor lamp at whose base they have arranged themselves is the one Mother so prizes—*Won't she be pleased to learn it still survives!* It had been a mail-order purchase, one of the rare parcels delivered to their house not to be sorted and held for a customer, but to stay. The filigreed cast-iron base came in one box and the stained-glass shade arrived separately, a week later, packed inside a crate with loads of cotton batting that Mother unwound with tremulous care. It looks like an upside-down bowl of fruit. Crimson clumps of cherries, amethyst bunches of grapes. Glad and Joy invent a game called picnic that consists of their slowly circling the lamp and laying claim to its goodies one by one.

I think I'll have that plum now.

Fine, I get the fig.

They point but do not touch. Touching is forbidden. Part of the game is how close they can hover their fingers near the brilliant glass shapes without making contact. They take turns choosing, miming the act of plucking and popping the fruits into their mouths. They show off their voraciousness by making bestial devouring sounds.

Once they squabble over the banana. One sister shoves the other out of the way, and the lamp is set rocking on its stem. Daddy, reading the *Rundle Junction Gazette* on the settee, shoots out an arm and steadies it without even looking, but Mother will not let them hear the end of it. *Selfish, selfish children! Have you no sense of the value of beauty . . . ?*

It was your fault, Joy says that night as they lie side by side under the eaves. *You're the one who bumped into the lamp.*

It's true. Gladdy is the irresponsible one. Gladdy is the one who breaks things, loses things, leaves things out in the rain or the snow or the woods. She is the one who trips, gets sick, talks back, won't behave. She is the one who makes Mother cry. As if a command had been issued at birth: *You shall be the little one, the reckless one, the sulk. You shall weep easily, lose your temper, accustom yourself to not getting your way.*

You shall have the smaller part, wear the bent wings, take the blame, come to harm, be rescued, be ridiculed, be lonely, be free. You shall be regarded as quirky, regarded as brave, called "an original," afforded a measure of respect, a place in the community, real affection. You shall be cared for, laughed at kindly, doted upon in your dotage. Little shall be asked of you, little expected. What ripples you make will be scant and modest. Except in duration. Except in time. For you will remain on earth many years, fourscore and counting; you will outlive all those who came before you and a great many of those who came after.

But why? Glad thinks, knowing this has always been the mystery, the core riddle of her life, perhaps of all lives, the question of usefulness: *Whatever is this long life for?*

And suddenly—*oh!* an answer suggests itself, at once obvious and strange: *For pleasure's sake.* Could that really be the crux of it, the point? *The receipt of pleasure. And of pain.* In the end, is that all that ever was wanted of her? To receive? Surely anyway this much is apparent: more and more, every day, every hour, pleasure and pain unveil themselves to her, unveil their dark, luminous secret, which is that they are not only not separable, they are not even separate. The border dividing each from each is illusory. More and more she is attuned to them in their bounteous and various forms. More and more she perceives the myth of their contrariety, is able to recognize both the abundance of their diverse blooms and their one joined root.

"LOOK." With his chin Tom indicates Aunt Glad, who is emitting the daintiest of snores. She projects the ageless sagacity of an infant in sleep. Thanks to a small, felicitous accident of symmetry, she is in fact mirrored by an actual sleeping infant: the baby Harriett in her father's arms. She, too, transported elsewhere. Her eyelids, the palest lavender tissue, astir with dreams. The one a recent arrival, the other soon to depart. They might be dreaming of the same distant land. They might be passing each other in the station.

Now Harriett's little features scrunch in her sleep. She looks for all the world as though she's wrestling a very great challenge, a point of Solomonic jurisprudence . . . a way around the second law of thermodynamics . . . the solution to Fermat's last theorem . . . an angel . . . She twists, reddens, emits a series of splurts from her nether regions, and relaxes, beatific once more.

"Impressive," says Tom.

Her father accepts the acclaim with a modest smile.

Earlier, out on the porch where everyone wound up having supper (as it happened, the new guests insisted on providing for all—a couple of massive salads and a stack of pizzas picked up from Mangiello's in town), Bennie had addressed him as Richard, as in, "Richard, can I bring you anything?" He'd been administering a slice of eggplant pizza to himself with one hand and a bottle to Harriett, nestled in her car seat, with the other. "Richard?" she repeated when he failed to respond. Instead the slovenly-shaggy dog, who'd been gazing adoringly at Pim's slice of pizza, had turned and thumped his tail.

"Who are you talking to, Mom?" whispered Clem. "That's Banjo."

"What?" Bennie whispered back.

"Harriett's dad? Is Banjo. Richard's the dog."

"Oh." Because she was embarrassed, Bennie added more acerbically than she intended, "I should have known."

"The pot calling the kettle black," Clem pronounced coldly.

Which stung the more for being unfair—after all Pim was the traditional Dutch nickname for William! And Mantha had been a perfectly ordinary Sam until six months ago; Bennie could hardly help it if her most willful child suddenly insisted on going by the latter syllables of her given name. But this was hardly the time or place to mount such a defense. Mother and daughter, reduced to furious silence, simply glared.

And so much congealed in that moment: Bennie's estimation of the newcomers; Clem's estimation of Bennie; the bitterness between the two; the injury in which each felt wholly and solely justified.

(Bennie's annoyance would only grow when, after supper, the newcomers pitched their tents, two of them, each sprouting from its peaked roof a pennant: one scarlet emblazoned with a golden apple, the other azure emblazoned with a silver swan. What about these flags—they were after all innocently jovial and evidently hand-stitched—did she find irksome? Was it the affectation? Or the territorial presumption? Her antipathy only ratcheted up when they proceeded to unload their car and carry into the barn—the barn! as if it weren't liable to collapse any minute now—a unicycle, a pogo stick, something that looked like homemade crutches, and what appeared to be painted flats of the sort a traveling theater might use. "What are those?" she asked Clem, who only trained upon her a Giocondian smile and said, "You'll see on Friday," so that Bennie was left again to wonder whether this wedding was sincere or a kind of trompe l'oeil, a piece of performance art that would make all the guests feel like dupes.)

Banjo, then: everyone turns to look at Banjo, the long-lashed man who sits rocking the infant, the look on his bearded face as he gazes down at his daughter matching her own. The mother is apparently rehearsing a play at some pop-up performance space in the city and won't get here until Friday. Which news Bennie registered with a click of gratifying disapproval: these selfish children playing at adulthood had no business bringing babies into the world and would plainly make a mess of it, to the detriment not only of their own offspring but of society as a whole.

And yet, she has to admit, there is no fault to be found in this moment, in this father-daughter portrait. It radiates only sweetness. Is fairly encrusted with sweetness, glinting with the crystalized syrup of parental love, and as such stands in painful relief against the mother-daughter portrait from just a few hours ago: Bennie and Clem on the lawn, the very emblem of connection gone awry.

Dave-Dave, who has been picking out "Summertime" on the uke, prompts, "Sing, Val," and now the person with the buzz cut begins to hum—Clem has informed Bennie that Val is genderfluid and should be referred to as "they"—producing a low satiny ribbon of sound. Clem is sitting in a half lotus on the floor behind Maya, who surrenders drowsily to the kneading of her vertebrae. The Ch/Hannahs have both flopped onto their backs, their limbs intermingled with a kind of carelessness, a kind of ease. They're like a couple of alley cats who, at the end of the day, without quite saying it was all a charade, shed their adversarial stances and concede to groom each other.

INTO THIS TRANQUILLITY comes a vivid pulse.

"Cops," observes Dave-Dave, so laid-back no one pays any attention.

Only when the lights strobe the room a second time, a carnival sweep of red and blue, and Dave-Dave stops strumming and repeats the word, do the others take notice. The Ch/Hannahs sit up. The little kids stop playing go fish. Richard the dog lifts his head from his paws. Sound of a car engine cutting out. The lights, close-up now, saturate the room in rhythmic rounds of hue. Walter sets down his beer and goes to the window, peers out for a moment, then strides into the kitchen. They hear the smack of the screen door, the rumble of voices on the porch. Then the door swings open and shut again, and there are footsteps, and Walter reappears.

"Tom?"

All heads swivel Tomward.

"Could you come out here, please?"

"Sure."

The exchange could not be more innocuous, nor, in its very minimalism, more foreboding. Walter's *please* occasions a flutter in Bennie's breast, but it's the way Tom responds—with such lightness of tone, as if Walter had just said *Could you give me a hand unloading the car?*—that ratifies her sense of dread. Dread of what, she could not say, but this much is clear: it's not nothing.

And there he goes. Tom follows Walter. Who did not bother to catch her eye. Neither to offer a look of reassurance, nor to brace her. He kept her in the dark like everyone else in the room. And whether he did this wittingly or no—but of course, of *course* it was witting! his failure to acknowledge her status and their link, their jointly held role as Tom's makers and protectors—there can be no question whether it was inadvertent. *Walter!* she would like to yell after him, *Walter, hey Walter—what happened to our foot?* But this she cannot do, being trapped onstage—for that's what the living room has become, with all these spectators. How often in life does the law come asking you to produce your child? How often in life does such a scenario turn out to be benign? A wave of protest swells in her, a wave of resentment at having her home wrested from her control and designated a public arena.

THIRD NOCTURNE

THE MOON

His own sobbing wakes him. He used often to wake sobbing when he was little, so little he doesn't remember, not as worded memory, anyway, not preserved in the aspic of language, but still there lurks, beneath this crushing liquid terror, a residue of something he has known before. Does that make the terror even more terrible? Yes. It senses him, knows him. He is caught inside the curling tongue of a massive wave; it tosses him mockingly, pricks of sand sting his skin, pricks of salt swarm his eyes and he cannot see, everywhere it's dark, he can't tell up from down and then something is reaching for him, a great suckered tentacle, and he wails and sidles away, his own scuttling motion appalling him. Nothing is stable, nothing as it seems, not even—most terrifying of all—himself.

Then he is grasped and hoisted from the queer dark airless rustle of the waves; limp with fright, he succumbs; he passes through fright into something numb. To resist somehow more horrific than to give in.

Give up,

give in,

wake up, Pim!

"Wake up. Pim. You're having a dream."

Walter draws to his chest the sweaty collection of limbs that is Pim. On the other side of the bed, Bennie does not stir. Normally a light sleeper, she has been succumbing more fully these past several weeks to the depths of first trimester slumber. The moon silvers the damp slick of hair at Pim's temple, and although his eyes are open they have a wild, remote look: he is still lost inside his dream. Or not dream, nightmare. Or not nightmare, night terror. *Pavor nocturnus* the doctor had called them when they sought help a few years earlier, back when Pim was having them several times a week. The worst thing they could do, Walter and Bennie had learned, was explicitly try to comfort. Overt eye contact, direct address, flagrantly consolatory touch: all of these only increased Pim's panicked confusion, made him skitter deeper into the crevices of his frightening unreality. They had learned instead to pay him only the most oblique attention. There were techniques. Hold him in one arm and casually say, as if to yourself, *I'm a little thirsty. Think I'll get a glass of water,* and then wander with him over to the sink. If you kept your tone light and your manner offhand, bit by bit then his breathing would return to normal and he might sip from the cup you abstractedly offered him, peer through the curtains alongside you, or rest his head on your shoulder and become a tired, ordinary boy once more.

Walter, yawning, lifts Pim and carries him first to the window (*Hello, moon,* he greets the aspirin-white tablet so far away), then across the hall to the bathroom where, without turning on the light, he lifts the seat and pees. Pim, his distress having passed, wriggles out of Walter's arms and, replicating in miniature his father's exact stance, adds his own tinkling cadence to the bowl.

THE MOUSE

High in the wall behind the eaves, under the attic and above the bathroom, in a nest soft as the lambskin upon which the Blumenthal children all lay when they were babies—in fact in a nest that is part lambskin, for the mother mouse while fashioning it had helped herself to liberal mouthfuls of the woolly thing that Bennie, after Pim outgrew it, had washed and packed carefully away in the attic for some future child; six months from now when she goes to retrieve it (not for a grandchild, as she had more or less supposed at the time, but for her own next soon-to-be-born child) she will find it depilated in patches, with signs of nibbling along one edge—five babies lie in a heap.

The babies are six days old. Hair just barely beginning to cover their pink nakedness. Snow-white peach fuzz. In the past twenty-four hours their ears have begun to perk up but they won't open their eyes yet for another week, won't stop nursing for another three. In the womb they'd had a sixth sibling but their mother ate it, the littlest, immediately upon giving birth.

These newborns share a lineage similar to that of the Blumenthal children whose lambskin they also share. Not genetically but geographically similar, all of them having descended from inhabitants of this house since its erection in 1891. The humans moved in upon completion in May of that year. By June there was a mouse family on the premises as well. For a hundred and twenty-three years the clans have coexisted, with varying degrees of oblivion and cognizance, under varying conditions of tolerance and pitched battle, fear and complacency. There have been acts of aggression on both sides: plunder and murder, soiling and eviction. There have been instances of communally endured hardship, countless blizzards and heat waves, sudden frosts and torrential downpours, that have proved challenging for all residents of this house. There have been, too, congruent experiences of well-being—good health and healthy births, full bellies, days of warmth and freshness, nights of good company—as well as corresponding burdens: disease, discomfort, discord, death. Loneliness.

Tonight, while just a few feet below them Walter and Pim pee side by side into the toilet, while more than two hundred thousand miles away the moon rolls across the sky like a lost pill, the baby mice are growing. Veering toward their respective fates. Their mother lies crosswise to them in the shape of a sickle moon.

She is a cousin, this attic mouse, of the downstairs mouse who two nights earlier was munching the beetle in the wall behind Aunt Glad's cot. She has cousins who live in the cellar as well, and cousins who live in the barn. She has cousins she's never laid eyes on, both here in these environs and farther afield, meadow cousins and woods cousins and those who live in other houses and other barns, and if we were to trace the clans back far enough in time, we'd see how she is in fact connected by blood to innumerable distant relations spread across the land today, relations who make their homes in habitats as diverse as libraries and train stations, synagogues and ice cream stands, old bowling alleys and new buildings under construction. Places beyond the imagination of this attic mouse.

Her progeny, just beginning to make sense of their newest sense, attune the delicate cups of their infinitesimal ears to the lullaby of her body. Lullaby of the nest. Synesthesia of sound and smell and touch and taste. Squirming, nursing, they are growing fat on the ancient hymn of milk and urine, feces and fur, mammalian warmth and sweet wood rot.

Blindly they suckle at this warm, white, silken, milky moon. Knead it with their paws. Whenever one gets pushed off the teat by a brother's foot or a sister's tail, it adds to the song a chirping sound of its own before scrambling back to latch on once more.

THE TRAITOR

Bennie draws back the covers and makes a crescent of her body for Pim, who's asleep again almost the instant he nestles back against her warmth. Before Walter can climb in, too, she whispers, "How's Tom?" which he understands to mean, *Go check on Tom.* Which he understands further to mean, *Since you were so keen to unilaterally assume control of the situation earlier.* Accepting the fiat as penance, he kisses her shoulder. Shuffles dutifully down the hall.

Tom's bed's empty.

Passing Mantha's room he receives a summons. "Dad, c'mere."

Treading carefully around Ellerby, fast asleep on the trundle bed, he goes to the head of Mantha's bed. She lies on her stomach with one arm, the broken one, by her side, the other flung radically above her head. Face turned to the side like a swimmer taking a breath. He smooths her hair, slightly damp in the warmth of the summer night.

"No, Dad, my feet." She hates it when her pajamas bunch up around her shins. Walter goes to the end of the bed, lifts the covers, smooths her cuffs down by her ankles, and gives her foot a double squeeze: *sweet—dreams.*

Walter continues on his mission. How biddable he is. The banister, polished by generations of hands, is soft as a pelt. In the darkness the house seems to expand around him; always in the middle of the night it feels more vast, more voluminously blue. Full of shadows, of shades, their inaudible histories stirring in the air, soughing in corners, shifting the hem of a curtain.

He finds his boy on the porch, occupying Aunt Glad's cane chair, the smell of cigarette smoke so obvious it seems pointless to mention it. Yet impossible not to. Stifling a yawn: "I wish you wouldn't smoke, Tom."

"I know, Dad."

"It's just a stupid thing to do."

"I know."

Walter sits. *So why do it*, he wants to ask. *So why don't you use your head?* and hears in the question so precisely the cadence of his own father that he almost laughs.

Myron. Myron Blumenthal. Deli boy, deli worker, deli manager, eventually deli owner, although even then, when he'd earned the right legally as well as spiritually, he never changed the name of the place. Fiebush's Deli it had begun and Fiebush's Deli it would remain until its demise, never mind that Myron had lived and breathed the place since the age of fifteen and given more than four decades of his labor to it by the time the establishment became his. *Establishment.* Fancy schmancy moniker for a shoe box of a shop down on Avenue C, with its fat and smelly cheeses, its braids of garlic depending like bellpulls from the ceiling, its slabs of lox and tongue gleaming pinkly in their glass cases, its oak barrels swimming with pickles, its soup of the day, whatever it was—mushroom barley, matzoh ball, kasha vegetable, borscht—steaming up the small window behind the counter.

For years the deli had closed early every Friday and stayed shut through Saturday, not because Fiebush himself observed the Sabbath but in deference to the bulk of his clientele, bearded men in black hats and vests with tzitzit, the fringes, hanging below the hem, women in long skirts and long sleeves no matter the weather, always with bundles of children in tow. Walter's mother had died (*Of a sepsis*, said one aunt; *Of meningitis*, said another; *It was her blood*, said his uncle, while his father always maintained *It was her heart, no good*) when he was not quite three, and as an only, motherless child, he'd spent most of his childhood afternoons and Sundays at the deli. Schoolboy memories of sitting on a stool behind the counter, his cheek bulging with a wad of Bazooka or a Mary Jane, looking up from his comic book or homework to make solemn eye contact with these other children who came in bunches, their neatly staggered heights a sign of their parents' faithfulness to the first mitzvah: be fruitful and multiply. The size of their families as exotic to young Walter as anything else about them.

His gaze would most often be drawn to one of the boys near his own age, a doppelgänger in yarmulke and *peyos*, intractably foreign to him, just as he was to them; that this foreignness existed on both sides was precisely clear, even in the absence of a single word spoken. Myron always referred to these customers as "the Hasids" in a tone that puzzled, seeming as it did to braid antipathy and respect. Over the years, as the deli became frequented by a more heterogeneous clientele—punk rockers and grad students, activists and artists, yuppies and drag queens, Puerto Ricans and Dominicans and Trinidadians and Taiwanese—the number of Orthodox customers dwindled and eventually, at Myron's urging, Fiebush's began staying open seven days a week.

Myron, who had always taken pride in the place—from his days as a pimply kid wielding a broom to his days as a young man wielding the meat slicer to his days as a balding widower wielding an adding machine in the tiny, airless back room—took that much more when old Fiebush at last, after years of demurrals, consented to be bought out. Fiebush, by then eighty-eight, liver-spotted as an overripe banana and prone to grinning in an unsettling way (his large, tawny false teeth always seemed to be on the verge of leaping free of his mouth); Fiebush, all at once Las Vegas–bound with his new wife, Essie (whom he proudly proclaimed to be, at seventy-six, a *spring chicken*); Fiebush had been by then only too delighted to sign the papers. Over Dixie cups of Manischewitz. Walter and Essie had been present for the auspicious occasion, like witnesses at a wedding following upon a decades-long courtship, each one standing just a little behind the key parties under a chuppah of braided garlic and flypaper. When the deal was done, the *l'chaims* and mazel tovs pronounced, and the drams of sweet wine downed, Myron had even teared up with the astonished gratitude of one who'd long ago resigned himself to his love remaining unrequited. But for all his deep attachment to the place, he'd forbidden Walter ever to work there.

"You don't know from the deli," Myron would scoff whenever Walter professed his desire.

"What are you talking about? I've probably clocked more hours of my life at the deli than in the apartment."

"Sure, eating jujubes and picking your nose."

"But I love the place," Walter would protest. He made his most ardent—and final—pitch just after dawn on the day after his father finally purchased the business. This was just months before his own graduation from college.

"Bullshit," Myron proclaimed. They were—where else?—in the deli, Myron getting ready to open, Walter hanging around before heading off to his actual summer job, working with at-risk youth in a program run by Hunter College. Myron ambled back from the refrigerator case with the day's first can of Cel-Ray—he ritually drank four a day, a practice to which he credited his excellent bowel function—and paused to ease himself onto the leather-upholstered swivel stool that had over the course of forty-two years molded itself perfectly to his ass. "Use your head, you should do me the favor, for one second, please. You got no feel how to run this place. How could you? Not one drop of sweat did you ever put into it."

"Because you never let me, Pop!"

"Why do you think?" Myron glared. His caterpillar eyebrows fairly vibrated. "Use your head. And by the way"—he took a long swig of the soda, then waited for the belch before continuing—"forget about inheriting. It'll never be yours."

Two weeks later, at age fifty-seven, Myron had a massive coronary and died the next day without regaining consciousness. Fiebush, already ensconced by then in his new Las Vegas high-rise with Essie-the-Spring-Chicken, outlived him by another decade. True to his word, Myron had written into his will a stipulation that the deli be sold to any qualified buyer not related to him by blood, with the profits to go to Walter. The *qualified buyer not related by blood* bit struck Walter as a kind of vaudeville gimmick, an exaggerated wink from beyond the grave, since Myron's only sibling, a brother, had died of polio in childhood and the extended Blumenthal family, cousins and such, had either perished in the Holocaust or moved to Israel.

At any rate, it came to pass that a buyer without genetic overlap with the Tribe of Blumenthal was found, and Fiebush's Delicatessen, Est. 1934, sold for what was deemed by the lawyers a fair price and what Walter, at his tender age, considered quite a bundle. Shortly thereafter the buyer, having managed to acquire not only the street-level business but the entire building, hired wreckers who put a two-ton ball of forged steel through the brick facade of the three-story tenement. He eventually constructed on its footprint a ten-story luxury condominium complex, anticipating the gentrification of the Lower East Side by a healthy and highly profitable margin. Walter used the money for a graduate program in Mass Communication, a field of study he chose because it sounded at once relatively easy and highly transferrable. That is, he figured he wouldn't have to think very hard to pass, and a degree in Mass Comm seemed like it might get him in the door for an interview at a wide range of jobs. This appealed to him because: (a) he couldn't imagine his grief ever dissipating enough to allow him to think sharply again, and (b) he couldn't conceive of any particular job he might want to do. A third reason for his gravitating toward this particular graduate program didn't occur to him until a few years later—until he met Bennie, in fact, that chilly autumn morning when he'd sat brewing coffee on the tiny camp stove. Only after he met Bennie, only after they'd struck up an intimacy he'd never before experienced, did the thought rise from his subconscious that the very name "Mass Communication" seemed to hold within it the prospect of bountiful connection, of linking together on a massive scale, and he had been at that moment in his life, in that newly orphaned moment, terrified of spending the rest of it alone.

Now here's Tom, occupying with princely ease the chair on the porch of the house in the village he has lived in his whole life, entirely innocent of his imminent ouster. For a moment, in the cricket-laced calm of the night, Walter contemplates spilling the beans.

Instead he says, "Anything else you want to tell me about the graffiti?"

"No."

Of course this was what the police had wanted to speak with Tom about—the vandalism at the new housing development. Security cameras had caught someone arriving on a bicycle and scaling the hurricane fence the previous night. Between 12:37 and 12:43, they said. Precisely. The beauty of time stamps. One of the officers down at the station had apparently coached the JV boys' soccer team last fall and thought he recognized Tom as the kid in the footage; the investigating officers were following up on his lead.

Walter had been surprised that they offered up the details so freely, even before dispatching him back into the house to get Tom. The officer who'd coached the soccer team—Walter had no memory of him. What did he look like? Had he been the head coach or an assistant? Did he himself have a kid on the team? Probably. He was probably one of those dads who had the time to attend every practice—a thought that produced in Walter a kind of defensive resentment. Who were they, anyway, these dads you always saw helping carry the equipment onto the field, knowing all the kids not only by name and position but by playing style, by stats? Many of them had probably grown up in Rundle Junction, had parents who'd grown up in Rundle Junction. They worked locally, for public services. Or as contractors. Small business owners who set their own hours, shift workers who got off at four. Walter might work at a socially conscious nonprofit in the city, Walter might write checks to the PTO and be an active participant in village meetings, but in Rundle Junction the fathers with real cachet are those who somehow know the exact moment to order the pizzas so they get delivered to the field just as the game is ending.

To feel forever inadequate: Is this simply the universal condition of being a father? Walter thinks about how few of Tom's games he actually got to last fall. How those times he had managed to attend he invariably reached the field late, so it had been approaching evening by the time he strode across the parking lot toward the field, the air already taking on that granular quality it gets on late-autumn afternoons, redolent with bonfires and the soft brown fragrance of apples beginning to ferment. By the time he reached the sidelines where the die-hard parents had been since the game began, well-established in their butterfly chairs with the built-in cup holders, their laps and legs snugly wrapped in the fleece blankets they kept in the cargo areas of their SUVs, the game would be in its final quarter. "Anyone know the score?" he'd ask, feeling guilty of a discourtesy he didn't quite understand. Perhaps the discourtesy *consisted* of his inability to understand, consisted of the fact that despite having lived here close to thirty years, marrying into one of the village's oldest families, sending four kids through the public schools and residing in the historic former post office, he would always be in some sense a trespasser.

Yet when the cops had come inquiring about an actual instance of trespass, for some reason he hadn't worried. Their willingness to divulge the manner in which they'd obtained Tom's name, coupled with Walter's own comfortable certainty about his kid's innocence, made him suppose the visit was a formality, a matter of protocol and due diligence, understood by all to be a required but ultimately pointless bit of police business.

"Tom, could you come out here, please?" he'd said, standing on the threshold between kitchen and living room, and it was what happened next, the way Tom had risen all too readily, as if he'd been anticipating the summons, that gave Walter his first unpleasant turn.

Once out on the porch—where one of the officers, tall and rangy, remained silent, and the other, a squat man with the face of an action-film star, questioned Tom with a kind of low-key charisma, sounding so casually friendly that Walter couldn't help but feel the cops must be on Tom's side—the second shock came. Without hesitation, without a blush, Tom acknowledged that yes: he had gone out the previous night a little past midnight, had ridden his bike over to the site of the new development, had scaled the fence.

"You're aware, Tom," said the compact one—he gave his name as Officer Vincente, but Walter couldn't help thinking of him as

Vin Diesel—"that's considered criminal trespass?" Only now the disarming cadence, along with the repeated use of Tom's name, struck Walter as less reassuring than calculating.

"No, I wasn't aware of that."

"Come on, Tom. You're a smart guy. You're telling me you didn't realize you were trespassing on private property?"

"Well it's obvious they don't want people going on the site," said Tom. "Or why put up a fence?" and Walter thought, *Careful, careful, don't be flippant, don't piss them off.*

"So you knew what you were doing was wrong."

"I don't know. Was it wrong?"

"You tell me, Tom."

"I don't know."

"Sure you do. You're a smart guy."

"I think it depends."

"Yeah? What does it depend on?"

"Whether you believe in the morality of private ownership."

Walter could feel actual beads of cold sweat slide from his armpits to his wrists.

But the Vin Diesel guy didn't get riled. If anything, his composure seemed to deepen, grow expansive. "I don't know about you, Tom," he said. "Me, I happen to believe in obeying the law of the land."

"Really?" asked Tom, his own insouciance a near match for the cop's; Walter's innards churned with a pileup of panic and pride. "In all situations? I mean, what about in the time of Jim Crow? Or the fact that we stole this land from the Native Americans in the first place? What about the idea that property is theft?"

Proudhon. Shit. Walter clenched his teeth. He was the one who introduced that idea to Tom in the first place. Not six months ago, at supper. Clem had been home on winter break, holding forth passionately about the ills of capitalism and the glories of socialism, and Walter had stepped in with a few innocent questions about human nature and ineradicable difference and freedom—*To revolt is a natural tendency of life*, he'd quoted Bakunin, and that had launched them into a discussion about anarchism and federalism and the revolutionary potential of the *Lumpenproletariat*.

The cop switched gears smoothly. You had to admire his equilibrium. "Look, Tom. We're not here to debate beliefs. You know the difference between right and wrong. You want to tell me your intentions in sneaking onto the property?"

"My intentions," repeated Tom, drawing out the word.

"What you were planning to do?"

"Yeah, no, I understand the question. I'm just thinking about the answer. I guess I'd have to say my intentions were to satisfy my curiosity." There was no one thing you could point to and say he was being disrespectful. Element by element—his face, his voice, his body language—all added up to a portrait of an earnest, cooperative boy.

"Well," said the cop, "you know what they say about curiosity, Tom."

"What?"

"How it killed the cat."

"It—what? I don't understand. What cat?"

Bile surged through Walter's gut. "Tom," he said.

"Tom, look. We all want to help you out here. Your father, Officer Gutierrez, and myself. We're not going to be able to help you out, though, unless you're straight with us. We need to know what you took onto the building site. You bring any supplies with you?"

"What kind of supplies?" Tom asked.

Too coolly, Walter thought, his heart racing as he pictured aerosol paint cans, then tried furiously to erase the image, as though the cops could detect his thoughts.

And the realization struck him physically—it was like a big stone plunging through his gullet—at some point he'd begun entertaining the real possibility that his son was in fact the culprit. Or one of the culprits. The officer continued to question Tom in a mild yet persistent manner, asking questions that suggested there might have been more than one graffitist. Who had he gone with, or planned to go with; who had he met there or expected to meet? Vin Diesel asked versions of the same questions over and over. Each time Tom responded that he'd gone by himself, had simply been curious to see the site, that he'd brought nothing with him, had only walked around. As the questioning went on (the dull repetitiveness oddly chilling), Walter found himself switching gears: rather than willing Tom to convey humility and show more cooperation, he found himself rooting for Tom to be no more than consistent and minimalist in his responses.

In fact, this is more or less precisely what Tom had done. The cops in the end had thanked him and Walter in a manner that would have elicited no complaint from Emily Post, had said they had "what they needed for now," and had taken off, putting their squad car in reverse and maneuvering down the driveway with intimidating speed and dexterity.

Now on the porch, Tom says, "I didn't do it, Dad."

"Do what?"

"The vandalism."

"Okay, Tom." And it is. What could be more okay than Tom's word? "You know who did?"

A beat. "I might."

Wind tosses the shagbark hickory above their heads, ruffles the leaves of the azalea bushes.

"I don't think I should say anything, though," Tom continues, "if I don't know for sure."

Tom's phrasing makes Walter think he wants to be persuaded otherwise. Wants to be coaxed to share his theory. Gingerly he ventures, "Kids?"

But after a long moment Tom only repeats, "I don't think I should say."

"Why'd you go?"

"Honestly? It's what I told the cops. Curiosity."

Walter rubs his chin, makes a skritching sound. An assertion of paternal authority. He doesn't do it consciously, but as soon as he hears the sound he recalls the way his father would do the same, scratch his stubble at key moments in a conversation. How eloquent, how economical the gesture. And how it used to madden Walter, especially when he was Tom's age and lacked the equipment to respond in kind.

"But not just curiosity—responsibility, too," says Tom. "I mean, don't we all have a responsibility to know what's going on? To make ourselves know. In general, in the world, isn't it our job to find out for ourselves. Figure out what we think." He's warming to his subject, speaking with a kind of passion—a kind of vulnerability, that is, self-exposure—he rarely permits himself these days. These days of cool witticism and urbane quip. It makes him seem at once more childlike and more grown-up. "I think we have a duty not to believe things just because it's how we were raised. I might actually—in the end, Dad, I might wind up thinking a lot of the same things as you. But if that happens . . . well I hope it takes a long time. You know?"

In the darkness, Walter nods. He does know. He does. And for some reason, in his mind he's sitting behind the counter of Fiebush's, watching an unbroken stream of souls processing down the aisle, a kind of surreal cavalcade encompassing several decades' worth of the neighborhood's ever-evolving populace: first the ultra-Orthodox, men in long beards and black hats, followed by a succession of others in Mao and Nehru jackets, then kurtas and saris, then guayaberas and halter tops, then biker vests and miniskirts, and finally hipsters—men in long beards and black hats.

He remembers asking his father once, *Why does one group move out and another take its place?*

Myron's reply, punctuated with a little troika of shrugs: *'S the way of life. How it is. Things change.*

"Listen, Tom," says Walter. "You challenge me and I love you. But don't say they're racist."

"What?"

"The Haredim. The thing you brought up the other night. About the effigy in New Ash—"

"But Dad, it was! It had dreadlocks and ev—"

"Yes—*it* was racist. The person, the member of that community who put it there, was racist. But what you said was 'they're' racist." He gives it a minute to sink in. "See what I mean?"

Leaves stir, changing the pattern of moon-coins scattered around the porch.

"Yeah," says Tom. "I see."

MEMORY

A train is coming. The slats on the departure board rustle and clatter. The wind is spinning them over and over very fast. She cannot read what they say. Their endless revolutions make her dizzy until she turns away.

And sees there white steam billowing into the station. A moving pillar of white, then a flurry of flapping as all the pigeons in unison rise—their violent ascension making her cover her head with her arms the way she did in the wagon, with the fairy wings on her back, having her picture taken on the way to the pageant, on the way to be a Little Fairy Attendant Upon the Hours—all beating their wings in concert as they congregate, circling toward the roof of curved metal and glass, impossibly high.

From far away down the tracks: sound of a whistle, sound of a horn. Horn of silver paper curved like a sickle moon. The moon worn on a ribbon worn round the neck of a bare-chested boy. He's blowing out a warning: *Be responsible! Stay together!*

She can feel him hidden within that billowing column of white, can feel him driving that train. The naked boy is draw-ing nearer. Baring his teeth. Here he comes with angel cake on his mind.

🌿 · 4 · 🌿

Episode Four. Thursday.

One Day Before the Wedding.

A little before five a.m. the eastern sky goes pale rose and the dawn chorus is overlaid by a heraldic blast. The startled birds hush, and from near and far—within the house, in every increasingly populated room from office to attic, out in the dew-sparkling trio of tents pitched by the barn, in every nest and burrow and warren on the property, even over at McElroy's farm, a field and a half away—the stirring reveille can be heard.

Carrie's sons, Otis and Hugh, never before having awoken in Rundle Junction, hear it and suppose it is a daily occurrence in this village. Instantly they are jealous.

Banjo's baby, Harriett, who has been awake for some time and regarding, from the crook of her father's arm, the configurations the sunrise choreographs along the ceiling of their tent, hears it, and her mouth goes into vigorous sucking motion.

Tom, who has only just gone to bed, hears it and pulls his pillow over his head.

Lloyd, having at last triumphed over his old nemesis insomnia and drifted into sleep, hears it in a manner so muffled by the whir of the box fan in the window and the derelict standing fan oscillating with its inebriate's lurch, that it becomes part of his dream.

His daughter, Ellerby, on the trundle bed one floor below, hears it and pokes the unresponsive leg of Mantha.

Mantha, who could sleep through a bomb going off, neither hears it nor feels her cousin's prodding finger.

Carrie, staying in the one attic room that is "finished"—it boasts a passable bed, a modicum of actual bedroom furniture, curtains, a couple of faded Currier & Ives prints, and, crucially, a window air-conditioning unit—always sleeps with foam earplugs. Between those and the AC no outside noise stands a chance.

Clem and Chana and Hannah hear it, the first two lifting their heads from their pillows. "What the—?" says Clem, and "What is that?" echoes Chana, while the third doesn't bother opening an eye. She merely groans. And diagnoses (accurately): "Fucking Dave-Dave."

Bennie and Walter and Pim, crowded together in the big cherry-wood bed, hear it and open their eyes. Walter, with the grumpy, confounded expression he always wears for the first several minutes upon waking, regardless of time or circumstance, scowls at Bennie. Bennie, as usual instantly lucid, sees his scowl and raises him bafflement. Pim is first to recognize the tune. He declares rapturously, "Superman!" His parents, realizing he's right, what they're hearing *is* in fact the theme from the John Williams film score being played on a French horn, exchange a second glance and, very much in spite of themselves, begin to crack up. Their attempts to stifle their laughter only increase their hilarity. Pim's, too: within moments all three are huddled snugly on their stomachs, mouths pressed into the bedclothes, positively heaving with mirth.

The perpetrator himself stands loin-deep in the pasture

between the barn and McElroy's property, saluting dawn with his lungs. Breath, flowing through the golden coils of his instrument, warms the metal from the inside. The just-risen sun warms it from without. Makes a halo of his macaroni curls. Bejewels the high wet grass that soaks him to the thighs. And begins to burn off the milk-white mist that hangs close above the fields.

Richard the dog, having followed Dave-Dave out of the tent, hears it and, although he has never been anywhere near a foxhunt, that part of him that is hound is galvanized deep in the blood. As if by some arcane canine circuitry he is able to recognize, in the opening fanfare of Gs and Cs, a bugle call. He halts, lifts both his snout and one delicately poised paw, and stands motionless save for the quivering, leathery moistness of his nose.

Aunt Glad, drifting in and out, hears it and is unsurprised.

He comes for me, she thinks. Little boy blue, close at last.

Her heart skips a beat.

In his nakedness, in his glory, with his horn he comes.

IN THE SILENCE that follows the final note Clem, lying awake in the tent, is flooded with butterflies. Today is Thursday. The day her beloved—from whom she has been separated for seven whole weeks—arrives. The flutters as visceral as if an actual bevy of winged creatures is churning inside her.

Thinking these words—*butterfly, churning*—makes her think suddenly of the old butter churn. She hasn't thought of that thing in years! More than half her life has elapsed since they dug it out of the barn, responding to a call for props for her third-grade play, a production about which she remembers virtually nothing except her costume—a mob cap and apron she had felt utterly, numinously transformed by—and her single line: *A woman's work is never done!* which she'd delivered with heartfelt conviction and which had gotten, unexpectedly and possibly offensively, a huge laugh. Where is it now, she wonders—a real old-fashioned butter churn she was lucky to have in the family, lucky since how many families stayed put (enjoyed the luxury of being able to *choose* to stay put, as Diggs has taught her to see it) long enough, and in possession of enough storage space, to house obsolete objects of cumbersome size?

Reabsorbed, no doubt, into the great glacier of detritus that has been consigned to the barn over the decades, from wrought-iron headboards to broken snowshoes to sleds with rusty runners; from steamer trunks stuffed with yellowed lace to a yellow Bakelite console radio the size of a steamer trunk; from a kerosene lamp and a set of currycombs to a Lava lamp and a set of electric hair rollers. Not to mention a wooden yoke, a galvanized metal icebox, a hand-crank ice cream maker, and last but not least—dismembered, its parts scattered about the heap—the venerable, retired Glendale stove. You could fairly taste the air, storied with molecules of ancient hay and manure; you could feel on your skin the way it held the imprints of past lives, lives of people responsible in some direct way for her own existence. How minor she always felt within the space of the barn, conscious that her own footprint, tiny and recent, was appended to so long and dense a history. It was oddly sweet, this reminder of her own insignificance.

Of course such a reminder is itself a luxury. For how many people are denied access to their family history, every route to their past rendered untraceable, the connections all rubbed out by empire and colonialism? *I don't think we go very far back on my dad's side of the family,* Clem had ventured once. *I think most of them stayed behind in Romania. Or Russia, whatever. And got wiped out in the Holocaust.* She was conscious of tendering the statement as not quite an apologia, but a kind of credential, an attempt to say, *See? Our lineage has gaps, too*—but even as she spoke she realized it was a false equivalency. To flee—even in the face of tyranny, even in the face of genocide—is one thing. To be brought in captivity is another.

All the more reason you should get what a privilege it is, then, Diggs had replied, sounding neither reproachful nor impressed. Her own family tree remained largely obscure, its roots traceable no farther back than a great-grandmother who, after emancipation, was supposed to have farmed rice and indigo in South Carolina. Even her family name, Diggins, was of course a blind alley, a crooked arrow pointing toward a history of slaveholders rather than shedding light on those who'd been abducted, sold, and stripped of their own original names. But Diggs didn't begrudge Clem. On the contrary; she encouraged Clem to value what she had, to be curious about it, to research and study it. *You're lucky, you know? To have even half your heritage so well-preserved.* As if her WASP ancestry were packed like so many peach slices in their own sweet syrup in a Mason jar.

The air in the tent is redolent of lady-sleep, their feminine attar of breath and oil and hair and sweat, their hodgepodge lotions and powders and sprays, their dew-damp backpacks and wadded-up balls of yesterday's clothes. Suddenly she is bursting with love for her friends, the Ch/Hannahs, in all their disheveled devotion, their absurdly beautiful willingness to play with her, to play. She marvels. How good they are, how innocent in their faith, how unfaltering in their allegiance. For not even they know yet all that she has planned, how she has scripted this, how she's approached this thing as an extension of her senior thesis, a kind of paratheater in which the border between art and life is dissolved.

Not even Diggs knows all the details, though she has given her blessing (while rolling her eyes) to being surprised. "Look, you know what? My parents already think it's subversive. You being a woman and all."

"And white."

"Wait—you're *white*?"

"I know, I was going to wait until our wedding night, but . . ."

"Damn." Diggs had gotten all serious, pretended to count on her fingers: "Woman. White. *Theater* major."

And Clem laughed a protesting laugh and whacked her on the shoulder.

But if their wedding is to be meta, or para, or pseudo, a kind of ersatz commentary on the institution of marriage, the love between them is all real. It pours. As uncontainable, as nectarous as the light filtering through the tent. That's pure Diggs, the scrambling-up of eros and fruit. *Clementina*, she's been known to intone, her face tipping up slyly from between Clem's thighs, her voice sweet and hoarse. *Clementina, Clementina*, she has rasped, *you taste like you're called*, only to disappear downward again, leaving Clem's field of vision to fill with the fan-shaped plaster swirls of her dorm room ceiling. This had been Diggs's first visit back to campus after graduating. On a long weekend last fall, well before they had spoken of marriage. Before they'd begun using the word *relationship* even. *This thing*, they'd called it then. When they were feeling brave: *This thing between us*. When that seemed too bold: *This "thing" between us, whatever*.

Clem had felt a kick of surprise when Diggs confirmed, after months of maintaining a supremely casual air, that she was planning to come up from law school to spend the long weekend. Not only that, she'd already purchased the train ticket.

"Really?"

"We planned this, duh?"

"Yeah no, I know. I just didn't—"

"Is it a problem? Have you other arrangements?"

Even over the phone it was easy to tell Diggs was hurt. The

giveaway being her diction. When she was upset it became impeccable, clipped. Almost British.

"No!" said Clem. "No other arrangements have I. It's just that . . . I honestly wasn't sure . . ." She touched her throat, which had gone dry. "I didn't want to . . . assume. When you said you would come. To assume you meant it."

"Are you demented?"

Clem had laughed.

"Why"—and how she loved this about Diggs, her way of asking a question point-blank, and now there was nothing clipped in her voice; it had pivoted from UK to DC—"why would you even want to be friends with a person who says shit she doesn't mean?"

So lo and behold: she had meant it, and she did come, and that weekend something had cracked open between them, some chary proscription on speaking of themselves as a couple with a future. They'd spent absurdly close to the entire seventy-two hours holed up together in Clem's dorm room under the eaves, during which time they both began to think—and not simply think but think out loud—that whatever said "thing" between them was, it had legs.

In any case it survived Diggs's graduation, a summer spent largely apart, and this entire past year of their inhabiting not just different geographies but different paradigmatic spheres, Diggs acclimating herself to the culture of legal studies in their nation's capital while Clem remained ensconced in a world of undergrads and play.

That's what Diggs maintained.

"How superior we've become," sniffed Clem.

It had been early November. After their glorious three-day weekend together it had become untenable to go more than a couple of weeks without seeing each other, and Diggs had taken the train north for the weekend again.

"It's true," said Diggs, sounding, as she always did first thing in the morning, like a rusty cat. "You're all about play. You live mostly in your imagination." (Clem thought of Mantha's classification system; didn't she have one category called Make-Believe Life?) "Case in point," continued Diggs, "this room: imaginary."

Clem, delighted at the preposterousness of the assertion, laughed.

They'd been in bed. It was early, overcast. The radiator pinged and clanged. "What's imaginary about it?"

"It's fairyland in here," Diggs insisted. "It's the gingerbread cottage. You're Rapunzel in her tower."

"You're mixing your metaphors, honeygirl. You're mixing your Grimms."

"Look. Case in point." Diggs jabbed a finger at the ceiling. "That shit's like Betty Crocker."

"Huh?"

"The ceiling."

"Er . . . I repeat: huh?"

"You know." Diggs gave an impatient click of her tongue. "Like the frosting on those old TV commercials. For cake mix. Like with the housewife standing there with the perfect lipstick?"

"Oh. And like a plaid dress with a belt?"

"And her hair all spray painted."

"Spray painted—like Banksy? Might you perhaps mean 'hair sprayed'?"

"Whatever. Okay, it's not *that* funny." (Clem was laughing so hard now she managed to fall half out of the bed. Diggs hauled her back.) "I'm saying. White people hair products are in her hair, okay? And she's standing there with her perfect cake."

From then on Clem could not look at her swirly-plastered dorm room ceiling without thinking of buttercream frosting. And fairy tales and mischief.

The wedding is mischief. Of a sort. Not in the sense of malice or harm, but of disruption. Playful disruption. Serious playful disruption. A kind of tricksterism, a turning inside out.

In school she'd been taught the etymology of theater: from the Greek *theasthai*, "to behold," and thence to *theatron*, "a seeing place." Stella Adler said people come to theater to see the truth about life. In her thesis Clem took up Grotowski's claim that the theater is a place of provocation, that it challenges by violating accepted stereotypes, then posited her own theory that this must necessarily be a two-step process. First mimesis, then disruption. Going on the idea that you need to give the audience familiar ground to stand on before whisking the rug out from under them.

It was in talks with Leopardi, her thesis adviser—a wizened man barely taller than five feet, with breath that reeked always of Fisherman's Friend cough drops—that she hatched the idea of building a practical, empirical element into the project. Together they dismissed the idea of anything so banal as an invited presentation or even an act of spontaneous improv or street theater that might take place somewhere on campus. They had lengthy discussions in which they imagined how she might co-opt a public ritual or planned community event as the basis for a performance, and toyed with the idea of Clem's disrupting her own commencement exercises as a form of outlaw art, but in the end discarded this as (a) unduly risky ("I have had tenure for more years than your feet have graced the earth, *cucciola*," Leopardi pointed out, exhaling a dank licorice gust in her direction, "but you—you will not yet have your two-hundred-thousand-dollar-sheepskin testimonium safely in hand") and (b) parasitic.

"If I'm really serious about this," Clem had decided, "I think I have to take ownership of creating the ritual I'm planning to disrupt."

"Ah but this," Leopardi had cried, coughing and wheezing,

then seizing an ethereal simulacrum of Clem's face in two hands and planting upon it an audibly moist kiss (after having twice been brought up on harassment complaints before the school's Title IX Hearing Panel, he had come to appreciate more fully the merits of pantomime), "this integrity, this assiduity, this *dedicazione*, this is why I love—is why you are among the top five or ten students I have known in the entirety of my career!"

And so, with Leopardi's blessing and counsel, she had begun to plan the experiential component of her thesis project: the creation of a public ritual she would then crack open. Like a sacrificial jug.

"HI HANNAH," says Tom as the former, attired in a gargantuan black T-shirt, yesterday's eye makeup having transitioned overnight into a footballer's eye black, ascends the stairs, cracked leather dopp kit in hand. Then, gutturally: "*Chai Chana,*" as a similarly dishev-eled Chana appears.

"Yuk yuk."

"I know." Tom lowers his lashes. "I'm a funny guy." Clad only in worn-to-gossamer pajama bottoms, he slouches against the wall opposite the bathroom, from behind whose door the sound of the shower can be heard (along with little bursts of Ellerby belting out, of all things, "I am sixteen going on seventeen"). He feels no shyness as a half-naked sixteen-year-old boy in the presence of two nubile young women. He has been liking his body quite a lot lately, in a marveling sort of way. Finds himself spending time alone before his full-length mirror studying it, learning it, appre-ciating the daily novelty of inhabiting it, and he yearns to have others appreciate it as well—almost without vanity, almost unre-lated to personal reward, the way if you saw something beautiful, a killer play by Messi, for example, or a perfect bacon cheese-burger with curly fries on the side, you'd want others to witness it, too. Simply because it exists, and is excellent, and ought to be re-marked. So he is not embarrassed when he feels both Ch/Hannahs' gazes traveling over his torso. But then, idly, he chances to notice that Hannah's V-neck is low and her cleavage on view—what a word, *cleavage*! what a concept!—and this, his susceptibility to becoming transfixed by the body of another, does rattle him, and causes him to announce officiously, "You're third and fourth in line, by the way."

"Why? Who's before you?"

"After me," he corrects, only to be drowned out by a ringing assertion from behind the closed door of Mantha's room: "Me!"

"No way," says Hannah. "No back cuts."

"It's not back cuts!" The disembodied voice sallies forth even more resoundingly. "I was already there before you! He's just hold-ing my place so I can get some rest!"

"And how's that working out for you?" Hannah mutters.

"Fourth?" squeaks Chana. "I'll never make it!"

"Dude. What do you have, like a permanent UTI?"

"No joke, you guys, I totally have to pee!" And relinquishing her claim on position number four she scurries downstairs to try her luck with the powder room.

Hannah, half serious, to Tom: "Think she's bribable, your sister?"

"Eminently."

"What would she go for?"

"Oh, straight-up cash."

Hannah's laugh: a little aphrodisiac. She slides down the wall to wait on the floor. Immediately Tom perceives the complication therein and tries to calculate his next move according to the rela-tive payoff: the naughty thrill of an enhanced view down her shirt if he remains standing versus the more subdued reward of self-commendation for chivalry if he lowers himself beside her. "So," she addresses him conversationally (he sits so fast his knee cracks), "are you for real an outlaw?"

"Wha—?"

"Are you a graffiti artist? A vandal? A neo-Nazi?"

"Oh that. Yeah. All of the above."

"Figured."

"Yeah?"

"Had you pegged. The moment I saw you. A young Himmler, I says to myself."

Now Tom laughs. "And you?"

"And me what?"

"What are your deep dark secrets? Anything you want to confess?"

"Well . . ." She turns to him with her very large, dark velvet eyes, framed by caked, flaked mascara and wanton smudges of kohl. Up close like this, in such a humbly intimate setting, pre-morning ablutions, he takes in, too, her seriously bitable lips (an attribute he has not previously noticed), her subtle and somehow childlike overbite, and the great unbroken tundra of skin sloping precipitously from her throat to midway down her bosom. ". . . between you and me . . ." she continues, lowering her voice to a whisper and bringing her mouth to within four millimeters of his ear, "I'm in love with the bride."

WALTER AND LLOYD exit the barn like a couple of strange beasts, encumbered by clusters of folding chairs swaying like extra appendages under each of their four arms. Behind them the door squawks on broken hinges. Sweaty already, they tramp past the little encampment, each of the three tents flying a festive little homemade flag. Strewn on the grass in every direction are assorted items—towels, jeans, onesies, underpants, sneakers, flip-flops, a baby bottle, a bicycle pump, earbuds, a stuffed rabbit—either laid out to air or simply abandoned in the midmorning sun.

"Let's just leave them here for now," says Walter when he and Lloyd reach the black walnut, against whose trunk they lean the chairs. "I don't know how Clem wants them set up."

Lloyd, hands supporting his lumbar region, arches his back and peers up into the branches, festooned with strings of LED lights and paper lanterns. A long time ago he used to write poetry up there, sequestered high above the earth, hidden from view except for his dangling legs. He'd sharpen his pencils with a pocketknife, let the shavings drop to the ground. He'd been a teenager then, both sisters off at college, both parents newly in their graves. Aunt Glad had given up her own apartment in town and moved back into her childhood home, in order to provide her nephew with an adult presence and a rotation of feebly seasoned but well-balanced meals during his last year of high school. He never told anyone about his poems—is that true? He cannot think of anyone he ever mentioned them to. He'd forgotten them himself until this morning. He used to stash everything—poems, pencils, pocketknife—in the tree, in a hollow made by rot. He wonders if any of it remains. Not the poems, surely, but possibly the pencils and quite likely the knife. He doubts he could climb that high anymore.

Ellerby could. She'd scamper up in about half a minute if he told her the tree might harbor artifacts of his youth. He lets a reel play in his mind, footage of an imaginary scene in which she ascends and finds all the treasures intact, the poems as well as the knife. The latter had been a gift from a maternal relative (some kind of elderly second cousin who'd kept impressing upon him the fact that it was *an heirloom, understand? an Erlend family heirloom*), given to him after his mother had died. At the funeral, in fact. Both of them, bestower and recipient, octogenarian and

teenager, ill at ease in their jackets and ties among the white bou-
quets. Both of them dry-eyed, both more than a bit sloshed.
"Every boy should have his own knife," the old man had said. Or
some such malarkey. "Now you've got an Erlend knife there, son.
I know you'll take good care of it."

All this connected to the very reason he won't actually tell
Ellerby. About any of it: the funeral, the knife, the poems in the
tree. Doesn't want her saddled with it. The weight of legacy. The
sad bullshit weight of legacy.

"You okay?" asks Walter.

"What?"

"Hurt your back?"

"No, no, I'm good." He regards Walter: kind aspect, sloe eyes,
large, snowy-maned head. He imagines telling Walter about the
lost poems—Walter who lives by jacket and tie, who bundles off
without fail every morning to catch the 6:54, briefcase in hand,
who attends village meetings and kids' soccer games, pays his taxes
on time and votes in local as well as national elections; Walter who
twenty years ago quietly and manfully assumed the mantle Lloyd
cast off: that of patriarch, preserver of the homestead, upstanding
upholder of the Erlend family foothold in Rundle Junction. Rubs a
hand across his mouth. "Let's keep going," Lloyd says.

They head back toward the barn, unaware they're being
stalked.

Slinking through the high grasses of the pampas, the hunter-
gatherers track the two water buffalo. The bigger members of the
hunting party carry ranged weapons (a bow and arrow for the one
they call Big Face and a spear for Big Eyes) but the littlest is armed
only with a melee weapon—a dagger stuck in the waistband of his
pants—and of course his astonishing skill and courage. Capable of
walking without making a sound, of spotting prey miles off, of

charging an enemy three times his size—even, the people say, of moving between raindrops without getting wet: he is their leader.

The pair of buffalo near. Almost pitiable in their ignorance of the lurking predators, they move without haste, grunting to each other. Now they draw parallel to the spot where the trackers hide. The leader holds out his arm, signaling to the men behind him to prepare for attack. He puts up a finger: *one*; then another: *two*; then his thumb: *now!* and with terrible shrieks they catapult from the cover of the pampas grass and set upon their luckless targets.

Big Face and Big Eyes attack the skinnier one, each grabbing a leg, while their leader takes it upon himself to go alone after the larger prize. In a single move he launches himself upon the back of the great white-maned brute and whips out his dagger.

"Whoa!" bellow the buffalo. "Whoooaaaa! We're under attack!" The lean one staggers and lurches but shows surprising stamina, bucking forward and back, then sideways, then the other way sideways, giving the hunters the ride of their lives. They make a sound that to the untrained ear might seem as laughter, but which a true hunter will recognize as a way of pacifying one's prey. The bigger beast, though less wild, proves harder to subdue. He halts, plucks his assailant handily from his back, and sets him on the ground. Squatting, he says, "What you got there, Pim?"

"My dagger!"

"But what is it? Let me see. That looks a little sharp for you, bud."

"It's mine."

"Where'd you get it?"

"It's mine! I porridged it."

"From where?"

He'll never tell. He can't help his eyes flicking toward the orange tent.

"It's a nail file, honey. Must be one of the girls'. Go put it back where you found it."

Pim sets off in a huff. A minor one, as huffs go. After all, he still has the pink poison tablets and the circus-colored jewel.

STILL IN HER NIGHTGOWN, shod in a pair of old rubber boots she found in the hall, Clem has left the property. She's rambling through McElroy's field, having decided it's more scenic than their own field, the wildflowers more copious and various. Chicory and loosestrife, daylilies and crown vetch, she names them aloud as she brushes her hands across their tops. She learned what they were called long ago from Aunt Glad, who used to come stay with her when she was little and her parents went away. They'd go on excursions through the fields, back along the skunky-smelling swamp, into the small woods between McElroy's and Garvey's farm, to visit a dried-up basin Glad said was once a swimming hole. *I used to disappear here for hours at a time. Sometimes with my sister but more often alone,* her great-grandaunt told her. *With no one but the squirrels and birds to testify to my existence.*

When she was a child the thought never crossed her mind, but now Clem wonders just how lonely Glad's life has been. And if it has been a lonely life, for what reason? Being a gay woman in a time and place when the cost of expression would have been too great? Bearing scars too disfiguring for a would-be lover to see beyond? Or does she bear scars of another, invisible kind? Could the trauma she experienced at age seven have caused adhesions in her soul? What made her *want* to disappear for hours at a time?

Clem, at once genuinely moved by these musings and rather pleased by being thus moved, plucks a black-eyed Susan and slides its stem behind her ear. She vows never to lose a sense of gratitude. How fortunate she is to be able to marry her beloved! How fortunate even to have met.

It was December of Clem's junior year. Diggs had been a senior immersed in law school applications and LSAT prep; Clem had been immersed, it must be said, in very little having to do with academics. At that point in her college career she was lavishing the bulk of her time and attention on participating in the extracurricular "happenings" staged by a renegade group of theater majors calling themselves This Is Not A Theater Collective.

It was thanks to one of their paratheatrical events, in fact, that Clem and Diggs came together. This particular event featured a dozen members of the collective, all costumed in vaguely post-apocalyptic garb (torn and tattered clothing, bare feet, gas masks on some, paper surgical masks on others). These actors infiltrated the main reading room of the library at precisely midnight and, from strokes one through twelve on the campus campanile, staggered among the studious, some threading their way through the stacks, others slithering down from the balcony or creeping on all fours across the floor. As the hour finished chiming, they assembled in the center of the room, at which point an accomplice pressed a button on an MP3 player and James Brown's "Doing It to Death" flooded the marble-walled, green-carpeted, vault-ceilinged space. At this point the zombielike figures began to writhe and gyrate right out of their masks and rags, stripping down to leotards and tights, in which they leaped upon tables with unbridled verve and proceeded, through the example of their own joyful intemperance, to unshackle their fellow students from the woes of completion week by whipping them into a festively frenzied dance party.

Sort of.

That, at any rate, had been the plan when the members of This

Is Not A Theater Collective had met the night before to come up with a concept. Their goal for this, as for all their happenings, clearly stated in the collective's manifesto (*This Is Not A Manifesto*) was to disrupt the "airless status quo" and deliver "the oxygen of unsought, unexpected, unorchestrated joy." The "unorchestrated" part invariably led to tension around planning their happenings, with members forever in dispute about how much planning would constitute a violation of the mandate versus how little would obviate the possibility of successfully disseminating joy.

For whatever reason, on the December night when she made her inaugural performance with This Is Not A Theater Collective, the joy part was not really forthcoming. Not for want of trying— Clem had put her all into the act, from her slinking entrance into the main reading room to the ecstatic shedding of her preliminary costume to her go-go-girl shimmying from the perch of a study carrel. Eyes shut, hips grinding, she had been thinking, *Man, this is college! Man, this is life!* when a voice undercut James Brown's promise to take them all *highhhhhhhh-er.*

"You people really need to leave." The voice was authoritative without being strident. "Seriously. This. Is. Fucked. Up."

Clem opened her eyes and looked around to gauge how other members of the noncollective were reacting. Most were still dancing, either truly oblivious or pretending (so well-trained had they been by their acting professors: *Don't break concentration! Don't break the fourth wall!*) not to notice.

"Hel-*lo!*"

Now Clem located the speaker, sitting at one of the long tables not far from her. It was the woman people called Diggs, someone she knew by sight. And, vaguely, by reputation: smart, studious, chip on her shoulder.

Clem stood frozen on her carrel in her pink leotard, looking down at the unsmiling face of Diggs. Diggs: so commanding she wasn't even standing. She sat behind a stack of books, elegant in a black turtleneck and horn-rimmed glasses, her hair worn natural and very short. And Diggs, having found at least one mischief-maker making direct eye contact with her, seemed to address the next thing she said specifically to Clem. Who wanted to die.

"You need," Diggs said, "to turn that shit off, get over your privilege, and let serious people study."

Someone disconnected the music.

What titters broke out among other students were quickly squashed. So it was to the more damning accompaniment of con-certed silence, broken only by the ruffling of pages and the sound of fingers tapping on laptops, that Clem and the other members of the noncollective slunk off their perches and shamefacedly col-lected the shed pieces of their costumes.

It was the way Diggs had said "Thank you" then—dignified, equable, with nary a gloat or a sneer—that roused something in Clem stronger than shame. Curiosity. And although Diggs had returned to her note taking, dropping her gaze back to her own papers and books, ignoring, but as if from courtesy rather than haughtiness, the inglorious exit of the dancers, Clem with beating heart went out of her way to stop by her table, to stand there until Diggs looked up and to whisper, burning-cheeked, "I'm sorry." Diggs merely nodded. No trace of a smile.

But after that Clem found herself running into Diggs every-where: in front of her on line at the bookstore, behind her when she went to refill her coffee in the cafeteria, on side-by-side ellip-ticals at the gym, waiting for the free shuttle into town, even do-ing laundry in the basement of her dorm (never mind that Diggs lived off campus). They went through periods of tentative friend-ship, then tentative flirtation, until eventually one freezing night on the library roof they engaged in what Diggs with adorably prudish understatement referred to as "smooching." There followed an agonizing fortnight absent any acknowledgment of their rooftop rendezvous, during which Clem made herself sick scrutinizing every speck of punctuation within their virtual communiqués, mulling over the multiple possible meanings of every word uttered, every breath held, every eyebrow arched, every micrometer of distance added or subtracted between them in their face-to-face conversations. Then their contact stopped. A week went by without her running into Diggs once. Then another week. Clem lost four pounds. Also all her notes for a research paper on Susan Sontag's ideological and romantic influence on the avant-garde Cuban playwright María Irene Fornés. Also her bike lock and then (not surprisingly) her bike.

"This has got to stop," said Hannah. They were squirreled in the dorm lounge under an old plaid comforter somebody had abandoned there, watching *Alfred Hitchcock Presents* and eating New York Super Fudge Chunk.

Actually Clem had not touched hers. "How?" In a hoarse whisper she addressed the bowl of melting Ben & Jerry's in her lap.

"Okay, please write this down. You need to call her up and (a) Tell Her How You Feel, and (b) Tell Her You Need to Know How She Feels."

"Okay," said Clem. Being lovelorn made her compliant. "When? How?"

"Oh my God," said Hannah. "Give me your phone." She took it, dialed it, handed it back. "Now give me your bowl."

And while Hannah slurped up the last of the chocolate by-now soup, Clem had lain bare her heart and Diggs had listened with vested interest, then pulled back the curtain on her own.

And now, tomorrow, a year and a half after first meeting, they will pull back the curtain together, the pair of them; they'll stand and plight their troth before family and friends, in a ritual marrying reality with theatricality. For isn't it always both? thinks Clem, wandering through McElroy's field. As much with the private scenarios we all act out inside our own heads as with grand works displayed for the public, theater is in the business of both reflecting and affecting reality. This was what she had concluded in her senior thesis: that whether theater aims (like the famous community pageant of 1927) to reinforce things as they are, or whether it aims (like Clem's own experimental theater piece, about to have its one and only staged performance tomorrow) to question and trouble our notion of reality, it is always a tool for motion.

Which she feels in herself: a sudden, urgent surge of motion. Tomorrow isn't just her wedding day, it's also her debut—not in the sense of an ingénue, but as a thinker, a contributor. She thinks of Diggs saying, *I arrived the day I came out my momma*. At last Clem has a sense of her own readiness to arrive. At the mercy now of a kind of ferocious excitement, she drops the flowers she has been gathering and breaks into a run. The midmorning sun seems to rear back before her, gilding the high grass as she parts it with her strides. Grasshoppers spark up in her path. She is smiling, broadly, with a kind of dumb happiness. For she has just seen something, or just had something revealed to her, something at once perfectly obvious and utterly profound—about the true nature of her privilege.

Bennie and Walter's marriage had never been a picture postcard of sweetness and light; in fact they fought not infrequently, and at times quite heatedly, all throughout Clem's life. But that, she sees now, is an essential component of what was so good about her childhood, which is simply the privilege of growing up believing that no matter what strife came between them, her parents would sort it out, survive. Not necessarily even that the marriage would survive. Just that everything, everyone, would in some large, vital fashion be okay.

This security, she wishes she could tell Diggs now—more than the family home, the land, the property, the barn stuffed to the gills with material treasure or debris—this is the marker of the ultimate privileged childhood. The abiding faith that everything remains in motion.

She stops, panting, halfway back to the house. For she has just seen something else: a man, a stranger, wandering about their yard. He peers into the branches of the black walnut tree, circles the ladder lying in the grass, then starts up the unused front walk. Funny, she thinks, that on a hot June day anyone would wear such a long black coat and hat.

"BUT DO YOU THINK? I mean *should* we? Ask Aunt Glad?" Carrie in the kitchen is stage-whispering to Bennie, who rolls her eyes. Because why stage-whisper? Because isn't that just so Carrie? The popeyed reverence for drama. All that energy wasted tiptoeing around, avoiding offense, all that fear of bruising one another. As if people were fruit. Please.

"If you're curious, ask." She taps the end of her pencil against the poor old scratched table, where she has been surveying and updating her little blue to-do lists. "Why make a big thing of it?"

It being the matter of the name Benjamin Erlend on the village memorial plaque.

"Because if it's her brother and we never knew, there must be a reason. That no one ever told us. Or talked about it. Man. Two years old. It's so sad."

"Look." Bennie shoves the pencil into her hair and pours more coffee into both their mugs. "She's ninety-four. If you want to ask, make it snappy."

"Don't you want to know?"

Bennie helps herself to a saltine from a nearly exhausted packet (this morning she's needed to insert one in her mouth every five minutes to keep the nausea at bay) and shrugs.

"But he's your namesake!"

"We don't know that."

"Bennie!"

"What?"

"I don't get how you can be so blasé."

Privately, Bennie shares some of Carrie's surprise: it *is* sort of strange that she doesn't care. Except it isn't really that she doesn't care. It's that she doesn't *want* to care. She finds that she's disturbed by what's implied: the idea that being related to one of the eighteen victims should make them feel something extra about that particular death. The idea offends her very sense of humanity. She rejects it.

All she says is: "Look, Car. I assure you the word *blasé* does not capture what I am feeling at this moment. All right? I have a houseful of people, a yard full of tents, cops showing up on my doorstep, a son who might have committed a felony, oh yeah and a wedding to host tomorrow"—she indicates the sheets of blue notepaper laid on the table, each covered with scribbles and crossings-out; truth be told she enjoys finding the rhythm in her litany of woes—"on a lawn that's somehow simultaneously bald and overgrown . . ." She looks out the window. Ridiculous. The ladder is still out there lying on its side, the black walnut tree has a mess of wires dangling from its branches, and a paltry assemblage of none-too-sturdy-looking folding chairs has been erected in haphazard fashion.

"But don't you want to know if she had a little brother?" Carrie practically wails. "It's your family tree!"

That's just the problem, Bennie thinks. Again: the almost giddy sensation of being up high, the atmosphere thin and cold, sharp and shiny as silver foil. *We go around caring so much about our own family tree—our own seedlings—that everyone who isn't us begins to look like a weed.*

At that moment Mantha and Pim and Ellerby come into the kitchen and Bennie catapults back to earth. For the preferential swell of her heart toward the first and the second of this trio serves notice: she is no better than anyone. She, too, loves her own blood best.

Ellerby slips around the door frame and looks at Mantha expectantly.

"We're bored," Mantha announces. "And hungry."

"There's a lethal combination," her mother observes.

"Can we have lunch?"

"Can you have *what*?" In a tone suggesting Mantha'd asked for lobster thermidor.

"What little brother?" asks Pim. He is wearing a shark-tooth necklace and nothing else.

"Pants," Bennie tells him.

"We want lunch, too!" Otis bursts into the room from the porch.

Hugh, hot on his heels: "Yeah, we're thtarving."

"What's his name?" Pim repeats.

"Who?"

Mantha, shoving aside ribbons, vases, and blocks of green floral foam, clears enough counter space to perch on it and rummage through the cupboards above. "For Christ's sake when's all this junk going away?"

"Don't say Christ."

"Why not? We don't worship Jesus."

"The brother," says Pim. "The little brother, Carrie said."

"Pants," Bennie tells him again. To Mantha: "Because some people find it offensive and I don't want you developing the habit."

"Fine. For *Pete's* sake when's all this junk going away?" Mantha grumbles, climbing down. "We don't even have room to pour our cereal." A grievance she lodges, incidentally, while pouring cereal, a bowl for her and one for Ellerby.

"That's all you want for lunch?" asks Carrie. "You don't want us to make you sandwi— ow!" She rubs her shin.

"If it ain't broke . . ." Bennie whispers.

"No, we do want sandwiches," Mantha clarifies. "This is just to keep us going until you make them. Tuna fish please. Anyway"— she turns to Pim—"they're talking about Benjamin Erlend, from the memorial plaque."

"Where is he?"

"Duh, he's dead."

"You're dead!" Pim runs her through with an invisible sword.

"Pim." There is steel in Bennie's voice. "Go Upstairs and Put on Pants."

"Why?"

"At the very least you have to put on underwear."

"But why?" he beseeches, turning to her, the shark tooth gleaming round his neck, the escargot of a penis all bland innocence. "Why do I?" Without a trace of impudence he asks, nothing but sweet-angel-lamb curiosity. Ellerby snaps his picture.

Bennie opens her mouth. Instead of speech there issues forth a long and terrible cry, beginning low in her throat, gathering steam, and ending as a ululating screech.

Each of those present—sister, son, daughter, niece, two nephews—pauses to gauge the significance of the eruption. Each independently arrives at the same conclusion: false alarm. It's only a performance of a woman at her wits' end, albeit a performance separated from the real thing by a mere membrane.

Pim, acting on sudden inspiration, crosses the room to where his mother sits, lifts her hand, bends over it, plants upon it a kiss.

This proves too much for Bennie, who buries her face in her hands.

"What's the matter?" Lloyd dashes headlong into the room. There's something gratifying about the sight of him, ordinarily imperturbable, so visibly alarmed. He must have been in the midst of his morning ablutions, judging from the shaving cream still clinging to half his jaw and what he is wearing: nothing but a towel wrapped around his loins.

"See?" Bennie exclaims a bit hysterically. She wipes her eyes and gestures: exhibit A. "Even Lloyd manages to put something on!"

Ellerby guffaws.

Lloyd looks flabbergasted. "What's going on?"

Nothing, nothing, he is assured . . . *Pim won't get dressed . . . Mantha said Christ . . . The kids asked for lunch and we never even gave them breakfast . . .*

"Who screamed?" This time it's Tom who pokes his head around the door frame.

"Just Mom," says Mantha. She and Ellerby carry their cornflakes over to the breakfast nook, where they slide onto the bench beside Bennie and Carrie, sloshing milk over the sides of their bowls.

"Er . . . are we expecting someone?" Tom jerks his chin toward the window.

"God help me," groans Bennie, "if Clem invited anybody else she didn't tell me about."

"How come I can't say Christ but you get to say God?" Mantha wants to know.

"Shut up and eat your goddamn cereal."

Mantha grins.

Bennie turns to see what Tom's talking about. "Who on

earth . . . ?" Something about her tone makes everyone gather around the nook's many-paned window. As the stranger progresses up the obsolete front walk, they all drift left to keep him in their sights: this man who looks like he has stepped out of the past. His black coat hangs past his knees. His wiry beard hangs past his collar. He wears a black homburg with a wide brim, a white shirt with no tie, eyeglasses with round black frames. He carries a black briefcase. Two long curls depend past his ears. As he mounts the steps he disappears almost entirely from their frame of view; en masse they list farther to the left. Finally only his elbow remains visible as it comes up and he presses, presumably, the long-defunct bell. They attend to the ensuing silence.

"He doesn't *look* like one of Clem's friends," Tom reflects.

"Maybe he knowth Uncle Walter," suggests Hugh. "They both have briefcatheth."

Clem creeps in softly from the porch door, unbridal in muddy nightgown and rubber boots. "There's some guy poking around out fr—" she begins, only to realize that's why they're all clustered around the window.

"It's the black hats!" Pim declares. "The black hats are here!"

"Shh." Carrie, giggling, claps a hand over his mouth, then quickly withdraws it, Pim having licked her palm.

They all watch as the disembodied elbow comes up once again. Another reverberant silence, during which no one moves: not the spectators joined in the strangely delicious activity of collective spying, nor the object of their interest, outside their line of vision but apparently continuing with impressive reserves of patience to await a response.

Bennie snaps to. "Where's Stalwart?"

"In the barn."

"Go get him, please, Tom. Better let Dad field this one."

"REAL ESTATE AGENT," says Walter some twenty minutes later. Hands on hips, he stands at the kitchen sink watching the stranger depart on foot.

"They have their own real estate agents?" queries Bennie from the breakfast nook.

She and Carrie are the only two remaining, everyone else either having been dispatched on chores or having scurried away in avoidance of that fate.

"Evidently."

"But why'd he come here?"

"To see if we're interested in selling."

"What, just randomly: Do we want to sell our house?"

"Yeah."

"But why us in particular?"

"They're asking everyone. Going door-to-door."

"Like the Fuller Brush man," says Carrie perkily. There is a thickness in the air between her sister and her brother-in-law, a quivering charge that makes her feel excluded. "Like the Girl Scouts," she adds. She is roundly ignored.

"They're doing it all over town." Walter joins them in the breakfast nook.

"How do you know?" asks Bennie.

"It's a thing."

"What do you mean, 'a thing'?"

"Jeff Greenberg was telling me. It's a thing they do. The ultra-Orthodox. When they're looking to expand into new neighborhoods, new towns, they start contacting homeowners, asking if you're thinking about moving. They offer cash, Bennie. Wait . . ." He searches the pockets of his shorts, pulls out a business card and tosses it on the table.

WALK 2 SHUL
WE BUY HOUSES
ANY CONDITION
FAST CLOSE
ALL CASH

"Jeff was telling me how it works," Walter continues, "how it's already gone down in towns like New Ashkelon. At first they'll pay above market value as an enticement to buy out residents. It doesn't matter if your house isn't listed. They're persistent, and they're patient, and they just go around asking, making impressive offers, and invariably they find some people who say yeah, why not? Pretty soon the demographic tips, the town becomes more and more majority Orthodox, the character of the community changes, public schools decline, and secular families that can afford it begin moving out. Then property values drop, and more Haredim move in."

All three of them turn and look out the window, as if they might catch a glimpse of other real estate agents out there, other black-coated, black-hatted, black-bearded men wending along the roads of Rundle Junction, each armed with a briefcase and quiet determination.

"I thought Jeff Greenberg was the guy you didn't like." Carrie's finding the whole political situation with the Jews and the trees and everything a bit confusing. It's a challenge to sort out who's on which side and which side, therefore, she's on.

"Jeff's a good guy," says Walter. "I don't always agree with him, but I have to say he's done a lot of research on this, and I think he's genuinely trying to look down the road and think about the best interests of the vill—"

"Walter!" cries Bennie. "You're saying now you agree with Jeff?"

"I didn't say that. Look, it's complex. It's seriously complicated. Listen, over in New Ashkelon the population has almost doubled in less than a decade, right? All from the Haredim. Well they've officially implemented—it passed last week, Jeff was just telling me—a no-knock rule to prevent real estate agents going door-to-door because it's gotten so bad—no, let me finish, Bennie—bad in the sense of real harassment. Intimidation. When homeowners would say no thanks to selling, they'd get asked, 'Are you sure? Why would you want to live in a Hasidic neighborhood if you're not Hasidic? Will your family really be happy if you remain?'—stuff like that. One guy says when he declined to sell, the real estate agent put a hand on his shoulder and told him he should reconsider. Like a scene out of *The Godfather*.

"Anyway, Ben, I thought you were more anti-them than I was. What about your whole 'I'm against fundamentalists of any stripe'?"

Bennie eats a whole saltine, brow furrowed, before responding. "Yeah, but you're making me think. With your whole white-flight analogy. Let's say the Orthodox do move in en masse. Let's say the character of the town totally changes. I mean: okay. What right do we have to insist on maintaining our status quo? If the demographic reality is shifting? We live in a democracy. If the majority becomes people who aren't like us, what—we just stop believing in majority rule? All this time, all this talk of democracy was just lip service? We're in favor of it so long as we come out on top?"

Walter, elbows on the table, massages his scalp. Sighs. "I don't disagree with what you're saying, Bennie." Fingers laced over his crown, he picks his head up, looks her in the eye. "But why bring it up now?"

In the way he says this—the tilt of his neck, the quiet stress on the last word, the privateness of his gaze—Carrie again feels this *thing,* a massive invisible hovering unvoiced thickness in the air between her sister and her brother-in-law.

"Is there something I don't know about?" she says.

Overhead a door slams. A shout. Almost immediately, a second slam. The flush of a toilet. Footsteps trundle up and down the hall, floorboards groan and a scintilla of plaster dust rains down upon the breakfast table.

"Mom!" Mantha summons from the top of the stairs. "We neeeeed you!"

Bennie takes another saltine. With scant conviction mutters, "It's nice to be needed."

From overhead, more thumping. More flushing. Shrieks of gleeful revulsion. Then another slam followed by another delicate drizzle of dust. Carrie places a hand protectively over her coffee mug.

Mantha: "Better bring the plunger!"

Bennie picks up the business card. "'Any condition,' huh?" Shoots Walter her best deadpan. "How much did he say he was offering?"

LESTER VILNO HAS BEEN CHASED OFF. His pace is not hurried, no visible throngs pursue him, but she knows his leave-taking is regretful. She sees it in the reconciled gait of his retreat down the drive, the bent of his head on which the big black homburg slopes.

Strange that he is on foot. What happened to his bicycle?

Stolen, she thinks. Or no—vandalized, she suddenly remembers. The men around the old Glendale said. Their voices as rumbly as the smell of Mother's coffee, dark as the grounds at the bottom of the pot. *The tires slashed.* Voices she has grown up knowing, voices familiar as her own hands. *The seat ripped off.*

Their own hairy-knuckled hands strong as vises, callused and cracked, with nails blackened from working in fields and sheds, in the woods and on the ice, some of them with fingers lopped off by axes or lathes or tractor belts; these hands she has grown up knowing, grown up watching them move backgammon pieces, shake dice, tap the dottle out of their pipes. *If that wasn't enough, the frame all mangled, too. Twisted like a pretzel,* they said. *Twisted like a tornado,* and someone made a phlegmy sound that might have been a laugh.

So old Lester Vilno had to leave on foot. Some said he walked all the way to New Ashkelon for the train. Some said he walked farther than that. With a bundle on his back bound with twine and a satchel in each hand, and no one ever knew what became of his marionettes, if he'd somehow managed to pack them all or if he'd burned them or what, but when they went into his little house after he left there was nothing in it but the furniture and a broom. *Left it neat as a pin,* people whispered. Hearth swept bare, dishes washed. *Empty as Satan's heart,* they told each other. Not a crumb, not a cobweb. *Even the windows,* they whispered: *scrubbed clean.* Those who set foot inside said the light streaming through the panes had an uncanny clarity. A luster to set your teeth on edge.

(*Well I'm glad he's gone,* says Mother late at night.

Now whatever did he do to you? says Daddy.

Glad, in bed, listening to them talk on the other side of the wall.

People should stick with their own.

Mary, says Daddy. *Listen to yourself.*

And Glad listens but all she hears is the bitter sound of nothing, her own blood whooshing past her ears, a black coat flapping in the empty night.)

Come back, Glad wants to call after Lester Vilno, receding.

Come back! He could have a glass of tea with her here on the porch, sit awhile in the shade of the climbing sweet peas.

Ah well. She understands.

She has a train to catch, too.

A FEW MINUTES AFTER FOUR O'CLOCK the barometer suddenly drops. Updrafts build towering cumulonimbus clouds above the Taconics. The earth cools rapidly as warm air is drawn skyward and the day darkens: a squall line forms across the foothills.

AT HALF PAST FOUR Bennie looks up from the dining table, which she has been setting with uncommon care, laying out her grandmother Joy's wedding china and her own mother's wedding silver for the prenuptial dinner with the Digginses. For a moment she leaves off counting salad forks under her breath and registers how dark the afternoon has grown. Abandoning with a long-suffering sigh the task at hand for a more pressing one (hastening out back to gather the still-damp laundry from the line), she lodges a mental complaint against Chana: Had she not, just a few nights earlier, thumb scrolling across her smartphone, promised fair skies for the rest of the week?

WALTER, IN THE KITCHEN, in his element: aproned, kneading, running through his entire repertoire of union songs—"Bread and Roses," "Joe Hill," "Which Side Are You On?"—in his most voluptuous baritone. The massing clouds beyond the windows give the yeasty kitchen the feel of a lighthouse: a bright haven in a tumultuous sea. As the outer world dims and the gusts come pushing through the screens, he responds by increasing both tempo and volume. *"When the union's inspiration through the workers' blood shall run / There can be no power greater anywhere beneath the sun / Yet what force on Earth is weaker than the feeble strength of one? / For the union makes us strong!"* Scooping dough from the bowl, sprinkling flour on the marble kneading board, he folds and presses, folds and presses, in time with the chorus, on which he is joined by his own two youngest and their cousins: *"Solidarity forever, solidarity forever / Solidarity forever / For the Union makes us strong!"*

The kids, having annexed the breakfast nook for their mail-making activities and transformed it into a riot of paper, tape, glue, scissors, stickers, markers, glitter, pencils, crayons, and, of all things, a cardboard box full of feathers (*Why are you bringing all that stuff into my just-mopped kitchen?* Bennie had demanded. *For decorating envelopes,* Mantha had replied in the manner of a high-ranking dignitary condescending to the ignorance of an underling. *Of course,* Bennie had replied, the patina of sarcasm lost on her audience. *Silly me.*), excited by the plummeting air pressure, contribute boisterously to the song.

RICHARD THE DOG, too, is sensitive to the barometric shift. He does what he is wont to do on such occasions: pee. Unfortunately, he is in the living room when the instinct overtakes him. Bennie, midway up the stairs with the rescued laundry, en route to drape the still-damp things across her bed, sees him squat (poor Richard, so unnerved he doesn't even raise his leg in the usual manner of his sex) and yells, "No!" He looks at her in abject apology, his long curly ears drooping, then averts his gaze as the puddle between his hind legs grows, a long golden tributary flowing toward the rug.

———————

AT A QUARTER TO FIVE, from where they have stationed themselves around the back of the barn, the roustabouts look up from their work and eye the sky. The roustabouts: Clem's gypsy friends, her own crew of patches, her personal band of rude mechanicals, that little indeterminate clan comprising Maya and Banjo and Dave-Dave and Val, the latter with baby Harriett presently asleep in a sling upon their chest. The work to which they've been entrusted is top secret, thus their location out of view of the house. *I need your expertise in merrymaking and mischief-making,* is how Clem originally enticed them. *The ceremony is going to be modeled after a pageant,* she'd confided, *consisting of five episodes.*

She'd promised them a place to pitch their tents and almost total artistic freedom, their response to which includes the scrolls they have been painting all afternoon on swaths of brown butcher paper spread in the dirt, corners weighted with stones. The stones keep the scrolls themselves from blowing, but now as the wind kicks up, dirt and tufts of dry grass are getting scattered across the still-wet paint, and *What do you think?* they've begun asking one another. They register the hairs standing up on their arms, gauge the anvil clouds forming in the west. Working in pairs, they hustle the scrolls into the already overstuffed barn.

LLOYD AND TOM, having completed their assignment of setting up fifty-three folding chairs in horseshoe-shaped rows around the base of the black walnut tree (Lloyd: *Why are we doing this now? What if it rains? Shouldn't we wait until tomorrow?* Tom: *Don't ask me. I just work here.*), have snuck off on bicycles. Pedaling down the county road they note the sudden change in temperature and the darkness, but continue undeterred on their impromptu, covert mission: Lloyd has asked Tom to show him the new housing development.

AT FIVE O'CLOCK CHANA, lying and every now and then whimpering upon her sleeping bag in the orange tent—which is really too small for three people and all their things, especially after three days of said things commingling until they give off a collective smell of damp Converse, damp socks, damp pillows filled with ancient duck feathers, plus whatever chemicals they use in the factory where they make the tent (whenever she gets a migraine she acquires literally nauseatingly supernatural powers of olfaction)— has known a storm was brewing for hours. She could feel its teetering approach behind one eye, could feel its weird tumescent luminescence building there. She has unzipped the window and door flaps to allow the strong breeze to wash over her, thinking it would soothe, but as the storm front closes in, the contrast with the warm spongy air of the past few days proves so intense that it's a kind of sensory overload. She feels she might really throw up.

"Here." Hannah slips in and crawls over to Chana with a glass of water, three aspirins, and a cold compress. She had stumbled upon Chana by accident ten minutes earlier, when she'd entered the tent seeking her nail file (*Dang, where is that sucker? I have a wicked hangnail. Did you filch it the other night when you went prowling through my things . . . Hey, what's the matter with you?*), and upon determining Chana was in real distress a new side of her had been revealed. It cannot be said Hannah exuded tenderness, exactly, but all shtick fell away—she had become quietly focused and gruffly kind. "You're such an idiot," she says now, case in point, supporting Chana's head as she lifts it so she can drink.

"You should have told us you lost your medication. Here"—taking out her cell—"call your doctor and tell them you need a new prescription, ASAP."

SITTING AS SHE USED TO when she was small, heels tucked against her bottom, knees hugged against her chest, Carrie perches on the swivel chair in the office and attends to the gathering gloom. A half hour earlier she'd deserted Bennie, with whom she'd been setting the dinner table, to help Aunt Glad get settled on her cot, the latter having expressed the desire for a "short sojourn" away from all the "hullabaloo," and she has been keeping the elderly woman company ever since. It's rather nice to take a break from all the animated busyness, not to mention from Bennie's peevishness.

At first they chat rather generally about the distant past, Aunt Glad responding now and then to Carrie's reminiscences with murmurs of recognition and the occasional gentle correction or elucidation. Emboldened, Carrie segues into asking questions about the pageant of 1927, and this leads quite naturally into telling about their discovery yesterday of the name on the memorial plaque. "Who was Benjamin Erlend, Aunt Glad, do you know?" There is no answer. "Is he a relation?" After a moment: "He must be a relation." After another moment: "He was two."

A sound of protest from the cot where Glad lies atop the trapunto coverlet.

"What was that? I didn't understand."

"*Three.*" A tattered squawk. "He was *three.*"

Oh, thinks Carrie. Just that, no thoughts or words other than *oh,* and a sense of something too massive to be easily understood, too massive to have its parameters glimpsed, let alone mapped, settles over her, and into her, seeps through all the world.

Then for a while there is just time passing, and noises coming from the cot, feeble, anguished, mangled noises, unlike any crying Carrie has ever heard. "Oh Glad," she murmurs, scootching the swivel chair on its casters up close to the bed. The older woman has covered her face with one hand; Carrie takes the other and holds it, egg-like, in both her own. "I'm so sorry."

Eventually Aunt Glad makes utterances, scratched and exhausted-sounding. Carrie has to lean forward to hear. "He was going to be three the next day. There was going to be a party. There was a kit for him to make little lead soldiers. The Coldstream Guards. An angel cake. Mother had baked it. There was a toy horn covered with silver paper. Little boy blue she called him. He was my—" Her voice breaks.

"Your what?" whispers Carrie.

Glad's mouth crimps shut. The hand that covers her eyes shakes.

"Your brother?"

"My *responsibility*." Her hand drops away and she meets Carrie's eyes with startling intensity. "And I didn't—" It breaks again, her voice. But she is determined, she is resolute. The near-weightless hand Carrie has been cupping now grips her back with sudden, painful strength. "I couldn't keep—I didn't keep—my word—I lost hold of his hand . . ."

"There were so many of us. Under the grandstand. And so much smoke. And so much noise. And Joy had my hand. I tried— I thought I tried—I had—I knew I was supposed to have his. But—I was afraid!" Her gaze bears into Carrie's with a kind of horrified radiance. "I was afraid. And I didn't—I didn't—"

Carrie leans closer.

But Glad is finished speaking. Finished with words. She releases her grip and Carrie returns her hand to the coverlet. Her body, her features, every molecule of her placid now. She cries, but softly, effortlessly, with untroubled breath. Tears spill from her eyes and roll sideways down her face, bathing her scars, flowing across the puckered, shiny skin.

After a while they cease.

Carrie sits with her. In the swivel chair, in her child's pose. Outside the sky has grown dark with clouds. Inside the air is striated with shadow. Carrie peers through the slippery dim: Glad's lips are ever so slightly parted. Her hands are folded, one over the other, upon her breast, which rises and falls at what seem like distant intervals.

A FEW MINUTES PAST FIVE the first drops break free of the clouds and Clem—who has moseyed restlessly down the driveway to sit on the big rock upon which every few years Bennie repaints their house number in a new color—sticks out her tongue and tilts her face to the sky. She came out to watch for the green Volvo Diggs has told her they will be driving, she and her father and stepmother. Clem has met Keith and Johnetta Diggins twice—once in a restaurant, and once at their house in Falls Church. The house had been cleaner than any Clem had ever set foot in. And Diggs's folks had been cordial to her in a way that made her wonder what they must have said later in private. When she confided her anxiety to Diggs, Diggs said she just didn't understand Southern manners. *I'm not saying you're not a stretch for them*, she'd allowed. When Clem's brow knotted up all woe-is-me at this, Diggs had given Clem's shoulder a shove. *C'mon, Swiss Miss. Like I'm not a stretch for your parents?*

But Clem fears she has further to go to prove herself with the Digginses. The fear of being wrong—being *in* the wrong—has never entirely left her. She cannot shake the notion that she keeps putting her foot wrong. The Swiss Miss epithet, however lovingly spoken, is just another reminder of the way she keeps putting her foot wrong. Even the occasion of learning her beloved's true name had been a minor disaster.

On paper Diggs is KC Diggins, which Clem initially assumed was her given name.

"You think my parents gave me initials for a name?"

"I thought it might be cultural. What?"

The look Diggs gave her seemed to Clem rich with sediment, the nature of which she couldn't deduce.

"I'm sorry. I'm learning, I want to learn."

"I know, *bambina*."

This had taken place just seven weeks earlier, the day after Clem's graduation and before Diggs began her internship in DC. They'd made an appointment with the Rundle Junction village clerk and sat waiting on a bench outside his office in the great gothic sandstone building, each with her birth certificate, social security card, government-issued photo ID, and twenty-dollar bill (they'd decided it was symbolic of their equal partnership to split the marriage license fee).

"So what's it stand for?"

Diggs made like she didn't hear.

Clem made to grab her legal documents out of her lap and a wrestling match ensued, brought to an abrupt halt by the frowning attention of the man who'd had them sign in on a clipboard. Giggles were suppressed; items of clothing were straightened; the girl with the peridot nose stud leaned over and hissed into the taller girl's ear.

"Come on, Chat. I'm going to find out in like five minutes anyway."

"First you have to swear never to tell."

"Okay."

"Not another living soul."

"Such drama."

"Swear."

"Fine, I swear. So what's your name?"

It was Keziah Charlene, information revealed in a mortified whisper.

"But that's beautiful! It's so pretty, Keziah. What's it mean? Is it African?"

"No, fool. Jewish."

"Nah."

"Old Testament."

". . . I don't think so."

Diggs arched an eyebrow.

"I mean, I never heard it before. You sure you're not thinking of the Quran? What?" For Diggs had turned away, and this pique was not in jest. "No, it's pretty." Clem scrambled. "I like it!" She had the horrible conviction she'd said something unforgivable, but knew neither what nor how. She moved to touch Diggs's arm, then thought better of it. "What'd I do?"

"Nothing."

"What's wrong?"

Minutely, without meeting her eyes, Diggs shook her head.

"Sorry." At a loss for anything else to say, she said it again: "I'm sorry."

"Stop. What are you even saying sorry for?"

Clem thought, *I have no idea*. What had she done? Nothing. By Diggs's own account. So why was she being punished? A needle of indignation began to crystalize in her chest. She looked at her beloved. Diggs remained turned away.

Clem stared out miserably across the hallway and found Clipboard Man looking back at her. How many couples fought moments before applying for a marriage license? How many couples were denied a license, and on what grounds? How many couples had this man personally witnessed sitting on this bench over the decades—for he looked as if he'd been here many decades, looked like a permanent fixture of this place, with his pinkish skin, upright gray hair, and shrewd blue eyes. What did he see when he looked at them, mixed-race, same-sex, here in little Rundle Junction? Clem sat up taller, uncrossed her legs, and angled her nose stud to glint in his direction.

As she did, something happened inside her, something at once tiny and immense: she saw reality. Saw that while she fantasized he was judging them, she most emphatically was judging him. And that was enough to cause her to lift her attention from the endlessly captivating whorl of her own existence and perceive three more things: that Diggs was suffering, that she did not understand why, and that she could ask. "Sweetheart?"

It was the first time in her life she had called someone that.

"Sweetheart?" Clem began.

SOME FIVE DECADES LATER, after they have split up and gotten back together and split up again; after Diggs has clerked for Sotomayor and served as General Counsel for the Virginia Department of Child and Family Services and then as Representative for that state's third congressional district; after Clem has gone through rehab and then doula training and attended the births of over three hundred babies and become an advocate for reproductive justice working especially in the area of women in prison; long after they have fallen out of touch and kept up with what the other is doing only through the occasional item on their social networks or newsfeeds; only then will the two bump into each other at a fund-raiser for the first transgender person to become

the presidential nominee of a major political party and resume—
or more accurately, strike up a new—close friendship.

Only then, when they are in their seventies and sitting by the
gas fire one winter evening in Diggs's Foggy Bottom town house,
Diggs (who, before reconnecting with Clem, won't have been
called Diggs by anyone in decades) nursing a bourbon and Clem
sipping ginger tea, will they speak of that moment outside the
village clerk's office when Clem had doubted the provenance of
Diggs's name, that moment when a chasm opened between them
there on the bench in the old sandstone building, a moment of
irredeemable distance, until Clem spoke across it, sent a question
("Sweetheart?") across the chasm like an arrow with a silken cord
tied to the end, and Diggs caught the arrow and shot it back with
another length of silk, and strand by strand then they began fashioning an earnest if tenuous bridge.

There in Diggs's living room, with its scarlet-and-rust-colored
rug and its floor-to-ceiling bookshelves and its mahogany wainscoting and glossy-leafed ficus, its tall windows with feathery
snow falling outside, its shadows softened by the light of orange
flames flickering in the grate; there Clem, bringing the black Jap-
anese stoneware mug to her chin and letting the fragrant vapor
envelop her face, will say, *I'm sure you don't even remember it but
I've thought of that moment—the moment I understood how much I
didn't understand, how much I would never understand, and how I
therefore, from that moment on, would always be responsible for
trying—I think of it, it's funny but I've always thought of it as the
moment I in a way became an adult, or no, became a person really, a
really and truly full human being.* And Diggs, in a voice raspy and
laden, suddenly, with something heavy, something making it crack
(Clem, looking over, will be amazed to see tears glittering in her
eyes) will say, *Bambina. That was the moment I started to believe we
were possible, you and me.*

LIGHTNING. IN THE KITCHEN all the windowpanes flare magnesium white for a split second, as if Ellerby's imaginary camera had a real flash. The scene she has just snapped: her uncle Walter in his striped apron baking and singing, her little cousins across the table from her, scribbling letters and singing along. The thunder that follows is a great cracking clap that makes the children scream, at first just the little ones but a split second later Ellerby, too, screaming for the fun of it and for the sake of belonging.

LLOYD AND TOM arrive at the building site at the height of the cloudburst. Everything's so slippery it takes Tom a few minutes to Kryptonite the bikes to the hurricane fence, but at last he gets the lock in place and the truth is neither of them minds the weather; they figure it's on their side because the place looks deserted. Sneakers squelching, they walk around the fence until they spot the swastikas, one on the side of the trailer, two on the new building itself. They're uglier than Lloyd had imagined, if you can say such a thing about swastikas: messily executed, as though done in a hurry, with copious drips.

"It's not who I thought it might be," says Tom.

"No?"

He shakes his head. "Whoever did this is no graffiti artist. That's bad can control. The guys I know take pride in their work."

Lloyd is amused by Tom's professional disdain. And made suspicious by it. "How's your can control?" he ventures.

"I suck," Tom admits. "But I've only tried it twice."

Hm, says the look on Lloyd's face.

When he'd asked his nephew if they could check out the

building site together, Tom had been visibly wary. "Why?" And when Lloyd said he wanted to see for himself what lay at the center of all the fuss over zoning and wetlands and anti-Semites and affordable housing and preserving tradition, Tom had been visibly surprised. "Mom always says you couldn't care less about Rundle Junction."

Lloyd had scratched his armpit. "She's not wrong," he said. "Rundle Junction qua Rundle Junction." He said *qua* in a way intended to show he was not really that guy who goes around using the word *qua*.

The truth is, he's more interested in Tom. Or more precisely: he's interested in Tom's interest. Not because it reminds him of himself at that age, but for the very reason that it doesn't. As if Tom's his converse, a version of who he might have been if he hadn't been himself. If he'd had a certain kind of appetite he's always lacked. That's it, really: he wants to fathom his lack.

Circling the site now in the downpour, they come to an unchained gate. Tom gives it a push; it yields.

"Security cameras," cautions Lloyd. This was not part of the plan.

Tom shrugs. "Then the cameras will show it was open—we didn't break in." He enters the construction area. After a moment, Lloyd follows.

THUNDER RUMBLING. Departure board tumbling. Wooden slat after wooden slat. Clatter of symbols juddering by. Too fast for the eye to decipher.

Train's approaching. Gusting into the station. Billowing behind it damp pearly plumes.

Who's Benjamin? someone's asking. Little boy blue. That's what we called him. Until we stopped calling him anything at all.

*Little boy blue, Mother calls, come blow your horn while the bath
is warm. He only chortles. Eels away naked down the hall.*

Naughty little angel. Never got his cake.

*Never mind. She's bringing some with her. It's in that bundle tied
with twine.*

RICHARD THE DOG, exiled, slinks miserably across the yard.
Drenched, he looks feral. Fear makes his hind legs tremble. Gives
him a furtive, diagonal gait. Lightning charges the world once
more as he reaches the barn, shivering and gaunt with his fur plastered to his body, only to find the great sliding doors have been
pulled shut. He paws them, barks. Waits. Barks again, sharply.
Paws again. Waits. Turns away, toenails skidding and slipping over
pebbles as he seeks alternative shelter.

INSIDE THE BARN at five fifteen the roustabouts lay the lengths of
butcher paper over heaps of old furniture and farm equipment.
They managed to get everything inside moments before the rain
began coming down in earnest and the painted words and images
are mostly intact; now they work to lay them flat so they can dry.
The deluge is deafening, as if the contents of a massive piggy bank
were crashing down upon the corrugated tin roof. *Careful, there's
a leak to your right*, they warn one another. *Can you move that back
a foot? Water's coming in over here, too.* Once the scrolls are settled,
they get to settling themselves, pulling up half-broken chests and
stools, a rusty icebox, an ice cream maker with a broken crank.
Val, still with Harriett slung around their chest, finds a place to
roost on what looks to be an old butter churn. Banjo produces
from the pocket of his carpenter shorts, as if it were the most
humdrum thing in the world, a dry-cured soppressata. Maya slides

a horn-handled penknife from the shaft of her boot and tosses it
to him. Dave-Dave fishes from his own pocket a bag of Swedish
Fish. They partake in a picnic of salami and candy while waiting
out the storm.

HAVING EVICTED RICHARD, Bennie snatches one of the freshly laun-
dered towels from the basket and uses it to sop his urine, at least
the portion that hasn't already seeped into the rug. For that she
goes into the kitchen to fetch paper towels and disinfectant from
underneath the sink, rehearsing in her mind: *Hello, Mr. and Mrs.
Diggins, so nice to finally meet you. What's that smell, you ask? Oh,
just a little dog urine. Won't you please make yourselves at home?* In
the kitchen she is greeted like Shackleton returning to Elephant
Island. *Mommy! Mom! Aunt Bennie, thee what we're making!* She is
clasped about the waist and led by both hands over to the breakfast nook to ooh and aah over the handmade cards, the envelopes
all painstakingly addressed to various guests. *We're almost ready to
start delivering them!* She tells them great job, tells them she can
see that neither snow nor rain nor the need to actually get things
done before fifty thousand wedding guests arrive will deter them
from their course. *Not fifty thousand!* she's admonished. *Okay,* she
concedes, *fifty,* and squats by Walter's legs to extract cleaning supplies from the cupboard. Another flash of lightning comes, then
immediately a thunder crack she feels in her throat. The children
all scream, transported by a kind of fearsome ecstasy, and the air
smells weirdly pink and she notices a big raised bruise on one of
Walter's shins, the sight of which, for all its ordinariness—*because
of its very ordinariness*—ambushes her with tenderness. *Our foot
hurts us,* she thinks. Welling with more affection, more gratitude
and pity, than she can possibly bear. No wonder she gets a head
rush when she stands again, Lysol in hand. She has to steady

herself against his chest. *You okay?* He encircles her waist with floury arms. She nuzzles his ear, murmurs, *Fucking dog peed the rug.* He squeezes her more tightly. She is as happy as she's ever been.

BY FIVE TWENTY, the puddle of rain gathered on the roof of the water-resistant nylon tent has begun leaking through. Hannah and Chana, side by side on their backs, watch drips collect in succession on the inside of the fabric, watch as each one swells and finally breaks free to descend with a fat splash on Chana's face. "It bizarrely helps," the migraine victim croaks, fraily optimistic.

"Getting rained on? Let's notify the NIH."

"More like the meditative thing of waiting for each drop to fall."

The next round of lightning brings a nearly simultaneous thunder crack. They feel it in their chests, feel it in the earth beneath their bodies.

"What about flirting with death?" Hannah asks. "Does flirting with death also help?"

A contemplative pause. "I think yes."

Hannah laughs. "That was funny."

"Really?"

"Literally."

The door flap is breeched by a large snout, rapidly followed by an entire dripping mongrel, tail declaring delight over having found sanctuary at last, paws trampling the lumpy terrain of sleeping bags, knapsacks, and bodies.

"Ow! Oh my God, Richard, could you please smell a little more like wet dog?"

They sit up, the Ch/Hannahs, trying unsuccessfully to fend off the particular excesses of canine happiness, each of them thinking

At least there's not enough room in here for him to shake just before he showers them and all their possessions with *eau de chien.*

"Okay, babe, that's our cue," says Hannah, taking matters (and Chana) in hand. They squeeze out of the tent and make a break for the house, Hannah still in her nursemaid role, leading the afflicted one; both of them with their bare feet sliding on the slippery mud and newly mown grass; Chana, her head still pounding but less acutely now, repeating a silent mantra of sweet surprise: *She called me babe; she called me babe!*

CLEM IS STANDING on one foot in the front hall, peering out the window to the left of the door nobody uses, which suits her purposes as just now she is wanting to be solitary, to watch in private for the arrival of her intended, whose face at the moment, disconcertingly, she can't quite recall. More disconcerting: neither can she at the moment recall why she thought this was such a good idea—holding a wedding, summoning family and friends to attend a ceremony of love and mischief, a subversive wink of a ceremony sure to evoke her thesis adviser's famously gabbling, hacking laughter when he is here tomorrow to take part in the ceremony. This is one of the surprises she has up her sleeve: he has agreed not merely to be one of the guests but to play an important role in the performance. (For a performance is, when you come right down to it, what the wedding—any wedding, but especially this one—is.) Her feet have tracked mud and grass clippings through the front hall, and where she stands a puddle forms. The hall clock reads five thirty-two. The Digginses are an hour late. An hour later than Diggs had said they'd be. Pushing away thoughts of slick highways, low visibility, and traffic pileups, rubbing her wet hair and then wiping her dirty feet with an embroidered guest towel (the very same one Bennie had laid, neatly folded, on the powder room vanity not an hour ago), she strains to make out the driveway through the rain-crazed glass.

WALTER, HIS ARMS still around Bennie's waist, his nose level with the top of her head, closes his eyes and inhales. His wife smells of the same no-frills brand of coconut cream rinse she uses to detangle Mantha's mop. He smells also the trio of loaves now in the oven, along with a charred aroma that means Tom has been making frozen pizzas again without bothering to put tinfoil on the lower rack to catch the drips. Although the new pregnancy has not yet declared itself in a publicly obvious way, Bennie's body is ampler today than it was a couple of months ago, and holding her now with the knowledge that she is holding, deep within her, yet another co-creation of theirs, he feels at once sated and hungry. The kids have stopped screaming but keep up a volatile chatter that spirals excitedly as the porch door opens. Without lessening his embrace he opens his eyes and sees, over the top of Bennie's head, the bedraggled Ch/Hannahs enter hand in hand. From behind them, just before the screen door slaps shut, a dark daemon comes streaking through the kitchen in a frenzy, toenails scrabbling over the just-mopped-this-morning floor. Even farther behind them, a light pulses red (*could it be lightning?*) then (*no it couldn't*) blue.

IT'S FIVE THIRTY-SEVEN when Carrie unfolds her legs and rises from the swivel chair. In a kind of slow motion, holding her breath for some reason she cannot name, she bends over the cot. The rain striking the window is so noisy and chaotic she cannot be sure—is the sense of movement coming from Aunt Glad a sign that she is dreaming, or is it merely the dance of liquid light across the trapunto coverlet, across her crepey skin? Is it just the storm that makes her eyelids appear to flicker with whatever visions sleep has brought? Or is it a function of whatever visions are visiting the old woman in her sleep? She brings her cheek close to Aunt Glad's nostrils.

Lightning rends the atmosphere.

A scorched smell, a splitting sound.

Rupture irradiates her very trunk.

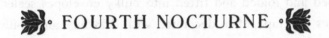 · FOURTH NOCTURNE ·

THE NIGHT MAIL

In the kitchen the letterboxes gleam dully. The dark tonight is like a canceling. The constellations are hidden, the moon no more than an idea. Visible or no, the letterboxes have become full of letters, their ordinary contents having been shifted and recombined—cardamom and coriander now intermixed with pot holders and egg timers, the lemon zester bedded with the strawberry huller, the candy and meat thermometers laid down like lion and lamb—in order to vacate two rows of cubbies for the children's missives.

Dear Clem, Happy wedding!!!! What flavor is you're cake?

Uncle Walter, Thanks for the bred. The sharp parts herted my mowth but its good.

Dear Aunt Glad, I like your skin the pink and wite parts are pretty.

Dear Diggs, Roses are red, violets are blue, if you have a paddle, you can canoe.

Hi Harriett, How's life?

Tom, Congrajulations on not getting arrested. Haha just kidding. Thanks for saving my place on line (bathroom).

Dear Mommy, When can we go to Chuck E. Cheeses? I'm bored.

Dear Lloyd, I am writing this in cursive. I am writing this in print.

Dear Chana, I have one VERY loose and one growing in. Three already growed. One cavity. Sharks teeth fall out every week. Also snails have teeth on their tongues.

Dear Benjamin, Sory you dide.

All these and more have been painstakingly composed and inscribed and folded and fitted into bulky envelopes sealed with staples and tape, then decorated with drawings and doilies and bits of ribbon, as well as food coloring and flower petals and feathers. They roost in silence, the letters, in the dark kitchen, nestled in their dovecote like a congress of living, dreaming sleepers.

Glued to one envelope is a border of what appear to be little pink beads. Moments ago, one of these beads was prized off and nibbled by the long yellow incisors of a mouse, misled by the sugar coating. Some twelve hours hence, it will be determined by none other than the letter's addressee that they are actually her own missing prescription tablets.

THE MOUSE

Poor little mouse. How delicious she found the round thing at first—the sweetness (nicely complemented by the savor of dried glue) delighted her taste receptors, and as she chewed her bright little eyes took in greedily the rest of the crooked pink row—but soon after swallowing the last bit she discovers it is not to her liking after all. Her heart races. Her appetite vanishes. Her whiskers twitch double-time while the rest of her body goes statue-still.

Is her anxiety triggered by the dose of synthetic estrogen and progestin she just ingested? Or by the bolt of lightning that just flashed? Does it remind her of last weekend's storm? For this happens to be the same young mouse who crunched the beetle three nights ago in the wall behind Aunt Glad's cot. Could she be remembering how the rain lasted four days and flooded her nest and drowned her first litter, all five pups, still hairless, still sightless, still with their earflaps pressed flat against their scalps?

MEMORY

Scientists have found evidence that mice have episodic memory—that is, the ability to recall who, what, where, and when. Not only that. Scientists have performed experiments in which they have been able to enhance mouse memory through the manipulation of a single gene. They claim to have successfully implanted false memories in mice. Perhaps most extraordinarily of all, they have demonstrated in mice the phenomenon of epigenetic memory—that is, the memory of an occurrence affecting one generation being genetically transmitted to the next. They report that mice conditioned to associate the smell of cherry blossoms with electric shocks bear offspring who, even in the absence of having experienced pain themselves, display an aversion to the same scent. The baby mice shudder when the fragrance is wafted before them. And their offspring in turn, the grandchildren of those who experienced the actual suffering, evince the same behavior. Without telling the story, without writing it down, without any tangible means of communication, some knowledge is being passed along from one generation to the next. Like a train that somehow makes its way from one village to another, or rather from one time to another, along unseen rails.

Now our mouse unfreezes. Gradually her heart rate returns to normal. She recommences her nocturnal scavenging, slipping deftly from her current cubbyhole to the one above, in which she finds nothing to eat. But a different treasure captivates her attention here: a plumulaceous feather of pearly gray that she tears with her long incisors from the piece of heavy construction paper to which it had been glued. She wants it for her new nest, which she is building under the front steps nobody ever uses.

Already a new generation is growing inside her womb.

THE MOON

Tonight in Rundle Junction for all practical purposes there is no moon. No sign of it is visible through the clouds. No dark marias, no pale highlands. No matter: our companion of four and a half billion years, our nearest neighbor little more than a billion feet away, isn't going anywhere. (Actually it is. Actually it is sidling steadily away, by minuscule increments: an inch and a half a year. But still we continue to exert influence over each other, the moon causing our oceans to slosh to and fro, the earth lashing the moon once a month with its magnetotail, stippling its surface with electrons and whipping up storms of lunar dust.)

The moon is by definition strange to us. Terra incognita, *unheimlich*, not-home. For millennia we have tried to fathom it: via selenography and selenomancy, poetry and algebra, robots and rockets. In 1994, a spacecraft named *Clementine* spent more than two months mapping the lunar surface. It sent back to earth in excess of a million and half images. This was the first expedition to offer evidence of water ice on the moon. Water! We know water. We have water, too.

The craft had been named after the old folk ballad, for it was understood from the beginning that, equipped with fuel enough only to complete its mission, it would after that time be *lost and gone forever.*

Clem Blumenthal had been at the time two. A full-bellied toddler who spoke to the moon in long strings of babble no one could understand. One June night her parents took her to the ice cream stand out on Route 7. Sitting on one of the benches with her cone she'd become so transfixed by the startling appearance of the moon—her same moon! the one she saw out of her own window at home!—which had somehow followed her here, that she'd let ice cream leak down her hand and drip off her elbow while she stood up on the bench and alerted all the unenlightened souls returning to their cars, beseeching, "Look, people, the moon! Come back! The moon!"

TRANSIT

For once it's midnight and neither Tom nor Lloyd is prowling about. Tom lies alone in the room he shares with Pim (who has already completed his nightly shuffle down the hall to their parents' bed), his strapping frame curled in the fetal position he still, at sixteen, has not outgrown. A rain-swollen breeze swishes through the open door of their tiny screened-in balcony and through the single large window at the foot of his bed, making the venetian blinds toss and slap, a sound he does not hear. Meanwhile Lloyd sprawls on the futon one flight up, naked except for his wristwatch. For once the little attic room is not sweltering. Now and then, out the window: a flash of violent, violet light, a sight he does not see. Both nephew and uncle, after having caused others a fair amount of unnecessary consternation on a day that was already highly eventful, are down for the count.

Those red-and-blue lights Walter had glimpsed over Bennie's shoulder mid-embrace in the kitchen earlier had turned out to be a squad car making its way, for the second time in two days, up the drive. The police had come this time not to locate Tom but to deliver him, along with Lloyd, the two of them emerging one after the other from the vehicle looking not especially remorseful. Walter did step outside in time to hear his son tell the officers, *Sorry, we kind of got your car soaked,* but dripping on the backseat of the cruiser seemed to mark the limit of Tom's range of contrition.

One of the officers was the same Vin Diesel guy from the other night. His partner this time was a woman who looked no older than Clem. Both wore police hats covered in a kind of elasticized plastic, like shower caps. They escorted Tom and Lloyd up to the porch and there, over the din of the rain, the female officer recounted to Walter the series of events leading up to this moment—how, while on routine patrol, she and her partner had observed two bicycles chained to the hurricane fence at the construction site and upon investigating the area on foot had found Tom and Lloyd eating an apple in the cab of a front-end loader, where they reported they'd gone to seek shelter from the rain. Seeing as the gate had been left unlocked; seeing as neither the minor nor the adult had any suspicious items on his person (no spray paint or any other tools that might be linked to intent to vandalize); and seeing as both had been cooperative, the officers had decided, after verbally collecting some personal information and inspecting the driver's license of the adult, to bring them both back to the minor's place of residence. *We will be filing an incident report,* Vin Diesel had apprised Walter in his heavy-lidded, thick-necked softspoken way, *and I can't say what the owner might do. Whether they're going to press charges.*

Tom, he said then, turning to face him directly. Walter both resented and admired the patience with which he waited until

Tom shifted his own gaze to meet the officer's before continuing. *I'm telling you now to stay away from that property. I don't want you going within a hundred yards of it. Understand?*

Walter expected his son to talk back, to inquire on what legal basis the police could place such a restriction on his mobility, something like that, but Tom was uncharacteristically docile. His *Yeah, I understand* was barely audible above the rain.

To Walter the female cop said, *We understand the other gentleman is your brother-in-law and his permanent residence is out of state, is that correct?*

Walter agreed that it was.

Then Vin Diesel said, *Can we speak to you alone, sir?*

Walter indicated they could. With a gesture, he sent Tom and Lloyd into the house, then listened as the cop, reducing his decibel level even further and thereby elevating the authority with which he spoke even more, told him they had reason to believe they knew who was responsible for the graffiti, and that neither Tom nor Lloyd was suspect. *I can't share any other information at this time. Reason I'm telling you is because I need you to keep them away from the property—understand? We got the guy, the last thing we need is to complicate things. Understand?*

Burning with resentment at being addressed like a child, burning with curiosity to know who had done it, and burning with anxiety over being made to promise something he actually had little power to deliver, Walter allowed that he did.

Not until the squad car was halfway back down the driveway did he go into the kitchen to confront Tom and Lloyd, slouching sheepishly near the pantry, only to find himself speechless. Again it was his own father who came back to him, the image of Myron glaring in disbelief after he'd committed some act of colossal stupidity; Myron saying, *What do you got, a loch in kop? A hole in the head.* Walter could feel himself glaring at Tom and Lloyd now in exactly the same way. The bozos, the lunkheads—what in hell were they thinking? That they were righteous revolutionaries. Yeah: Che Guevara and Nelson Mandela as portrayed by Cheech and Chong.

Involuntarily, the two bozos glanced at each other. Big mistake. They found themselves in a pitched battle to suppress bouts of laughter.

Half an hour earlier, sitting in the cab of the front-end loader, Tom had been on the verge of lighting the apple pipe he'd carved earlier that day when they saw a couple of cops traipsing across the building site. *Shit*, said Lloyd. *We're cool*, Tom assured him. *Easy for you to say—you're a minor. I'm a middle-aged indigent.* But Tom was unfazed. *Here, eat up.* He handed the weed-packed apple to Lloyd, tearing off a large chunk with his own teeth first. Between them, passing it back and forth and crunching with applied muscle and speed, they managed to devour it to the core—which Tom stuck in the baggie that had held the weed. He shoved his lighter in the crack of the seat just as the officers reached the truck and ordered them to climb out, still chewing. By then what was left of the pipe looked as wholesome as anything a mom would find cleaning out a lunch box after school. In fact—it was a genius touch, for Tom could have stuffed the baggie down inside the seat along with the lighter—it made Tom look like a nice kid, a kid who'd been brought up not to litter, not even something biodegradable like an apple core.

In two weeks' time it will be public knowledge that the graffitist is neither a neo-Nazi railing against the spread of Orthodox Jews in Putnam County nor a lackey of the Grand Rebbe trying to increase sympathy by staging an anti-Semitic threat, but what the newspapers will call a "troubled teen" with a "history of mental illness," whose mother is a Reconstructionist rabbi and whose father is a clinical neuropsychologist.

But for now, unaware of all this and beginning to surmise from the look on Walter's face just how much trouble they may yet find themselves in, if not with law enforcement then with their own flesh and blood, Tom and Lloyd launched into a welter of apologies and declared their readiness to submit to any kind of labor Walter wanted to assign them.

Again Walter opened his mouth—only to be interrupted three times in quick succession: first by a crack of lightning so close he felt it in his sternum; second by the sight of a late-model pine-green Volvo with Virginia plates gliding up the drive; and third by Bennie. Who came into the room with a tentative, almost tiptoeing tread. And looked at Walter with bewildered, silent effort for several seconds, as though waiting for her voice to swim up from wordless depths, before saying, "Something's wrong with Aunt Glad."

AUNT GLAD HAD BEEN UNRESPONSIVE when Bennie, summoned by Carrie, had first gone in to see her. Carrie said she thought Aunt Glad was not breathing, but when Bennie accompanied her back into the room, they were both able to see the rise and fall of her chest. Her color seemed off, but then the whole room seemed off, what with the storm, which had a flattening effect, like an emerald-gray iron bearing down on all light.

Bennie took one of Glad's hands and held it much as Carrie had earlier, between both of her own. It was mottled and noticeably cool. She stroked it gently and spoke with quavering intensity. *Aunt Glad? It's Bennie. Can you hear me? Aunt Glad? Do you feel all right? Are you sleeping? Do you hear me?* And then, shifting gears, summoning a kind of soothing sturdiness, as if she were speaking to one of her children, sick with fever or lost in nightmare: *We're with you, Aunt Glad, Carrie and I are both here by your bed, and it's raining outside, and it's summertime, and all is well, everything is okay. We're here.*

She looked meaningfully at Carrie, then laid Aunt Glad's hand by her side, while Carrie smoothed the coverlet more comfortably over her feet. They stepped outside the office and held a whispered conversation.

Should we call someone?

Like who?

An ambulance?

She's peaceful now.

True.

Did you see her hands?

Did you see her nails? They're blue.

What would they even do?

Who?

An ambulance.

We're not calling an ambulance.

I agree.

Can you imagine all they'd do to her at the hospital? Lights, IVs, monitors, for what?

I agree.

She's peaceful. She's home.

Agreed.

Another fantastic crack of lightning simultaneous with thunder. They both whipped their heads to look at Aunt Glad, but she remained perfectly still. Carrie had gone back into the room to sit with her then, while Bennie had gone to find Walter, and of course this was precisely the moment when their daughter's beloved arrived at last from Falls Church, the moment when Diggs, all but a stranger to them, was, along with her father and stepmother, stepping out of the green Volvo and hurrying through the rain toward the porch.

It was an evening of convergences, an evening of dizzying motion, people revolving in and out of rooms, shifting together and apart like bits of colored glass in a kaleidoscope, and there were both public and private roles to be performed, depending on where one found oneself and with whom, so that it felt a bit like a theater with one set of rules applying to conduct onstage and another set entirely in the wings. Bennie did her best to behave as a welcoming hostess and auspicious future in-law, offering to take the Digginses' raincoats, bringing them drinks, groping to remember what other things she had planned to do (put out cheese and crackers? ask about the drive? show them around the house?), while Walter, true to his nickname, dispensed hearty hugs and handshakes even while being the one to keep dinner progressing as planned, remembering to take the chicken from its marinade and arrange it on rack and pan—they would do it under the broiler this evening instead of grilling out in the rain—and Clem and the Ch/Hannahs materialized with, respectively, shrieks of greeting for Diggs and more dignified niceties for her parents. They looked unabashedly slovenly, with bits of mud and grass stuck to their bare legs, and their hair matted and stringy from various escapades out in the storm. Sometime during all this the roustabouts traipsed in from the barn, Harriett howling like a banshee (it was gratifying to have proof she was a normal baby after all, though the timing of her fussing could have been more felicitous), and then there was Bennie pulling Clem aside, pulling her into the powder room, in fact, because with all the bodies swirling around the downstairs it seemed the only immediate option for discreet communication (*What? Mom!* was Clem's initial piqued response), and there by the sink, with the little shell-shaped guest soaps they never used and that looked unfriendly and pretentious to them both, Bennie told her about Aunt Glad's seeming to have slipped into a kind of *not coma, I wouldn't call it, but something . . .*

no, Clem, I'm not being dramatic, if anything we may be under . . . though I don't think, at her age, more intervention would . . . well anyway: we're just going to wait and see, but I thought you should know.

And poor Mr. and Mrs. Diggins (Keith and Johnetta, they insisted on being called), who beneath their gracious expressions of concern (because of course the Blumenthals didn't, in the end, try to keep it a secret that Clem's great-grandaunt had taken a sudden turn and was lying unwell in the back room) seemed understandably weirded out, said they couldn't possibly stay for dinner (*But we have plenty of food, and we've been so much looking forward to this!*) under the circumstances, but would just finish their drinks and go check in at the Garrison Inn.

Their drinks: white wine with an ice cube for Johnetta, who wore a beige crepe blouse and a shell-pink skirt a few shades lighter than her fingernails; coffee with cream for Keith, who wore an apple-green polo tucked into single-pleated slacks that fell beautifully from his trim waist. For Diggs, water. Diggs looked both ill at ease and stunning in a sleeveless black ribbed body-con dress, silver gladiator sandals, silver bangles. How evident, in this environment, was their foreignness—the Blumenthals' foreignness, that is, their thoroughgoing oddness, not to mention the eccentric ramshackle shabbiness of their home. All three Digginses comported themselves with an elegant economy of motion, a kind of kinesthetic self-control. Not that they were stiff. Johnetta had laid an easy hand on Bennie's arm when the latter, explaining the situation with Aunt Glad, had choked up and gone silent mid-sentence, and the touch had not been perfunctory; on the contrary, the other woman had pressed her fingers really warmly against Bennie's arm. And Keith emitted the extravagant munificence of a certain kind of Christian outreach worker (he did, in fact, Clem would later report, teach Sunday school in addition to coaching a K–1 soccer team)—he asked Tom if he had an opinion about whether the Yankees were going to the Series this year (Tom allowed that he did not), asked Otis how he managed to tell himself apart from his brother (Otis blinked, slack-jawed, until Mantha clued him in: *He's being funny*), and hailed Pim as Little Man (Pim, after a moment's pause, let it be known that the correct appellation was Iron Man).

Diggs herself was quiet. But is that true? No one besides Clem knew her very well; now it was hard to remember whether she'd been more gregarious on those earlier occasions or if this was simply her way. Next to Clem she did seem notably . . . what was the word? Adult. Not only her sartorial élan, but her whole comportment, the way she sat on the gold settee beside Johnetta (in Glad's spot, the family could not help but think), sipping her water and patting her mouth every now and then with one of the red paper cocktail napkins that Mantha, of all people, had remembered to fetch from the kitchen and pass around. Clem, whose fluttering nerviness might have been partly due to seeing for herself Aunt Glad's precipitous decline (after the powder room conference, she slipped into the office only to emerge minutes later red-eyed and strangely excited, as if charged with new, directionless urgency), and partly run-of-the-mill pre-wedding jitters, sat on the floor with her bridesmaids and dispensed for the benefit of her fiancée and future in-laws a rush of breathily patchworked stories about Aunt Glad's life. Was there something more to her disquiet, though? A few times she reached up to grasp Diggs's fingers, Diggs, who only gave her a brief squeeze before removing her hand back to her lap. "I waited for you on the rock at the end of the driveway," Clem whispered at one point, going up on her knees to bring her mouth close to Digg's ear. "That's why I'm all wet!" The smile Diggs gave in acknowledgment struck those who noticed as reserved.

Other family members rotated through, some gathering in the living room to exchange pleasantries with the Digginses, others making their way discreetly into the office; an unspoken consensus having arisen, it seemed, among Glad Erlend's descendants that they would not, while she hovered in her ambiguous state, allow her to be unattended. Lloyd was first to relieve Carrie at Glad's bedside (he was only too happy to have reason not to socialize with the newcomers). Perhaps he was slightly less than grateful when, a little while later, he was relieved by Tom, who was himself replaced in turn by Bennie and Walter, the one leaning back against her husband's chest, the other with his chin lightly touching the side of his wife's head. During this the younger ones drifted in and out, all of them grave of mouth and unnaturally graceful of posture, full of finely meshed respect and curiosity. At some point someone turned on the floor lamp, which cast a warm yellow glow at the foot of the cot. At some other point someone brought in the old pink mohair blanket from the cane chair on the porch and spread it on top of the trapunto coverlet. And at still another point the chicken, forgotten in the oven, set off the smoke alarm and brought Walter running into the kitchen, where he set with a clatter one blackened sheet pan on the floor while he reached to pull out the other, and at this opportune juncture Richard the dog galumphed along, dove with nary a pause to seize in his jaws one burned breast, and fled with it through the porch door. Shortly thereafter the Digginses, Diggs included, shook hands all around and fled through the same.

As did the roustabouts, who—bless their initially unwelcome hearts—embarked on their second pizza run in as many days.

Bennie and Carrie went back into the office to check on Aunt Glad, who lay just as they had left her: eyes closed; hands, patterned lace-like with purple and white, crossed just below her breast. "Like Snow White," said Mantha solemnly. She was sitting at the end of the cot.

"Get down," said Bennie.

"What? I'm not bothering her." But Mantha slid off. Then lingered, placing a hand over one of Aunt Glad's feet beneath the covers.

"Sweetheart, you might be. We don't know." So rare was it for Bennie to say *sweetheart* that tears came to Carrie's eyes.

Otis and Hugh and Pim appeared in the doorway, holding between them the old Parcheesi game whose box depicted an elephant in magnificent robes, with a little throne thing perched high on its back. "Can we play in here?" asked Otis.

Eyes solemn behind his glasses, Hugh said, "We promith to be quiet."

"That's not—" began Bennie, but Carrie stopped her with a look.

"Why not?" she granted the boys. To Bennie, in a private register, "If she is . . . sentient, what could be sweeter than—?" And she indicated the children arranging the game now with great gingerly decorum on the office floor. Their movements held the intentionality of a tea ceremony. And their care was contagious; Mantha sank beside them and asked which color she could be. Pretty soon Ellerby found her way into the room, too, for once not in paparazzi mode but just to play.

And so it came to pass that on the night Aunt Glad at last embarked on the initial part of the journey she had long if disjointedly been anticipating, her youngest descendants were there to see her off.

❀ · 5 · ❀

Episode Five. Friday.

The Day of the Wedding.

Walter's the first one up. Leaving his wife and son in bed (by the time he reaches the door and glances back he sees they have already performed their magic trick of expanding in their sleep to fill the space that so recently accommodated him), he crosses the hall to the bathroom where he pees, flushes, yawns, regards himself blearily in the mirror, stretches his back in the way that has recently become a necessary part of his morning routine, and is uncapping the toothpaste before it hits him what is special about the day. *Clemmy.* The sun has finally risen on the day he knew would come, the day whose beginnings originated with her birth: one of his children is leaving the fold. Little old Clemmy. Who forbade him as she was boarding the bus her first day of kindergarten ever to call her that again. He sees with sudden exactitude how she had turned, halfway up the bus steps, to reprove him. She'd had the physique of a dumpling, been dressed in a yellow corduroy jumper, and as she'd wagged her finger at him for good measure she had given him such a jolt of pleasure and pain as he would not have thought possible.

Not until he takes the toothbrush from his mouth and spits into the old enamel sink does he remember what else is unusual about the day. *Aunt Glad*. He, Bennie, Carrie, and Lloyd had agreed to take turns sitting with her throughout the night. Lloyd, who'd volunteered for the last shift, brought *The Tibetan Book of the Dead*, along with his pillow and sheet, down from the attic and stretched out below her on the braided rug. It was lost on no one that when Lloyd had been orphaned during his last year of high school Aunt Glad had been the one to move in and keep him company. What must that duet have looked like? Walter imagined them as celestial bodies: teenage Lloyd, moody and rangy and newly bereaved, and a younger, more kinetic, more strikingly odd-ball Glad, the two of them slinking and flitting respectively around this old house, aware of each other's presence while sticking, for the most part, to nonintersecting orbital paths.

Squirting shaving cream into his palm, he unnerves himself with the thought that Glad might have slipped away in the night. In a kind of countermove, he then forces himself to think of her alive—more than that, to think of her whole life. To hold in his mind the enormity of one human existence. He contemplates Gladys Erlend. Who just yesterday morning, as he was helping her get settled in the cane chair with a cup of hot tea and the moth-eaten mohair blanket over her lap, had given him grooming advice. "Stalwart," she'd said—he can't remember her ever having used the nickname previously, yet she said it quite naturally, as if it were what she'd always called him—and then continued with her deliberate, beautiful syntax, "I hope you will allow me the liberty of pointing out something I couldn't help but notice, and suspect you may not have." He'd set the teacup and saucer on the wicker table and turned to her, bending at the waist. But she'd beckoned him in even closer, then lowered her voice as if, he'd felt, she wished to avoid causing him undue embarrassment. "You are in need of a haircut." He'd managed to cover his laughter with a bow of thanks.

That had been a high pleasure: Aunt Glad finally deeming him worthy of being the recipient of such intimate, not to say presumptuous, counsel. After so many years of marriage, to be considered family at last.

Lathering his face, he turns his attention to the Digginses. The next new family to commingle with the Erlend line. And rebukes himself: he should have been more hospitable, should have pressed harder for them to stay for supper. Sure, things had been a bit chaotic, but wasn't that one of the signal characteristics of family: being together in messiness as well as in presentability?

Immediately he rebukes himself again: Why focus on their imminent kinship if true hospitality is ungoverned by tribal affinity? He should have pressed for them to stay regardless of clan attachment.

An image floats up before him then: the man from yesterday with the business card and the beard, the big black hat and the long black coat, and the way he'd left on foot when the transaction was finished, the way he'd receded without haste down the drive. Walter lifts his gaze from his foam-covered jaw in the mirror to look himself in the eye. *I should have offered him a glass of water,* he realizes. *I should have given him bread.*

He recalls something Glad—of all people!—said. How strange. Just yesterday morning, after disapproving of his hair. At the time it had made no sense to him and he'd chalked it up to her doddering mind.

"We must have those new people over."

Assuming she was doing her thing of weaving in and out of time, memories of the past leaking into the present, he'd just smiled.

But she'd clutched his arm. "I really feel we should. It is happening, you know."

"What is, Aunt Glad?"

Her deep-set eyes fixed upon him so intently he felt himself blush.

"The—new people?"

Perhaps this satisfied her, for she released him. Then added, inscrutably, "We must always try to embrace reality."

What had she meant by it? he wonders now, drawing the razor across his face. *Reality*. It makes him think of Mantha and her taxonomy of the various forms of life: Past, Future, Dream, Make-Believe, Private, Public, Real, and so on.

Something stirs in the darkness of the hall. Walter snaps his head to look and cuts his cheek. A filament of blood draws itself up through the white foam. It's Richard the dog. His snout nudges the bathroom door wider; his body flows in after. With limpid, licorice eyes he gives Walter a look. Such a look. As if to say, *I do not want for faith that you will treat me well.*

THE LIVING ROOM, when Walter comes down the stairs, holds a slumbering sprawl of roustabouts and bridesmaids cocooned in sleeping bags, having been driven from their tents by last night's rain.

The office, when Walter sticks his head in the door, reveals two more sleepers (really? he lingers to make sure he hears—yes: two distinct beings sketched in breath, a tuneless two-part song).

The world, when Walter opens the back door, is washed with brightness, every still-wet jeweled place touched by the just-up sun kissing back a different color of the visible spectrum. Richard the dog half closes his eyes and does reverence with his nose. Then out he bounds.

AN HOUR LATER BENNIE finds Mantha, already in her flower-girl dress (a daffodilly thing with a satin bodice and tulle skirt she had been allowed to pick out herself), sitting on the edge of Glad's cot eating an ice cream sandwich.

She widens her eyes furiously, shakes her head, and points her finger to the door.

"But Lloyd said—" begins Mantha.

Bennie's pointer moves sharply to her lips.

Mantha hushes, slides off the cot, and steps just outside the office. "But Lloyd said I should stay with her while he went to get ready."

"And did he say you should have that ice cream sandwich?"

"I didn't know how long I was going to be in there!"

"Keep your voice down." They both look, not unhopefully, to see if Aunt Glad has been disturbed by their voices. She has not. Her valise, on the little bench under the windowsill, is still open. The sight of her nightgown, impeccably folded, palest pink *batiste* with buttons to the chin, stops Bennie. Something ascends inside her chest and collects at the base of her throat. She swallows, and forces her attention back to the kid with the contraband breakfast.

"You already got some on your dress."

Mantha looks down at her shiny yellow front, marked now in places with vanilla ice cream and pasty-soft bits of chocolate cookie. She wets her finger and works at the splotches. Succeeds only at grinding the mess deeper in.

"Why are you even wearing that now? The wedding's not till five. I have a million things for you to do between now and then."

Mantha's eyes fill. "Oh, *Mama!*"

Bennie narrows her eyes with professional skepticism. "What?"

"Aunt *Gla-aaa-ad!*" Mantha's lower lip trembles, the tears that had been wobbling in her eyes now flood their banks, and the new drip that has been collecting at the base of her ice cream sandwich plops onto the buttery yellow tulle of her skirt.

"Hm." Either these are the greatest crocodile tears ever or some *there-there*-ing might be in order. Still, Bennie is as Bennie does. First she takes the ice cream sandwich from Mantha's hand, leads Mantha into the kitchen, deposits the melty thing in the trash, and dabs with a wet cloth at the splotches on her dress. Then and only then does she embrace the weeping child, allowing the sob-racked shoulders to convulse against her own burgeoning middle, where new life is developing in its private amniotic sea. *Meet your big sister. Meet your new little something or other.* Bennie makes the silent introduction between Mantha and her tadpole sibling, which is even now engaging in a sustained and awe-inspiring flurry of growth, the measure of which it will never again reach, that it might become viable on land.

To think: all the industry going on within her is silently outstripping all the activity going on without. Bennie knows practically by heart the stages of fetal development. Now is when its wispy limbs are beginning to articulate, its formerly webbed fingers and toes beginning to differentiate and sprout translucent nails; now is the time its tiny kidneys, intestines, brains, and liver are all beginning to function. Oh fig-size life, you who will in seven months emerge to have a name, an identity, and a particular series of adventures (you who will someday in point of fact be known as Glory Aviva Blumenthal, have copious dark curly hair and, at age twelve, an operation for scoliosis; you who will, despite this, become a modern dancer and one summer, while in residence at Jacob's Pillow, fall in love with a puppeteer of Uzbek descent and travel through Central America with him and members of his troupe in a VW bus; you who will, years later, things having soured with the puppeteer, return to the States with your son, attend culinary school, and open a pie shop in Poughkeepsie specializing in late-night delivery to college students; you who will, when your widowed mother at age ninety goes on home hospice care, be the child who moves back in with her for those last nine weeks of her life, managing the schedule of the nurses and aides, administering the medications in the comfort kit yourself; you will by then be forty-five, the very age she was when she had you), oh little soul: for now you remain tenuous, provisional.

Every child she has delivered into this world, Bennie has delivered also into the arms of Aunt Glad, who would move in with them after each birth. The lengths of her stays varied according to her age. With Clem she had stayed the longest, a couple of weeks right at the beginning, when Bennie herself was still so young, and weepy and motherless and untried. How momentous it had been for Bennie to place Clem, still in hospital swaddle, in Glad's arms, and hear her pronounce *Clementine* (in a low, private voice, as if it were a matter strictly between her and the child), *dear little mouse*. How vital, especially in those early days (Walter, still finishing his graduate studies and just beginning to work as a junior research assistant at the Ujima Foundation, had been so rarely at home), to have her great-aunt by her side. Glad had been seventy-two, and helpful in numberless ways. She'd pushed Clem in a pram, let her lie out naked on a blanket in the grass, washed spit-up from sweaters she'd crocheted herself, folded endless onesies, endless darling minute socks. She'd stood shoulder to shoulder with Bennie at the kitchen sink and helped administer Clem's first bath. She'd massaged olive oil onto Clem's scalp and combed gently, patiently, night after night, to remove the cradle cap. And after Bennie's sole attempt to pare Clem's fingernails, when she'd horrified herself by drawing blood, Aunt Glad had taken over manicure duty, abjuring both scissors and clippers in favor of the method she claimed to have used on Bennie's own mother as well as Bennie herself: biting them.

With each successive child she'd stayed a shorter amount of time, yet her presence and participation had remained vital. As the years went by, her repertoire dwindled a bit—she could no longer lift the children or take them places in the car—and the frequency with which they saw her dropped off sharply after she'd moved into the assisted living center over in Fishkill. But for Bennie there continued to be something indispensable in the ritual of setting each of her children for the first time in that same pair of arms, of seeing the bright whisky-colored gaze travel thoroughly, attentively over each new arrival, as if studying, chronicling, and finally blessing each one's inchoate singularity.

Only this fifth child, this last, will never receive her welcome.

Bennie reaches behind her until she connects with the box of tissues on the counter and, one-handed, blows her nose.

"Gross." Mantha pulls away.

"Hey! You're the one rubbing your snot all over my stomach."

"Hardy har har." Mantha wipes her face with her hand.

"Use a tissue," says Bennie. "Better yet, go upstairs and wash your face. And take off that dress and put on something schlumpy. I wasn't kidding about chores."

WALTER IS DEEP in the woods by now. He hadn't intended to take such a long walk—on this of all mornings—but by the time Richard the dog found a place that suited him well enough to deposit his morning excrement they had already passed the gully, at which point he reasoned it made more sense to keep walking until they came to the county road rather than reverse direction. When they do emerge from the trees, he sees they've come farther than he'd thought, all the way to the edge of Garvey's property. It occurs to him that some part of his mind might have led him here on purpose, curious to see up close what the place looks like now with the Haredi family installed. He hustles a little guiltily to cross the field and reach the road, aware that back at the house people must be awake and starting to attend to all the wedding-day details on his wife's little blue lists. Still, he can't help noticing that the yard, which in Garvey's time had been divided into a luxuriant, well-kept lawn and a bountiful vegetable garden, has gone entirely to seed. The aluminum siding is bearded with mildew and one long section of gutter hangs at a precarious diagonal. If not for the banged-up minivan in the driveway, the place would seem abandoned.

"Excuse me."

Walter startles.

A man is standing in the yard. Pale, unmuscled, with a sparse beard and corkscrew *peyos*. Black pants, white button-down. Behind small gold-rimmed glasses, his eyes are gas-jet blue. He's young—couldn't be much older than any of the roustabouts—and barefoot. If not for the tzitzit, the long fringes dangling from the *tallit* under his shirt, and the yarmulke pinned to his blond curls, he might be one of Clem's friends.

"Why are you on my land?" The accent is not quite foreign.

"I'm sorry. I was just taking a walk in the woods with"—Walter, hesitating over the minuscule lie, waves his hand toward Richard— "my dog."

The man's gaze doesn't stray from Walter. In a tone that is neither aggressive nor friendly he repeats, "But why are you on my land?"

There is something uncanny about the question. The man seems too young to refer to the land as his. Or perhaps it's the way he said *land* instead of *property*.

"We—uh, lost our way," Walter begins, then doubles back to clarify: "I'm your neighbor." And corrects himself: "Your neighbor once removed." Is it his subconscious that comes up with an attempt at humor evocative of familial connection? He hastens to explain: "We live on the other side of McElroy's." He gives another little wave, but the gesture—he feels it—comes a beat late, as if he's an amateur actor in a bad play. "I'm Walter Blumenthal," he says, recovering ever so slightly. Surely the other man will recognize the name as Semitic. Walter extends his hand.

"Amos Klein," says the younger man. He pronounces it Ah-*mohs*. His hand in Walter's is like powder. Like the theory of a hand. Then it is gone. Back at his side. "I must ask you not to walk here." He speaks with zero ire, zero apology. "My wife, my children, you understand. They were alarmed."

"I'm sorry." A flare of unaccustomed shame and incredulity. The unaccustomed shame because as a white man in the suburbs Walter hasn't much practice thinking of his appearance as a cause for alarm. The incredulity because this kid already has a wife and children, plural? But he should have expected as much. That's how it works; they marry young, reproduce often. "How many?"

"Yes?" The way he says it—in place of *excuse me?*—again suggests he is a foreigner, someone for whom English is a second language. As of course it is, assuming this man grew up speaking Yiddish at home, Hebrew in shul.

"How many children do you have?"

"Four, thank God. And one on the way."

"Me too!" exclaims Walter. As if this is proof of something. "I also have four and one on the way." He flushes. Until this moment he has told no one about the new baby, respecting Bennie's wish to keep the news private until after the wedding. Now he has taken it upon himself to tell a stranger. Out of a desire he can't account for, a desire to establish fellowship with a man whose interests are almost certainly opposed to his, a man who in all likelihood would vote against a tax override for the schools, who in all likelihood would not support local businesses that stay open on the Sabbath, who in all likelihood would not shake hands or even exchange a *Good morning* with Bennie or any other woman he might pass on the street. A man who in all likelihood regards him, Walter, as *shaygetz*.

The word comes back to him from childhood. *Abomination.* A term for a non-Jewish man, but more pejoratively a term the Haredim applied to Jews like them, like Walter and Myron and even Fiebush, for that matter (never mind that Fiebush was at shul every Friday night, it was the wrong shul). A term for Jews who were insufficiently Jewish. He remembers one time, he'd been sitting behind the counter at Fiebush's reading a comic book. The bell on the door tinkled and he'd glanced up to see a Haredi woman enter with her horde in tow, seven or eight kids in long sleeves, long pants, long skirts. That was not unusual, but what happened next was. Unwritten custom dictated Walter would slide his eyes back down to the comic without offering any kind of greeting or acknowledgment, as indeed no Haredi children ever acknowledged him. But there was one boy among this group who must have been Walter's age—not just his age but in some ineffable way his very likeness—and as if he, too, recognized a similarity, a sameness between them, this boy broke with convention and allowed himself to make eye contact with Walter for long unblinking seconds, long enough for a smile to test itself upon Walter's lips, before the boy turned to one of his younger brothers and whispered that word: *shaygetz*.

Walter looks the young man in the eyes and says with deliberate warmth, "Welcome to the neighborhood."

"*Tate, Mama zagt bite kumin!*" A child's voice, coming from a window. Walter looks up in time to catch a flurry of movement, little bodies scrambling from view.

"You understand," Amos Klein says again, neither courteous nor discourteous, making his meaning clear by sweeping his palm toward the street. As though he has no agency in the matter. As though it is all entirely out of their hands. Each must act in accordance with what he has been taught. Walter does understand.

Amos Klein remains planted there while Walter, after whistling to Richard, makes his way down the drive. Walter feels himself watched as he goes. Much as he stood yesterday, watching the departure of the man who wanted to pay cash for their house. The man he later regretted not having offered a glass of water. A piece of fresh baguette. Not until he reaches the road does he hear behind him the sound of footsteps crossing the porch, the front door creaking open and shut. The sound of vigilance relaxed.

Agitated, even short of breath, for some reason he does not understand, Walter finds himself suddenly questioning whether they should put their house on the market after all. Jeff Greenberg has been sending him links to articles detailing all the myriad problems faced by towns where Haredim live in large numbers. Last night in bed he'd finally clicked on a few, only to become immersed in tales of insurance fraud, tax fraud, social security fraud, food stamp fraud, Medicaid fraud, election fraud, voter harassment. He'd read up on investigations of ultra-Orthodox communities by the FBI, the ACLU, the Office for Civil Rights. Story after story describing how lawyers specializing in religious loopholes help the Haredim drain secular coffers while spurning secular society. Reading on the laptop beside his sleeping wife his insides had roiled: he'd felt sick and sad and righteous and angry and resolute.

All he feels now, walking along the county road in the fat of the June morning, bees lumbering about the wildflowers, gold pollen stains patterning the asphalt where the rain ran in rivulets overnight, is a single desire: to be acceptable. To be seen and recognized as good. *Menschlich.* How he hates being regarded as an intruder, a threat. How intolerable it is—here in his own village! *I meant no harm*—he finds himself formulating this protest in his head, but to whom is it addressed? To Amos Klein? To the unseen wife and children he is supposed to have alarmed? To the elders of Amos Klein's community, the synagogue administrators, the guardians of modesty, the yeshiva teachers, the rebbe? *I pose no threat, I mean no harm.*

But this is not true. His very appearance—his very existence— serves as evidence of the vast world that lies beyond the boundaries of Orthodox life. The Haredim, he knows, brook no Internet use, no television, no exposure to secular thought. If you need a cell phone you have to use a "kosher" one: a phone on which inappropriate content has been blocked. It's not that these things in and of themselves violate halakhic law; it's that more and more, modernity encroaches. The community is living under growing threat of losing members to the allure of life off the *derech*, off the path.

Now he draws even with McElroy's house and the lawn sign so prominently staked: CITIZENS FOR THE PRESERVATION OF RUNDLE JUNCTION. And he thinks: Isn't that the ultimate hubristic banality? The wish to keep things as they are, to triumph over impermanence.

So what if the Haredim do move in en masse, get their own elected to the school board and the village trustees, establish yeshivas and *eruvs*, alter the very character of Rundle Junction? How is that different from the myriad other examples of migration and evolution that make up the history of life on this planet? Before the Haredim, the Erlends. So what? Before the Erlends, the Wappingers. Before the Wappingers, the dinosaurs—and it's not as if anyone sits around saying, *Oh what a shame* Homo sapiens *came along! If only the Mesozoic Era had lasted.*

What was it Glad had told him? Only yesterday morning, gripping his arm. With such queer, startling intensity. *We must always try to embrace reality.*

And what would Bennie say if he came to her now, after all their arduous deliberations, after finally, finally reaching their difficult decision, only to tell her: *I've changed my mind. I don't think we should move after all.* What if he were to say, *Let's stay.* Not in order to dig in with the resistance and push the Haredim out. But because—well because they live here, and life is change, and you can't avoid or outrun change no matter where you go. Or who you are. The Haredim are also going to change, he realizes. They can't not. The point isn't to fight it but to be curious, attentive to, in dialogue with the reality of change, the ever-changing reality. To sing along with it. Help make up new verses.

Walter's a little frightened by the strength of this sudden conviction: that they should remain, should be part of whatever shifts and strife and growth may happen in the community. But the feeling is so much clearer than any he experienced around their earlier decision to leave. He's invigorated, wants to break into a run, wants to go find Bennie and take her by the shoulders, tell her right away: *Listen, listen! I think we should stay.* And will she be mad at him for changing his mind? Probably. And after being angry will she be happy, too, after all, to stay? He doesn't know. In any case, he will keep from saying anything until after the wedding.

Rounding the bend now between McElroy's property and their

own, he stops short. And stares. Hardly able to make sense of what he sees. The immense black walnut, ripped out of the earth, split and prostrate on the lawn.

"WHAT?" BENNIE SHUTS the faucet and yells to Lloyd, who has just yelled something to her on his way through the kitchen.

"I SAID WE'RE GOING TO THE STRIP MALL! TRY TO SCORE SOME MORE UMBRELLAS!"

It is threatening to rain again.

Bennie, loading the dishwasher with the last of the lunch dishes (*That's it*, she announced not ten minutes ago, realizing the wedding is less than three hours hence, *no one eats anything else until after the ceremony*), nods and gives him a thumbs-up. Ellerby, his accomplice, makes sure to photo-document this gesture of approval.

"BUT DON'T DAWDLE!" yells Bennie after them.

Lloyd, halfway through the doorway, turns back. "WHAT?"

"COME STRAIGHT BACK! I NEED YOU!"

He salutes. His accomplice salutes. The door bangs shut.

"WHERE'S LLOYD AND ELLERBY GOING?" Mantha scampers into the kitchen.

"WHAT?"

The question is duly repeated.

"UMBRELLAS!" comes the cryptic reply.

Either Mantha's synecdochical gifts are extraordinary or their destination is beside the point. "CAN I GO WITH THEM?"

"NOT ON YOUR LIFE! I HAVE MORE CHORES FOR YOU!"

Her bottom jaw slides into its trademark sulk. Bennie, stooping to shake soap powder into the little plastic tray, makes a point of not noticing.

"WHATH EVERYONE THOUTING FOR?" Hugh comes in.

"NOTHING!" Mantha gives a casual wave of her cast. "WE'RE JUST YELLING SO WE CAN HEAR!"

"WHAT?"

Bennie turns on the dishwasher, adding a new layer of noise.

Mantha makes an athletic but wholly unsuccessful attempt to communicate through hand gestures, then shouts for good measure, "STUPID CHAIN SAW!!!"

The chain saw is McElroy's. Their dour neighbor, bless his heart, has come to carve some semblance of order out of the severed and toppled black walnut.

When Walter returned from his walk earlier that morning, he'd broken the sad news and everyone had traipsed out en masse to survey the scene. The centuries-old tree had come down sometime during the night, bowing at last to the combined forces of time, soaked earth, and wind. Its trunk had flattened the majority of the metal folding chairs, and its crown splayed its massive reach across almost the entirety of the lawn. The paper lanterns and LED lights that Clem and the Ch/Hannahs had spent half a day hanging were all crushed or lost amid the great fractal labyrinth of branches.

"It's so sad."

"It's so gigantic."

"Is your mom crying?"

"*Cool.* Look at the *roots*."

"It ripped up the whole ground."

"Can we keep it like this?"

"I heard it fall."

"Did not."

"Did too—it woke me up. I thought it was an explosion."

"That tree was like a hundred years old."

"It's older than Aunt Glad!"

"Much."

"It's been here since the Civil War."

"Even longer."

"Since the Revolution?"

"Maybe."

"It's basically a miracle it didn't hit the house."

"Or a tent."

"Or a car."

"Or a person."

"Do you think Aunt Glad knows?"

"Look, your mom *is* crying."

The tree's wrecked anatomy covered so much ground that it did seem little short of miraculous it had managed to avoid so many precious marks. On the other hand, the mark it *had* struck— pretty much the exact footprint of the wedding venue—presented predicament aplenty.

"What," wondered Bennie aloud, "are we going to do now?"

"There must be a tree removal service that would come on short notice?" Carrie suggested, sounding as if she very much doubted it.

"If you explain the reason we need it done today . . ."

"Not just today, but like, ASAP, because even then—"

"What are we going to do about seating? The chairs are toast."

"The chairs are toast! The chairs are toast!" The children, enchanted, took up the cry.

"We should've waited to set them up," opined Lloyd.

"Thank you, Lloyd, that's helpful."

"Maybe Dad knows someone from the village? Like a public works guy?"

"Why does everyone think I have an in with the village officials?"

"Well you do go to all those meetings," said Bennie.

As it happened, Stalwart lived up to his name—though not by calling public works. He had a better idea. Went and knocked on McElroy's door, asked if he might borrow a chain saw.

McElroy twisted his mouth sideways. "Ever use one?"

"Not personally." Only after the words were out did Walter realize how lame this sounded. "I'm familiar with how they work," he added, again realizing a moment too late the unlikeliness of this helping his cause. "I once used a skill saw?"

Such a substantial expectorating sound came from McElroy's throat that Walter seriously considered stepping out of the way. Instead of phlegm, however, McElroy produced only his verdict: "Can't let you borrow it." He shut the screen door, saying, "Give me ten." Not seven minutes later he appeared in their yard decked out in safety visor and steel-toed boots, chain saw in hand.

He's a lifesaver, is McElroy. Or a weddingsaver. And he looked improbably gallant, striding up in all that regalia with his usual saturnine expression.

He's been at it for hours now, long enough for the family to have come up with the name Operation McElroy for what has turned out to be a stroke of genius: as McElroy saws the limbs into logs, the rude mechanicals collect and arrange them into rows upon which the wedding guests can perch. Cut by cut, the dead tree grows smaller and the demolished folding chairs are replaced by the very source of their demolishing.

THEY HAD, OF COURSE, considered whether to go ahead with the wedding or not. All four of the adults who had taken shifts with her through the night believed Aunt Glad was in the process of dying. Walter had never experienced the particular intimacy of accompanying someone through the end of life, but each of the three siblings had been present during their parents' final days—their mother's at home and their father's at the hospice center across the river—and they recognized the signs. Lloyd, who saw her open her eyes and move her hands before her face in the early-morning hours (*Almost like she was folding a piece of cloth, or playing cat's cradle*, he reported), recalled his father also moving his fingers with unhurried absorption through the air before him, as though tracing complex, invisible geometries.

For Bennie it was the breathing—or rather the intervals of apnea during which Aunt Glad drew no breath—that brought back memories of her mother's last twenty-four hours, the arrhythmic respiration that had made a crazy quilt of time, scraps of rattling calico stitched willy-nilly to lengths of plush velvet loosely basted to edgings of broken lace.

During Carrie's watch Aunt Glad had not just awoken but actually spoken. *Who's here?* she suddenly asked.

It's me, your great-niece Carrie, Carrie replied. *I'm right here beside you.* She described to the others how the older woman's face had knitted into a mask of intense concentration then, as if trying not simply to discern but to divine the answer to a compound riddle.

Who else is here? Glad insisted without lifting her head. *Who is that over by the door?*

Carrie had looked. *No one*, she replied. *It's just the two of us.*

And Aunt Glad, after seeming to hang on to her question for several speechless moments, had at last given a small nod and lapsed back into her sleep state.

In the end, they let Clem decide whether to proceed with all the intended festivities or to modify things. She was reached by phone over at the Garrison Inn, where she'd spent the night with Diggs (the brides had intended to spend their final night of singledom apart, but wound up scrapping even this minor and frankly tongue-in-cheek concession to tradition in a wedding otherwise very nearly devoid of any), and apprised of the situation.

"Oh, I'm sure Aunt Glad would want us to go on with everything!" Clem declared without hesitation. Bennie, though wounded by the blithe selfishness she inferred from the speed of Clem's response, nevertheless did not disagree with the verdict. None of them did.

And so it was determined the day would continue as planned.

AT TWO THIRTY, after three and a half hours of work, McElroy switches off his chain saw for the last time, wipes his brow, chugs the glass of lemonade Bennie brings across the lawn, holds out the drained glass for someone to take (Mantha, to her own surprise, steps in), nods, and without further ado hoists his heavy blade and tromps back across the property line. Glistening with sweat and sawdust, wearing his flipped-up safety visor as gloriously as any Greek warrior ever wore his helmet, he inspires not only a chorus of gratitude in his wake but a musical tribute: Dave-Dave runs and grabs his French horn off the front porch and manages to get out the first several bars of "Fanfare for the Common Man" before McElroy, declining to look back but raising his hand in a parsimoniously heroic acknowledgment, reaches his own front door and disappears inside.

Now the sweet ruffians are gathering and tying the last bits of black walnut refuse together with twine. The lawn is starting to look almost orderly. The bent chairs and crushed paper lanterns have been toted out of sight behind the barn. The remains of the black walnut—the massive clump of vegetal viscera resembling nothing so much as a giant earthen heart, a vital organ sculpted of wood and soil, complete with ventricles, atria, branching arterial and venal roots—have become a kind of altar around which the log benches are arranged in concentric rows. The remnants, all the leafy branches too small to be used for seating, are bundled and tucked around the circumference of the new-fashioned amphitheater, and then as a final touch are studded with sparklers: a surprise for when darkness falls.

This is how the setting for the wedding comes to include a spectating area with seats made of wood, ringed by materials known for their flammability.

AND WHERE ARE THE BRIDES? They've taken Diggs's parents' car over to the train station in New Ashkelon, to meet the two forty-five from Grand Central. Unhappily, the two forty-five has come and gone, discharging onto the platform a scant handful of passengers, among whom the person they were expecting did not number. They watch its silver segments grow smaller and smaller and finally disappear around a bend.

"O-kayyyy," says Diggs.

"Where is he?" moans Clem.

"Text him."

"You think he fell asleep?"

"Or just didn't haul ass. How old is he?"

"Mid-eighties? But super-spry."

The parking area has emptied out. Diggs shades her eyes and peers up and down the barren tracks. "Shit."

"Sorry."

"Clem? You've got to stop doing that."

"What?"

"Saying sorry."

"Okay."

"I mean it. You say sorry way too often, and half the time I don't even know what you're saying it for. Hell, half the time *you* don't know what you're saying it for. "

Clem draws breath to protest but it is a knee-jerk reaction, impulse outpacing content, and no words come.

Diggs says, softly, "It's like you're scared all the time."

"Maybe I am. I am."

"Of what?"

"—"

"Me?"

"Displeasing you. Offending you."

"Why? Am I so easily offended?"

"No—I just." But then she cannot think of what else to say.

"Look, Chat. Do you trust me?"

Clem nods.

"Do you trust yourself?"

A more tentative nod.

Diggs laughs.

"What?"

"You should see your face."

Now Clem mugs, pouting exaggeratedly.

But Diggs no more allows her to flee the moment with a comic turn than she allows her to commandeer all the vulnerability in the relationship. "Are we getting married today?" she asks. Very softly. As if really checking.

"Oh Diggs." Clem is flooded with remorse, tenderness, protectiveness, conviction, rededication. Love. "Yes. Yes."

After they finish kissing, Diggs returns to the practical. "He text back yet?"

Clem checks her phone. "No."

And they stand there, Clem trying to look up routes and schedules on her phone, Diggs squinting without much hope into the distance, until she says in a voice riven with disbelief, "Is that him?"

On the other side of the tracks, way down near where the tail end of the train had been stopped, an unlikely figure appears. Bantam-size, moving with sprightly dexterity, it appears to be ambling in their direction. At first, so far away, it's distinguishable mainly by the almost vertical shock of yellowish-white hair. As it draws closer, they begin to make out a fuchsia bow tie, a pair of lilac bell-bottoms. Pastel-blue seersucker jacket. Eyeglasses pinging bits of sunlight at them.

"Leopardi!" yells Clem, waving. "Leopardi!"

"*Cucciolina!*" The figure halts and begins semaphoring madly with both arms.

Diggs directs the scene sotto voce: "Okay, great: you see us, we see you, everybody sees each other. Now keep walking, baby."

As if heeding her instructions, Ignazio Leopardi resumes his progress in their direction with an infusion of vigor and speed (Diggs, alarmed: "You don't actually have to *run* . . ."), all the while beaming, pausing every now and then to wave, as if to remind them he really is on his way, and talking a blue streak (not that they have any idea what he's saying; he's too far away for the words to carry, besides the fact that his speech is interrupted by fits of boisterous coughing, neither of which—the distance or the cough—seems to trouble him in the least). Drawing opposite them at last, he stops, looks both ways like a child crossing the street, and lifting his knees high, tromps across the metal rails.

"*Cucciolina!*" he exclaims in a voice even more laryngitic than usual. "And her inamorata!!" He has to go on tiptoe to reach each of their cheeks with his moist lips, fairly fumigating them with the sooty odor of his Fisherman's Friend cough drops. Then he seizes their hands, unable to contain himself, and, standing between them, swings their arms back and forth. "Welcome, welcome!" he cries.

Clem and even Diggs are laughing helplessly, breathlessly, not without a tinge of hysteria. "But you're the one," Clem manages to point out at last, "who traveled here."

"Yes!" he agrees, his enthusiasm, not to mention his grip on their hands, undiminished. He looks skyward and gives a shake of his cottony mane, as if at the wonder of it all. Or perhaps just at the wonder of himself. "Welcome, me!"

What can one possibly say in such circumstances?

"Welcome," they respond.

The officiant has arrived.

"WHEN ARE WE GOING TO EAT?" A question Otis has put to his mother at least five times already this afternoon.

"Later," she has told him repeatedly. Now she has gone to shower and he addresses his query more generally to anyone who will listen.

"Nobody's eating anything until after the ceremony." Mantha parrots what she has heard her own mother say.

Otis makes a sound of utter wretchedness.

"Don't whine," says Tom.

"I'm not whining."

Tom snickers and Mantha, with triumphal glee, declares, "You just did!"

Otis screams. "I hate it here! I hate all you Blumenthals!"

Tom blows a raspberry.

"My father does, too, you know—that's why he didn't come! He says your sister's a lesbun!"

Tom's mouth forms a giant O.

More or less informatively, Mantha says, "That's not how you pronounce it."

But Otis is past the point of distinguishing information from insult. "I hate you! I hate your whole family!"

"Well," says Mantha. "We hate yours."

Otis's rage rises beyond the recourse of speech. He stomps over to the fridge.

"Don't," warns Tom.

Otis yanks it open. When he turns to give Tom a nyah-nyah look, Mantha throws herself between him and the food.

What is he to do then but shove the heavy door against her, knocking her into the racks. She clubs him with her cast. Tom rushes to intervene and moments later all three are sprawled on the ground, along with a bottle of ketchup, a dozen eggs, a basket of blackberries, and a carton of milk, seeping tranquilly across the kitchen floor.

THE COMMOTION REACHES Bennie at Aunt Glad's bedside, and Walter coming down the stairs. Hearing his tread, she calls softly, "Stalwart?" and he comes to the door of the office.

Even now she can get brought up short by his handsomeness. He's always sharp in his navy suit, which he's paired today with his special-occasion tie, splashed with pink and yellow flowers. "You look like you're about to host the Oscars."

He appraises her, still in T-shirt and jeans. "You look like you're about to—"

"Don't say it."

A soundless laugh blooms at the corners of his eyes.

"Do you know what that's all about in the kitchen?"

They listen, but the ruckus has subsided.

"Shall I investigate?"

She shrugs. "Nah. Hey, have you seen any sign of Clem?"

"Yeah, they finally just got back from the train a little while ago—she and Diggs and her old theater professor, Leonardi, Leopardavinci, something? Listen, have you seen her ring?"

"What ring?"

"She says she's missing the ring she bought Diggs."

"For the wedding?"

"An opal."

"I haven't seen it. Not that I knew about it. Not that she bothered mentioning it to me. But with all the tents and the sleeping bags and the rain and the moving around, I'm sure—"

"Yeah, I said basically the same thing. We'll keep an eye out."

"Fine. Meanwhile, I'm going to go change, so will you keep an ear out? For Aunt Glad, I mean. In case . . . ?"

They both look over. At this hour a kind of lemonade light streams in the office window, pouring libations over the lower half of the cot and illuminating the gold-speck constellations revolving above. Glad looks smaller than ever under the wispy pink mohair, aglow like spun sugar in the sun. She looks not simply reduced but somehow concentrated, as if all that has evanesced was superfluity, while all that remains is essence.

"Has she been awake at all with you?"

Bennie shakes her head no. "I don't think someone has to be in the room with her every second, but—"

"Yeah, no, Ben. You go." Walter sits. "I'll be here."

NO SOONER HAS Bennie gone than the guests start to arrive, first in a trickle, then in a stream; now in cars snaking up the driveway, now in cars clogging the driveway, until they can be Tetrised into spaces along the periphery of the lawn one by one by Tom. Only too glad to extricate himself from the kitchen (everyone in the clash of cousin against cousin had ended up feeling a similar shamed remorse), he'd flung himself into the role of parking attendant unbidden and unrehearsed. He's proving quite a natural. Lanky, bare-chested (having shed his button-down in the late-afternoon heat) and chewing a long stalk of wild onion grass, he guides drivers into space-saving, geometrically intricate and (as will become evident only at the end of the party) well-nigh-impossible-to-back-out-of slots.

They arrive, the guests, in dribs and drabs and then all at once, accruing in the yard and on the porch and in the house, kitted out in a miscellany of long dresses and Converse high-tops, of miniskirts and tuxedo jackets, of lace mantillas and porkpie hats, of kilts and harem pants and army boots and feath-ered mules. They come almost to a one bearing covered dishes (so Clem had been neither disingenuous nor delusional when she'd claimed to have the food under control), which, at a glance, run the gamut from the crudest of crudités and supermarket hummus to more eclectic contributions (tubs of yogurt, bags of homemade horehound lollipops, a pot of plain brown rice, a whole watermelon) to the truly culinarily grandiloquent: some-one made a mocha *marjolaine* and someone else a towering *cro-quembouche*.

They bring not only vittles but bottles of wine and brightly wrapped gifts, also knapsacks and musical instruments and camping chairs and bedrolls. More than a few come toting what look suspi-ciously like tents. More than a few come with four-legged plus-ones—no one ever gets an accurate count, but at least five or six dogs seem to be loose around the place, not including Richard, who wel-comes the newcomers with the magnanimity of one whose preemi-nence is beyond dispute; he spends the rest of the evening monitoring the pack with benign but unassailable authority.

Walter, replaced at Aunt Glad's side by Carrie, steps out onto the lawn, ever the emcee. Pinned to the lapel of his jacket now is a sprig of fresh myrtle. "From Clem," he tells everyone who com-pliments him. He'd been surprised and touched when she'd ap-proached him, in a halter dress of palest green, matching the tiny peridot in her nostril, to pin it on his lapel herself—and only slightly deflated when he saw the foppish old fellow with her (*You remember my adviser, Leopardi?*) already sporting its twin. Or its sextuplet, as it happened, for she has similarly provided for her father-in-law-to-be, and Lloyd, Tom, and Pim. ("What do you want me to do, stick it behind my ear?" the still-shirtless Tom offers when she tracks him down. "In your teeth," she counters, "like Carmen." "Oh go clothe your naked villainy," advises Hannah, coming up and draping an arm over Clem's shoulder, silently commending herself for managing to flirt with two Blumenthals—the puckish adolescent and his Shakespeare-loving sister—at one go. "Give it to Otis," decides Tom. "Tell him it's from me. Peace offering.") Now Walter strides about, big and handsome with his silver mane and sonorous voice, hailing friends and strangers alike, shaking hands with one and all.

Diggs, for her part, has gotten matching corsages for Johnetta, Bennie, Carrie, Mantha, and Aunt Glad. ("Aunt Glad," Clem breathes, removing the final corsage from its plastic clamshell, then turns to Diggs, her eyes wetly shining. "You never even got to meet her.") They consider bringing it into the office and laying it where Aunt Glad might spot it if she opens her eyes, but just then they notice Ellerby lurking shyly at the end of the porch, and Diggs kneels before the slender brown girl in green cowboy boots. "This is yours," she says, sliding the elastic band onto her wrist.

Ellerby, finding it itchy, transfers it as soon as Diggs is out of sight to the ankle of one of her boots. Mantha, declaring hers itchy, too, transfers it from her naked wrist to the one with the cast. Feeling resplendent in her daffodil tulle (never mind that it's speckled now not only with remnants of ice cream sandwich but with a medley of blackberry and ketchup stains as well), she has commandeered one of the card tables set up on the lawn and turned it into a satellite post office branch. Arrayed before her are the familiar props: pens, pencils, paper, scissors, tape, glue, glitter, feathers, stickers. Through a paper bullhorn she tries to drum up business. "Step right up to the Nuptial Post! Come write a letter to the happy couple! Free of charge! Delivery included!" Beside her, the wicker wastepaper basket from her bedroom masquerades as a mailbox.

"How does this work, exactly?" inquires a prospective customer, and when Mantha sees who it is she is overcome.

"Mom! You're so pretty!"

"Lipstick. Try sounding less shocked." But she is pleased all the same, even more so when Mantha, unable to contain herself, flings both arms around her.

LLOYD LOOSENS HIS TIE, kicks off his shoes, and relaxes on the office floor. He couldn't be happier to have won the position of designated companion to Aunt Glad during the ceremony. For one thing, it excuses him from having to witness the exchange of vows, which would have been uncomfortable not, as his sisters might suspect, because he's opposed to the codification of human relationship, but because he himself failed in his one attempt at marriage and it still hurts. For another, remaining here with Aunt Glad offers something close to solitude, a thing he's accustomed to quaffing in large doses and of which he's been deprived these past several days. He reclines against the wall and finds an almost sensuous pleasure in the cool, hard plaster on his back and head. All about him the house crackles with vacancy, is fairly animated by it, that particular heightened sense of vacancy that derives from knowing everybody else is gathered out of doors.

The wedding has begun.

Even tucked away at the back of the house, Lloyd can hear its official commencement: Dave-Dave playing "Here Comes the

Sun" on his French horn. Now he watches as the other roustabouts convey from the barn three long banners of brown butcher paper. He can just make out the hand-painted script through the office window as the young people process toward the amphitheater:

WEDDINGS:

A WITHERING CRITIQUE OR,

AN ODE TO UNFETTERED LOVE

· · ·

A PAGEANT IN FIVE EPISODES

He can tell they have reached their destination by the sound, moments later, of what strikes him as tentative laughter from those assembled. Himself, he grins. When the next generation does not fear offending the previous one, he thinks, this bodes well for the species. Not only that: it's the ultimate tribute. The children's way of telling their elders, *Behold your success. You raised us to be free.*

OUT ON THE LAWN the wedding is unfurling with much the same effect as the banners themselves—that is, eliciting from those gathered a mixture of insult and indulgence, curiosity and amusement, and an expectation of pleasure increasingly surmounted by niggling dread.

The first "episode," proclaimed as such by yet another banner, bears the title "Chattel Bride" and involves a perplexing but evidently intended-to-be-funny skit in which Hannah, costumed in a derby hat, kipper tie, and Oliver Hardy mustache, holds up an old metal birdcage (pilfered from the barn) on whose dangling perch has been glued a plastic figurine of a bride, and Chana, wearing a white terry-cloth bathrobe and a long white beard made out of cotton balls, scrambles up the aluminum ladder, now decorated with cardboard cumulus clouds. ("Ith that thuppothed to be God?" asks Hugh. "Shh," whispers his mother, who is wondering the same thing.) There is some dialogue between the two, which does indeed having a biblical ring ("She is my goods, my chattels; she is my house, my household stuff, my field, my barn, my ox, my ass, my any thing!" cries Hannah, spluttering a little to get the mustache hairs out of her mouth; meanwhile the false beard renders Chana's lines largely unintelligible), and then the roustabouts shout, from upstage, "Release the chattel bride!" whereupon Hannah opens the birdcage, removes the cake-decoration bride, and flings it, à la bouquet, into the audience. Tom catches it and promptly tucks it in his breast pocket, in lieu of the boutonniere he bequeathed to Otis. With many blown kisses then and an abundance of ornate bows, the Ch/Hannahs exit the stage.

The second episode, "The Ghost Bride," alters the tone radically. Guests, seated on log benches that only yesterday were part of a single towering organism, crane around as a new sound, woody and aching, floats through the air from behind them. Dave-Dave has vanished and in his place stands Maya, playing a Chinese folk melody on a bamboo flute. Heads swivel back the other way as a stilt-walker approaches, all in white, its identity concealed by a featureless mask that closer inspection reveals to be a paper plate. Upon reaching the front of the amphitheater, it executes a deep curtsy and everyone can see it is wearing wings made of wire and netting, decorated with real flowers and paper butterflies. ("Is that supposed to be a ghost?" asks Otis. "Shh," whispers his mother. "It's an angel." But on her other side Hugh says, "It'th Aunt Glad," and those seated nearby see in their minds the powder room photo: the girl in the wagon on her way to the pageant as a Fairy Attendant Upon the Hours.)

LEAH HAGER COHEN

In stylized slow motion, with the strains of the bamboo flute wheeling and threading like birds on currents of air, the figure does a dance that—although the movements could not be simpler, the round white face no more expressionless—makes gooseflesh rise on the arms of those who watch. As the last prolonged note dies, the figure bends in another curtsy and this time draws up the hem of her long white dress. The outer layer is gauze, and when she raises it up, all the way up to cover her face, it becomes both shroud and bridal veil. When she gathers up the underskirts, too, tucking them in at her waist and thereby exposing the long wooden sticks to which her legs are bound, they appear entwined, swallowed, consumed by flames of red and copper foil.

Now the bamboo flute emits a series of birdlike pips, and the figure becomes alert, searching hither and thither, until she appears to spot what she seeks. She extends both arms toward—the audience turns to see—a second stilt-walker, approaching from across the meadow. This one is all in black, even its mask, and it runs, actually *runs* through the tall grass on its spindly limbs, shockingly precarious and shockingly light. The guests suck in their breath. Upon reaching the outer row of ringed benches, the black figure stops—it is somehow unmistakably a suitor—reaches into the pocket of its under-any-other-circumstances-comically-long pants and produces from it an outsize jewel box, which he holds out toward the white, winged figure, opening it to reveal not a ring but a fiery sunflower. The ghost bride, for surely that is who she is, presses together her palms—delicate and mortal, almost piteous relative to her overall stature—and in that prayerful posture, proceeds down the middle aisle to receive the burning helianthus, which she presses to her breast.

Now the bamboo flute resumes, and the stilt-walkers stride away hand in hand, lifting their impossible legs over the high grass with stick-insect grace.

"IS IT OVER?" asks Lloyd, for Bennie has come into the room, but she says, "No . . . no," and then just stands there, looking at Glad with a stricken expression.

"Are you okay?" asks Lloyd, but she says, "No . . . yes," and then just continues to regard, with more naked emotion than he is accustomed to seeing on his sister's face, their great-aunt.

"Why aren't you out there?" asks Lloyd, and only now does she really seem to notice him, sprawled on the floor in sock feet, his necktie resting across his lap.

"This"—a sip of air, a shake of her head—"is a very weird wedding." She joins him on the floor. "I think they just acted out kind of like a memorial, or—a *wedding*, actually—for Aunt Glad."

He must wait while she regains control of her voice, then he listens as she recounts the details of "The Ghost Bride."

"That's a real thing, you know, in China," he says. "Marrying off the souls of the dead."

"I know, I remember. That course Clem took. Critique of the Marriage-Industrial Complex or something. She said it's how women who don't want a husband can avoid it. Get married to a dead guy."

"Maybe," says Lloyd. "I thought it was so unmarried souls don't have to be lonely. To give them peace."

"Do you think Aunt Glad was lonely?"

They both mark her use of the past tense.

Softly he answers, "I don't know anyone who's not."

Together they look up at the cot. So slight is the mass occupying it that from their angle it could be uninhabited, if not for the faint sound of a breath expelled. Together they listen. With all their being they listen. Until, after a longish interval, it is followed by the sound of a new inhalation.

Bennie, surprising herself, says, "I'm pregnant."

Lloyd, surprising them both, turns and kisses her on the temple.

OUTSIDE THE GUESTS are being entertained—or if not entertained, then edified—or if not edified, then bemused—by Episode Three: "Jumping the Broom," another shift in tone.

The whole gang is involved in this one. First the Ch/Hannahs plunk a couple of apple crates center stage, upon which Banjo and Val rest a large wooden frame displaying a paper scroll with a painting of a broom. As they crank handles on either side, the image of the broom travels off to the right and a painting of a globe inches in from the left. Meanwhile Dave-Dave narrates through a bullhorn in the dramatic baritone of an old newsreel. *The origins of the custom called Jumping the Broom have been the subject of much cultural dispute.* As the low-tech slide show illustrates his points, he gives a brief history of various similar rites found among the Romany, the Welsh, the Asante people of West Africa, and enslaved people on antebellum plantations in the southern part of the United States. Then Maya comes forth and with a twirl, deposits an antique broomcorn besom (this, too, pilfered from the barn) on the ground in front of the wooden frame. The roustabouts all insert kazoos in their mouths and razzily hum, *Here comes the bride.*

There is a ripping sound—the brown paper scroll is slashed from behind—and Clem and Diggs leap through the opening, jumping over the broom and landing with a smack. Much clapping, cheering, stomping, whistling, hooting, and catcalling ensues.

Episode Four: "The Act Itself," announces the next banner. Now the roustabouts depart the playing area, clearing away all props and scenery as they go so that the happy couple remains alone against the backdrop of the epic, calamitous uprooted stump of the ancient black walnut. Still holding hands, visibly breathless and visibly happy, they appear in the brilliance of the solstice's long golden light to be nearly fluorescing. Ellerby, knowing a photo op when she sees one, stands on her log and lifts her invisible camera to her eyes.

Mantha also rises. Catching her sister's eye, she points at her own chest and mouths, *Now?* Clem nods and Mantha gathers the froth of her flower-girl dress in the manner of ladies in olden-time movies (a move she has been practicing lo these many weeks) and sweeps toward the back of the amphitheater where her basket of wildflowers, gathered that afternoon in McElroy's field, awaits. At the same time, a little musical combo arranges itself on the lawn beside the stage. It consists of Dave-Dave, Banjo, Maya, Val, and Chana, armed respectively with French horn, ukulele, bamboo flute, claves, and concertina. Anyone wondering how this idiosyncratic mishmash of instruments will sound will have to wait, however, for the ensemble, once prepped, remains silent, evidently awaiting some cue yet to come. People begin looking around, shifting their bottoms on the log benches that are beginning to register as less than ergonomically ideal.

And still the wedding fails to progress. Not only the audience but also the betrothed are now craning in all directions and engaging in murmured consultation. The musicians raise their eyebrows inquisitively; the flower girl can be heard wondering to no one in particular what the heck is going on; the brides look frankly concerned; the guests smile with forbearance all around. If their thoughts could be aggregated and distilled, here is what they might sound like: *We are with you, don't you worry . . . oh how we are with you . . . more than you realize, more than you can know . . . do not worry about us; we don't mind the mishap, and after all there will be so many mishaps, so many moments such as this and many far worse . . . even if you believe it, even if you believe in the idea of it, the idea of mishaps and of soldiering through, even if you believe all it takes is remaining—remaining in place, in conversation, in communion, unswerving, still—you don't yet know what it means (how could you? when only time can teach us, when nothing but experience— those tiny bits and pieces that by themselves are nothing and that in sum compose a life—when only this can grant such knowledge, this and nothing else—no amount of intellect, no amount of imagination, preparation, study, faith), you cannot yet know these things because you are babies both of you, never mind your senior thesis, never mind your LSAT; you are not really so different from Harriett either of you, Harriett whose milk-blue veins show through the lantern of her skin, Harriett whose diamond-shaped fontanelle pulsates between the bones of her still-forming skull, Harriett whose open toothless mouth sucks avidly now on Carrie's pinkie knuckle; you, like her, are so new still and wide open to everything, to drinking in your unknown future even as you fall farther and farther away from the memory of wherever it was you left, the memory of the time or place that came before (or the no-place that came before, the nameless, placeless, timeless soup of something-that-is-not-nothingness), even as you fall farther and farther away from the ancestral memories you came into this world somehow bearing—like a yellowed letter written in a forgotten alphabet—these memories you came bearing in strands of nucleotides and in dream symbology: stowaway memories of love, of death, of fire, of celebration, of forced migration and emancipation, of ghettos and shtetls, of calendars that follow the moon and calendars that follow the sun, of singed feathers and wooden boats, of train stations and oceanic undulations, of cherry blossoms and fear . . . you are—we can see it in your eyes, in your glowing faces, in the shininess that is part flop sweat, part elation; we can sense it in the air of mischief and impatience, of luminous expectation rolling off you like fragrance—you are still newly hungry, both of you; like Harriett you are ready to put everything in your mouth, to learn its character by gumming it, licking it, and biting down, and we forgive you your beautiful foolishness as we forgive ourselves our disenchantments and our longing; we bless you both and bless every scrap of sadness and happiness you have yet to encounter.*

And if there is such a thing as a wedding, if the act of "wedding" exists in any way beyond pure abstraction, if it could be thought of as an active verb, a concrete force or occurrence, then does this spontaneous, unspoken benediction, conceived collectively and received unknowingly by the lovers under the invisible fermata created by human error, by a glitch in timing, by (not to put too fine a point on it) Leopardi's letting himself doze on the porch while awaiting his entrance—does this constitute the moment their union is sacralized?

It is true that by the time Leopardi makes his way to the amphitheater, seersucker jacket accidentally left draped over the back of the cane chair so that not only his rainbow suspenders but also his half-moons of armpit perspiration show, wiping a bit of spittle from his chin, there is a sense that the climactic moment—"the act itself," as the banner put it—has already occurred, so that whatever Leopardi's role in the ceremony may be (look what a to-do he is making now, positioning himself smack between the couple, where he grins a bit wildly up at each bride in turn, then grants himself license to bodily rearrange them so that he is not upstaged) is of little consequence.

At last the Ch/Hannahs hoist their homemade chuppah, and while the guests shift on their makeshift benches (how patient they have been, how tolerant of all the shenanigans, but now they are bent on standing and stretching, moving into the shade, quenching their thirst, and heaping their plates), Leopardi goes on at immodest length, making some kind of nuptial remarks that no one can follow thanks to the dual impediments of laryngitis and the fact that he is, frankly, bonkers, and his speech would make little sense even if they had access to a transcript. Apparently it's very witty, if the fact that he keeps cracking himself up is any indication. The sun, even as it continues its flaming descent, swells and intensifies, its own color growing more deeply yolky as it ignites a riotous palette of pigment across the residual tatters of cloud. It drops another notch and each stalk of grass in McElroy's field is illuminated like a glass rod, while the insects arcing above the grass become lit en masse like so many flecks of spume above a cresting wave.

At last Leopardi finishes his treatise. He directs the brides to kiss and a smattering of applause breaks out. Then, on the reasonable assumption that the official joining is complete, the guests rise, clapping, cheering, whistling, hooting.

"Wait, wait!" Leopardi roars, though it comes out as a rusty mew. He waves his arms overhead in a canceling motion, calling off the ovation. "It's not over! Be quiet!" he entreats. "There is still more!"

The final banner is raised.

EPISODE FIVE: "UNFETTERED LOVE"

"BEN, YOU BETTER COME." Walter stands in the doorway, absorbing the tableau of his wife and his brother-in-law sitting on the floor, shoeless, lolling against the wall, bottles in hand. Bennie's, he sees, is root beer; nevertheless. "What are you doing in here, anyway? Why did you leave?"

Bennie flushes. Right. As she'd left, she did whisper to him, "Going to check on Glad," but clearly she has overstayed. "I got— I was a little overcome. I wanted—I just needed to see Aunt Glad. Did I—? Shoot." Scrambling up, smoothing her dress. "Did I miss the—is it over?" Talking fast, compensating for the guilt that is taking hold. "It just seemed like it was going on and on. And on." She laughs and instantly stifles it: how snide she sounds. Using Walter's arm to brace herself while she slips her feet back into sandals, she steals a glance at his face. He's granite-jawed. Contrition knits her into its corrective corset. "Oh Stalwart, did I miss it? That's terrible. I didn't mean to stay away so long."

"You must have meant it," he says. "On some level."

Her neck grows warm. "I didn't." But she sounds like Pim, denying getting into the candy jar with chocolate all over his chin. "I really didn't do it on purpose. I lost track of time." How unconvincing that sounds. "I may not be thrilled with the way Clem's orchestrated everything, but truly—I didn't mean to miss her wedding."

"Well." He still bears a residual glower, but his tone is less severe. "You didn't, exactly."

"What do you mean?"

Walter fills them in.

Leopardi, despite having enthusiastically agreed over the phone to Clem's outline for the final episode, "Unfettered Love" (it was to have involved a pair of intricately hand-carved marionettes they'd come across in the barn; he would be the puppeteer, but a bumbling one; the strings would become entangled and need to be cut, at which point the brides would step in and, in a sort of variation on cat's cradle, weave the strings into a fine, airy bridge suspended between them), had taken the prerogative of changing his mind. As he proclaimed, with laryngitic, self-adoring exuberance, he'd dispensed with the script entirely in order to reveal the *regalo stupendo* he'd decided to give the couple. *Ahem!* (He'd actually pronounced the word *ahem*, Walter says, as if under the impression it was English for *May I please have your utmost attention.*) While completing the online application to become a Universal

Life minister so that he could legally perform the ceremony, he'd experienced an epiphany.

"And what epiphany was that?" Bennie inquires.

An epiphany that caused him to realize that the greatest gift he could give was not to help them tie the knot, but to leave them *meravigliosamente* unknotted! Therefore he had mercifully, providentially, and very cleverly never completed the application but exited the program without entering his credit card information, and was therefore now thrilled and honored to be able to assure one and all that his role as officiant this day was entirely symbolic! Thus leaving the *care ragazze* free to enjoy *sinceramente vero* unfettered love! Upon which, after a protracted moment of stunned silence all around, Clem had let out a choked sound and fled the amphitheater, stumbling, her hands hiding her face, up the aisle and across the meadow toward the little encampment, where she'd zippered herself into the orange tent.

"That fucker," says Bennie.

"You should go to her, Ben."

"Yes." She starts out of the room, doubles back, takes him by the lapels, and kisses him on the mouth. "Stalwart."

IN THE AFTERMATH of the non-wedding wedding (obvious echoes of This Is Not A Theater Collective, a parallel her friends tactfully refrain from pointing out to its chief architect, also its chief disappointee), the startled guests behave with spontaneous, uniform gallantry. They pitch in to expedite the serving of food—peeling foil off trays, lighting Sterno, whisking cold items from coolers—while chatting one another up with concerted good humor, avoiding all critiques and analyses of the unconventional ceremony and its even more unconventional finale. Walter invites Keith and Johnetta Diggins into the relative privacy of the living room, where he pours them each a scotch and they all digest what just happened—or more to the point, what didn't. The roustabouts ferry the props and scenery back to the barn, and even Leopardi is rescued from the glare of ignominy (not that he's in need of rescue, appearing wholly unabashed) by a squadron of his most devoted alumni, for whom no outrageousness in the name of art could be too much.

For her part, Bennie stands sentry, positioning herself outside the orange tent in which both brides have taken respite, itself encircled by other tents, which together comprise a little enclave not unlike the one in which she first encountered Stalwart on a frosty morning a quarter century ago, brewing coffee in the dark. Her cause today is less global, perhaps, than his had been, but she feels no less ferocious about pursuing it: defending the fragile bond between the lovers (for what bond constructed of love isn't fragile?) by guarding their privacy as they suture this Leopardi-inflicted laceration. She assigns herself the task of keeping well-meaning intruders at bay. It isn't lost on her that she herself is now a member of that camp. She, who had once been closer to Clem than any other human being, she whose very body had been Clem's dwelling place, the incubator of Clem's becoming; she who had been not only mother but motherland, is now relegated to defending the periphery. A role she takes up gladly in the wake of the bungled wedding. And with what noble humility, what wise restraint does she stand outside the closed flaps of the tent. (From whence it is hardly her fault she can overhear the voices within.)

Ah, Chat . . . How can you kiss me? . . . Yes it is . . . it is my fault, it was my idea—ridiculous—to ask him . . . I'm sorry I'm sorry I'm sorry . . . I know, but it won't be the same . . . God, your parents must really love me now . . . It's mostly Clem's words she can discern, whether because she knows Clem's voice better or because Clem in her emotional state is simply louder. Diggs's voice comes through as a plush murmur, intervals of rumbles trading off with Clem's chimes of distress. *What do you mean I asked for it? . . . You think this is what I wanted? . . . Anyway how come you're so calm? Anyone would think you didn't actually want to get married . . . Chat! Is that supposed to be funny? . . . No, now I'm upset for real! Why would you say that? . . . don't tease . . . don't call me cracker, pudding . . . you heard me, Kozy Shack . . . oh . . .* Silence, then laughter, then silence again, then a deeper silence ribboned with hints of movement, rustling fabric, the metallic harrumph of a zipper, the hiss of whispers, the click of lips . . . until embarrassment wins out over maternal longing and maternal prurience, and Bennie moves several yards away.

"Avast," she says.

Pim, in a soldierly mood, is marching toward the tent.

Blocking his way: "We're not going in there, bud."

"But I have to deliver something."

Thinking he must mean letters from Mantha's Nuptial Post, she begins, "Not right now you don't—" but cuts herself off, for on the flat of his hand he is holding forth a small black velvet box. "What do you have there?"

"The crown jewel."

She narrows her eyes at him, swipes it, and peers inside: an opal ring. "William Myron Erlend Blumenthal!"

Miraculously, he manages to forestall whatever censure she may be about to deliver with nothing but his impeccably martial bearing. Not only that, his manner is sufficiently impressive that when he holds out his palm once more she actually returns the box to him and steps aside, allowing him to continue on his way to the tent, at whose ramparts he calls, "Madam!"

From within, rustlings and shushings.

"Madam!" He issues his summons again. "Important news!"

The zipper is lowered, the little box deposited through the

flap, and after several moments the beneficiary's head emerges, hair mussed. "You little brat!" says Clem.

A dignified blink. "I porridged it."

"What does that mean? You're a thief!"

Pim bows. "My lady." And judging this an opportune moment to take his leave, he turns and high-steps in the direction of the party.

Clem, spotting Bennie, slips fully out of the tent. "Did you see that?" she demands. "I can't believe—he must have snuck in and taken it right out of my—" And then with no transition at all she cries, "Mommy!" a name she has not used in who knows how many years, and buries her face in Bennie's neck. "I'm so sorry," she cries. "I'm sorry," over and over on an anguished loop while Bennie holds her, while Bennie luxuriates in the opportunity to hold her, this girl, this inimical, impossible, beloved eldest child, this turncoat who is betraying her, betraying her whole family, as all healthy children one day do, by leaving home. "Shh," says Bennie. "You have to stop saying you're sorry."

Clem gives a teary laugh. "That's what Diggs says."

Bennie, looking over Clem's shoulder, catches the eye of her all-but-in-law daughter-in-law, also now emerged from the tent, her own hair mussed, her own lips softly swollen, wearing on her left ring finger the opal ring. The two of them exchange a smile. "In that case," says Bennie, and gives Clem a look that completes the thought: *Need I say more?*

"Oh, but Mom! I *am* sorry—sorry I haven't been very nice, and sorry about all the tents and not telling you how many people were coming and acting like you were uptight for wanting to know, and I'm sorry I didn't manage this whole wedding very well, you were right, in the end it was, it *was*—just a stupid show. A stupid, botched, make-believe, amateur . . ." Weeping takes over again.

"Clem," says Bennie, stern now. She puts her hands on her daughter's shoulders. "Open your eyes. Listen. You know something? *All* weddings are just a show. *All* weddings are amateur." She gives her a little shake. "Marriage is what's real. Weddings are just pageantry." She laughs. "Did you hear what I just said? Pageantry, Clem! You got it exactly right."

"LOOK," says Otis. "Amish."

It's a half hour later. Guests are milling round, sitting on the lawn, balancing paper plates on palms and laps. Otis has been playing Revolutionary War Spies down along the driveway with Pim and Hugh, but now he comes running up to joggle his mother's arm—"Look!"—and point out the cluster of men in long black coats and round fur hats passing along the edge of the lawn.

"Shh," says Carrie, transferring her cup to the other hand and checking to see whether any red wine spilled on her dress.

"Why do I have to be quiet? The ceremony's over."

"Because it's impolite. Anyway they're not Amish."

"What are they then?" asks Hugh. He and Pim have come up to log their official reports alongside Otis's.

"Black hats," says Pim.

"What are they really, Mom?"

Carrie lowers her voice. "Jews."

"I'm a Jew." Mantha of the uncanny hearing wanders over, eating a piece of watermelon. "What are you guys talking about?"

The boys point.

Now they can see, along the far side of the road, a second cluster, this one comprising women and girls in long sleeves and dark stockings below their skirts. A few push strollers.

"Oh," says Mantha. "Not *that* kind."

"Hold this." Ellerby hands Mantha her watermelon. "I want to get a picture."

Mantha rolls her eyes but accepts the watermelon. "Hey Dad," she calls. Walter stands nearby, carrying on a conversation with Keith Diggins. "Hey Dad, look—it's those ones you've been talking about."

Both men turn with their plates of ribs and follow the sight of the Haredim processing slowly along the road. The sun is sinking rapidly now toward the horizon and the air is cooling, turning lavender.

"Where are they going?" asks Mantha.

"To sound the alert," says Pim. "One if by land, two if by sea."

"Where are they really going, Dad?"

To the old Garvey house, he supposes. Then corrects himself: to the house of Amos Klein.

Aloud he says, "It's the Sabbath. They must be gathering to pray." To Diggs's father he says, "This is new here, the uh, establishment of an ultra-Orthodox community in Rundle Junction."

Keith, sucking barbecue sauce from his fingers, nods. "We have the same thing. With Muslims. On our street alone we have a few. There's an Iraqi family down the block. They've lived there, must be three years now."

Johnetta comes over and hands him a napkin. "The Khouris are from Iran."

Keith accepts both the napkin and the correction. "And now a young couple from Yemen just bought the place across the street."

"They have the cutest little boy," says Johnetta. "Eyelashes out to here."

Walter watches the men round the bend. In a moment, he knows, they'll draw even with McElroy's lawn sign. He entertains a fantasy of running ahead and ripping it out of the earth before they see it. Not that they are likely to be shocked. Not that they are unversed in the experience of being unwelcome. They vanish from sight, the bottoms of their long black coats belling slightly in the evening breeze. How many such signs have they encountered? And their ancestors, how many did they encounter? Over the generations, over the centuries. Winding back through the branches of history to where their roots and his are one.

"They look so old-fashioned," says Mantha.

But they're the future, thinks Walter. *The immediate future of this place. And also its temporary future. All futures being no more than temporary.*

Twenty feet away, Lloyd brings his plate of food over to join Bennie on the sagging front steps, those ancient treads leading to the front door no one uses, the door whose broken bell has not trilled in decades. This is not to say the steps have no function. At this very moment they are providing a roof, a shelter for the new nest under construction by the newly impregnated mouse, the very same whose first litter was drowned in last weekend's rain; who then built a second nest behind the baseboard in the office, but abandoned that one, too, last night—for there had come an odor that made her whiskers twitch and her small heart clatter. Not the odor of cherry blossoms—something else, something beyond comprehension. Beyond what a mouse knows, though not what a mouse smells. Perhaps the scent of a train coming into a station.

The mouse does not mourn. Each time a nest is destroyed, each time danger looms and it becomes necessary to move on, she wastes no time on sorrow. She is a creature attuned purely to exigencies. Even now she freezes: the roof over her head creaks. Is it a threat? She listens. Her whiskers quiver. Her tiny heart pumps blood through her veins. The five fetuses in her womb continue their own undiluted pursuit: to grow.

Gradually, the mouse unfreezes. Resumes the activity of life: gathering material for a new nest.

Oblivious to all this unfolding beneath them, Bennie greets Lloyd with a question. "Is anyone with Aunt Glad?"

"Clem and Diggs."

That feels right. Feels beautiful, somehow. She sticks her own fork into the watermelon and feta salad on Lloyd's plate.

"New neighbors," he says.

"Huh?"

He points toward the road with his corn on the cob; she looks and sees the long-skirted women and children passing by.

"Neighbors." She tastes that ordinary word. "I guess they are." She entertains a fantasy of running after them, calling, *Come back! Look—we have cake!* And suddenly remembers how Clem, one summer night when she was little, had stood on a bench at the ice cream stand out on Route 7. How she'd called after the customers returning to their cars, called to them with the soft serve running down her elbow: "Come back, people! Look, the moon!" She'd been—what? No more than two.

We should stay.

The thought settles upon her like a fine mist. All the talk of putting their house on the market and moving to another town seems suddenly foolish, pointless. This is their home. Whether they move or whether they stay, all homes are no more than temporary.

We'll stay, she thinks. *Come what may.*

(Though God only knows what Stalwart will say.)

She won't mention it tonight, that's for sure. But her heart is beating fast with it, the conviction. The clear and sudden relief of seeing the real.

Meanwhile the cousins have drifted together toward the road, drawn as if toward a parade. None of the Haredim so much as glance in their direction, or register any awareness of the secular festivities taking place. The men are already out of sight. The women and children process with unimpeachable focus like characters in a play, indifferent to the existence of an audience.

As the tail end of the group is passing by, Pim does a very Pim-like thing: raises a hand to his temple. Across the street, the child bringing up the rear stops in her tracks. Slowly she turns. And among all the people on the Erlend lawn, she locates him, as surely as if he had called her name. She doesn't do anything so grand as salute back; instead for several seconds she simply stands, regarding him. Her expression and his each alike in fortitude. Until, with a solemn nod, he lowers his hand. Only then does she dart ahead, scurrying to catch up with her people.

WHEN THE FIRST STARS come out it's time to light the sparklers. All around the yard: a syncopated dazzle as silver-gold spikes of light geyser here, then there, then there, then there. Heads swivel. Conversation trails. For a minute or more everyone's mesmerized by the wheeling, whirling sparks.

Everything seems darker once the sparklers go out. The band packs up, what's left of the food is put away. Coolness shimmies over the yard like a nightgown. One by one the guests depart, saying their goodbyes and extricating their cars with considerable patience and toil from the convoluted geometry wrought by the overly zealous parking lot attendant, until at last the knot comes loose and headlights snake down the driveway. Those who remain disperse across the lawn, drift through the empty amphitheater, wander toward the fringes of the property, collect in the encampment, from the direction of which the oily, herby perfume of weed begins to waft.

When will it happen?

If Aunt Glad were sentient, would she be wondering this? Alert to the danger? Would she feel the old alarm clang in her marrow, would a kind of cherry blossom premonition scamper through her blood?

Two pageants, eighty-seven years apart. The first scripted to fortify the myths upon which the institution of this nation was built. The second scripted to dispel the myths upon which the institution of marriage was built. The first sabotaged by anarchists or by accident. The second sabotaged by a solipsistic fop. The first featuring bales of hay. The second featuring bundles of sticks. *And doesn't history repeat itself?* Aunt Glad might ask. *Haven't we been taught that tragedy recurs?*

What recurs more often than not is possibility. Opportunity. Odds. The groundwork laid, the conditions met, the stars aligned, the critical mass reached. What happens then may go either way. One generation's unforgivable error becomes the next generation's act of grace. One generation's narrow escape becomes the next generation's foot put wrong. One generation's epic lament becomes the next generation's comic relief. One generation's reconciliation becomes the next generation's rift. The same threads surface again and again, but the weave is riddled with deviation, tessellation, transformation. No design replicated verbatim.

This is the ecstasy of life. Ecstasy from the ancient Greek *ek*, "out," and *histanai*, "to stand in place." Ecstasy: the condition of being not fixed, not fettered, not set in stone.

To know we are ever in motion.

This is happiness.

THE FIRE STARTS a little before midnight. The cause is a match. One of the sparkler-lighters (a guest long since departed), upon completing his mission, had blown out the match and tossed it in the nearest garbage. So he thought. He was half-right, twice over. Though he'd put out the flame, he'd failed to extinguish the livid glow at its base. And though his receptacle of choice was indeed a wastepaper basket, it was the one Mantha had brought down from her bedroom as part of the Nuptial Post, and it was full of unde-livered missives: dry, crumpled paper. Tinder.

After a few hours of flameless combustion, during which time it produces tendrils of smoke too visually and olfactorily insignif-icant to draw notice, the smoldering at last crosses the frontier into actual fire—although even then the tongues of orange that lap and lick at the folded sheets of construction paper remain ini-tially modest. When the wicker basket itself erupts, the effect is more dramatic: all those good wishes intended for the newlyweds are released from the prison of material form. Paper and ink are transmuted into heat and light, the written word atomized into the lingua franca of spark and smoke. By now, however, no one remaining on the property stands in the immediate vicinity, and the blaze goes unnoticed.

Who does remain? Ignazio Leopardi bid farewell ages ago, dis-tributing a flurry of impenitent air kisses before catching a ride back to the city. Keith and Johnetta Diggins, having rolled with all the punches with seemingly indefatigable good humor, finally de-clared themselves fatigued and retired to the Garrison soon after. The not-quite newlyweds themselves followed suit an hour later, in a car that took almost that much time to extricate from Tom's vehicular maze. The car (Chana's Buick wagon) turned out to have been appointed by the roustabouts in surprisingly conven-tional fashion (*It was the one traditional thing about the wedding,* Carrie will later remark), and it made a great disturbance, tin cans on strings rattling noisily over the gravel drive, as they pulled away. Their departure signaled bedtime for the kids, who were herded upstairs by Bennie and Carrie, both of them pining for their own pajamas. Tom is taking a turn sitting with Glad. Lloyd and Walter are tidying up the kitchen. And Richard the dog has led his pack back from their crepuscular investigations in the woods; having sated for the moment their vestigial wildness, they allow their domesticated selves to steer them over to the ring of tents, where a dozen or so humans are passing around a flask of arak and a couple of joints and debating the pros and cons of state funding for the arts.

Chana, lying with her head in Hannah's lap, is the first to notice the blaze. *Sweet,* she thinks, *someone's made a bonfire,* an observation she attempts to share with those around her, but they assume her use of the word *bonfire* is metaphorical, or perhaps a reference to a particular form of protest art, which gets them talking about Guy Fawkes and effigies and Burning Man. "No, no, you guys—*literally,*" she says (for once using the word accurately), but she is too sleepy and the others too araked-out for the message to transmit.

Shortly after this, the first bundle of black walnut branches catches. The smoke blows toward Bennie and Walter's bedroom window. Bennie, lying awake (barely) beside Pim, who is lying asleep (soundly) in the crook of her body, smells something burning. *Clem's friends must have built a fire,* she thinks. *They really have turned out to be awfully responsible,* she tells herself, sorry now that her first reaction to them had not been more felicitous. *And Stalwart's up and about; he'll make sure they've got it under control.* She snuggles her boy closer, tucking her face against his hair (ah, the perfume of dried sweat and hot dogs), and elects to have faith that all is well.

In the next room, Carrie is so preoccupied with the challenges of tucking her overstimulated twins into bed that she notices nothing. In fact, so intent is she on getting them both to stop bouncing around the room and to submit once and for all to their sleeping bags that when Hugh says, "Thomethingth burning," she shoots back (not sure whether to be aghast or quite pleased that she sounds a lot like her sister), "Yeah, that's the smoke you'll see coming out of my ears if you don't settle down this instant."

Farther down the hall the girl cousins are fast asleep. On the dresser top sits the dollhouse that is a replica of this house, backlit by the night-light's artificial moon. Gradually it acquires a secondary light source: an animating amber glow flickering through the window, growing brighter by the minute and reaching farther up the wall.

Not until the fire has pounced on three more of the roped bundles, found a pathway along the discarded lengths of butcher paper, and begun caressing the side of the barn does anyone take serious note. Lloyd, carrying out the trash, is the first to register not simple *fire* but the scale of the problem: *Fire!*

Walter, to celebrate having washed the last dish of the evening, has just hacked himself another slab of wedding cake, which he eats standing up at the sink. He's positive it's not what he ordered— he distinctly remembers having relayed to the baker what Clem herself had specified: chocolate cake with apricot jam between the layers and lemon buttercream frosting—but when he picked it up this afternoon it had been far too late to waste time arguing, and this combination anyhow has proved strangely delicious: the angel cake lighter, more ethereal, than anything he's ever eaten, and the penuche icing somehow at once exotic and familiar. It has a sort of burned taste, he thinks now, savoring this midnight slice.

"Walter!" Lloyd bangs opens the porch door and with improbable assertiveness pushes Walter away from the sink, where he shoves the big spaghetti pot and turns on the tap full force. At nearly the same moment Tom barrels through the other door, crying, "Dad! The barn is on fire!"

It's more pots and multiplying bodies, then, a whole stream of roustabouts tramping in and out of the kitchen as if they'd trained all their lives for a good old-fashioned bucket brigade. Voices outside. Calm yelling, if that's a thing. People trying to drag the garden hose around from the spigot on the driveway side of the house but it doesn't reach. More voices, less calm. Voices upstairs and on the porch and outside, all overlapping, and footsteps, disciplined hurrying, the air crosshatched with smoke, people coughing, dogs barking, windows lighting up throughout the house, windows lighting up at McElroy's, too. A siren, plaintive and distant at first, swells to near bursting only to cut out abruptly. Sound ruptured by silence. A great dinosaur of a truck lumbering up the drive, veering diagonally across the lawn, scarlet-lit, its tires plowing deep ruts in the earth.

Firelight casts phantasmagoria upon the office walls. They flicker across the desk, the floor, the cot, they lick at the curtains, tongue the ceiling. A puppet show of shadow-flame, a writhing saraband of orange and gold.

For the first time since she embarked on this final leg of her earthly journey, no one attends her. No one is here to notice how, while her body lies still, she is drifting, traveling, her rootedness fully behind her now. She is beyond stasis, in motion.

There once more—the sound of a horn. Something within her inclines toward that voice. The smell of smoke. Something within her reaches for a hand. The spreading flame, the flaming warmth, and something within her is not afraid. Fire makes steam, steam powers engine, train approaches. How beautiful a train.

All that remains her advances toward the fire and its promise: to set matter free, release spirit from form, reunite atom with atom.

AND WITH THIS LIBERATION, the final trace of Lester Vilno is lost.

Although the man himself died decades ago (on a park bench in Chicago on June 21, 1941: another solstice, also the eve of Operation Barbarossa, the Nazis' massive invasion of the Soviet Union, in which they marched into territory formerly known as the Pale of Settlement), something of him had continued in what scraps of memory persisted among the living. There had never been many of these, for even before his exile from Rundle Junction in 1927— even before he caught a train out of town, wearing his long black coat and holding what scant possessions he took with him in a single bundle tied with twine—he had been a man of few acquaintances. Afterward, living in one SRO after another, he'd been known only skimmingly and never by any one person for very long: a gaunt, limping, bearded figure, eyes like stones at the bottom of a well, more caricature than human being. As if he had become one of his own painstakingly crafted marionettes.

Glad Erlend had been the last to furnish what meager nourishment a ghost requires: a place at memory's hearth, a setting at the spectral table. Now with the expiry of his lone remaining host, the shade of Lester Vilno vanishes wholly from this world.

AND IS THIS HOW IT HAPPENS, how the old Erlend homestead, formerly the village post office and general store, passes on? Not by changing hands, but by conflagration? As if the house itself were programmed to resist change, to refuse the advent of newcomers, strangers of any ilk? Is this how the family finally departs, not by choice but by chance, uprooted rather than pulling up roots?

No. It takes the firefighters all of eighteen minutes to get the fire under control. Good thing, they say, the fuel was damp. Be thankful for last night's rain. Be thankful the tree was alive until yesterday, the branches still green, slow to burn. Be thankful the wind wasn't stronger. Be thankful it wasn't blowing in the direction of the house.

For the house, miraculously, is untouched. The barn's ruined, but good riddance—the moldering structure has been an albatross, its store of artifacts an encumbrance. All of it gone now. The firefighters, still holding their hoses, won't let anyone near the contorted, collapsed, dripping timbers, among which some lesser flames still leap intermittently here and there, but even from a distance it's clear everything's lost, nothing salvageable or even recognizable except perhaps—is that the old Glendale? In the darkness, with steam rising from its cast-iron chimney, it looks like a small locomotive.

They should have donated the barn's contents to the Rundle Junction Natural Historical Museum long ago, but perhaps this is even better. To be done with the responsibility of owning all that. No longer in charge of its preservation, no longer beholden in that way.

Still, thinks Walter, his heart rate not yet returned to normal, it's humbling all around. The judgmental benevolence of the fire chief. The mixture of efficiency and jocularity among the firefighters as they put their equipment away. The spate of dogs slinking around, sniffing at the edges of soaked, smoking debris. The roustabouts beaming as if something marvelous has taken place, gratified that they were called upon to help and they did help, all of them holding their empty pots and jars and jugs like medals of valor. Banjo in long johns singing "There's a Hole in the Bucket" as he walks Harriett in circles to calm her. The squad car pulling slowly, belatedly up the driveway, its very torpor seeming to say *Not these idiots again*, discharging none other than Vin Diesel (what's his name again? maybe it's time to start calling him Officer Vincente), whose nod of greeting is so professionally devoid of affect that Walter feels he might as well resign here and now: as father, as householder, as man. McElroy, too, clomping over in his steel-toed boots and flannel bathrobe and precious little else, if his pale shins are any indication, ready to bail out his neighbors for the second time in one day. Bennie and Carrie and the little ones in their pajamas huddling by the azaleas, the kids all holding hands as if someone told them to and not let go. Carrie still in her sleeveless dress, shivering. Lloyd stepping up from behind to wrap his arms around her. Bennie slipping away from the others now and coming over to where Walter stands talking to the cops. She places her hand on his lower back. That's all. Just her warm, steady hand.

And Walter thinks, *There are worse things than being humbled.*

And Pim comes over, too, now and stretches his arms for Walter to lift him up, and this time he doesn't say, *Don't hold me.*

So Walter lifts and holds him both.

But wait.

What are these new shapes drifting across the lawn? Two, three, four figures, four dark entities emerging from the darkness of the county road. *Look, Daddy!* whispers Pim. Placing a hand on either cheek, turning Walter's head so that it points in that direction. *Look, they're coming!* They advance, the four men, spectacles glinting as they near the light, heavy beards obscuring their mouths. Long black coats hanging at their sides like wings at rest. The fringes of their *tallitot* silvered by the moon.

Look, breathes Pim. *People.*

ACKNOWLEDGMENTS

Hannah Judy Gretz, your gift—from a stranger to a stranger—continues to astonish me. I loved my time at Ragdale and thank all the people there who support and nourish art, but no one more than you and the gesture of your gift.

I'm beyond grateful to work with an editor who is not only committed and wise but also willing to challenge me, and challenge me, and challenge me again. Sarah McGrath, you are extraordinary. I'm fortunate to have you help me grow. Likewise the excellent and talented Danya Kukafka, Lindsay Means, and Alison Fairbrother. Thanks to Chandra Wohleber, for copyediting in a way that is an art, a craft, and a blessing all in one, and to Claire Vaccaro for somehow translating my linguistic babble into visual sense. My deepest gratitude to Geoff Kloske and the whole Riverhead crew.

With no less feeling but at the limit of my capacity to articulate it, I thank three stalwarts: Barney Karpfinger, Stuart Pizer, and Oscar Cohen, and three inspirations: Joe, Rosy, and George.